QUEENS NOIR

QUEENS NOIR

EDITED BY
ROBERT KNIGHTLY

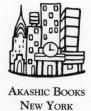

AKASHIC BOOKS
NEW YORK

Published by Akashic Books
©2008 Akashic Books

Series concept by Tim McLoughlin and Johnny Temple
Queens map by Sohrab Habibion
Editorial and technical assistance by Carrie Beehan

ISBN-13: 978-1-933354-40-8
Library of Congress Control Number: 2007926099
All rights reserved

First printing

Akashic Books
PO Box 1456
New York, NY 10009
info@akashicbooks.com
www.akashicbooks.com

Also in the Akashic Noir Series:

Baltimore Noir, edited by Laura Lippman
Bronx Noir, edited by S.J. Rozan
Brooklyn Noir, edited by Tim McLoughlin
Brooklyn Noir 2: The Classics, edited by Tim McLoughlin
Chicago Noir, edited by Neal Pollack
D.C. Noir, edited by George Pelecanos
Detroit Noir, edited by E.J. Olsen & John C. Hocking
Dublin Noir (Ireland), edited by Ken Bruen
Havana Noir (Cuba), edited by Achy Obejas
London Noir (England), edited by Cathi Unsworth
Los Angeles Noir, edited by Denise Hamilton
Manhattan Noir, edited by Lawrence Block
Miami Noir, edited by Les Standiford
New Orleans Noir, edited by Julie Smith
San Francisco Noir, edited by Peter Maravelis
Twin Cities Noir, edited by Julie Schaper & Steven Horwitz
Wall Street Noir, edited by Peter Spiegelman

Forthcoming:

Brooklyn Noir 3, edited by Tim McLoughlin & Thomas Adcock
D.C. Noir 2: The Classics, edited by George Pelecanos
Delhi Noir (India), edited by Hirsh Sawhney
Istanbul Noir (Turkey), edited by Mustafa Ziyalan & Amy Spangler
Lagos Noir (Nigeria), edited by Chris Abani
Las Vegas Noir, edited by Jarret Keene & Todd James Pierce
Manhattan Noir 2: The Classics, edited by Lawrence Block
Mexico City Noir (Mexico), edited by Paco I. Taibo II
Moscow Noir (Russia), edited by Natalia Smirnova & Julia Goumen
Paris Noir (France), edited by Aurélien Masson
Rome Noir (Italy), edited by Chiara Stangalino & Maxim Jakubowski
San Francisco Noir 2: The Classics, edited by Peter Maravelis
Toronto Noir (Canada), edited by Janine Armin & Nathaniel G. Moore
Trinidad Noir, edited by Lisa Allen-Agostini & Jeanne Mason

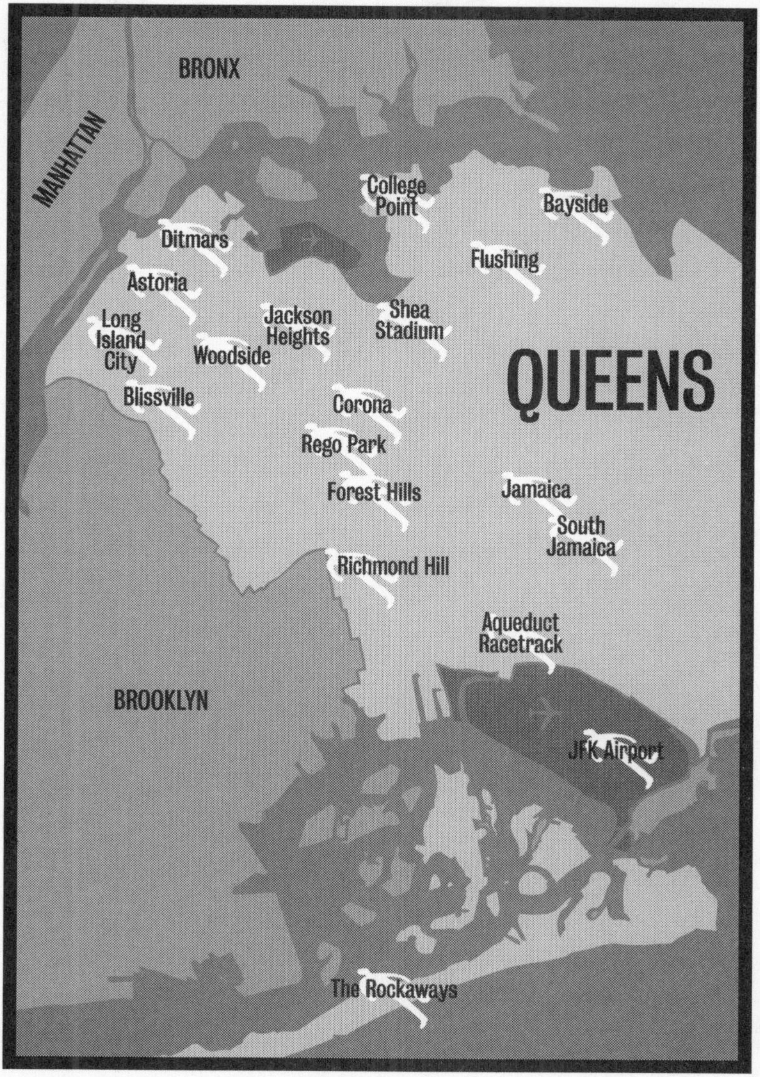
BRONX
MANHATTAN
College Point
Bayside
Ditmars
Flushing
Astoria
Long Island City
Jackson Heights
Shea Stadium
Woodside
QUEENS
Blissville
Corona
Rego Park
Forest Hills
Jamaica
South Jamaica
Richmond Hill
Aqueduct Racetrack
BROOKLYN
JFK Airport
The Rockaways

*To the women in my life: my beloved wife Rose,
without whom this book would still be a thought;
and my precious sisters, Maureen and Lillian.*

TABLE OF CONTENTS

INTRODUCTION
QUEENS HAS ATTITUDE

Queens is New York City's biggest borough, with the most parks and cemeteries, both major airports, Shea Stadium, the city's only racetrack, and 150 languages spoken by more foreign-born residents than live anywhere else in the U.S. No wonder Queens has attitude. And plenty of noir to go around. That's the premise of *Queens Noir*. I chose these nineteen authors for their solid connections to the borough, not to mention their skewed worldviews. This introduction is organized as a tour of the neighborhoods. It begins at the point where a traveler from Manhattan touches down in Queens.

Leave Manhattan (a.k.a., New York City to Outlanders) and drive over the Queensboro Bridge (a.k.a., the 59th Street Bridge) that spans the East River. Take the outer roadbed; on your descent, mark the Citicorp Building (Queens' only skyscraper) looming on your right; then, close in, the Silvercup Studios sign big and in your face as you touch down in Long Island City. Overhead is the rotting steel skeleton of beams and girders that support the elevated tracks for the N, W, and 7 subway lines, all converging at the Queensboro Plaza station. The 7 line is sometimes called the Orient Express: Of the 2.2 million souls in Queens, forty-eight percent are foreign-born, the majority Asian.

Look around this commercial hub. Seedy Queens Central. Note City Scapes and the other two "gentlemen's clubs" within three blocks. At night, the strip joints are lit in neon; prostitutes work the johns on Queens Plaza South and across the roadway on Queens Plaza North; all-night donut shops give sustenance; the bus from the Rikers Island jails disgorges discharged inmates at the bus stop at 3 a.m. every weekday. Yet Queens politicians are talking a bright future for Queensboro Plaza, involving $1.2 billion to be invested in development here and on the Long Island City waterfront across the river from Manhattan. And Silvercup—formerly a baker of bread, now a purveyor of illusions—is leading the pack. Here, in *Queens Noir*, you can visit the movie lots and TV studios with actress-writer Kim Sykes's Josephine, a security guard in "Arrivederci, Aldo."

Continue up Queens Plaza South till it intersects with Queens Plaza, Northern Boulevard, and Jackson Avenue. As you turn right onto Jackson, catch in your rearview mirror the clock-face tower of the Bridge Plaza Tech Center, previously named the Brewster Building—built in 1910 to make horse-drawn carriages—looming above and behind the elevated train tracks (it's our cover photo). Proceed a ways down the avenue to the core of old Long Island City with its fine Italian-American restaurants, wood-frame aluminum-sided homes, and factories chockablock with the ateliers of the arrivistes. Make a left onto the Pulaski drawbridge over the Newtown Creek into Polish Greenpoint, Brooklyn. Take a left at the foot of the bridge onto Greenpoint Avenue, then you're riding alongside the creek but it's hidden from view by the huge wastewater treatment plant, which may or may not be making a difference. Note the stink. (Greenpoint has always stunk.) Continue over the Greenpoint Avenue drawbridge—a hop, skip, and a jump—into Blissville, Queens.

Blissville is a four-square-block neighborhood bounded by

Van Dam Street to the west, the Long Island Expressway to the north and east, and First Calvary Cemetery to the south. First Calvary was opened by St. Patrick's Cathedral in 1846 to take in the poor Irish who had become too many to be laid down in Manhattan. "There are more dead in Queens than alive." (This classically noir line is Ellen Freudenheim's in her fine guidebook, *Queens*—told me things I didn't know and reminded me of what I'd forgotten.) Having spent my first forty-four years across the waters in Greenpoint and having worked one summer digging graves in First Calvary (a much sought-after position), I was led to write my story in this volume about the ghosts that can haunt even a very young life, shadowed by the high stone walls of First Calvary.

Take Greenpoint Avenue east through small-town Sunny-side till it becomes Roosevelt Avenue, and continue on, with the 7 train overhead on the elevated tracks. Roosevelt Avenue is a main east-west road that passes through the heart of Woodside, Jackson Heights, and Corona—Queens' version of the Casbah. Tibetans, Irish, Mexicans, Filipinos, Colombians, Ecuadorians, Koreans, Indians, Bangladeshis hawk food, clothing, jewelry, appliances, phone cards, forged or stolen drivers' licenses, phony Social Security cards—from storefronts, push-carts, stalls, alleyways, doorways, street corners. The denizens of the Casbah, and the 100,000 bill-paying customers of Con Edison in Astoria, Woodside, Sunnyside, and Long Island City were left in the dark when the Con Ed generators blew on July 17, 2006 during a heat wave. The blackout lasted ten days. Author Liz Martínez records the terrible consequences for one compulsive shopper in "Lights Out for Frankie."

Detour to the north on the Brooklyn-Queens Express-way (BQE) to nearby Astoria and Ditmars: the Greek lands. Other settlers include Egyptians, Italians, Bangladeshis,

Bosnians, and a mélange of artists and young people fleeing Manhattan rents. The Kaufman Astoria Studios at 36th
Street and Thirty-Fourth Avenue have been making movies for ninety years. They were busy in the late 1920s while
one block away the Irish were taking over the bars from the
Germans who had preceded them. In "Only the Strong Survive," Mary Byrne spins an old Irish morality tale with more
twists and turns than an Irish country road. Moral: Bar owner
is a perilous profession.

The neighborhood jewel of Ditmars is Astoria Park and
its landmark pool that lets in 3,000 on a summer's day. The
park sits on the shore under the Triborough Bridge and along
the Hell Gate channel, the most turbulent and deepest water
in the New York Harbor. In "Last Stop, Ditmars," Tori Carrington has situated the Acropolis Diner at the intersection of
Ditmars Boulevard and 31st Street underneath the last stop
on the N line. It's a small domestic Greek tragedy: Think Arthur Miller's A View from the Bridge.

Hop back on the BQE at Astoria Boulevard and then get
off at Roosevelt Avenue/74th Street. You're now in Jackson
Heights, in the epicenter of Little India. Visit the Jackson Diner
for a *masala dosa*, check out the gold emporiums, pick up the
latest Bollywood flick at the video store. In Shailly Agnihotri's
droll tale, "Avoid Agony," you can walk in the footsteps of Raj
Kumar, who runs the only astrological readings/matrimonial
investigations agency on the street. Raj, from his office above
a sari shop, looks to the heavens for direction while trolling
for prey on the Internet.

Continue up Roosevelt to Junction Boulevard and you
cross into Corona: Colombians, Argentinians, Brazilians, Koreans, Mexicans, Ecuadorians pack the streets and the stores;
the predominant sounds are dialects of Spanish and Portug-

ese. Corona is on the doorstep of Shea Stadium, a stop or two away on the 7. K.j.a.Wishnia's female P.I., Filomena Buscarsela, is tight with her Ecuadorian neighbors. The neighborhood is awash in Mets fever, as well as diluted antibiotics peddled from local *farmacias* and *botánicas* that have caused a boy's death. Filomena, tracking their source, is on everybody's case in "Viernes Loco."

Shea Stadium is located in Flushing Meadows–Corona Park, site of the 1939 and 1964 World's Fairs. Joe Guglielmelli's protagonist is seemingly just another subway passenger en route to a game, who falls into conversation with a Boston Red Sox fan. You never heard so much baseball talk in your life as in "Buckner's Error" . . . until the final inning.

Ride the 7 for one more stop and it's the end of the line at Roosevelt Avenue/Main Street. Main Street is packed all the way up to Kissena Boulevard with peddlers, fish markets, phone stores, fast-food shops—all the signs in Chinese characters. More Chinese live in Flushing than in Manhattan's Chinatown. Author Victoria Eng, who knows the turf, takes us off-street to Bowne Park, a tiny oasis in a sea of commerce, for a coming-of-age story. A bad move in the park, however, and you might not get any older.

Bayside and College Point are middle- to upper-class neighborhoods in northeast Queens, off the Cross Island Parkway. In "Under the Throgs Neck Bridge," Denis Hamill's two jogging characters cover a lot of Bayside landscape. One, however, is unaware that it's a race to the death.

College Point sits across Flushing Bay from LaGuardia Airport. You know you live in Queens if you are airplane-conscious: There's always a flight path directly over your house. But that's not police officer Jill Kelly's problem; hers is an itchy trigger-finger. In "Crazy Jill Saves the Slinky," Stephen

Solomita spins an Irish domestic drama where family ties run deep—deep as a grave.

Take the Whitestone Expressway to the Grand Central Parkway south, exit at Queens Boulevard. You're in Kew Gardens, the seat of political power in the borough. On your right is the Queens Criminal Courts building, which appears to have a piece of a flying saucer buried in its face, a silvery metallic canopy over the entrance, reminiscent of *The Day the Earth Stood Still.* Not a surprise: Both the movie and the building are from the 1950s. Keep heading west on Queens Boulevard—a twelve-laner so hard to cross even with the light that it's called the "Boulevard of Death"—to Forest Hills and Rego Park, high-income and alike as two peas in a pod. Typical of both these old communities is block after block of high-rise co-op and condo buildings lining both sides of the boulevard. Jews have predominated here for decades. Recent immigration has added Russian, Israeli, Middle Eastern, and Bukharan flavors. Alan Gordon opts for the traditional in "Bottom of the Sixth," setting a tale of the Hasidim on a Little League baseball field in Rego Park. Batter up! Watch out for flying lead!

Megan Abbott returns to yesteryear, the 1970s, in "Hollywood Lanes," set in a venerable bowling alley. The building still stands on Queens Boulevard and Sixty-Seventh Avenue—vacant like a haunted house harboring the violent passions that erupted therein on a summer's night.

Take the Van Wyck Expressway south, exit at Jamaica Avenue in Richmond Hill. Before World War II, the Hill was middle-class comfortable, and its historic district is still intact with 1,000 Victorian homes. These days, the area is the center of the city's Guyanese immigration, also home to Hindus, Sikhs, Pakistanis, and West Indians. Jillian Abbott keys us in to the emotional life and ultimate fate of a misfit al-Qaeda mole in "Jihad Sucks; or, The Conversion of the Jews."

Take Atlantic Avenue east to the Jamaica neighborhood, with the largest African-American community in the city. It's also the destination-of-choice of Filipinos. West Indians, Chinese, and Salvadorans also abound. Belinda Farley sets her story amidst a law-abiding Haitian family in their modest dwelling on Guy R. Brewer Boulevard and 108th Avenue in the heart of Jamaica. "The Investigation" has its roots in the "locked room" mystery.

Move south on Guy R. Brewer to Baisley Pond Park in South Jamaica, where playground basketball is king, where Glenville Lovell's second-generation West Indian gangsta has an out-of-body experience.

Aqueduct Racetrack is due south. You can get there by the A train or drive along Rockaway Parkway. It's 113 years old, though it has fallen on hard times; attendance is in the toilet. The real estate jackals are salivating while the governor sings that old song: Urban Renewal. But Maggie Estep (the smartest horsewoman on the planet) celebrates the breed in "Alice Fantastic," a twisty tale of Fatal Attraction among the Usual Suspects in the clubhouse.

Head south on the Van Wyck to the end: John F. Kennedy Airport. It's huge. Playing against the grain, Patricia King (a globe-trotter herself) takes us into the mind of an ordinary woman as she deplanes and makes her way through the terminal to collect her bags. The unexpected intervenes in "Baggage Claim," and suddenly you're in *The Twilight Zone*.

Last stop: the Rockaways, the southernmost point in Queens, a ten-mile peninsula flush against the Atlantic Ocean. A lot of beach. In 1993, a ship loaded with smuggled Chinese foundered off the coast here. A few made it to shore. "Golden Venture" is the story of one of them—well, not exactly. This is novelist Jill Eisenstadt's comical riff on what might have happened later.

Queens!—this sprawling Babel—an ethnic stew best sampled by dipping into the stories up ahead. You can almost taste 'em . . .

Robert Knightly
Queens, New York City
November 2007

PART I

Queens on the Fly: by Sea, Horse,
Train, Plane, and Silver Screen

ALICE FANTASTIC

BY MAGGIE ESTEP

Aqueduct Racetrack

I'd been trying to get rid of the big oaf for seventeen weeks but he just kept coming around. He'd ring the bell and I'd look out the window and see him standing on the stoop looking like a kicked puppy. What I needed with another kicked puppy I couldn't tell you, since I'd taken in a little white mutt with tan spots that my cousin Jeremy had found knocked up and wandering a trailer park in Kentucky. Cousin Jeremy couldn't keep the dog so he called me up and somehow got me to take the animal in. After making the vet give her an abortion and a rabies shot, Jeremy found the dog a ride up from Kentucky with some freak friend of his who routinely drives between Kentucky and Queens transporting cheap cigarettes. The freak friend pulled his van up outside my house one night just before midnight and the dog came out of the van reeking of cigarettes and blinking up at me, completely confused and kicked- looking. Not that I think the freak friend of Cousin Jeremy's actually kicked her. But the point is, I already had a kicked puppy. What did I need with a guy looking like one?

I didn't need him. But he'd ring the bell and I'd let him in, and, even if I was wearing my dead father's filthy bathrobe and I hadn't showered in five days, he'd tell me, *You look fantastic, Alice.* I knew he actually meant it, that he saw something fantastic in my limp brown hair and puffy face and the zits I'd started getting suddenly at age thirty-six. It was embarrassing. The zits, the fact that I was letting this big oaf come over to nuzzle at my unbathed flesh, the little dog who'd sit at the edge of the bed watching as me and Clayton, the big oaf, went at it.

My life was a shambles. So I vowed to end it with Clayton. I vowed it on a Tuesday at 7 a.m. after waking up with an unusual sense of clarity. I opened my eyes to find thin winter sunlight sifting in the windows of the house my dead father left me. Candy, the trailer trash dog, was sitting at the edge of the bed, politely waiting for me to wake up because that's the thing with strays, they're so grateful to have been taken in that they defer to your schedule and needs. So, Candy was at the edge of the bed and sun was coming in the windows of my dead father's place on 47th Road in the borough of Queens in New York City. And I felt clear-headed. Who knows why. I just did. And I felt I needed to get my act together. Shower more frequently. Stop smoking so much. Get back to yoga and kickboxing. Stop burning through my modest profits as a modest gambler. Revitalize myself. And the first order of business was to get rid of the big oaf, Clayton. Who ever heard of a guy named Clayton who isn't ninety-seven years old, anyway?

I got into the shower and scrubbed myself raw, then shampooed my disgusting oily head. I took clean clothes out of the closet instead of foraging through the huge pile in the hamper the way I'd been doing for weeks. I put on black jeans and a fuzzy green sweater. I glanced at myself in the mirror. My semi-dry hair looked okay and my facial puffiness had gone down. Even my zits weren't so visible. I looked vaguely alive.

I took my coat off the hook, put Candy's leash on, and headed out for a walk along the East River, near the condo high-rises that look over into Manhattan. My dead father loved Long Island City. He moved here in the 1980s, when it was almost entirely industrial, to shack up with some drunken harlot, right after my mom kicked him out. Long after the harlot had dumped my father—all women dumped him all the time—he'd stayed on in the neighborhood, eventually buying a tiny two-story wood frame house that he left to me, his lone child, when the cancer got him last year at age fifty-nine. I like the neighborhood fine. It's quiet and there are places to buy tacos.

"Looking good, *mami*," said some Spanish guy as Candy and I walked past the gas station.

I never understand that *mami* thing. It sounds like they're saying *mommy*. I know they mean *hot mama* and, in their minds, it's a compliment, but it still strikes me as repulsive.

I ignored the guy.

As Candy sniffed and pissed and tried to eat garbage off the pavement, I smoked a few Marlboros and stared across at midtown Manhattan. It looked graceful from this distance.

The air was so cold it almost seemed clean and I started thinking on how I would rid myself of Clayton. I'd tried so many times. Had gotten him to agree not to call me anymore. But then, not two days would go by and he'd ring the bell. And I'd let him in. He'd look at me with those huge stupid brown eyes and tell me how great I looked. *Alice, you're fantastic*, he'd told me so many times I started thinking of myself as Alice Fantastic, only there really wouldn't be anything fantastic about me until I got rid of Clayton. When he would finally shut up about my fantasticness, I'd start in on the *This isn't going to work for me anymore, Clayton* refrain I had been trotting out for seventeen weeks. Then he'd look wounded and his arms would hang so long at his sides that I'd have to touch him, and once I touched him, we'd make a beeline for the bed, and the sex was pretty good, the way it can be with someone you are physically attracted to in spite of or because of a lack of anything at all in common. And the sex being good would make me entertain the idea of instating him on some sort of permanent basis, and I guess that was my mistake. He'd see that little idea in my eye and latch onto it and have *feelings*, and his *feelings* would make him a prodigious lover, and I'd become so strung out on sex chemicals I would dopily say *Sure* when he'd ask to spend the night, and then again dopily say *Sure* the next morning when he'd ask if he could call me later.

But enough is enough. I don't want Clayton convincing himself we're going to be an everlasting item growing old together.

Right now Clayton lives in a parking lot. In his van. This I discovered when, that first night, after I picked him up in the taco place and strolled with him near the water, enjoying his simplicity and his long, loping gait, I brought him home and sucked his cock in the entrance hall and asked him to fuck me from behind in the kitchen, and then led him to the bedroom where we lay quiet for a little while until he was hard again, at which point I put on a pair of tights and asked him to rip out the crotch and fuck me through the hole. After all that, just when I was thinking up a polite way of asking him to leave, he propped himself up on his elbow and told me how much he liked me. "I really like you. I mean, I *really* like you," looking at me with those eyes big as moons, and even though I just wanted to read a book and go to sleep, I didn't have the heart to kick him out.

All that night, he babbled at me, telling me his woes, how his mother has Alzheimer's and his father is in prison for forgery and his wife left him for a plumber and he's been fired from his job at a cabinet-making shop and is living in his van in a parking lot and showering at the Y.

"I've got to get out of Queens soon," he said.

"And go where?"

"Florida. I don't like the cold much. Gets in my bones."

"Yeah. Florida," I said. I'd been there. To Gulfstream Park, Calder Race Course, and Tampa Bay Downs. I didn't tell him that though. I just said, *Yeah, Florida*, like I wasn't opposed to Florida, though why I would let him think I have any fondness for Florida, this leading him to possibly speculate that I'd want to go live there with him, I don't know. I guess I wanted to be kind to him.

"Just a trailer is fine. I like trailers," Clayton said.

"Right," I said. And then I feigned sleep.

That was seventeen weeks ago. And I still haven't gotten rid of him.

Candy and I walked for the better part of an hour and then headed home, passing back by the gas station where the moron felt the need to repeat, *Looking good, mommy*, and I actually stopped walking and stared at him and tried to think of words to explain exactly how repulsive it is to be called *mommy* and how it makes me picture him fucking his own mother, who is doubtless a matronly Dominican woman with endless folds of ancient flesh, but I couldn't find the words and the guy was starting to grin, possibly thinking I was actually turned on by him, so I kept walking.

Once back inside my place, I gave Candy the leftovers from my previous night's dinner and sat down at the kitchen table with my computer, my *Daily Racing Form*, and my notebooks. I got to work on the next day's entries at Aqueduct. No matter how much I planned to change my life in the coming weeks, I still had to work. It wasn't much of a card, even for a Wednesday in February, so I figured I wouldn't be pushing a lot of money through the windows. But I would watch. I would take notes. I would listen. I would enjoy my work. I always do.

Several hours passed and I felt stirrings of hunger and glanced inside my fridge. Some lifeless lettuce, a few ounces of orange juice, and one egg. I considered boiling the egg, as there are days when there's nothing I love more than a hard-boiled egg, but I decided this wasn't one of those days. I would have to go to the taco place for take-out. I attached Candy's leash to her collar and threw my coat on and was heading to the door when the phone rang. I picked it up.

"Hi, Alice," came Clayton's low voice.

I groaned.

"What's the matter? You in pain?"

"Sort of."

"What do you mean? What hurts? I'll be right there."

"No, no, Clayton, don't. My pain is that you won't take *No* for an answer."

"No about what?"

"No about our continuing on like this."

There was dead silence.

"Where are you?" I asked.

"In the parking lot."

"Clayton," I said, "I know you think you're a nice guy, but there's nothing nice about coming around when I've repeatedly asked you not to. It's borderline stalking."

More silence.

"I need my peace and quiet."

After several moments: "You don't like the way I touch you anymore?"

"There's more to life than touching."

"Uh," said Clayton. "I wouldn't know since you won't ever let me do anything with you other than come over and fuck you."

Clayton had never said *fuck* before. Clayton had been raised in some sort of religious household. He wasn't religious himself, but he was reserved about cursing.

"My life is nothing. Clayton, I go to the racetrack. I make my bets and take my notes. I talk to some of the other horse-players. I go home and cook dinner or I go to the taco place. I walk my dog. That's it. There's nothing to my life, Clayton, nothing to see."

"So let me come with you."

"Come with me where?"

"To the racetrack."

"I'm asking you to never call me again and get out of my life. Why would I want to take you to the racetrack?"

"Just let me see a little piece of your life. I deserve it. Think of it as alimony."

I couldn't see why I should do anything for him. But I agreed anyway. At least it got him off the phone.

I took the dog out to the taco place. Came home and ate my dinner, giving half to the dog.

I'd told Clayton to meet me the next morning at 11:00 and we'd take the subway. He offered to drive but I didn't trust that monstrous van of his not to break down en route. He rang the bell and I came downstairs to find him looking full of hope. Like seeing each other in daylight hours meant marriage and babies were imminent. Not that he'd asked for anything like that but he was that kind of guy, the kind of guy I seem to attract all too often, the want-to-snuggle-up-and-breed kind of guy. There are allegedly millions of women out there looking for these guys so I'm not sure why they all come knocking on my door. I guess they like a challenge. That's why they're men.

"Hi, Alice," he beamed, "you look fantastic."

"Thanks," I said. I *had* pulled myself together, was wearing a tight black knee-length skirt and a soft black sweater that showed some shoulder—if I ever took my coat off, which I wasn't planning to do as I figured any glimpsing of my flesh might give Clayton ideas.

"I'm just doing this 'cause you asked," I said as we started walking to the G train, "but you have to realize this is my job and you can't interfere or ask a lot of questions." I was staring straight ahead so I didn't have to see any indications of hurt in his eyes, because this was one of his ruses, the hurt look, the kicked puppy look, and I was damn well sick of it.

"Right," said Clayton.

We went down into the station and waited forever, as one invariably does for the G train, and all the while Clayton stared at me so hard I was pretty sure he would turn me to stone.

Eventually, the train came and got us to the Hoyt-Schermerhorn stop in Brooklyn where we switched to the far more efficient A train. I felt relief at being on my way to Aqueduct. Not many people truly love Aqueduct, but I do. Belmont is gorgeous and spacious and Saratoga is grand if you can stand the crowds, but I love Aqueduct. Aqueduct is down-on-their-luck trainers slumping in the benches, degenerates, droolcases, and drunks swapping tips, and a few seasoned pro gamblers quietly going about their business. My kind of place.

Thirty minutes later, the train sighed into the stop at Aqueduct and we got off, us and a bunch of hunched middle-aged white men, a few slightly younger Rasta guys, and one well-dressed suit-type guy who was an owner or wanted to pretend to be one.

"Oh, it's nice," Clayton lied as we emerged from the little tunnel under the train tracks.

The structure looks like the set for a 1970s zombie movie, with its faded grim colors and the airplanes headed for JFK flying so low you're sure they're going to land on a horse.

"We'll go up to the restaurant, have some omelettes," I told him once we were inside the clubhouse. "The coffee sucks but the omelettes are fine."

"Okay," said Clayton.

We rode the escalator to the top, and at the big glass doors to the Equestris Restaurant, Manny, the maître d', greeted me and gave us a table with a great view of the finish line.

Then Clayton started in with the questions. He'd never been a big question guy, wasn't a very verbal guy period, but suddenly he wanted to know the history of Aqueduct and my history with Aqueduct and what else I'd ever done for a living and what my family thought of my being a professional gambler, etc., etc.

"I told you, I have to work. No twenty questions. Here's a *Racing Form*," I said, handing him the extra copy I'd printed out. "Now study that and let me think."

The poor guy stared at the *Form* but obviously had no idea how to read it. Sometimes I forget that people don't know these things. Seems like I always knew, what with coming here when I was a kid when Cousin Jeremy still lived in Queens and baby-sat me on days when my father was off on a construction job. I'd been betting since the age of nine and had been reasonably crafty about money-management and risk-taking since day one. I had turned a profit that first time when Jeremy had placed bets for me, and though I'd had plenty of painful losing days since, for the most part I scraped by. I'd briefly had a job as a substitute teacher after graduating from Hunter College, but I hated it. So I gambled and supplemented my modest profits with income from the garden apartment in my house. Not many people last more than a few years gambling for a living but, for whatever reason, I have. Mostly because I can't stand the thought of doing anything else.

I was just about to take pity on Clayton and show him how to read the *Form* when Big Fred appeared and sat down at one of the extra chairs at our table.

"You see this piece of shit Pletcher's running in the fifth race?" Fred wanted to know. Big Fred, who weighs 110 pounds tops, isn't one for pleasantries. He had no interest in being introduced to Clayton, probably hadn't even noticed I was with someone; he just wanted confirmation that the Todd Pletcher–trained colt in the fifth race was a piece of shit in spite of having cost 2.4 million at the Keeneland yearling sale and having won all three races he'd run in.

"Yeah," I said, nodding gravely. "He'll be 1-9."

"He's a flea," said Fred.

"Yeah. Well. I wouldn't throw him out on a Pick 6 ticket."

"I'm throwing him out."

"Okay," I said.

"He hasn't faced shit and he's never gone two turns. And there's that nice little horse of Nick's that's a closer."

"Right," I said.

"I'm using Nick's horse. Singling him."

"I wouldn't throw out the Pletcher horse."

"Fuck him," said Fred, getting up and storming off to the other end of the place, where I saw him take a seat with some guys from the *Daily Racing Form*.

"Friend of yours?" asked Clayton.

I nodded. "Big Fred. He's a good guy."

"He is?"

"Sure."

I could tell Clayton wanted to go somewhere with that one. Wanted to ask why I thought some strange little guy who just sat down and started cursing out horses was a good guy. Another reason Clayton had to be gotten rid of.

One of the waiters came and took our omelette order. Since I'd mapped out most of my bets, I took ten minutes and gave Clayton a cursory introduction to reading horses' past performances. I was leaning in close, my finger tracing one of the horse's running lines, when Clayton kissed my ear.

"I love you, Alice," he said.

"Jesus, Clayton," I said. "What the fuck?"

Clayton looked like a kicked puppy.

"I brought you here because I thought it'd be a nice way to spend our last day together but, fuck me, why do you have to get ridiculous?"

"I don't want it to end. You're all I've got."

"You don't have me."

"What do you mean?"

"Clayton, there's no future. *No mas*," I said.

"No who?"

"*No mas*," I repeated. "No more. Spanish."

"Are you Spanish?"

"No, Clayton, I'm not Spanish. Shit, will you let me fucking work?"

"Everything okay over here?"

I looked up and saw Vito looming over the table. Vito is a stocky, hairy man who is some kind of low-level mafioso or mafioso-wannabe who owns a few cheap horses and fancies himself a gifted horseplayer.

"Everything's fine," I said, scowling at Vito. Much as Clayton was pissing me off, it wasn't any of Vito's business. But that's the thing with these Vito-type guys at the track: What with my being a presentable woman under the age of eighty, a real rarity at Aqueduct, these guys get all protective of me. It might have been vaguely heartwarming if Vito wasn't so smarmy.

Vito furrowed his monobrow. He was sweating profusely even though it was cool inside the restaurant.

"I'm Vito," he said, aggressively extending his hand to Clayton, "and you are . . . ?"

"Clayton," said my soon-to-be-ex paramour, tentatively shaking Vito's oily paw.

"We all look out for Alice around here," Vito said.

Go fuck yourself, Vito, I thought, but didn't say. There might be a time when I needed him for something.

"Oh," said Clayton, confused, "that's good. I look out for her too."

Vito narrowed his already small eyes, looked from me to Clayton and back, then turned on his heels.

"See ya, Vito," I said as the tubby man headed out of the restaurant, presumably going down to the paddock-viewing area to volubly express his opinions about the contestants in the first race.

A few races passed. I made a nice little score on a mare shipping in from Philadelphia Park. She was trained by some obscure woman trainer, ridden by some obscure apprentice jockey, and had only ever raced at Philadelphia Park, so, in spite of a nice batch of past performances, she was being ignored on the tote board and went off at 14-1. I had $200 on her to win and wheeled her on top of all the logical horses in an exacta. I made out nicely and that put me slightly at ease and reduced some of the Clayton-induced aggravation that had gotten so severe I hadn't been able to eat my omelette and had started fantasizing about asking Vito to take Clayton out. Not *Take Him Out* take him out, I didn't want the guy dead or anything, just put a scare into him. But that would have entailed asking a favor of Vito and I had no interest in establishing that kind of dynamic with that kind of guy.

The fifth race came and I watched with interest to see how the colt Big Fred liked fared. The Todd Pletcher–trained horse Fred hated, who did in fact go off at 1-9, broke alertly from the six hole and tucked nicely just off the pace that was being set by a longshot with early speed. Gang of Seven, the horse Big Fred liked, was at the back of the pack, biding his time. With a quarter of a mile to go, Gang of Seven started making his move four wide, picking off his opponents until he was within spitting distance of the Pletcher horse. Gang of Seven and the Pletcher trainee dueled to the wire and both appeared to get their noses there at the same time.

"Too close to call," said the track announcer. A few minutes later, the photo was posted and the Pletcher horse had beat Big Fred's by a whisker.

"I'm a fucking idiot!" I heard Fred cry out from four tables away. I saw him get up and storm out of the restaurant, probably heading to the back patio to chain-smoke and make phone calls to twenty of his closest horseplaying friends, announcing his own idiocy.

"Guy's got a problem," Clayton said.

"No he doesn't," I replied, aggravated. While it was true that Big Fred had a little trouble with anger management, he was, at heart, a very decent human being.

I got up and walked away, leaving Clayton to stare after me with those dinner plate–sized eyes.

I went down to the paddock, hoping that Clayton wouldn't follow me. I saw Vito there staring out the big viewing window, his huge belly pressing against the glass. As I went to find a spot as far away as possible from Vito, I craned my neck just to check that Clayton hadn't followed me. He had. I saw him lumbering around near the betting windows, looking left and right. He'd find me at any minute.

So I did something a little crazy.

"Vito," I said, coming up behind him.

"Huh?" He turned around.

"Favor?" I asked.

His tiny black eyes glittered. "Anything, baby," he purred.

I already regretted what I was doing. "Can you scare that guy I was sitting with? Just make him a little nervous? Make him go home?"

Vito's tiny eyes got bigger, like someone had just dangled a bleeding hunk of filet mignon in front of him.

"You serious?" He stood closer to me.

I had a moment's hesitation. Then thought of Clayton's love pronouncements. "Yeah."

"Sure. Where is he?"

I glanced back and didn't see Clayton. "Somewhere around here, let's look."

Vito lumbered at my side. We searched all around the betting windows of the ground floor, but no Clayton. Then I glanced outside and spotted him standing near an empty bench, hunched and cold and lost-looking under the dove-gray sky.

"There," I said.

"You got it, baby," said Vito. Without another word, he

marched outside. I saw him accost Clayton. I saw Clayton tilt his head left and right like a confused dog would. I thought of Candy. Later this afternoon, I'd go home to her and just maybe, thanks to Vito, I wouldn't have to worry about the big oaf turning up with his big eyes and his inane declarations. Me and Candy could have some peace and quiet.

Now Clayton and Vito had come back inside and were walking together. They passed not far from where I was standing. Where was Vito taking him? I figured he'd just say a few choice words and that would be that. But they seemed to be going somewhere.

I followed them at a slight distance. I didn't really care if Clayton saw me at this point. They went down the escalator and out the front door. Vito was only wearing a thin button-down shirt but he didn't seem to register the bite of the February air. Clayton pulled his coat up around his ears.

They headed over to the subway platform. I saw Clayton pull out his MetroCard and go through the turnstile. Then he handed his card back to Vito, who went through after him.

What the fuck?

I stopped walking and stayed where I was in the middle of the ramp leading to the turnstiles. The two men were about a hundred yards in front of me but they had their backs to me. There wasn't anyone else on the platform.

They started raising their voices. I couldn't hear what was being said. There was wind and a big airplane with its belly low against the sky. Then the sound of an oncoming train and a blur of movement. A body falling down onto the tracks just as the train came. I braced myself for some sort of screeching of brakes. There wasn't any. The train charged into the station. The doors opened then closed. No one got on or off. The train pulled away. There was just one guy left standing on the platform. He was staring down at the tracks.

My fingers were numb.

I slowly walked up the platform. Found my MetroCard in my coat. Slid it in and went through the turnstile. I walked to the edge and looked down at the tracks. There was an arm separated from the rest of the body. Blood pouring out of the shoulder. The head twisted at an angle you never saw in life. I wasn't sure how the train conductor had failed to notice. The MTA has been very proud of its new One-Person Train Operation system that requires just one human to run the entire train. Maybe that's not enough to keep an eye out for falling bodies.

I felt nauseous. I started to black out and then he steadied me, putting his hands at the small of my back.

"He was talking about you," said Clayton, staring down at Vito's big mangled body. "Said you were going to blow him in exchange for him getting rid of me. He was just trying to upset me but it was disrespectful to you. I wanted to scare him but he fell onto the tracks." Clayton spoke so calmly. "He was talking shit about you, Alice," he added, raising his voice a little.

"Well," I said, "that wasn't very nice of him, was it?"

Clayton smiled.

He really wasn't a bad-looking guy.

UNDER THE THROGS NECK BRIDGE

BY DENIS HAMILL

Bayside

Times change, she thought. People don't.

Nikki reread the last of three diaries written by a dead woman named Eileen Lavin, took a deep breath, and spied Dr. George Sheridan through the Zhumell Spotting Scope mounted on a tripod in front of her sixteenth-floor window in her Bayside condo. He was leaving his luxury shore-front home over in Douglaston.

It was 8:55 a.m. on a sunny Mother's Day in Queens. Dr. Sheridan was dressed in his blue and white Abercrombie & Fitch tracksuit and Nikki's zoom lens was so powerful that even clear across the half-mile of Little Neck Bay she could see the double-G imprinted on his $375 dark-blue Gucci sneakers. She knew from watching him since New Year's that he wore a different tracksuit and rotated his designer sneakers every day.

"Mmmm-hmmm," Nikki whispered, knotting her yellow cotton tank top at her sternum and tying the laces on her New Balance sneakers, sweat socks bunched at the tops. Her white spandex shorts could not have been any tighter, accentuating her twenty-five-year-old ass that she'd slaved to sculpt into bubble perfection on the butt buster, StairMaster, and at the aerobics dance classes in the gym in the Bayview condo complex where she'd rented an apartment for six months.

Two things she'd noticed about all the women Dr. Sheridan chased—all were in their twenties and all had bubble butts.

Several minutes later, Nikki peered through the telescope again. The sun twinkled on the blue eye of Little Neck Bay as Sheridan boarded his forty-two-foot Silverton bearing the name *The Dog's Life* at his private dock behind his modernized Queen Anne–style house on a cul-de-sac off Shore Road. He climbed to the fly deck, fired up the twin engines, and aimed straight at Bayside Marina a half-mile across the water. Nikki knew Dr. Sheridan would moor *The Dog's Life* there before moving down the marina walkway to the jogging path. He would run south to the end of the asphalt path at Northern Boulevard, then make a U-turn and jog three miles north to Fort Totten, where he'd turn and head back to the marina to complete his daily six-mile route along one of the most idyllic stretches of waterfront in New York City.

"He's mine," Nikki whispered, before hurrying out of the apartment and down the sixteen flights of stairs to work up a good sweat before jogging out into the Bayside streets, passing the old colonials, the Queen Annes, the Tudors, and the gruesome McMansions and boxy two-family condo units that looked to her like they had been designed by shoemakers.

She huffed east on Thirty-Fifth Avenue and over to the secret little emerald called Crocheron Park. Nikki ran past a fraternity of dog walkers who let their pets chase taunting squirrels through the underused meadows. She legged past the fields where a father in a Mets jacket towered fly balls to his son who wore a Yankees hat. She nodded to three chunky women joggers who gasped counter-clockwise on the one-mile inside roadway and watched a tennis volley between two seventy-something men wearing white designer shorts with indoor winter tans. They stopped the volley to ogle Nikki. Since Viagra, seventy is the new seventeen, she thought. She slowed to a walk as she approached the southern-most of the two gazebos stationed on the steep leafy hill overlooking the jogging/bicycle road parallel to the humming Cross Island Parkway. Through the budding trees she would momentarily clock Dr. Sheridan making the southbound leg of his run.

It was 9:17 a.m. now. She knew his moves better than he did. Glistening with sweat, her red headband securing her long dark hair, she gulped some Poland Spring water, then poured out all but an inch from a twenty-ounce bottle. Through the verdant trees she saw him, running hard, like someone fleeing from his own footprints.

Nikki bounded down the long stone steps from the park to the Cross Island overpass. She leaped from step to step in a graceful ballet, her body taking blurry flight between footfalls. She cut over the six lanes of the Cross Island, busy with Mother's Day travelers, about half of them on their way to visit Mom now living in some old person's orphanage, with a name like Shady Acres, after having been abandoned by the very ingrates she had brought into the world. Nikki gazed right and here came Dr. Sheridan hoofing toward her just as she bounced down the final ramp onto the jogging path, her breasts heaving, sweat lashing off her face in a spray of tiny sunlit diamonds.

They exchanged glances. Dr. Sheridan smiled. Nikki didn't. A lifetime of running had kept his forty-five-year-old body as trim as Nikki imagined it had been when he was twenty. She pivoted, sprung, and ran ahead of him, ham muscles bunching in the damp white Spandex like sins waiting to be committed. Her thigh muscles rippled as she passed fishermen in rubber suits standing hip deep in the tame bay where swans and geese and mallards and ducks looped around the sailboats. A spotted hawk circled and a pair of fat black crows exploded from the wild reeds into the high trees of Crocheron.

A lone whooping crane stood on one leg on a sand spit, bleating like a traffic cop. Nikki watched a pair of young lovers, a pretty Asian girl and a skinny white boy with mousse-spiked hair, sharing the two earplugs of an iPod and strolling hand-in-hand as if never wanting this song, this walk, this morning to end. The girl gave her companion a gentle bump of her left hip in the first movement of their ephemeral dance of spring. Love him till it hurts, Nikki thought. She knew Dr. Sheridan was behind her undressing her with his eyes.

Up ahead she saw the sun gilding across the long steel bones of the Throgs Neck Bridge. A cabin cruiser grumped beneath it. Nausea rose in Nikki like a dirty tide. She contained it with her sense of mission. She was gonna make a bad thing right.

Nikki knew Dr. Sheridan would shower and change in the luxury salon of his boat before hopping in his two-door silver BMW Z4, with the *MEOW1* vanity plate that he kept in one of his two rented parking spots by the marina—the second spot was for babes who spent the night on his boat. Then he'd drive the five minutes to work at his Menagerie Animal Clinic across the street from the Bay Terrace Shopping Mall. There, even on Mother's Day, he would give comfort to the daily parade of heartsick pet owners, most of them women—divorcées, young and single, widows, unhappily married and happy to cheat—who came whenever Fido or Fluffy so much as sneezed, just to hear the soothing timbre of Dr. Sheridan's deep voice. Observing him over four months, from winter until spring, Nikki had deduced that Dr. Sheridan didn't mix business with pleasure. He mixed pleasure with more pleasure, she thought. Never with friends or clients. Only with strangers.

With his handsome and gray-only-at-the-temples good looks, a multimillion-dollar bay-front home, his own luxury boat, a Beemer and a Benz in his driveway, a lucrative veterinarian clinic, and membership in the local community board, Dr. George Sheridan possessed one of the most sought after naked left ring fingers in eastern Queens.

Fat chance, girls, she thought. For on Thursday night, Ladies' Nite, when Cosmopolitans were free for babes in most of the crowded bars along Bell Boulevard, Dr. Sheridan could usually be found at the three-deep mahogany bar in the ambient bordello lighting of Uncle Jack's Steakhouse, dressed in an Armani or Hugo Boss, with open-necked shirt, Botticelli loafers, no socks, sipping Grey Goose and tonic through a swizzle straw.

When he met the right hot chick, never older than the French formula of half-his-age-plus-seven, he'd buy her drinks. After two rounds he'd ask if she was hungry and then treat her to the famous crab cakes, shrimp the size of mandolins, and the porterhouse steak that he insisted was as good if not better than the ones served at Peter Luger's over in Brooklyn. "Meal whores," Nikki had overheard Dr. Sheridan call his prey to other middle-aged men on the prowl on Ladies' Nites.

Dr. Sheridan always paid with cash when he left and usually had one of the Cosmo'd babes plopping her bubble butt in the leather bucket passenger seat of his Beemer on his way home to Douglaston. But Nikki knew—as did he—that those consenting adults in high heels were as much on the make as Dr. Sheridan. He wanted to get in their pants; the ladies wanted to get on his left ring finger. It was a game, though he was the one who stacked the deck.

In the mornings after, through her all-revealing telescope, Nikki had seen many of those young women stagger out of Sheridan's house, or the salon of his boat, still dazed and woozy. He'd drive them back to the cars they had left on Bell Boulevard the night before.

Of late, however, with spring prickling the air, Dr. Sheridan was fond of taking his lady friends for a nightcap at the elegant, brilliantly lighted Caffè on the Green overlooking the Throgs Neck Bridge, a high-end restaurant that was once home to Rudolph Valentino and Mayor Fiorello LaGuardia. And then for a moonlight cruise on his $300,000 luxury Silverton, replete with living room, salon, wide-screen satellite TV, quadraphonic sound system, full-service kitchen, elegant dining room, master bedroom with queen-size bed, and smaller guest bedroom. Nikki would watch him drop anchor under the Throgs Neck Bridge, where he and his young dates would spend the night rocking in the tide.

Nikki knew his routine. A month ago, she had positioned herself alone at the bar of Uncle Jack's so that Dr. Sheridan would spot her wearing her skin-tightest jeans, high spaghetti-strap heels, and matching tight red leather waist jacket. He offered to buy her a drink and she asked for a bottle of Heineken, no glass. As she drank the beer, she watched him sip his Grey Goose in careful measures through the swizzle-stick straw.

"Real guys don't suck straws," she said, pulling it from his mouth.

He laughed. She clinked her bottle against his glass and he drank from the lip.

"Real guys offer to buy beautiful women like you dinner," he said.

"Maybe some other time. I just stopped off for a cold one before work."

"Where do you work?"

"Queens."

"Queens? Queens what? Queens Hospital? Queens College? Queens Supreme?"

She slugged more beer. "Nah."

He laughed. "Okay, doing what?"

"My job."

She wanted him to remember her. Nothing makes a rich man remember you like a little bit of mystery and declining a dinner invitation, she thought. Go to dinner, fuck his brains out, and tell him your life story . . . and you are as memorable as yesterday's Dow index. Turn him down, keep your pants on, tell him nothing, and he'll never forget you.

He wrote his cell number and his private e-mail address on the back of his embossed business card and handed it to her. She opened her pocketbook and stuffed the card into her wallet, then discreetly slipped the swizzle stick in a clear plastic bag. She finished the beer, said thanks, and left for work.

The job consisted of sitting in her dark-blue Jeep Cherokee with tinted windows, parked up the block on Bell Boulevard. Three hours later, after bar hopping along the same street, Dr. Sheridan left a place called The First Edition accompanied by a gorgeous wobbly blonde with a bubble butt and pants so tight they looked like they hurt. Nikki figured her fake ID said she had turned twenty-one the day before.

Nikki followed Dr. Sheridan's BMW to the Bayside Marina, where he and his date boarded *The Dog's Life*. Later, Nikki watched them through her telescope from her condo window as he pulled the boat under the Throgs Neck Bridge. After one glass of bubbly, the young woman got up from a deck chair and staggered sideways. Dr. Sheridan helped her into his salon and closed the door.

Hours later, Nikki watched him come up on deck wearing only boxer shorts, gabbing on a cell phone. The second time he came up he was completely naked, spraying Windex and wiping off the railings and deck furniture. Nikki turned away, but then felt compelled to look back with the zoom lens because something seemed odd. A close inspection through the telescope revealed that Dr. Sheridan was a man completely devoid of body hair. Shaved from neck to ankles, like a toy poodle in summer. Nikki could think of nothing less sexy than a completely hairless naked man doing housework. *Retch-ro-sexual*, she thought, suppressing a wave of nausea.

The girl never reemerged. Not until morning when Dr. Sheridan had to help her off the boat on her wobbly platform shoes. Through the telescope the woman appeared to be dazed, confused. He stroked her hair, shook his head, kissed her, and patted her cheek, as if reassuring her that nothing sexual had happened. Then he tapped his watch and helped her into his Beemer, and drove her back toward Bell Boulevard where she would have left her car the night before. Some hangovers you never recover from, Nikki thought.

Now, on this sun-filled Mother's Day, Nikki jogged just ahead of Dr. Sheridan along the wooden planks of the Bayside Marina, knowing he was watching her. She slowed to a sweaty, panting walk. Asian and Latino fishermen crowded the end of the marina, casting their lines into the dark waters. A bride and groom stood posing for pictures that would keep them forever young, even when married life got old before they did. Nikki nodded to a grizzled dock hand running the boat-rental concession and entered the snack shop at the end of the pier, opened the soft drink refrigerator door, grabbed an ice-cold bottle of Poland Spring, and approached the cashier. She patted her hips as if just realizing she didn't have her jogging pouch with her.

"Damn it," she said. "Forgot my money." She turned to return the bottle, counting: *One Mississippi, two Mississ—*

"Let me buy it for you," she heard Dr. Sheridan say in that soothing, deep voice that sounded like a priest giving absolution.

She looked up. "Nah, thanks anyway." She opened the refrigerator door.

"C'mon, don't you remember me?"

"Sorry?"

"Uncle Jack's? Several months ago. You said I looked gay sipping a straw."

She snapped her fingers and pointed at him. "I didn't say you looked gay. I said that real guys don't suck straws."

"Dr. Sheridan . . . um, George. I'm a veterinarian. I offered to buy you dinner."

He paid for her water and bought some for himself.

"Yeah, well, thanks for the water, doc." She turned for the exit.

"You said you'd have dinner with me some other time."

"I'm positive I said *maybe*."

"*Touché*. Is maybe still an option?"

She smirked. "Look, I don't date married guys and you look like the married ty—"

He held up his bare left hand. "Never."

She cracked open the water bottle, took a long gulp, her neck muscles and veins bulging, her face and pronounced clavicle bones gleaming with a patina of fresh sweat. She rolled the cold plastic bottle on the back of her neck. "Italian?"

"Caffè on the Green?"

"Promise not to suck straw?"

He laughed and nodded. "Promise."

She swigged more water. "When?"

"Tonight? Eight? I'll pick you up. Where do you—"

"See you then."

"Hey," he called out, "I don't even know your name . . ."

But she was already on the hoof, buns bunching, hair flapping in the wind off Little Neck Bay. Got him, she thought.

Over dinner at a window table in the spacious Caffè on the Green, decorated with polished Italian marble, Oriental carpeting, lustrous mahogany, looking out on the glittering Throgs Neck Bridge, Dr. Sheridan asked Nikki dozens of questions. "Why won't you tell me your last name?"

"I only give my last name to people who pay me. Friends call me Nikki."

"Like Madonna? Or Cher? You a singer? Or fugitive or something?"

"Something."

"Family?"

Nikki told him that she had no siblings. That her mother had died when she was young. That her father had never really been in her life. That she had fended mostly for herself since moving to New York after college.

"What school?"

"You never heard of it."

When he asked what she did for a living, she said, "IT."

"Aha, the IT Girl. Information technology for whom?"

"Freelance," she said, eating an arugula salad. "I work for online database companies that locate people."

"Like old sweethearts and schoolmates?"

"Yeah, and for estate lawyers looking for beneficiaries, private investigators looking for abducted kids and dead-beat parents, orphans who want to find their birth parents, bail bondsmen searching for bail jumpers, people who need criminal background checks on potential spouses or prospective employees."

"Cool. How'd you get into that line of work?"

"Doing my family tree."

"Fascinating."

"Can be."

"How do people find you?" he asked.

"I find them. I choose my own hours. But I'm gonna launch a website soon."

"Awesome! Need any investors?"

"Nope."

The more he probed, and the more evasive she got, the more intrigued he became. Everyone loves an enigma, she thought.

"So what brought you to Bayside?"

"Enough about me," she replied, then asked about his family.

He poked at his branzini filet with lemon, garlic, and capers. "I'm an only child," he said. "Lost both my parents when I was seventeen. Drowned in a boating accident." He pointed out the window at the bay, where the lights of the 1800-foot-long bridge reflected in the night waters. "Right there, under the Throgs Neck."

"Sorry."

"It was a long time ago."

"Some things hurt forever."

He nodded.

After she declined coffee and dessert, he invited her for a nightcap at his house, where she could see his menagerie of exotic animals.

"Nah."

He seemed surprised. He asked if she'd like to join him for a midnight cruise through New York Harbor.

"Nah."

"Cold Heinekens on board. Or Roederer Cristal champagne."

"Cristal's tempting but I never put myself in a hump-or-jump situation on first dates."

He laughed. "Then how about on a second date?"

"Maybe."

"How will I know?"

"I still have your card."

Dr. Sheridan paid the bill in cash, like a man who didn't want to leave a trail. Like a body-shaved man who wipes away fingerprints with Windex.

They left Caffè on the Green and walked across the sprawling lawn toward the parking lot, passing the duck pond that reflected the moon shining through the hundred-year-old willows. An ornate marble fountain burbled, and a thousand tiny white lights dotted the shrubbery like immortal fireflies. A frail breeze sighed off Little Neck Bay and Nikki imagined Rudy Valentino putting the make on some hot flapper here long before the Throgs Neck was even imagined.

Dr. Sheridan offered to drive Nikki home, but she declined. In the well-lit parking lot she thanked him for dinner and said, "Goodnight, doc," then shook his hand. His palm was damp. He leaned in to kiss her and she backed away, sliding her hand from his, and before the valet could retrieve Dr. Sheridan's Mercedes 450, she clacked her high heels off into the night, looping home through the dark drowsy side streets of eastern Queens.

* * *

Nikki watched Dr. Sheridan through the telescope for the next two weeks. She watched him jog along the Cross Island Parkway each day, ogling the female joggers, chatting them up, handing them business cards. He took a young woman on a boat ride just before sunset one evening. When he dropped her off at a small weed-shrouded fishing dock halfway between the Bayside Marina and Fort Totten after dark, Nikki saw her stumble up the jogging path to her car in one of Dr. Sheridan's two parking spots. She collapsed into the driver's seat and appeared to fall fast asleep.

An hour later, Nikki jogged up to the car, stopped, knocked on the window, and asked if everything was okay. "S'all right," the glassy-eyed girl slurred. She asked the time while stifling a yawn. Nikki told her it was almost 10 p.m. The girl was astonished. She sat up, shook her head like a wet hound, and started her car. "My fuckin' husband'll kill me," she said. Nikki asked if anything bad had happened to her on the boat. The girl blinked several times and said, "Boat?"

"Were you sexually compromised, hon?"

"Fuckin' lesbo freak," the girl shot back, powering up the window and squealing off onto the Cross Island.

At night during this period, Nikki sat in her Jeep Cherokee staking out Dr. Sheridan as he cruised the local bar scene on a mobbed Bell Boulevard. There were a dozen bars in this four-block strip that brought young people from all over Queens and Nassau County by car or the Long Island Rail Road. She watched Dr. Sheridan, big fish in a small, well-stocked pond, sample Uncle Jack's, Bourbon Street, Sullivan's, KC's Saloon, Dempsey's, Donovan's, Monahan's, Fitzgerald's, No No's, and The First Edition. On Thursdays, Fridays, and Saturdays, Dr. Sheridan left with different young women each night. He spent the night aboard *The Dog's Life* with each one, anchored under the Throgs Neck Bridge. No one's that lucky, she thought.

On a Friday morning in the second week of June, Nikki received the results from Dr. Sheridan's swizzle straw from the DNA lab. All that she'd suspected was now scientific fact. The DNA on the drinking straw confirmed everything that the woman named Eileen Lavin had contended long ago to her family, friends, church, and the authorities—and in her diaries.

Dressed in her jogging gear, Nikki sat down in front of her telescope with Eileen Lavin's diaries and went over everything again. Lavin had told police that she went aboard a boat with a guy named George Sheridan who said he had some golden Labrador retriever puppies from which she might choose a mascot for the orphan kids she was working with as a novice in the order of the Sisters of Mercy. Eileen had finished three years at St. John's University, lived in a convent in the Bronx for eighteen months, and had taken all the temporary vows of poverty, obedience, and chastity. She had met George Sheridan when he attended a St. John's swim team meet against rival Wagner College. That night, beautiful Eileen Lavin, who was on a full athletic scholarship, led the Johnnies to a major victory over the Seahawks. A series of photographs in the *St. John's Torch* student newspaper showed young Lavin in a team bathing suit. She was gonna be a nun, thought Nikki. But she had a bubble butt.

George Sheridan was a St. John's senior majoring in veterinary medicine. Eileen Lavin was studying social work, working toward her BA. She was also preparing for her final vows of sisterhood. Sheridan ate lunch with her at school several times. He cheered at her meets. Then one afternoon after school, Sheridan invited her aboard his boat. He said he would gladly take some of the poor inner-city orphan kids she was working with out for a day of fishing and sightseeing. He also told her about some pedigree puppies he had at home and said that he'd like to donate one to the orphanage. Late that afternoon, Eileen went out on the boat with Sheridan. Her diary said that he was a perfect gentleman at first and took her for a cruise around New York Harbor. On the way back to his home in Douglaston, he dropped anchor under the Throgs Neck Bridge. As the sun went down over Queens, he asked Eileen to pray with him for his parents who'd drowned in those very waters. Then he served popcorn and gave her a glass of lemonade before they were to head back to his home in Douglaston and select a puppy. The last thing she remembered were the lights of the Throgs Neck playing on the night waters of Little Neck Bay.

Then, according to her diary, total blackout. When she awoke in the predawn, she was sitting on a bus stop bench down the road from her Novitiate House. She was groggy and very sore between her legs.

Years later, after an exhaustive Internet search, Nikki had found the old police report and Eileen Lavin's Family Court records. She had tracked down Eileen's father, a broken old man who still lived in Bayside. She told him who she was, and he had let her read his daughter's diaries. Eileen's mother had since died, never really recovering from the scandal, shame, and sorrow her daughter had brought upon the family with the out-of-wedlock pregnancy, expulsion from the convent, withdrawal from St. John's, and then her suicide.

The diary entry recounting Nikki's boat trip with George Sheridan said that she had bled most of the next day. She didn't want to believe that she had been drugged and raped by the kindly schoolmate. She had no memory of any such monstrous thing happening and she had woken up fully clothed. She was not beaten or bruised. She had no memory of seeing any puppies. She called Sheridan, but he didn't return her calls. She had no proof that she had ever been with him, in his car, his house, or on his boat. Never mind his bed.

Afraid she would be punished, or asked to leave the Novitiate, she kept her dark fears of having been raped to herself. She did not go to a hospital or to the police right away. Instead, she prayed. She did a Novena and the Stations of the Cross. She lit votive candles. She worked with orphan children who had more problems that she could ever know. She went to confession in Manhattan where no one would recognize her. She kept a diary for her and God's eyes only.

The diaries revealed that after the night on Sheridan's boat, Eileen missed a menstrual cycle. Then a second. After three and a half months without a period, she confided in her Mother Superior that she feared she was pregnant. That she'd been raped. The stern, skeptical, no-nonsense head sister who'd seen many a young novice surrender over the years to the weakness of the flesh before taking final vows asked why Eileen hadn't told anyone till then. Eileen said she'd been afraid.

"You were afraid of going to hell," Mother Superior said.

"I wasn't sure I was raped. Or even pregnant. Until now."

"The alternative being that you are the second coming of the Blessed Virgin?"

"I was afraid! Afraid of you. Afraid of the shame to my parents. Afraid of God."

"And so now, three months later, you blame a young man, a good Catholic boy from St. John's studying to be a veterinarian? You aren't even sure he ever laid a hand on you. You have no memory of any such thing. No evidence. Yet you accuse him and bring shame on him, upon a great Catholic university, to make up for your own weakness? Your own mortal sin?"

"You have it all wrong. I was a virgin when I stepped on his boat!"

"You've violated your vows," Mother Superior said. "You've committed the sin of fornication. You are bringing a child out of wedlock into the world. Stop pointing fingers at others. Go home and point the finger at the dirty girl in the mirror."

When she was four months pregnant, Eileen Lavin was told she could not take her vows of sisterhood. She had not kept her temporary vow of chastity. She'd sinned, covered up that sin, compounded the sin by lying about the original sin, and now she was carrying a bastard child. "There is no room for untruthful, unwed mothers in the sisterhood," Mother Superior said.

The diaries revealed that when Eileen finally contacted the police, they asked why she'd waited four months to report a rape. They asked why she hadn't gone to a hospital. Why she hadn't contacted police right away. They asked why any woman would give birth to a rapist's baby. She explained that she was a devout Catholic, and could never abort any baby. The skeptical detectives from the 111th Precinct made a cursory call on Sheridan. He denied ever having Eileen Lavin aboard his boat or in his house. He invited them to dust for fingerprints. He said the woman was delusional. That her nickname was Sister Psycho.

The cops believed Sheridan. They apologized for bothering him. "We cannot indict a man on the word of a defrocked nun with no memory of the alleged crime," said the Queens District Attorney's office who investigated the case in 1982. "There's no proof the baby is Sheridan's. A blood test could only eliminate him, not identify him." There was no definitive DNA test in 1982.

Eileen's devout, old-world, immigrant Irish Catholic parents ostracized her. They had been shamed by a whispering campaign in their Bayside parish where they had previously bragged about their pious daughter going into the convent. Eileen had become just another unwed, knocked-up college slut. Gossip swirled. Neighbors snickered. Friends didn't return her calls. Because of the pregnancy, she lost her swimming scholarship. She was forced to drop out of her last year of St. John's and had the baby shortly after she turned twenty. Her mother refused to have anything to do with the child. Or Eileen. After the baptism, Eileen reluctantly gave the baby up for adoption.

Then, the diaries showed, Eileen went into a period of deep and prolonged depression. She reapplied for the Novitiate a year later, but Mother Superior said she was psychologically, morally, and spiritually unfit for the sisterhood. She had no family to turn to. Her religious dreams were shattered. She tried in vain to retrieve her baby from the adoption agency. The Queens Family Court refused to restore custody of her child because she was too emotionally and financially unstable. In thorough despair, Eileen ventured out onto the Throgs Neck Bridge one summer night and jumped 120 feet into the inky waters where she had lost her virginity on George Sheridan's boat.

On a Friday morning in the second week of June, a quarter-century later, Nikki spied Dr. George Sheridan through her telescope as he left his house in Douglaston for his morning run. She timed it so that she ran into him twenty-two minutes later while descending from the Crocheron overpass of the Cross Island. He undressed her with his eyes so blatantly that she feared he'd leave a stain. Then he sidled up and ran alongside her toward the Bayside Marina.

"What are you doing on Sunday night, doc?" she asked.

"I'm free."

"Thought I might take you up on that moonlight cruise."

"Fabulous. Want to eat somewhere first?"

"I'll pack dinner."

"I'll pour you champagne. Where do I pick you up?"

She told him she'd be waiting at 8 p.m. sharp at the little fishing dock alongside the Cross Island between Bayside Marina and Fort Totten.

"Date," he said.

She promptly jogged up the ramp of the next overpass and he headed on toward the Throgs Neck Bridge.

On Sunday night, Dr. Sheridan showed Nikki how to start, stop, and steer *The Dog's Life* as they cruised back to Little Neck Bay from their tour of New York Harbor. Nikki wore black Spandex clam-diggers, a black halter top, a black Mets jacket, and a black Mets cap, which she tilted up when they sailed under the chilly shadow of the Throgs Neck. Sheridan cut the engines and suggested they go down on deck to "eat, drink, and be silly."

"Okay," Nikki said.

He dropped anchor under the bridge as Nikki opened the picnic basket and served chicken and broccoli tossed in a cold penne with olive oil and thinly sliced red bell peppers, seeded Italian bread, and a tomato and basil salad. He walked into the salon and she watched as he poured a flute of champagne from an already opened bottle of Roederer Cristal chilling in a silver ice bucket. He made himself a Grey Goose and tonic.

They headed back out of the salon and he handed her the champagne as *The Dog's Life* lolled on the night tide.

"You aren't having champagne?"

"Real guys drink Grey Goose," he said. "From the glass."

She smiled and they sat down and started to eat. She watched champagne bubbles rise in the flute glass, each one like a long buried corpse popping to the surface.

"You like it out here?" he asked.

"Nah."

"Why?"

She stood and carried her glass to the railing. She leaned over it and swept her free left hand across the Throgs Neck as she carefully poured her champagne into the bay with her right hand, out of Dr. Sheridan's view.

"Too beautiful a place to die," she said, her back to him, lifting her empty glass and pretending to guzzle her champagne. She turned to him and forced a belch into her fist.

He said, "Die?"

"You told me your parents drowned here under the Throgs Neck."

He ate a bite of pasta, took a sip of his Grey Goose, and leaned back in his deck chair. "You have a very good memory."

"Yeah." She waved the empty champagne flute as she took a sideways step across the deck. She knew it took most date-rape drugs about fifteen minutes to kick in. She excused herself and tottered into the luxurious salon that was bigger than some Manhattan apartments. She spent about ten minutes in the bathroom, then staggered out, tripping over the step at the threshold to the deck.

"You okay?" he asked.

She grabbed her head and lurched across the deck. He looped his right arm around her waist.

"Easy," he said.

"Feel funny."

"Maybe you should come inside and lie down."

"Tryin' to 'memba . . . something I gotta tell ya . . ."

He led her inside, slammed the salon door closed, and shoved Nikki onto her back on his couch. He pulled off his shirt in a single flourish. "Now the fucking fun starts, mama."

Nikki lay motionless on the couch, hands in her jacket pockets. "Whajoo give me?"

"Ketamine," he said, unbuckling his pants. "Horse tranquilizer. When it wears off you'll remember nothing. But tonight you're mine, for any fucking thing I please." He stripped to his boxer shorts, turned his back to hang up his pants. Then he kneeled before Nikki and slid his two index fingers under the waistband of her Spandex pants. "Now, let's see what you have here for the ass master."

Nikki pulled her right hand out of her jacket pocket and rammed a .25 caliber Colt automatic to his left temple. "What I have here is the end of your miserable life, motherfucker," she said.

Sheridan froze, still kneeling in front of Nikki. "Please . . . It's a joke."

"Real side splitter," she said. "Let's see if you remember the same old joke you pulled on a girl named Eileen Lavin."

His face collapsed into a spasm of tics, coming apart in pieces like a mosaic held together by a lifetime of lies. "Who?"

"Maybe a little champagne will improve your memory."

Nikki stood up, pointing the gun, grabbed the bottle of champagne, and poured.

"Drink," she commanded. He looked at the bubbling flute, his eyes skittery. He licked his dry lips. "Drink the fucking champagne, Dr. Sheridan."

"No, please—"

She shoved the pistol into his left ear again and yanked back the metal slide. "Then I will blow your sick fucking brains across your boat and leave you for the gulls."

He drank the entire glassful.

She poured another. "Drink, motherfucker."

He downed it.

She said, "Eileen Lavin was going to be a nun."

"Her? She was a nut. Everyone called her Sister Psycho."

"You took her on your father's boat. Out here where you take all the young girls, because this is the spot where your parents died all right. But they didn't drown. No, this is the spot where your father discovered your mother screwing his best friend on his boat. The place where he killed them, in a jealous rage. And then shot himself. When you were seventeen. I found all this with a few keyboard strokes. *Jilted Hubby Kills Wife, Lover, Self.* Nice. And so what was it, doc? When you wanted to get even with Mom, you took poor Eileen Lavin out here to the same spot? On the same boat? Here, under the Throgs Neck Bridge, you drugged and raped her. Over and over and over again. All night."

"No girl gets on a boat with a man unless she wants to go with the flow."

"Like your mother? Your father found out she was going with the flow on his boat while he was busting his ass at work to pay for it. He heard talk, slipped out here in a dingy, snuck aboard, and made her pay. And you're still making her pay, aren't you, you sick fuck? Every time you take another young girl out on your boat, you're getting even with Mom. Am I right? But you got careless with Eileen Lavin. You didn't use protection. Or maybe the rubber broke because she was a virgin. Something went wrong. And you knocked her up. But it was 1982. Before DNA testing was refined. She couldn't prove it was you."

"You're as nuts as Sister Psycho," he said, yawning.

"She was a fucking virgin! You took her out here, you drugged her, you raped her, you knocked her up. She had to give the baby up for adoption. Then she tried to get her baby back. Everyone abandoned her. You destroyed her life. You destroyed her soul. You destroyed her mind. Until she went up on that bridge and jumped. And died right about here, right where we're anchored."

"You can't blame that on me. And why the hell do you care? What's it to you?"

"That baby she put in the orphanage? That baby was adopted by a good family, a nice elderly Greek family in Astoria. They called her Nicola. They died when the kid was twelve. Then that baby was bounced around the foster system like a meal ticket. Treated like, well, a bastard. Scroungy orphan. Second-class citizen. She was beaten, abused, neglected. The only time anyone paid any attention to her was when she grew a pair of tits. Then she couldn't get the filthy bastards off her! Then she became a party favor."

"Fuck . . . you . . . talking 'bout?" His voice was becoming disjointed.

"I'm talking about your own daughter, asshole! The one you made when you raped Eileen Lavin. The rape-baby that caused her to jump off that bridge." She pulled the diaries out of her jacket pockets and read wrenching portions of Eileen's words to Dr. George Sheridan.

"She . . . wush . . . fucking nuts!" he said, his voice slurry and his jaw slack. "Jush . . . like . . . joooo." His eyes were bloodshot and glazed, like stained glass. He stood and staggered sideways, a straw man, his body devoid of muscle control. Nikki pulled a pair of driving gloves from a jacket pocket, wiggled them on, and led him back onto the rear deck of *The Dog's Life*, rocking in the bay under the Throgs Neck.

"You started using the horse drug as a veterinary student. You used it on Eileen Lavin. You literally fucked her out of a life." Nikki paused and looked up at the bridge, crowded with cars under the crescent moon. "You also fucked me out of a mother. And you gave me a fucking monster for a father. When I was old enough, I went into computers just so I could trace my biological parents. I found out who my real mother was from the old baptismal records. My first adoptive mother told me the name of the church where I was baptized. I was the only girl baptized there the year I was born without a father's name on the certificate. Once I had my mother's name, Eileen Lavin's father—my grandfather, that piece of sanctimonious dogshit—gave me her diaries. From them I found marvelous you. Times change. People don't. Your hardwiring is the same. Crisscrossed, short-circuited. You're fucking *e-vil*, doc. Twenty-five years later, you're still taking girls my mother's age out on your boat. Drugging them. Date raping them. Only now you're more careful. You use a rubber. You shave your body. You pay for meals in cash. You wipe away all fingerprints. You leave no trace of anything. But you are still getting even with your mother, aren't you? Before you tried to rape me, you even called me *mama!*"

"I never . . . hurt anybody," he said. "I just fucked 'em, thass all."

Nikki shoved him into a deck chair, pressed the button for the mechanical winch, and the anchor rose. She climbed to the fly deck and started the twin engines. When she was done here, she would simply steer the boat to the small fishing dock, hop off, and let the tide take *The Dog's Life* back out into the dark bay. But first Nikki descended to the deck and packed up the picnic basket which she'd take with her, then washed the flute glass, filled the champagne bottle with water, and threw them into the bay. She used the Windex to wipe her fingerprints from everything she'd touched on board. She'd get rid of her sneakers before she got home, in case they left footprints.

Nikki led Dr. Sheridan, who was barely able to walk, to the edge of the aft deck. She opened the entry gate and looked him in his bleary eyes. "Do you know what today is?" she asked.

His head flopped like a bobble doll's. "Shuuunday."

"It's the third Shuuunday of Juuuuune, assbag," she said, mocking him. "That's the day my mother, Eileen Lavin, jumped from this bridge twenty-five years ago."

"Fuckin' nutjob." His voice sounded like it was coming out of a deep well.

She opened the gate. "Fuck you."

"How . . . can joo do thish . . . to me?"

"Easy," Nikki Lavin Sheridan replied, shrugging. "I have your blood in my veins."

"Please . . ."

"Happy Father's Day, Dad," she said, and pushed him into the black water. She watched him flail and kick. The ketamine was paralyzing him. He tried to scream but his mouth filled with water, and Nikki watched Dr. George Sheridan slip into the same grave that had swallowed her mother under the Throgs Neck Bridge.

GOLDEN VENTURE

BY JILL EISENSTADT

The Rockaways

He's waiting for her to die, Rose knows. She's no dummy. It's June and her son, Paulie, is once again thinking about inheriting her house on Rockaway Beach.

"You're getting up there," is this year's phraseology, as if turning eighty-five begins her ascent. Up and up, she'll levitate a little higher each birthday, while Paul, Maureen, and the kids line up on the sand waving bye bye. Paulie's latest brainstorm is to just move in now—this weekend. "We'll take care of you," he insists, somehow oblivious to the way this sounds.

"Maureen's a doctor, after all. You'll get to play with your grandkids. All the time!"

"Oh, they'd sure love the free baby-sitting . . ." Rose is telling her new Chinese friend, Li. "But at fourteen and ten? Those kids think I'm boring and smell weird. And I am. And I do! I'm no dummy!"

This strikes Rose as so hysterically funny that soon she's collapsed in a stained dining room chair, cradling her arthritic elbow. Harboring an illegal alien is one of her first ever crimes (give or take a little parking on her late husband Vincent's handicapped permit). She feels Sambuca giddy, puffy with pride. If Vin, may he rest in peace, could see Li lying here in his favorite shirt—the ivory one with black piping and breast pocket snaps—he'd surely be impressed. Donning their cowboy best, Vin and his buddies from the social club used to spend each Sunday morning riding around Belle Harbor on their mopeds. "The Good Guys" they called themselves, and went looking for good deeds to do. But Vin had never risen to this Robin Hood level: A good deed and a crime too!

"It was mostly his excuse to get out of church," Rose adds and crosses herself; a reflex.

"*Yesu Jidu!*" Li suddenly claps from his spot beneath the dining room table, an awkward choice of seating conversation-wise but okay; maybe it's cultural.

"*Yesu Jidu? . . . Parla Inglese?*" Maybe he's dreaming with his eyes open. So weak and emaciated, it's like taking care of a child again. Like Vin in the end. But this fellow can't be much older than thirty. A large bruised head on a skeletal frame and wet-looking hair even now that it's dried. In one hand he clutches a Ziploc bag containing a small roll of bills and a phone number written on a scrap of newsprint. With the other, he points a shaky finger at the iron crucifix from Calabria hung over Rose's marble sideboard.

"*Yesu Jidu,*" he repeats. "Me!"

At last, Rose gets it. "You're Jesus Christ! Well, no wonder we're hitting it off!"

And not an hour ago, he was on his knees, in his undies, puking up the Atlantic Ocean all over her shower house.

For some reason, this cracks her up all over again.

When the helicopters whirred her awake, the phone was ringing too. Rose fumbled for her bifocals. Three a.m.

"Are all the doors locked?" Paulie panted. "Turn on the TV! There's a boatload of illegal chinks out—!"

"Who taught you to talk like that?"

"I'm comin' over."

"Who said?"

"Don't you get it? They're washin' up by—what?"

"What?"

"I heard something."

"Helicopters?"

"Oh, Christ, Ma! Get up! Turn on the TV!"

It was easier to just push aside the window curtain. Yes, the giant metal insects were out there hovering. But that was not so unusual here on the shore where they're often called in for drownings, drug traffickers, and big-wig airport transport. And what with that 120,000-pound dead whale that just washed up in Arverne Friday, the sky had been pocked with press copters all week. But this new swarm buzzed the other end of the beach, up near Riis Park, and seemed to be composed of police and Coast Guard choppers.

"Get Dad's gun; I'll feel better."

"Paulie . . ."

"Get it, Ma, or they'll be stormin' our fuckin' house."

"Who taught you that language?" *Our* house.

"If you don't get it, I'm comin'."

So what choice did Rose have but to slowly unload herself from the bed? She'd never get back to sleep now anyhow. Instead of a robe, she preferred one of Paul's old red surf-shop sweatshirts. Instead of slippers, flip-flops. Better to accommodate a hammer toe or two.

The gun, still loaded and ready to guard Vincent's Bootery on 116th Street was hidden, appropriately, in one of Vin's old cowboy boots. It was painful, physically and every which way, for Rose to crouch in the closet and extract it. Yet she lingered, running her hand along the familiar broken-in black leather and fancy white boot stitching, letting herself miss the husband she mostly despised. The revolver sagged heavily in her big front sweatshirt pocket but the feeling was not altogether unpleasant, a little like a baby there. Vincent's Bootery was now a cell phone store.

The backdoor sticks. To open it, you have to lean with your whole weight, *wham*, shoulder-first. Each time Rose does this, she imagines falling onto the brick patio where she'll lay in crumpled agony until 8:30 a.m. when, obligated, Paulie comes to check she's not drinking, and forevermore forces her to wear that medical leash with the button to press in case of emergencies.

"I know you would have come and rescued me," Rose says, as she shuffles toward Li with a breakfast tray. "If I were out there wailing in pain, I know you would."

Li just bows (or has a cramp). He reaches clumsily for the tray and a bowl skids off, smashing. Together, the two wrestle the food down to the scratched-up dining room tile. Can he hear all her joints popping? she wonders. His smooth black eyes both avoid and study her as if she's a phantom or royalty, the Queen of Queens maybe.

"The Queen of Queens and *Yesu Jidu* will commence to dine. Choice of Fiberall, orange juice, Sambuca."

It's a far swim from the meals she used to make, for her daddy, then her husband, then her son, for the endless stream of relatives from Italy and Bensonhurst, for Good Guys and Bad Guys, their loud wives, sandy children, pets! On a Sunday like this, she'd be expected to serve the antipasti and the pasta, two meats, a vegetable side, dessert, espresso, and mints. She prayed for a daughter to help her. When that didn't work, she prayed for an air conditioner. Finally, "I just prayed they'd leave me the fuck alone, excuse my Italian. And here I am. Until Paulie gets his way. Or the whale saves me."

"*A bacterial time bomb,*" the papers are calling the washed-up finback. If the city doesn't get rid of her before the next high tide, she could infect the whole waterfront. Rockaway's summer of '93 would be an environmental disaster, a PR nightmare! A blessing for Rose. No one will bother coming near her house if the beach is closed. Rose will live happily ever after for one more summer. Rose and Li—

Sadly, no one's ever seen a Chinese person in Rockaway besides the delivery boy for Wok and Roll. People would definitely notice. Li's dark hair and busy eyebrows are actually a lot like young Vin's were, but there are those nearly lidless eyes to give Li away, high cheekbones, a nose like some kind of exotic sliced mushroom. He sniffs with what might be disgust at the box of Fiberall cereal.

"If Paulie hadn't had my gas turned off, I'd make you my famous cutlets and escarole," Rose apologizes. "Or some soup—I know your people like soup. The nerve of that kid after forty-five years of scarfing my rigatoni. On a Sunday like this, I'd serve an antipasti and a pasta, two meats—

Eyes closed, Li begins quickly eating the cereal, with his hands, from the box, no milk. He's got a way of chewing with his whole head that Rose has never seen before. And Rose has seen a whole lot of people eating.

"I'd go easy on that Fiberall," she warns.

He streaked across her lawn just as she made it out the back-door, without falling. There goes the neighbor's huge black lab, Blacky, off its leash again, she'd assumed. And though she'd noticed his bark sounded odd, like a croup, she was too distracted, thinking how the wretch had gone to pee in his favorite spot against her shower house. No point reasoning with the owners, people so deeply unoriginal that they'd name a black dog Blacky. Didn't they also want her property? Eager to buy and tear down the place Paulie was born in to build something they called a *solarium*. Owning things others covet might make some feel powerful, but it just filled Rose with fear.

In the distance, Ambrose lighthouse pulsed on, off, on, but its usual soothing rhythm was jangled by searchlights roaming the dark, chaotic waves. She could hear sirens. Screams? The helicopter din made it hard to make out. Then that lumpy policeman appeared, bouncing around the side of the house.

"What!" Rose snapped, clutching her sweatshirt closed. She'd been hassled by the law once before, after starting a fire on the beach. Had she really fallen, this officer would have been the one to find her. Quite by accident, while coveting the ivy climbing up her façade, the decorative inlaid tile, flowering shrubbery, large picture windows, his flashlight would have suddenly illuminated what was left of her, Rose Camille Maria Impoliteri. A shriveled, bloodied human carcass. An ugly, used-up thing requiring removal. A nuisance.

"We were ringin' but you were out here, I guess," the policeman said, and only then remembered to flash a badge. "O'Donnell."

Behind him, a second, trimmer uniform materialized. This one trailing a nightstick along the beach wall and whacking now and then at Rose's ornamental grasses. He looked so much like an old classmate of Paulie's. Kevin? Kieran? But then they all did. Those fair-haired Rockaway lifeguards and rangers, cops, firefighters, Coast Guard; they could all pass for larger versions of the St. Francis High School bullies who tagged her son "Guido" and "Greaseball Wop," "Guinnie Rat" and "Zipperhead."

"Stop!" her frail voice failed to yell. "Why's he doin' that?"

"Just checkin' around." O'Donnell smiled, still bouncing, in place now. "You see anything unusual?

"Yeah. Over there, your partner beatin' on my plants."

"Any Chinese, I mean. Boat ran aground on a sandbar off a Breezy," he explained. "*The Golden Venture.* Full of Chinese illegals. They're drownin' and runnin' so we're s'posed to check around." With a couple more bounces for punctuation.

"I know about that," Rose said. "You need to use the men's room?"

A genuine offer but O'Donnell ignored it. "Anyone else wit ya here? Husband? Kids? Some kinda companion?"

Rose snapped. "What makes ya think that? I can take care a myself! I am—"

Which is when Blacky started up barking again, barking from inside the house next door, the same old bark she was used to. So Blacky wasn't actually out there, Rose got around to understanding. So it hadn't even been a dog that ran past her just—

"Wait," she called uselessly. By the time her mind had gotten here, the two officers had set off to search the garage. "Wait. You can't do that."

Her elbow throbbed and flamed from opening the door, but still she followed.

"You can't do that! Wait!" Kicking off her flip-flops to try and move faster. "No, I think you're not allowed to do that. Without a warrant." Was this true? She hadn't the faintest idea. All she knew for sure was, "This is *my* house!"

The backdoor sticks, the tile is scratched; the basement floods every time someone cries, Vin used to joke. But according to the brokers who periodically call, the brick rectangle is now worth two million easy. Ten thousand was what Rose's daddy paid for it brand new, back in the '40s.

"Germans came ashore then, did you know that? German spies in Rockaway!"

Now total strangers regularly stroll up and make offers on the house over the beach wall.

"But I'm gonna fool them all, Li," Rose all of a sudden decides. "I'm gonna leave the place to *you*."

The Good Guys didn't help anyone that much. Other than a lady who let them load up her car with groceries in the Waldbaum's parking lot, the Good Guys never really helped anyone at all. Vin said they tried but no one was interested. Even the lady with the groceries, Vin said, probably she just felt sorry for them. So the Good Guys took to drinking instead. Then they'd drag race their mopeds up and down Beach Channel Drive. Vin would stagger into Sunday dinner to alternately love up and criticize Rose. *My favorite flower. You call this turd a meatball? My soft, fragrant Rose. Lazy bitch can't go to Bensonhurst for some decent bread!*

"It was that and more, and I took it until the day he says, *Rose*, he says, *do me a favor. Don't serve this grease when my cousins come from Calabria.* In front of our Jewish friends, he says this in front of the Friedmans. He calls my sauce grease."

Li can't possibly understand the story, yet he tilts his head at its tone of hurt and even stops eating while she speaks. If Paulie and his atheist wife ever showed her half the deference, she might have invited them to live here already. *If.*

"That night, I burned the table leaves," Rose continues. "This table here. I dragged those two heavy planks one by one across the floor—see here these long scratches?—that's from draggin' them, and mind you, by myself, since Paulie's too busy

upstairs with Vin watchin' detectives chase each other or pro-
fessional wrestlin' . . . But I know you would have helped me,
Li." At that, he tries to give Rose the wad of bills from his
Ziploc bag and she pretends not to notice.

Once she finally got to the garage, all the chairs and cushions
she'd paid the grandkids to stack at the end of the summer
had been tossed across the dirty floor, and still the officers
were going at it, knocking over beach umbrellas, tossing paint
cans. What would they do if they actually found a person?
Her father had come over just like this, on a boat from Sic-
ily. And Vin had arrived in an Armani suit on a plane. But
the ways they'd been harassed would be nothing compared to
what they'd do to a poor Asian soul stuffed on a freighter, for
months it had to be, now half-drowned and frozen from kicking for his life in the frosty June chop. Just thinking about it
made her sure she heard the croup again, that someone was
there.

"Someone's here," Kevin or Kieran said, but he meant
Rose. "Hey. Hi. Ma'am. Ya really shouldn't be out."

"At my age?"

"At this hour. With that cough." One of his green eyes
was lazy, drifting. Rose thought to cough again to cover for
the stranger. She wondered if the wok she'd long ago ruined
had wound up here in the garage. She'd cleaned it wrong and
it had rusted or—

"Let me take you back inside," Kevin or Kieran insisted,
grasping her elbow. *Ow.* "Mrs.—"

"Don't you even remember me?" The way it came out
sounded like begging. "Paulie's mom?" Of course, it had been
years since she was even that in any meaningful way. She
touched the bulge in her sweatshirt. It had been years since

she'd been in her own garage, let alone had a car, driven a car, ridden a bike, fired a gun. The beachy gas smell pulled her back to all those sticky cousins of Vin's, of endlessly boiling pots, gritty towels, crumbs, bones, and water rings that slowly led her down to the sand dragging those two heavy planks that signified: *Company. Two leaves, two meats, the vegetable side—*

Kevin or Kieran claimed to not have grown up around here. But too bad, he'd kill for a house like this, on the beach. At the door, he gave her a card. In case she saw anything unusual. Then O'Donnell was beckoning him away, to the neighbor's, setting Blacky off all over again.

"Fires on the beach are illegal; you should know that," said the policemen when they arrived, that first time. "We could give you a ticket. Burnin' some good wood there too, looks like oak. We could haul your crazy ass in." When they'd finally gone, it took Rose a long time to bury the rest of the charred leaves beneath the sand. And still, a dog had it partially dug up by daylight. Vin saw it and said, "So?" If Rose wanted a buffet, well, he'd just invite more company. Then he drag raced his moped into a Green Line bus.

The kids on the beach used to always say they were digging a hole all the way to China. And once, for a few months somewhere in the '70s, she'd fashioned a hair ornament out of chopsticks like she'd seen on that actress, what's her name, in that film, whatsitcalled?

"Other than that, I gotta admit, when it comes to things Oriental, I'm one big dummy."

Li starts to nod but an involuntary shiver overtakes him. His eyes close. He slumps against the table's pedestal. Rose imagines his mother teaching him to swim. A river it must have been, not a curly, raging ocean. A nice, manageable river.

* * *

At first, he looked like some kind of sea monster soaked through and wrapped in the moldy shower curtain. You could see his chest go in and out, but close up that rusty, tentative sound it made scared her. Every now and then he'd erupt with the cough. The shower house itself was a dank lair, reeking of vomit and adorned with wet leaves, cobwebs, and the butts of cigarettes she'd long suspected her teenage grandson of smoking.

"I can help you," Rose said. "My daughter-in-law is a doctor."

The stranger bowed, moaning himself up onto his hands and knees, but then he heaved up saltwater and collapsed again.

"You come into my house," she insisted. "I have a nice house."

"Ma! Ma! You okay? Did ya trip? What are you doin' down here under the table? The traffic, ohmygod. That Golden Adven— Why don't you have the TV on?"

"I'm sleeping?" Rose opens her sticky eyes to see a short, wide man with a graying goatee wheeling several bulging Samsonites. "What are those for?" She pushes up on to her forearms, blinking.

"Thought I'd start the process. Since I was comin' anyways." Paulie crosses his furry arms.

According to the window it's now morning. Low tide. Soon enough he's eying the empty bottle of Sambuca near her foot and swearing.

"You know you're not allowed—"

"I thought she was decaying. I thought they were closing the beach!"

"You're still talking about a damn whale? MA! A dozen or two people drowned right out there last night—"

Her confusion clears, leaving panic. "Where is he? What did you— Oh!" Li's beside her, his chest moving up and down, kind of. "Call Maureen!"

But Paulie's too busy hating her to notice. "They got some cement trucks to bury the big ugly fish, all right? The beach is safe. NOW CALM THE FUCK— Oh god, not again!"

Now he's spotted his father's shirt—the ivory cowboy number.

"You keep tellin' me you don't need takin' care of, so how come every time you get blicked, you gotta carry this shit around?" Grabbing for the sleeve, he—"Aah!"—discovers there's an arm inside it, and there's a man under the dining room table attached to the arm.

Rose can't help but giggle. She was waiting for that. "You should see your face, Paulie!"

"What the hell—"

And it just keeps getting funnier. "SHHHH," Rose has to gasp between laugh spurts. "This is Li. He's not well."

"Have you gone fuckin' nuts? Where did you—why—"

"I was hoping Maureen—"

"What? You can't ask her to do that."

"Why not?" With effort, Rose pulls Li's dented too-still skull onto her lap. "He's a Christian."

"You mean *criminal!*" Paul yells, patting his khakis. "And she's a vet."

"Then call a priest."

"I'm callin' the cops is who I'm callin'!" Paul starts rifling through his suitcases. "If you'd please shut your trap." Sounding exactly like Vin.

"When you find your weapon, let me know," Rose says,

reaching into her sweatshirt pocket to cock the gun. "Then you can just kill me and get my house."

"What? Where's my phone. I just had—"

The kick of the gun knocks Rose down where Paulie is also heading with a sashay–low twist combination that leaves him slumped right over his bulbous luggage. The movements seem so foreign that she actually finds herself wondering, *Did he just get a bad haircut or something?* Then she remembers to thrust the gun into Li's dead-cold hands, their life about drained from them. Fingerprints, right? Rose didn't endure years of *Columbo* for nothing.

She is waiting for Li to die before crossing herself, a reflex, and calling the number on the detective's card. Not Kevin or Kieran but Andrew—her new friend. He'll be the one to do her the favor. *Andrew Volishskya.* Not from around here.

.

BUCKNER'S ERROR

BY JOSEPH GUGLIELMELLI
Shea Stadium

I followed him to the platform for the 7 train at Grand
Central, a place so far down below the street that I ex-
pected to meet devils with pitchforks on their way up
from Hell. The tail was easy. After a couple of days on the job,
I saw that he always wore the same kind of clothes, like a uni-
form or that crazy detective on cable. White Oxford shirt with
the sleeves rolled up, beige khaki pants, and brown loafers.
But today he added a cap—navy-blue with an antique capital
B on the front and little red socks at the back. A brand new
Boston Red Sox baseball cap.

I noticed more people in the city wearing Boston caps after the team had won the World Series. Always brand new,
never faded from the sun or stained with sweat. It was like
they were previously ashamed to walk the city's streets broadcasting their loyalty or were afraid that crazy Yankees fans
would chant "1918" at them when they went for a quart of
milk or to pick up their dry cleaning. I say, your team is your
team no matter what and no matter what anyone says. I wore
a Mets cap that wasn't new when they won the Series in 1986,
and carried a copy of today's *Post* in my back pocket. The two
of us waited, on this warm June night, for the 7 train to take
us to Shea Stadium where the Mets and Red Sox would play
the first of three interleague games.

He stood quietly on the platform, leaning against the elevator with his hands in his pockets. He stared off into space with no paper or book to read. The stale, sticky air did not seem to bother him. Next to him, a fat guy in a crappy suit with his polyester tie at half-mast, tired and heading home to Queens, mopped his face with a rumpled handkerchief. Three Korean women who could have been anywhere from forty to seventy years old stood silent and still, holding shopping bags filled with vegetables and other groceries. I disregarded them. Further down the platform, college kids wearing black away-jerseys with the name and number of their favorite Mets players on the back were obviously going to the game. The kids were playful and laughing but I knew they wouldn't get in my way when the train pulled in. I didn't expect the subway car to be sardine-can crowded until we got to the Queens stations.

A blast of cooler air signaled the arrival of a 7 express, which meant fewer stops and fewer chances for screw-ups. When the train stopped, we stood in front of the last car. He didn't move to rush the doors like so many subway riders do. He followed the tinny, distorted message over the car's loud-speakers and let the passengers off the train before getting on. I maneuvered my way into the car so that I was standing in front of him and holding the same pole in the middle of the car. A little guy wearing blue mechanic's overalls and reading *El Diario* had grabbed a piece of the pole to my left. A teen-aged black girl on my right was lost in the music playing from her iPod, swaying in time to the song. I was lucky that it was '70s Philly soul leaking from her headphones, not some rap shit.

I knew that I had to make my play before Queensboro Plaza, the first stop on the ride to Shea with connections to other subway lines. The express rattled through the first two under-ground stations, making so much noise that I couldn't even talk to myself, forget about talking to anybody else. When the train left the Hunters Point station and emerged into the evening sunlight five or six stories above the Queens streets, the clatter lessened to a normal din.

He was humming along with a Delfonics song from the girl's iPod and staring out of the windows at abandoned buildings covered from rooftop to ground floor in graffiti that appeared to be carefully designed and painted, rather than the work of random punks with spray cans. He held onto the pole with both hands. He seemed not to be in the subway car but in a private place with a look of contentment on his face. It was the same expression that my second ex-wife had when she did yoga in the morning.

I startled him when I told him that he was a brave man. I saw in his eyes that he was confused and did not know whether to ignore me, to ask me what I wanted, or, like any true New Yorker, to tell me to fuck off. I continued to make eye contact and said, "You're a brave man to be wearing a Red Sox cap to Shea."

He relaxed and smiled, never questioning how I knew where he was going. "Oh, I don't think so. It's not like going to Yankee Stadium when the Sox play. The crowds there can get rowdy. Besides, we Red Sox fans have a lot in common with you Mets fans," he said, taking one hand off the pole long enough to point to the cap on my head. "We both hate the Yankees."

I smiled back at him. "Good point, good point. But I don't know, man. We snatched Pedro from under your nose. And if Manny stands at home plate admiring a home run ball to show off for all his Washington Heights homeboys, it could get ugly."

Still smiling, he shook his head but was fading back to his

own personal place with his own thoughts, not the thoughts of some joker on the subway. He turned away from me to look at the midtown Manhattan skyline that now dominated the view from the left side of the train after it had pulled away from the Courthouse Square stop. I needed to keep this conversation going.

"I'm sitting up in nosebleed country. I'm gonna need one of those guides that mountain climbers use to find my seat. But what do you expect when you decide to go at the last minute? Where are you sitting?"

He still didn't know what to make of me but was polite. "My friend's family has season tickets. Field level behind first base." I knew all about the friend. I was standing in front of him because of the friend.

"Nice. I've sat around there a couple of times. I've been going to Mets games since my dad first took me when I was six. Most of the guys I know follow the teams that their dads followed. It is like an inheritance, to my mind. He was a big Brooklyn Dodgers fan. I mean, a huge fan. My mother says that when O'Malley took his team to California, my father said words that he never said before or would ever say again in all the years they were married. So growing up in a National League house it was only natural that we would follow the Mets. But if the Dodgers were in the World Series or in the playoffs, my dad, until the day he died, would root for the other team. Even if it meant rooting for the Yankees." I whispered the last part as if I were sharing a shameful family secret.

I had hooked him just in time. The subway car was beginning to get crowded as more people going to Shea got on at Queensboro Plaza. He could have easily moved away from me to grab one of the metal railings in front of the benches of filled seats. Despite the crush of Mets fans and homebound workers boarding the car, we were still standing together like two buddies having a night out at the ballpark.

"So, *your* dad take you to Fenway during the glory days of Yaz?"

He flinched at the question. I thought I'd overplayed my hand and lost him. I hoped that the look on his face was just the result of a sudden burst of sunshine hitting his eyes. "No. My father never took me to a ballgame. I don't think I ever saw a baseball game when I was growing up. My college roommate freshman year dragged me to Fenway with some of his friends because he thought I studied too much. It was love at first sight, the minute I stepped into the ballpark. After the first pitch I knew that I belonged right there. I never liked the taste of beer but must have had five that day. I loved the cheering and yelling of the crowd. I loved the hustle and grace of the players on the field. When we left and the Sox had beat Baltimore 5 to 4, I was hoarse and my hands were sore from clapping. I went to dozens of games before I graduated. I read the *Globe* and *Herald* sports pages religiously and any baseball history or biography voraciously. All these years I've been true to the Boston Red Sox. I never get to see the team live enough, working here. Now I have one of those cable packages that allows me to see almost every game, but it's not the same as being in Fenway."

I gave him a name and told him that I worked on Wall Street selling mutual funds to retail brokers. I knew enough details about this kind of job that I could BS my way through a conversation if he wanted to talk about work. I know a little about a lot of things so that I can talk to almost anybody about anything, a talent I find useful in my line of work. It would have given us something else in common, though I was certain we wouldn't be talking shop for the rest of the ride. Only baseball.

"I'm Jack Buckner," he said, mentioning he worked for an elite, privately held Wall Street firm that only handled old-money clients whose net worth was a minimum eight figures. He did not mention that it was his friend's family firm.

"Any relation to Bill? A cousin maybe, returning to the scene of the crime after so many years? Bill Buckner . . . letting the world championship roll between his legs during the legendary Game 6 of the '86 World Series."

"Billy. Buck. Did. Not. Lose. The. World. Series." Jack emphasized each word. I'm certain that he would have poked me in the chest on the beat of each syllable if the train had not roared past a local station with enough speed to cause him to keep both hands on the pole.

I have seen criminal defense attorneys sum up before juries in high-stakes trials with flair and with eloquence. Imagine Darrow in his heyday. Think Cutler and Gotti. Remember Cochran arguing on behalf of that piece of crap? None of them showed the passion that Jack did defending Bill Buckner. Hell, years later, all I remembered was the tenth inning. Jack could practically tell you the entire game pitch by pitch.

"First of all, McNamara should never have taken Clemens out in the seventh with a one-run lead," he began. "He claimed Clemens asked to be taken out because he had a blister on his finger. This man will be the AL Cy Young winner and the league's MVP. You keep him in unless he needs immediate surgery on his pitching arm in the dugout. Besides, Clemens said that he never asked to be taken out, but only after McNamara was fired. In my opinion, Clemens was very honorable because he didn't undermine McNamara's authority in the clubhouse by contradicting him. When I look at how he has pitched since leaving Boston, the awards and the rings, I cannot believe that he quit. However, I confess that I have a soft spot for the Rocket. The Sox quit on him. He did not quit on Boston."

He went on about some Italian relief pitcher named Calvin letting the tying run score in the eighth. Never met too many guys from Mulberry Street named Calvin. But then again, I thought Rudolph was a name for only Nazis and reindeers before Giuliani came along.

Jack was analyzing and dissecting the plays in the tenth inning when the 7 passed Fisk Avenue. So intent on making his points, he didn't see the joke of talking about the 1986 Series above a street that shared the name of the great Sox catcher. "Bob Stanley had already tied the game on a wild pitch, so the damage was done before Wilson ever hit the ball toward Billy. At that point, Buckner should never have been in the game. Because his ankles were bad, McNamara had taken him out of every other post-season game in the late innings and put in Dave Stapleton for defense. What was he thinking? It was not as if Billy's bat would be missed. He went 0-for-5 in Game 6. Nevertheless, I firmly believe that even if Billy makes that play, Wilson beats him to the bag. Billy was too beat up and Wilson was too fast . . . And, of course," Jack added as we were about to leave the Woodside stop, "there was still Game 7. You can't blame Billy Buck for what happened in Game 7. They would have been the champions if they'd won that game." He paused for a breath and checked his watch when the conductor announced that the train was being held in the station.

While Jack had been commandeering facts and stats to make his point, I noticed that each platform for the local stops along this stretch of the 7 line had stained-glass windows. I could not make out the designs as the train raced by, but I was sure that they were not pictures of the Stations of the Cross.

We even passed a giant red neon cross on top of a Korean church of some Protestant denomination. With each word out of Jack's mouth, I kept thinking about that movie with Susan Sarandon and how she belonged to the Church of Baseball. Jack was certainly a member of that congregation.

When the train finally left the station, Jack said, "Buckner was the butt of a lot of jokes afterwards. But my sympathies were later with Donnie Moore."

The name rang a bell but I couldn't place it.

"He was the other goat of 1986. He was the relief pitcher for the Angels, who were one strike away from winning the American League pennant when Moore gave up a home run to Dave Henderson that tied the game. The Angels lost that game in the eleventh inning. They lost the next two games and the pennant. At the time I was, of course, very happy that Boston was going to the World Series. However, Moore was never the same pitcher due to physical ailments. He was hounded out of Anaheim by boorish fans and a mean-spirited front office in the middle of the 1988 season. About a year later, he shoots his wife in front of his own children and kills himself with a bullet to the head."

With a sigh, Jack continued, "Anyway, I couldn't believe that when Moore's suicide became public, a reporter called Buckner to ask whether he considered killing himself after the 1986 Series. Billy said, 'Of course not. It's only a game.' I can never decide whether that's a cheery or depressing thought."

"Depends on the day, my friend," I said. He went quiet as the train pulled into Junction Boulevard and 103rd Street.

I tried to keep the conversation casual for the rest of the ride, just bar talk between strangers, but I could tell that Jack's thoughts were drifting away again. He agreed with a curt "yes" that the Zambrano-for-Kazmir trade was the biggest heist since Lufthansa. I asked him who he was going to the game with, when the windows of the subway suddenly darkened. Trees densely filled with leaves surrounded the car, blocking the sunlight. It was as if, for a minute or two, the subway had left the trestles above Roosevelt Avenue and plunged into a forest. Just as suddenly, the train emerged from the tree cover and Shea, all blue, gray, and orange, appeared in front of a slowly setting sun, a stunning joyful sight. I never got an answer to the question, only a curious stare.

Even before the subway came to a full stop at the Willets Point station, the chants of "Let's Go Mets!" could be heard. When the doors opened, everyone in the car poured out onto the elevated platform and made their way to one of the metal stairways, freshly painted a puke-green color. I was right behind Jack as we left the car. As distant and formal as when I first addressed him, he turned and said, "Nice speaking with you. Enjoy the game." He headed off toward the stairs and began to blend into the crowd, anxious to meet his friend.

I yelled at him over the head of a father holding the hand of his young son: "Jack, wait up! Let me give you my card and I definitely want to get yours."

He reluctantly stopped, letting people pass him to get to the staircase. We stood by a large green garbage can so we would be out of the way. He pulled a thin gold case out of his pocket to take out a crème-colored business card. I fumbled with a frayed leather case that dropped between my feet. I squatted down to pick it up, watching Jack stare at the diminishing crowd on the platform and impatiently tapping the business card against his thigh. I also removed the ice pick that was taped to the inside of my right calf and concealed it under my sleeve. The platform was now empty except for the stragglers at the top of the staircases. A quick glance across the tracks at the Manhattan-bound platform found only a teenaged couple too busy making out to notice a pair of middle-aged guys exchanging business cards.

Jack again said goodbye and turned to walk away. But he stopped beside one of the black wooden benches on the platform when he saw that the name of his boss, the name of his friend's father, was printed on the business card I had given him.

I could imagine the confused look on his face as the handle of the ice pick slipped down into my hand. I focused on my target. There is a small indentation at the base of the skull, just below the Velcro strap of a baseball cap and aligned, in this case, with a cartoon pair of red socks. A blade thrust into this depression will sever the spinal cord from the brain. Your muscles go limp so you cannot run away. You cannot breathe so you cannot cry for help. You go into shock as your blood pressure drops to nothing. You become unconscious with barely another thought. Death is almost immediate if an expert wields the ice pick. I am an expert.

I caught him as he began to fall like a puppet whose strings had been cut. I placed him on the black bench, arranging the body so that the Mets fans exiting the next trains would think that he was just waiting to board. I took his wallet, card case, and BlackBerry so that the cops would have the always popular and distracting motive of robbery to think about. I put the *Post* from my back pocket in his lap so that Jack appeared to be reading the sports page with Pedro on the cover. I left the ice pick there with no prints and no trail back to me. I was halfway down the stairs before the next train pulled in.

When I came up on the Manhattan side of the platform, the young couple were still at it hot and heavy and wouldn't have noticed me if I had shot Jack with a .45. Standing in the evening breeze, I could see the body on the bench. The latest trainload of fans was hurrying down the puke-green stairs to get to the game. No one was giving him a second look. The starting lineups were about to be announced.

Jack's mistake was thinking with the head between his legs, not the one on his shoulders. People with assets worth in excess of eight figures don't care who or what you fuck so long as you are discreet. When the details of your sex life appear on the disapproving lips of some dried-up matron whose name is in the Social Register, or in a blind item in a sordid tabloid gossip page, those people might take their assets to another investment boutique. But that's just money. There is always more money to be made somewhere.

It becomes trouble when whispers and innuendos reach the ears of your boss. It becomes real trouble when, after a little snooping and a little window peeping, he learns you are screwing his college freshman son. It becomes big trouble when you tell your boss that you are the only thing that keeps his firm from being a comical relic on The Street and that, if he continues to interfere in your personal life, you will take his business and his son. Blood and money are very personal. That's when, through a middleman or a cutout or a guy who knows a guy, I get a call.

But who knows? Maybe it wasn't a mistake to fall for the kid. If they had baseball in common, that would have been plenty for Jack. His error was not how he used his mouth with the kid, but opening his mouth to the father. It was the blow-up, not the blowjobs. My mother often said: Be careful because a big mouth will always get you in trouble.

A Manhattan-bound local pulled in and I got on. Below me, a young man waited outside of Shea Stadium with two tickets for tonight's game that wouldn't be used. Probably wearing a brand new Boston Red Sox baseball cap.

Jenny put a Guinness in front of me while NY1 played on the plasma screen over the wooden bar at my local Woodside pub. I could see some reporter standing with Shea in the background, but with the sound low and the jukebox blaring Bono, I couldn't hear anything. Because it was the top of the hour, I figured he was not reporting on the outcome of the game.

"Can you believe it?" Jenny said. "They had this story on before. Some poor guy is going to a ballgame and gets stabbed to death. You can't ride the subway anymore without some wacko trying to kill you with a knife. First that kid from Texas gets stabbed in the chest. And I get the creeps just thinking about that poor guy and the handsaw. I'm taking buses everywhere from now on."

"More importantly, love, did the Mets win?"

She slapped my hand playfully. "You're bad." She walked to the other end of the bar where a couple was signaling for a refill.

Yes, tonight I think I am.

BAGGAGE CLAIM

BY PATRICIA KING

JFK Airport

Read. Just keep reading. She had to try to lose herself in the story. Let it block out the shaking and shuttering. She gripped the book with sweating hands. She rubbed her knee. There was no way in this cramped space to ease the throbbing.

The man in the seat next to her was sleeping. He had changed places with a Hasid who had refused to sit next to a woman. When this new guy first sat down, he had scared her. He looked like an Arab. His pockmarked skin gave him a sinister appearance, and she had tried not to think of him in such a prejudiced way. He had a nice smile. But hijackers could smile.

"Are you going home or do you live in the UK?" She had worked up her courage to question him while she waited behind him in line for the loo. She kept saying "loo" now, after a week with the people in the London office.

"Home," he had said. That smile again. It did look kind of threatening. "I'm from the Bronx, and I can't wait to get back."

The accent was unmistakable. Bronx, for sure. He was probably Puerto Rican. "Me too. Riverdale." She tried to smile back at him. The last word came out sounding apologetic. People from the real Bronx hated Riverdale; she was sure of that. It shamed her to have suspected him. He seemed so benign now. He could be a victim, not a terrorist.

The plane touched down with a jolt that woke him.

She wiped her palms on the rough fabric of the seat. Rivulets of rain ran over the window glass.

"*Welcome to JFK,*" an intimate and humorous voice began over the loudspeaker. "*If I hadn't just spent nearly eight hours cavorting with all of you on this plane, I would think we were still in London, given this gloomy weather.*"

Friday. The traffic would be awful. And she had her car in long-term parking. The Triboro Bridge would be backed up. And the rain would make it worse.

She got her black rolly down from the overhead bin and waited in the aisle to get off the plane.

"*Thank you for flying Virgin Atlantic,*" they said by way of goodbye.

The walk to Passport Control went on forever. The specter of having to drive over the bridge haunted her. Suppose she got stuck in traffic in the middle of the bridge with her heart beating out of control. She would have to get off. She would have to. This started back in October of 2001, returning from Washington on a Sunday night—at dusk on a misty evening, driving along, sipping the latte she had picked up at the rest stop. The bottoms of her feet had gotten sweaty when suddenly there was the Delaware Memorial Bridge— the double span sticking up above some light fog. It would have looked pretty, if it hadn't frozen her heart. She couldn't drive up there.

She had moved behind a blue Volkswagen Passat in the middle lane and hung onto the steering wheel for dear life. She had stayed behind that car and couldn't look left or right until they got through the toll on the other side. Heart still pounding, she had pulled over at the first opportunity. It was almost an hour before she could get back on the road.

A few months later, she had gotten lost trying to get back to Manhattan from Newark without driving on the Pulaski Skyway. Worse and worse. Two weeks ago, she had driven down through New Jersey and gone through the Lincoln Tunnel and back up to the Bronx, just to avoid the George Washington Bridge. So ashamed, she hadn't even told her sister. But when she finally mentioned it to Roger, who was hardly a close friend, he immediately asked, "Did this start after 9/11?" The idea had shocked her.

"Go to line twenty-seven." The short, sharp-faced African-American woman at Passport Control jabbed a finger in the direction of a booth.

The officer's face was round and kind, but he looked at her with hard, searching eyes. She handed him her passport. He scanned it and watched the screen, then handed it back with a perfunctory, "Welcome home."

The baggage was slow. The rain, she guessed. The Hasidic guy stood near her, waiting. The rainy weather made her knee worse. She tried to keep her weight off it.

On 9/11 she had been down in Soho, getting physical therapy. She hadn't gone to the office that morning. A lot of people weren't at work for odd reasons. They were late. They called in sick. She had heard a lot of stories like this. A woman who went to pick up her new eyeglasses and never got up there. A guy from Jersey whose little girl had cried and said, "Daddy, don't go." The father had stopped so long comforting his kid, he missed his train. The kid had saved her father.

Her knee had saved her. By rights she should have been on the ninety-seventh floor.

After her therapy appointment, while icing her knee, she felt the gym go quiet. They were all staring at the burning skyscraper on the TV, asking each other, "Which building?" "What kind of plane?"

Her office would be flooded with light. On such a sunny day, the intensity of the light always made her giddy. Working up there made you feel important, even if all you did was put numbers into spreadsheets all day. Gerry and Margaret, sitting at their desks, would be silhouetted against the windows on a day like this. Like ghosts. Only black. Only they couldn't be sitting. Not with this going on in the other tower.

She stood, gazing at the burning building, completely silent, feeling guilty that she was thinking about how much it would hurt her knee to be walking down all those stairs with them. The second plane hit. "Terrorists," was all she said. She went and put on her clothes.

She had a portable radio in her gym bag. Only one station was broadcasting. One tense male voice.

On her way out, she glanced over at the knot of people gathered in front of the big TV near the treadmills and Stair-Masters. Radio to her ear, she left without looking at the screen.

Out on Broadway, the air was acrid with smoke and stung her throat. People streamed up the sidewalks. Ambulances and firetrucks careened south toward the towers. An EMT vehicle with the words *Valley Stream Rescue Squad* on its side went screaming by. *How the hell could they have gotten here so fast?*

A crowd gathered around her. "What are they saying?" A short guy in a snug gray suit pointed to the radio. She held it out to him. The battery was weak and the street so noisy that he had to put his finger in his opposite ear to hear it. Two big African-American women with tears streaming down their faces stopped and asked for news. She just shrugged and gestured to the guy holding her radio.

One of them was sobbing uncontrollably. "They are jumping out of the top floors."

They couldn't be. No one would do that. Gerry wouldn't do that. Harry Ardini wouldn't do that. She looked at the other woman, who just nodded and pulled her friend away, up Broadway.

She pictured the wide expanse of her office. The fichus tree next to her chair burning. The light from it shining in the frame on her desk. Her sister's picture smiling through the bright red reflected flames.

The guy handed the radio back to her. She put it to her ear and started walking north with the herd.

The voice on the radio was suddenly hysterical. *"We're losing it! We're losing it! OMIGOD!"*

She turned and looked down Broadway. Her building was collapsing. *Boom! Boom! Boom!* Like one of those structures in a demolition movie. A huge cloud of thick gray dust rushed toward them up the street. She turned again and ran. Past the church with the pealing bells. The sexton had thought to do that. As if he were in some medieval village that had the plague.

She had walked all the way to Riverdale that day. Over the Henry Hudson Bridge. Her knee never recovered, had not stopped hurting since. She never returned to physical therapy. Just the thought of physical therapy brought back that picture in the papers the next day. The guy falling though the air. Head down. The familiar building behind him. She had looked and looked at that picture. Sometimes she was sure it was Harry. Other days, it didn't look like his hair.

The buzzer on the luggage carousel sounded and the metal belt started to move. Bags moved down the slope onto the belt in front of her. The Hasidic guy peered at a huge black one, frowned, and then let it pass. It came around again. Blood dripped from a small opening where the zippers met at the top. Bright and shining, it pooled onto the metal of the conveyor. She breathed in to scream as it went by. She held her breath. People would call her a hysteric. Seeing blood all the time, knowing that if she had jumped that day her body would have liquefied. That's what they said. That a body hitting the ground from such a height just liquefies. The bottoms of her feet were sweating. Just like driving over a bridge.

Her bag came tumbling down the slope. She saw the green ribbons on the zipper. Not red. Not blood. She grabbed her bag, turned in her card at Customs, and dragged it to the nearest restroom. She couldn't drive over the bridge. She just couldn't.

In the handicapped stall, she sat on the toilet and laid the big bag down. Inside was her toiletries kit, with all that stuff you can't carry with you on a plane anymore.

She unzipped it and pulled out a pink disposable razor. She wedged it under the toilet paper dispenser and pressed hard. It bent but would not break. She put her foot against it too and finally it popped with a loud metallic crack.

"Are you okay in there?" a voice from another stall called.

"Fine," she said.

She retrieved the razor blade from the floor and held it carefully between her thumb and forefinger. This is better, she thought. She could stop the pictures in her head of Harry liquefying on the sidewalk. She could finally do what she was supposed to have done. She cut along the blue veins on her wrists. She held out her arms and let the blood drip on the green ribbons, running them red, like the blood in baggage claim.

ARRIVEDERCI, ALDO

BY KIM SYKES

Long Island City

I love my job. How many people can say that?

I could be working security in a department store over in Manhattan, where they make you follow old ladies with large purses and mothers with baby strollers. Or in an office tower doing Homeland Security detail, looking at photo IDs all day and pretending I care whether you belong in a building full of uninteresting lawyers and accountants, most of whom come to work hoping I'd find a reason to stop them from going in. Or guarding a bank where you're so bored that you consider robbing it yourself or kicking one of those lousy machines that charge two dollars to do what a bank is supposed to do for free.

My friends tell me I got it pretty good because I work security at Silvercup Studios where they shoot television shows, movies, and commercials. Not to mention the fact that it's not far from my walkup in Long Island City. My neighbors treat me like I'm a celebrity. Which is pretty funny since my mother worked at Silvercup in the '50s baking bread and nobody ever treated her like she was somebody, except me and my father.

Yeah, okay, I see lots of good-looking men and pretty girls, famous singers and movie stars. No big deal. They're just like you and me. Especially without the makeup and the fancy clothes. They all come in with uncombed hair, comfortable shoes, and sunglasses. Some of them got egos to match the size of the cars they drive up in. They arrive with their assistants and their entourages carrying everything from little dogs to adopted babies. Some of them pride themselves as just folks and come in on the subway. The one thing they all got in common is that I make them sign in. It's my job. They might be celebrities, but I treat them all the same.

There *are* exceptions, like the directors and the producers. They don't bother to sign in. Every day they walk past my security desk and one of their "people" will whisper to me who they are. You'd think they were royalty or something. I check their names off a special list the office gives me. The boss says that they pay the bills and we should make them happy no matter what. I guess when you're in charge of making multimillion-dollar movies, it's the little things that matter, like not having to write down your own name.

Then there's everybody in between, the ones who are not movie stars—the supporting and background actors, backup singers, and the hoochie girls in the music videos. When they come in, all eager and excited, they usually put their names in the wrong places and walk through the wrong doors. Especially the first-timers. They don't pay much attention to anything except the hopes and dreams in their heads.

Last, but not least, there's the crew. Most of these guys I know by sight. They come in when it's still dark outside and that's usually when they leave too. They walk past me half asleep. It's hard work getting up before dawn every day, unloading, setting up and breaking down and loading up again—not to mention looking after all those people. So sometimes I try to make their days a little easier. If I've never seen them before, they sign in. If I know them, I let them go through, but you didn't hear that from me. You see, we got thirteen studios and they're in a constant state of shooting something. So sometimes I have to bend the rules.

The phone at my security desk rings and I almost fall backwards in my chair. It's probably the boss's office telling me about an unexpected delivery or adding a name to the list. You see, they got it under control up there. The next day's schedule and sign-in sheets are usually done at midnight and placed on my desk for the following morning. We run a tight ship around here, so when the phone rings it's pretty important. I answer it on the second ring.

"Yes, sir?" I straighten up in my seat. It's the boss himself.

"Listen, Josephine, we got an intruder walking around the premises."

I can hardly believe my ears. The news makes me stand up and grab hold of my nightstick, my only weapon.

"I'm sorry, sir," comes tumbling out of my mouth. I feel as if I've let him down. Being the only woman in security here at Silvercup, I know I have to work harder than everybody else.

"He's walking in on sets, Jo. He's ruined a shot in Studio 7, for Christ's sake. See who the hell this guy is, will you? Probably some damn background actor looking to be discovered."

It happens occasionally that extra players, bored with waiting around, go exploring the place in hopes of finding the next job. Sooner or later a production assistant spots them and sends the poor thing back to where he or she belongs. The fact is, Silvercup is the last place you'll be discovered. By the time actors get here, they're just numbers in a producer's budget. If you're not in the budget, you're not in the shot. Of course, there are exceptions to every rule, but I can count them on one hand.

"Anybody say what he looks like?" I ask my boss.

"White, around thirty. Wearing clogs."

"*Clogs?*"

"That's what they tell me. Just take care of it, Jo."

"Yes, sir."

There are thirteen studios here at Silvercup, and at least two sign-in sheets for each one. We're talking hundreds of people. It's barely 10 o'clock and the place is packed. This is not going to be easy. On one of the sheets, a couple of wise-asses signed in as Mick Jagger and Flavor Flav. They came in early. I can tell by the names before and after them. That means these comedians are with the crew. I take a moment to remember who came by my desk just before dawn. There was nobody I didn't know. And I would have remembered a guy wearing clogs.

The new guard, Kenneth, is checking out the *Daily News* and eating his second meal of the morning. His plate is piled high. He is reading his horoscope and is oblivious to my panic. I watch him dunk a powdered donut into milky coffee and drip the muddy mess on his blue vest. I hand him a paper napkin and look past him at the tiny security screens mounted on the wall. Like I said, there are thirteen studios here, with at least three times that many bathrooms, not to mention dressing rooms, storage rooms, production offices. These little screens are useless to me. You'd think we'd have better video equipment here, but we don't.

Still, nobody-but-nobody gets past me. I pride myself on that. I'm famous, if you will, for keeping the place tight and secure. Okay, I'm not going to make it seem like I'm guarding the U.S. Mint, but we get a lot of people trying to come in here, like rag reporters or crazed fans or desperate actors. They don't have weapons but they have things that are far more lethal to us like pens, cameras, and unrealistic expectations. It's my job to protect Silvercup and everybody inside from all that. My job and reputation are at stake, and I'm not going to let some clog-wearing twerp or donut-eating knuckle-head ruin it.

Just my luck, my other two colleagues are at lunch. That leaves me and the munching machine, who since he got here has been visiting the different sets and mooching free meals. I watch him fold the *News* and start the *Post*. He reminds me of myself when I started on the job years ago. After the rush of the morning, it slows down to a crawl. Keeping yourself awake is a chore. Thanks to plenty of coffee, newspapers and maga-zines, and hopefully some good conversation, you can remain alert most of your shift.

Then there's the food. Each production has it's own ca-tered breakfast, lunch, and if they're here long enough, din-ner. My first six months I gained twenty pounds and it's been with me ever since. One day it's fresh lobsters from a restau-rant chain shooting commercials, then it's a week of birthday cakes from a television show. Here, at any given time, some-one somewhere is eating something. Makes you wonder where the term "starving actor" came from.

I'm not too confident in this boy's abilities, especially after I see him bite into his breakfast burrito and squirt half of it on his lap. But he's the only guy I got on the desk right now, since the other two have gone off on a break. So I tell him to keep an eye out for a white guy wearing clogs and to call me on the walkie if he sees anything suspicious. He doesn't bother to ask me what's going on or about the clogs even, and I don't bother to fill him in. I give him two weeks, if that.

I take today's schedule with me. I have to be careful not to excite or disturb the productions going on. Today we've got four commercials, two cop shows, three sitcoms, one movie, and two music videos shooting, not to mention the Home Shopping Network, which has it's permanent home here. That means hundreds of actors and crew roaming the place. I decide to go up and work my way down. I don't bother with the top floor where the boss's office is. I figure a guy in clogs is not interested in that. A guy in clogs wants attention. He wants to be discovered. And that means I got to go where the directors and the actors are. I take the freight elevator to the second floor.

When the doors open, I see a herd of suits, some eating bagels, others reading or having intense conversations. It's like I just walked in on a business conference at some firm on Wall Street, only the men are wearing makeup and the women have rollers in their hair. I move past them to Frank, a production assistant I know pretty well. He's worked here at Silvercup almost as long as I have.

"Yo, Frank, all your people accounted for?" I ask him.

Frank silently counts the actors.

"Yeah. Why?"

"We got somebody walking around the place. He screwed up a shot in 7."

"Moron."

"Yeah. You see anyone who doesn't belong, call me."

"You got it, Jo.

"Oh, and he's wearing clogs."

Frank raises an eyebrow.

"Don't ask," I tell him.

I walk to the other side of the building. Past storage rooms that have complicated lock systems installed. You have to have a combination or a special key. On some of them you need both. I try the doors anyway. Better to be sure.

My schedule says they're setting up a music video in the

next studio. Whether they want to or not, they usually start shooting later in the day. Pop and rap singers don't like to get up in the morning. They can afford not to. The crew was there, however, installing stripper poles for a rap video.

"What's shaking, Jo?" says Dimples, a pot-bellied Irishman carrying heavy cables. I cross the studio floor toward him.

"You won't believe it," I say as I approach. "I've got some guy walking around the place messing up shots."

His cheeks flushed, betraying his nickname. "Was he wearing clogs?"

I nearly choke on the chocolate-covered peanuts I just snatched from the Kraft table. "Yeah, you seen him?"

"About ten minutes ago. He walked in here asking for Tony Soprano. I thought he was joking." Dimples takes off one of his thick gloves and scratches his bulbous nose. "He had an accent. Italian, or maybe Spanish. It's hard to tell. Tiny guy, though. No bigger than my leg. Kept stuffing bagels into his pants, like he was saving them for later. He creeped me, so I chased him out of here."

"Which way did he go?" I ask, licking chocolate from my fingers.

"I followed him out to the hall and watched him take the stairs down. That's the last I saw of him."

"Thanks."

I run toward the exit and take the steps two at a time. I figure if I move quickly enough, I can catch up with him. Besides, how fast can a guy in clogs go? But when I get to the bottom landing, I have to sit down. They say, if you don't use it you lose it. And after all these years, I have definitely lost it. When I was younger, if somebody had said to me I would be tired after running down a flight of stairs, I would have kicked his ass. Now the very thought of lifting my foot

to carry out my threat exhausts me. Not counting vacations
and holidays, I have mostly spent my time sitting behind the
security desk watching others come and go. The last time
I chased anyone was awhile back when a mother-daughter
team tried to get an autographed picture of Sarah Jessica
Parker. They would have succeeded if they hadn't been as
out of shape as I was.

I look down at my ankles. They're swollen. It makes me
think of my mother, who would come home from work, worn
out, same swollen feet as mine, in the days when this place
supplied bread for schools in Queens and the Bronx and parts
of Manhattan. Now, instead of filling their stomachs with
dough, we fill their heads with it.

The mayor keeps telling us that New York City has grown
safer now that violent crimes are at the lowest rates they've
been in a decade. That's true everywhere except on television
and in the movies. It's as if Hollywood didn't get the memo.
Production companies spit out cop show after cop show, movies full of mobsters and gang-bangers who kill and rape, rob
and shoot one another—in the name of entertainment. It's
not Silvercup's fault. We don't write the scripts. We just provide the space to film them in.

I push myself up from the steps and enter the first floor. First
thing, down the hall, I see two guys about to come to blows.
Any moment the fists are going to fly. I stand quietly off to the
side and watch. I know that when the time comes for one of
them to throw the first punch, they'll calm down and probably
laugh or pat each other on the back. This time they do both.

"Hey, Jo, what's up?" Edward, the one with the perfect
teeth, calls me over. I shake his manicured hand. He plays a
serial killer on one of the cop shows. He's on for the whole
season. Nice guy, great family man, good kids.

"Same ole, same ole," I answer. "You seen a guy running around here in clogs?"

The actors laugh, thinking I am about to tell a joke.

"I'm not kidding." I say this with my best poker face.

Ed drops his grin. "No, just us up here running lines before our scene. Why?"

"Nothing serious. Sorry I interrupted you."

"Don't worry about it," the new guy chirps. He has a shaved head, which from a distance made him look thuggish, but now that I'm closer to him, I can see that he's a kid barely out of school. Must be his first big part. This morning when he signed in he was a little anxious around the eyes; polite though. Probably right out of college and here he is playing a street thug, the kind his mother and father sent him to university so as not to become. If this script is like all the others, his character's going to be shot or killed and sent off to prison by the afternoon. That's show business.

I stick my hands in my pockets. It's cold in here, I want to get back to my desk where I keep a space heater tucked down below. The boss has the thermostat in the low sixties, even in winter. He says it keeps everybody on their toes.

The next studio is dark except for the set, which looks like a doctor's office. They're rehearsing a scene for a pharmaceutical commercial. A very nervous actor in a doctor's coat is having trouble with his lines. When he gets to the part about the side effects, he starts to laugh. But no one else thinks it's funny. Time is money and everyone is frustrated, including the director, who makes the actor even more uncomfortable by sighing loudly and storming off between takes.

After my eyes have adjusted to the dark, I glance around the room. The crew, producers, and other actors are standing around, quietly waiting for the next take, hoping this day will come to an end so they can all go home. Everyone except what I will later describe to the press as a deranged imp—no more than five feet tall. He's standing off to the side, eating a bagel that he has just pulled out of his tights.

He has on a billowy white shirt that looks like it's from one of those Shakespearean movies—it's hanging over his wiry shoulders and flared out past his nonexistent hips. On his small feet are a pair of genuine wooden clogs.

We make eye contact and he quickly figures out why I'm here. The actor and the director head back to the set. I search around for a couple of guys who I can recruit to help me. When I turn back, the little guy is standing right next to me.

"Have you seen Tony Soprano?" he whispers in an Italian accent. His eyes are bright, even in the dark, and his breath smells of cheese.

"Quiet on the set!" The alarm bell rings, signaling that the camera's about to roll. I grab his skinny arm but he twists around and frees himself from my grip.

"Action!" The director cues the actor, who begins his lines.

"*I'm a doctor, so people are surprised when I tell them that I suffer from irritable bowel syndrome.*"

No one is watching me or the imp as he makes his way behind several clients from the pharmaceutical industry who are engrossed in the actor's performance. Imagine spending a good part of your career having meetings and conference calls about irritable bowels. I squeeze past them and follow my quarry who is creeping closer to the set.

"*If you suffer from irritable bowel syndrome, do like I did. Call your doctor. Side effects include stomachache, fever, bloody stool, and on rare occasions, death.*"

This time the actor does not laugh, but the imp does, as he dashes right in front of the camera.

"Cut!" What the . . . ?" The director is about to have a nervous breakdown.

I know better than to follow the imp in front of the camera. I figure there will be enough people waiting to kill him for messing up this shot. Someone switches on the overhead lights just in time to see him open the door and scurry out.

The first year *The Sopranos* shot here were my hardest as a security guard. We had the press, fans, everybody coming by asking to speak to the fictional mob boss, Tony Soprano. We even had real gangsters come around. It wasn't easy turning these kinds of fans away. We had to hire two extra security guards to handle the crush. But now the show is winding down. The actors are bored. The reporters have moved on. Things were getting back to normal until this clog-footed fruitcake came along.

I go out into the hall but there is no sign of him. I call Kenneth on the walkie but he doesn't answer. He's probably in the john, making room for another meal. Did I say he'd last two weeks? Make that one.

As I struggle to put my walkie back in its cradle, the imp exits a john and sprints into the stairwell. By this time I'm joined by the actor/doctor, the director, and several guys from the crew.

We follow him up one flight. My heart is thumping. He better hope I catch him before the director does. I can see the tabloid headline: *IMP MAIMED AT SILVERCUP.* We chase him down the narrow hall toward the Wall Street herd waiting to go on set. Because he's limber and small, the imp cuts through the crowd barely touching anybody.

"Stop him!" I yell out.

A few of the actors look at me like I'm a 300-pound woman who just walked into a gym. Let's face it. In a place where there are actors and little guys in clogs, I'm the odd one. Thankfully, a banker type catches on and grabs the imp from behind, lifting him off the ground. An actress who looks like an H&R Block agent screams. Everyone panics.

Coffee and bagels splatter and fly into the air. This is the imp's second big mistake. You don't mess up a director's shot and you don't spill coffee on an actor's wardrobe before he goes on. I start to feel sorry for the little guy, until he reaches back and grabs his captor by his private parts and gives them a yank.

"Aaaah, Christ!" groans the actor, who lets go. The imp lands on his feet and darts toward the east end of the building.

Now this is where it gets interesting. I couldn't make this up if I wanted to. It's the kind of stuff that Hollywood pays big bucks for. I got to remember to put that in the screenplay I'm writing. Did I mention that I'm writing a screenplay?

The light outside of the Home Shopping Network set is flashing red. This means only one thing: No one can enter. They're shooting. I've seen movie stars stop in their tracks when they see it. Directors, producers, even the boss. But the imp ignores it and, once again, goes in without hesitation.

I move to stop the others from following him, but then I realize I don't have to. The consequences of entering a set when the red light is flashing differs from set to set. It can be anything from a stern talking-to, to getting punched out by a Teamster, to having the cops called in to haul you away. Home Shopping has a full-time bodyguard and ex-cop named Zack, who carries a .38. Whatever happens, it's going to be the last set the imp crashes.

I wonder how long it will take for Zack to spot him. As soon as I finish the thought, the doors burst open and Zack emerges with the imp tightly pinned under his arm and a meaty hand clamped over his mouth. None of us say anything.

Ready for revenge, we all silently followed Zack down the hall to the bathroom. It's like watching David and Goliath. Man, the little guy is *strong*. His arms bulge like small canta- loupes and his legs are like iron rods. Every time Zack tries to go through the door, the imp's arms and legs stop him. This goes on for a while until the imp bites down on Zack's hand. The ex- cop screams like a eunuch and drops him to the ground.

We don't waste time. We all dive on top of him, arms and legs grabbing and pulling at other arms and legs. I swear I have him until I find myself pinned to the ground by a sweaty stockbroker. A Teamster has to be stopped from strangling the director. By the time we realize what's going on, the imp has wiggled out from under us.

"Ciao!" he calls over to us before entering the stairwell a couple of feet away.

I watch Zack and the others follow him up. The next floor is administrative and is rigged with an alarm. His only option is the rooftop, and from there he'll be trapped. So I save my- self the climb and take the freight elevator to the roof.

A couple of years ago, the boss had a series of solar panels and plants installed to help generate electricity for the build- ing. I thought it was a crock myself, but apparently it works. At least it's gotten the boss off our backs about portable heat- ers and keeping the doors open for too long, and in August I can take home all the tomatoes I can eat.

On three sides of the building, Silvercup Studios is en- circled by two exit ramps to the Queensboro Bridge and the elevated subway tracks of the 7 train. Four flights down is the street. Unless the imp can do like Spiderman and climb brick, he's mine.

Row after row of raised square planting beds lie next to solar panels angled to the east. Large generators, the size of trucks, stand off to the west side harvesting the energy. Above me is the towering *S* of the famous *SILVERCUP* sign that lights up the entrance to Queens from the bridge at night. The sign stretches from one end of the building to the other, above the elevated tracks of the subway.

I walk to the west to get a better view of the roof and spot the imp standing under the *P*, waving at me like I'm his long-lost sister.

I don't like coming up here when it's not warm, especially on days like today when there's nothing but gray clouds and a damp wind that cuts through my thin uniform right to my bones. I can't wait to get my frozen hands on this little creep. But before I start after him, Zack and the others come bursting out of the rooftop door like the Canadian Mounties, only without the horses.

We spread out and begin walking slowly toward him, just like in the movies, but the closer we get, the further he backs away, until finally he reaches the far edge of the building. Listen, I don't want the imp to jump. His death is the last thing I need on my conscience, so I motion for everyone else to hold back while I try and talk to him, even though the traffic from the bridge and the trucks unloading below make that impossible.

I wish I could tell you that I get him to move from the edge or that he drops that stupid grin and runs sobbing into my arms, but things like that only happen on television. Real life is much more complicated. Instead, he rubs his hands along his thighs and then, with an operatic flourish, he calls out to us, "*Arrivederci!*" Then he turns around and jumps.

I must've looked like the wide-mouth bass in the window of the fish store on Queens Plaza South. At least that's what I felt like: a cold dead fish. I ran with the others to the edge, expecting to see Italian sauce splattered all over the pavement below. Just one story down, however, there's the imp, rubbing his hands on his thighs again and grabbing hold of a rope hanging from the 25A exit ramp of the Queensboro Bridge.

I forgot that this end of the building has an extension to it: a freight garage that's only three stories high, connected to the main Silvercup building. It looks like he got into the building by lowering himself from the exit ramp to the garage and then climbed up the emergency fire ladder to the main building. When I tell the boss about this, he's going to lose it.

I decide not to follow him, especially since he's scurrying up that rope faster than an Olympic gymnast. Besides, now that this jerk's off the premises, he's no longer my problem. If this were a television show, it would be a good time to cut to commercial. I could use a donut and a hot cup of coffee, only my curiosity is getting the better of me.

We all stand there and watch as he scurries up the rope jammed between the crack of the concrete barrier and onto the exit ramp to 25A. He loses one of his clogs but it doesn't faze him. Like a tight-rope walker, he steps along the ledge, against traffic, to exit 25, which runs parallel to 25A, but then veers off and under the elevated subway tracks of the 7 train. Once he's on exit 25, he crosses the lane and hops up on the ledge again and reaches for another rope. This one is tied to the iron gridwork that holds up the track, and instead of going up, he goes down. We lose sight of him behind the Silvercup parking lot, so we all rush to the west end of the roof just in time to see him running, with one clog, up Queens Plaza South toward the subway entrance a block away.

The End.

Or so I think.

* * *

A week later, I'm sitting with Kenneth at the desk (yes, he's still here and he's five pounds heavier) and we're reading the *News*. A headline screams, *ALIEN ACTOR NABBED BY HOMELAND SECURITY*, and there's a picture of the imp, smiling for his close-up.

His name is Aldo Phillippe and he's a street performer from Naples who overstayed his visa. He came to the United States to do three things: meet Tony Soprano, get discovered for the movies, find a wife.

According to the paper, Aldo decided that a good way to get publicity was to climb to the top of the Statue of Liberty, crawl through the window of her crown, and sit on her head. You probably think they caught him because they have better security over at the Liberty, but it wasn't that. According to the article, they had to close the visitors' center and chase him around for over an hour. The only way they caught him was by cornering him at the tip of the island, and evidently Aldo can't swim. If he's lucky, they won't send him to Guantánamo Bay.

I keep Aldo's clog on my desk filled with pens for people to use when they sign in. No one notices it except when the director and actors who were with me that day come back to work. Everybody else is too busy making entertainment.

PART II

OLD QUEENS

HOLLYWOOD LANES

BY MEGAN ABBOTT

Forest Hills

The way their banner-blue uniforms pressed up against each other—the wilting collar corners, her twitchy cocktail apron and his regulation pinman trousers—I was only a kid, but I knew it was something and it made my head go hot, my stomach pinch. Eddie worked the alley, made the lanes shine with that burring rotary machine. Carol slung beer at the cocktail lounge, heels digging in the heavy carpet, studded each night with peanut skins, cigarette ashes, cherry stems.

They were there every day, at 3:30, in the dark, narrow alley behind the pinsetting machines. And I saw them, saw them plain as day while I sat just outside the machine room on a metal stool, picking summer scabs off my knee. First time by accident, just hiding out back there, where it was quiet and no one came around.

Eddie'd been there a month, he and his wife Sherry, who ran concessions with my mother over by the shoe station. He had blue-black hair, slick like those olives in the jar at the Italian grocery store. When he walked through the joint, coming on his shift, everyone—the waitresses, even old Jimmy, the sweaty-faced manager—lit up like a row of sparklers because he was a friendly guy with a lot of smiles and his uniform always finely pressed and the strong smell of limey cologne coming off him like a movie star or something.

No one could figure him and Sherry. Sherry with the damp, faded-blond features, eyes empty as the rubber dish tub she was always resting her dusty elbows on. Cracking gum, staring open-mouthed at the crowds, the families, the amateur baseball team, the VFW fellas, the beery young marrieds swinging their arms around, skidding down the lanes, collapsing into each other's laps after each crash of the pins, Sherry never moved, except to shift her weight from one spindly leg to the other.

Just shy of thirteen, I was at Hollywood Lanes every day that summer. Husband three months gone, my mother was working double shifts to keep me in shoes, to hear her tell it. I helped the dishwashers, loading racks of cloudy glasses into the steaming machine, the only girl they ever let do it. Some days, I helped Georgie spray out the shoes or use Clean Strike on the balls.

But I always beat tracks at 3:30 so I could be behind the pin racks. Eddie and Carol, his hands spread across her waist, leaning into her, saying things to her. What was he saying? What was he telling her?

Sherry's face looked tired in the yellow haze of the fluorescent pretzel carousel. "Kid," she said, "you're here all the time."

I didn't say anything. My mother was stacking cups in the corner, squirming in her uniform, too tight across her chest.

"You know Eddie? You know him?" Sherry gestured over to the lanes.

I nodded. My mother spun one of the waxy cups on her finger, watching.

"I know what's what," Sherry said, looking over at my mother. I felt something ring in my chest, like a buzzer or school bell.

"You don't know," my mother responded, looking at the rotating hot dogs, thick and glossy.

"I got eyes," Sherry said, gaze fixed on the lanes, on Eddie running the floor waxer over them jauntily. He liked using the machine. He kind of danced with it, not in a showy way, but there was a rhythm to the way he moved it, twirled around on it like he was ice-skating. Billy, the last guy, twice Eddie's age, looked like he would fall asleep as he did it, weaving down each lane, hung over from a long night at Marshall's Tavern. His hands always shook when he handed out shoes. Then he threw up all over the men's room during Family Night and Jimmy fired him.

"Don't tell me I don't got eyes," Sherry was saying.

"We all got eyes," my mother said. "But there's nothing to see." Her brow wet with grease from the grill, her eye shadow smeared. "There's not a goddamned thing to see."

I didn't say anything. I rarely said anything. But something was funny in the way Sherry was looking at Eddie. She always had that blank look, but it used to seem like a little girl, a doll, limbs soft and loose, black buttons for eyes. Now, though, it was different. It was different, but I wasn't sure how.

Back there in that space behind the pins, it was like backstage and no one could see even though all eyes were facing it. As soon as you walked in a bowling alley, that was where your eyes went. You couldn't help it. But you never imagined what could be going on behind the pins, so tidy and white.

And each day I'd watch. It was a hundred degrees or more back there. It was filled with noise, all the sharp cracks echoing through the place. But I was watching the way Carol trembled. Because she always seemed so cool and easy, with her long pane of dark hair, her thick fringe of dark lashes pasted on in the ladies' room one by one. ("They get her tips, batting those babies like a raccoon in heat," Myrna, the old lady who worked dayshift concessions, said. "Those and the pushup brassiere.")

Carol was talking to Diane, the other cocktail waitress. Diane used to work at the Stratton, but to hear her tell it, the minute her tits dropped a half-inch, they put her out on her can. She hated the Lanes. "How much tips can I get from these Knights of Columbus types?" she always groaned. She worked at Whitestone Lanes too and had plenty to say about the customers there.

I was sitting at a table in the cocktail lounge, looking at pictures of Princess Grace in someone's leftover *Life* magazine. I wasn't supposed to be in there, but no one ever bothered me until happy hour.

"She can jaw all she wants," Carol said, eating green cherries from the dish on the bar. "It's all noise to me." She was talking about Sherry.

"She should take it up with her man, she has something to say about things," Diane said.

"I don't care what she does."

"What I hear, she can't show her face in Ozone Park. They all remember her family. Trash from trash."

"I'm going to haul bills tonight, I can tell. Look at 'em," Carol said, surveying the softball team swarming in like bright bumblebees.

"Yeah, good luck," Diane added, then nodded at Carol's neckline. "Bend, bend, bend."

In the bathroom once, right after, I pretended to be fixing my hair, snapping and resnapping a rubber band around my slack ponytail. I knew Carol would be in there, she always went in there

after. When she came out of the stall, I looked at her in the mirror.
Her face steaming pink, she brushed her shiny hair in long strokes,
swooping her arm up and down and swiveling a little like she was
dancing or something. She was watching her own face in the mir-
ror. I wondered what she was watching for.

I saw the dust on her back, between her shoulder blades. I
wanted to reach my hand out and brush it away.

Eddie was oiling the lanes and saw me watching, eating french
fries off a paper plate at the head of lane 3. "And there's my
girl." He said it like we talked all the time, but it was the first
time he'd ever said anything to me. "Stuck inside every day.
Don't you like to go to the Y or something? Go to the city
pool?"

"I don't like to swim," I answered. Which was true, but
my mother didn't want me to go there by myself. When summer started, she let me go once to a pool day with the kids
at school, but when I got home, she was sitting on the front
steps of our building like she'd been waiting for me for hours.
Her face was red and puffy and I never saw her so glad to see
me. That was the only time I went. Besides, she'd never liked
it. Mr. Upton, before he left, was always telling her I'd get dis-
eases at the public pool.

"All kids like to swim, don't they?" Eddie was saying. He
tilted his head and smiled. "Don't girls like to show off their
swimming suits?"

I ate another fry, even though it was too hot and made my
mouth burn, lips stinging with salt.

"I always liked to go, just splash around and stuff," he said.
"You got no one to take you, huh?"

"I don't really swim much," I said.

He nodded with a grin, like he was figuring something out.

"I get it. Well, I'd take you, but I guess your daddy wouldn't like it."

I felt my thigh slide on the plastic seat. I looked at the far end of the lanes. I felt my leg come unstuck and slide off the edge of the seat and it was shaking. "He's gone," I said.

Eddie paused for a flickering second before he smiled. "Then I guess I got a chance."

Fred Upton was my mother's husband. My real old man died when I was a baby. He had some kind of infection that went to his brain.

There were some guys in between, but two years ago it was all about Mr. Upton. We moved from Kew Gardens when she got tangled up with him and quit her job at Leona Pick selling dresses. She'd met Mr. Upton working there, sold him a billowy nightgown for his fiancée, and he took her out for spaghetti with clams at LaStella on Queens Boulevard that very night. They got hitched at City Hall three weeks later.

Before he left, times were pretty good. It was always trips to Austin Street to buy new shoes with t-straps and lunch at the Hamburger Train and going in the women's clothing store with the soft carpet, running our hands through the linen and seersucker dresses—with names like *buttercup yellow, grasshopper green, goldenrod, strawberry punch*. One day he bought her three dresses, soft summer sheaths with boatneck collars like a woman you'd see on TV or the movies. The sales lady wrapped them in tissue for her even when my mother told her they weren't a gift.

"They're a gift for you, aren't they?" the lady had said, her pink–cake-icing lips doing something like a smile.

Those dresses were sitting in the closet now, unworn for months, yellowing, smelling like stale perfume, old smoke.

Never saw my mother out of one of her two uniforms these days, except when she slept in the foldout couch, usually in her slip. Some days I tugged off her pantyhose while she slept.

"He said he was going to Aqueduct," I heard my mother say on the telephone to a girlfriend soon after he left. "But his sister tells me he's in Miami Beach."

It had been three months now, and wherever Mr. Upton went, he wasn't in Queens. Someone my mother met in a bar told her he'd heard Mr. Upton was dead, killed in a hotel fire in Atlantic City the same night he'd left. That was the last I knew. I didn't ask. I could tell she didn't want me to. I hoped she'd forget about Mr. Upton and marry a mailman or a guy who worked in an office. As it was, I figured us for six more weeks of this and we'd be moving in with my grandmother in Flushing.

"She's got ants in her pants, that one," Myrna was saying to Sherry. Myrna had a big birthmark on her cheek that twitched whenever she disapproved of something, which was a lot. She was talking about Carol, who she called "Lane 30," because that was where the cocktail lounge was. "Thinks she's got it coming and going."

"Don't I know. She better watch where she shakes that," Sherry said, face tight and sallow under the fluorescent light. She looked like a sickly yellow bird, a pinched lemon.

"You got ideas."

"Sure I got ideas. And I'm no rabbit. Maybe she needs to hear that."

"I'll see she does."

Sherry nodded. Those flat eyes were jumping. That slack lip now drawn tight. Her face all moving, all jigsawing around. She looked different, more interesting. Not pretty.

It was all too much for pretty. But you couldn't take your eyes off it.

I wasn't supposed to be back there at all. Once, years before, some kid, not even fifteen years old, was working at the Lanes. He got stuck in the pinsetter machine and died. There were a million different stories of how it happened, and ever since, no one under twenty one was supposed to be back there. But I never got near the clanging machine. I stayed in the alcove where they kept the cleaning equipment.

From there, I could see them and they never saw me. They never even looked around.

Sometimes, Eddie would be whispering to Carol, but I couldn't hear.

They were just pressed together, and when the machine wasn't going, when no one was bowling, you could hear the rustle of their uniforms brushing against each other.

The more he moved, the more she did, and I could hear her breathing faster and faster. He covered her and I couldn't see her except her long hair and her long legs wound round. I was too far to see her eyes. I wanted to see her eyes. It was like he was shaking her into life.

"Things are getting interesting," Mrs. Schwartz said to my mother, who was resting against the counter, slapping a rag around tiredly. *You can lean, you can clean,* Jimmy always said.

"Don't count on it," my mother replied.

"Sherry might try harder, wants to keep a man like that," Mrs. Schwartz said. She was the head of one of the women's leagues. She was always there early to gossip with Diane. I think she knew Diane from the Stratton, where Mrs. Schwartz met her second husband. They liked to talk about everybody they knew and the terrible things they were doing. "Looks like a singer or something," she added, twisting in her capris. "A television personality. Even his teeth. He's got fine teeth."

"I never noticed his teeth," my mother said.

"Take note." Mrs. Schwartz nodded gravely.

Diane walked up, clipping her name tag on her uniform. No one said anything for a minute. They were watching Sherry walk into the ladies' room, cigarette pack in hand.

"She can't even be bothered to put on lipstick," Mrs. Schwartz said, shaking her head. "Comb her hair more than twice a day."

"Her skin smells like grill," Diane commented under her breath. The two women laughed without making any noise, hands passing in front of their faces.

Mrs. Schwartz left to meet her teammates surging into the place with their shocks of bright hair and matching shirts the color of creamsicles.

Diane was watching Sherry come out of the bathroom. "Trash," she said to my mother. Then, in a lower voice, "They used to live upstate. Her father's doing a hitch in Auburn. Got in a fight at a stoplight, beat a man with a tire iron. Man lost an eye."

"How do you know?" my mother asked.

"Jimmy told me. He gave her hell for making a call to State Corrections on his dime." Diane shook her head again. "Mark my words, she's trouble. Trash from trash."

I looked over at Sherry, leaning against a ball return to tie her apron. She had her eyes on them, on all of us. She couldn't hear, but it was like she did.

"Mark my words," Diane said. "Blood will tell."

That whole summer, I'd lie in bed at night waiting for my

mother to come home from her shift waiting tables at the tavern. I'd lie in bed and think about Eddie and Carol. It was like how I used to think about Alice Crimmins, the Kew Gardens lady who killed her kids so she could be with her boyfriend. I couldn't get her face from the newspaper out of my head. Two, three times a night, I'd run around testing all the window latches, the window gates.

Now, though, it was all about Eddie and Carol. I'd stay under my sheets—cool from sitting in the refrigerator for hours while I watched television and ate Chef Boyardee—and think about how they looked, all flushed and pulsing, how you could feel it coming off them. You could feel it burning in them. It made my throat go dry. It made something ripple in me, like the time I rode the rollercoaster at Fairyland and thought I just might die.

Then I'd start thinking of Sherry standing behind that counter all day. When she'd first started she cracked gum and looked bored, went in the bathroom twice a day to wash hot dog sweat off her hands and spit out her gum in the sink.

But lately she didn't look bored. And nights, she'd get into my head. Standing there like that, her head dropping, eyes lowered, watching. I wondered when she was going to make her move. Was she waiting to see it for herself? Hadn't she figured out yet when and where it was happening, right behind the wall of pin trestles that she—we all—stared at every day all day?

Each day it seemed closer and closer. Each day you could feel it in the place, even as the clean and fresh-faced Forest Hills kids pounded their bright white tennis shoes down the alleys; even as the shiny-haired teenagers hunched over the pinball machines, shoving their hips, twisting their bodies, like they wanted to squirm out of their skin; even as the customers at the bar, steeled behind smoked glass by lane 30, cocooned from the pitch of the squealing kids and mooning double dates, cool in their adult hideaway of tonic and beer, crushed ice and lemon rinds and low jazz and soft-toned waitresses with long, snapping sheets of hair and warm smiles, and a bartender who understood them and would know just what to do to make them happy . . . even with all that going on at the Lanes, it was going to happen.

"I don't like the way they talk about her," Diane was whispering to my mother, leaning over my mother's counter, tangerine nails tapping anxiously. "Sherry and Myrna and Myrna's friends from the Tuesday league."

"Talk's just talk," my mother answered, loosening her apron.

"Listen," Diane said, leaning closer. Looking over at me, trying to get me not to listen. "Listen, she deserves something. Carol does." Her voice even lower, husky and suddenly soft. "Her mom's at Creedmore. She's been there awhile. Took a hot iron to Carol when she was a kid. She was sound asleep when it happened. Still a scar the shape of a shield on her stomach."

Diane was looking at my mother, looking at her like she was asking her something. Asking her to understand something.

My mother nodded, eyes flickering as the fluorescent light made a pop. "You got a customer, Diane," she said, pointing toward the bar.

I was thinking they might stop. Might take a few days off, let things cool off. But they didn't. They only changed it up a little. From what I could tell, Carol came in the back way for her shift and met Eddie first. Met him back there before anyone even saw her. But they didn't stop. And one day Eddie came out with a streak of Carol's lilac lipstick on his bleach-white collar, just like in a story in a women's magazine.

I watched him walk across the place, lane by lane, with the stain on him. I glanced over at Sherry, who was leaning against the pinball machine and watching him. I thought: This is it. She's too far to see it, I thought to myself. But if he moves closer. If she moves closer.

Yet neither of them did.

When I saw him later, the lipstick was gone, collar slightly damp. I pictured him in the men's room scrubbing it off, scrubbing her off. Looking in the mirror and thinking about what he'd done and what he couldn't help but keep doing.

The kids from Forest Hills High School were all over the place that afternoon, all in their summer clothes, girls with tan legs and boys freshly showered and gleaming. The rain had sent them, some straight from lounge chairs at the club, others from lifeguarding or the tennis courts. I always noticed the fuzzy edges of my summer Keds around them. I always wondered how the girls got their hair so shiny, their clothes so crisp, their eyes so bright.

I had a feeling it was going to happen that day. I couldn't say why. Before Sherry even got there. But when she did, I knew for sure.

She looked like she'd been running a fever. There was this gritty film all over her skin and red blotches at her temples. Her uniform was unwashed from the day before, a ring of grease circling her belly.

She was late and I'd just left my post, just left the two of them. *They never took their clothes off, ever, but sometimes he'd lift her skirt so high I could see flashes of her skin. I was searching for the scar, but I never saw it.*

Her fingers pinched around his neck, the rushed pitch to her voice . . . it felt different this time. It felt like something was turning.

Maybe it was something in the way his hands moved, more quiet, more careful. Maybe something in her that made her move looser, almost still.

I got it then. And I knew for sure when I saw them break apart and each look the other way. She dropped her skirt down with a snap of one wrist. He was already walking away.

I flicked off the last piece of the strawberried scar on my knee. The skin underneath was still tender, puckered.

And now there was Sherry. I was coming from the back and she was right in front of me, talking at me, her voice funny, toneless.

"I saw you sitting over there yesterday. By the machine room."

"No one's at concessions," I said, wondering where my mother had gone.

"It was the same time. I saw you come out from there at the same time yesterday."

"I guess," I said.

It was ten minutes later, no more, when we all heard the shouting. Jimmy, Myrna, Eddie, two guys putting on their bowling shoes—we all followed the sounds to the ladies' room.

Carol was hunched over, hair hanging in long panels in front of her. She seemed surprised, her mouth a small "o." It looked like Sherry'd just punched her in the stomach.

But then I saw it in her hand. The blade was short and Sherry held it so close to her, elbows at her waist. The blade was short enough that it couldn't have gone deep.

Jimmy backhanded Sherry. She cracked her head on the stall door and slid slowly to the floor, one hand reaching out for Jimmy's shirt.

The knife fell and I saw it was one of those plastic-handled ones they used to open the hot dog packages at concessions.

Eddie pushed past Jimmy and knelt down beside Sherry. She had a surprised look on her face. He was whispering to her, "Sherry, Sherry . . ."

Carol was watching Eddie. Then she looked down at her stomach and a tiny blotch of red against the banner-blue.

"That ain't nothing," Myrna said, birthmark twitching. "That ain't nothing at all."

Myrna taped up Carol with the first-aid kit. Then Jimmy took all three of them to his office. I walked over to concessions, but no one was there.

That was when Diane came running in, shouting for someone to call an ambulance.

"We don't need no ambulance," Myrna said. "I hurt myself worse getting out of bed."

But Diane was already on the phone at the shoe rental desk.

We all ran down the long hallway and up the stairs to the boulevard. Someone must have already called because the ambulance was there.

At first, it was like my mother had just lain down on the street. But the way her neck was turned looked funny. Like her head had been put on wrong.

Diane grabbed me from behind and pulled me back.

That was when I saw a middle-aged man in a gray suit sitting on the curb, his face in his hands. His car door was open like he'd stumbled out to the sidewalk. He was crying loudly, his whole body shaking. I'd never heard a man cry like that.

Diane was telling everyone who would listen, "She said she saw him. She said she saw Fred Upton pass by on the 4:08 yesterday. But he'd never take a bus, would he? That's what she said. So she wanted to watch for it at the same time today.

See if it was him. You know how she always thought she was seeing him somewhere. No one must've hit the bell because the bus didn't stop. And she just ran out onto the street after it. That car didn't have time to stop."

She looked over at the man, who started sobbing even louder.

"Hit her like a paper doll," Diane continued. "Nothing but a paper doll going up in the wind and then coming down."

Later, I would figure it out. My mother, nights spent looking out diner windows, uniform steeped in smoke, thinking of the stretch of her thirty years filled with glazy-eyed men stumbling into her life— all with the promise of four decades of union wages like her old man, repairing refrigerators, freezers in private homes, restaurants, country clubs, office buildings—for her whole life never stopping for more than one Rheingold at the corner bar before coming home for pot roast at the table with the kids.

Those men came but never for long, or they came and then turned, during the first or second night in her bed, into something else altogether, something that needed her, sure, but also needed the countergirl at Peter Pan bakery, or four nights a week betting horses at the parking garage on Austin Street, or a night watching the fights at Sunnyside Garden even when it was her birthday, and, yeah, maybe he needed the roundcard girl he met there too.

There was a dream of something and maybe it wasn't even a guy like her old man or the one in the Arrow Shirt ad or the doctor she met at the diner, the one with the big apartment in the new high-rises, the view from the bedroom so great that she'd have to see it to believe it, he'd said. Maybe it wasn't a man dream at all. But it was something. It was something and it was there and then it was gone.

ONLY THE STRONG SURVIVE

BY MARY BYRNE

Astoria

> *It wasn't the boys from Carrickmacross*
> *Or the boys from Ballybay*
> *But the dealin' men from Crossmaglen*
> *Put whiskey in me tae*

My father announced this from a comfortable arm-chair by a window. Clad in good pajamas, he had "showered, shat, and shaved," as he put it himself. In fact, this had been engineered and executed by an obese but energetic Polish lady of some thirty-eight years who was now about to leave after the graveyard shift. An old phono-graph exuded Johnny Mathis or Andy Williams, I don't know which. Or care. Schmaltzy music kept my dad quiet. It was almost as important as the nurses.

The Pole bustled back into the room, sweating already, and hung about with bags and baskets.

"A proper scavenger," said Dad.

"You can talk," the Pole shot back.

"Live where you'd die. Build a nest in your ear." He eyed me crossly. We exchanged stares.

"I weel not take much more of thees," said the Pole. "He's gotta be put in a home. Those opiates are bedd for his hedd. Hallucinations again last night, squirrels climbing the bed-room vall and someone up a ladder—"

"She's cleaning the house out little by little," said my dad, "hence the multifarious bags."

"—not to mention the insults and the smell of his excreta," she went on.

I stood up, hoping she'd get the hint. I had no desire to discuss Dad's excreta—or anyone else's—with a sweaty and exhausted Pole.

"Get someone to relieve me a few nights," she ordered, heading for the door. "I gotta lotta werk on."

She was mixed up in illegal sweatshops, and perhaps even illegal aliens. A true wart on the heel of humanity, she even had her own off-off-illegal sweatshop, in which the most desperate of Eastern Europeans put together for her benefit little trinkets and zippered bags made from the offcuts of the real thing.

"When you kill a pig, nothing goes to loss but the squeal," Dad pronounced as she flounced out the door.

We were alone. My son Sean hadn't come home last night, an increasingly frequent occurrence. The big house was silent but for the ticking of old clocks, Dad's only hobby and luxury. Every room had several of them. "Are them things gonna be bongin' all night?" my wife had said the first night we slept there after the honeymoon.

Naïma, the day-shift nurse, was late. Normally my wife dealt with any kind of overlap problem before going off to her museum job. But she was absent at the moment, as she was more and more these days.

"Where's the Swamp Rat?" asked Dad, as if reading my thoughts.

Nulty Jr. eyed Nulty Sr. I wondered just how senile the old man really was.

"Some art shindig in St. Petersburg," I replied. I wondered why I bothered.

"Home to the swamps," said Dad.

"No, the other St. Petersburg, the Russian one."

That seemed to silence him, or else his thoughts wandered off to something else. He dubbed my wife the Swamp Rat as soon as he heard she came from Tampa, Florida. At the time, I was offended for her. I was in love with this dark little hustler—she reminded me of Edith Piaf. I called her La Piaf. *Then.* But little by little the very things that pleased me at first made me hate her later: her bustling ass, the way she crimped her thin frizzy hair, a moue thing she did with her mouth as if to strengthen up facial muscles. I soon saw her thrifty housekeeping as meanness. She was prepared to spend money on no one but herself. She even squeezed enough for little facelifts and gold wire here and there over the years. This was on top of sports clubs, gyms, dance classes, and trainers. The house was feng shui–compliant, another recent source of trouble and expense.

By now, I approved the nickname. She'd been in it for the money from the start, and I had been reeled in, hook, line, and sinker. I suspect the facelifts and staying in shape were preparation for getting away from me in the best possible circumstances. Women always went away—my mother took off without a by-your-leave.

I left the old man alone for a minute and went down to collect the mail. Although I received my business mail in the bar we owned on Broadway, The Two Way Inn (because there are two ways in), the family's private mail arrived here. Sometimes Naïma or Old Jessica left personal mail lying around for days. I disapproved of such a risk. Dad trained me to structure my day around things like that: "Get the unpleasant stuff out of the way first. Leave nothing lying to fester."

There was a postcard from the Swamp Rat singing the praises of St. Petersburg. I knew she was there with the big Armenian, her latest conquest, but I could prove nothing and was waiting for something to come to a head. There was junk mail for my son Sean and more for my daughter Maureen, who had just moved out for the second time with a second man. Rectitude hadn't made it to the third generation.

At the bottom there was a letter with a Canadian postmark from a lawyer's office in Québec. My heart gave a lurch. Suddenly Naïma was behind me. I smelled her perfume before I turned to face her. She was flushed.

"Musing again?" She had a light, assured voice. I envied her calm contentment. In another life I would have loved her and this would have done me good.

I looked at the letter then looked at her.

"Come on, I'll make you a decent coffee before you go." She took my elbow.

I walked to the bar each morning as Dad once did. This always cleared my head. There was no spring in New York this year. There never is. I left the house huddling against a cold wind blowing off the river, but by the time I reached Mt. Carmel Cemetery, the summer had arrived. Here it was, late, when we'd almost given up hope.

I paused for a moment to look at the broken, half-buried headstones of Irish-born immigrants from famine times, people who'd worked in the factories, greenhouses, and homes of the nearby rich. *Every dog has his day*, I could hear Dad say, although I knew the old man always felt a bit of a fraud in the mansion on 12th Street. It was the house which had so impressed La Piaf at first. I heard my father again: *Not a house for a humble tiller of the soil.* Somehow it was bearable because it wasn't ours. It belonged to Dad's brother, Uncle Eddie, Canadian millionaire. The Two Way Inn belonged to him as well. No one knew exactly how Eddie Nulty had made his money. Fact is, he was the eldest of ten, had come out around the time of the Irish Civil War, worked in bars at first, then got on the ladder and sent for his little brother.

The further I walked, the more my step steadied and took on a rhythm independent of my thoughts. I could hear the reassuring rattle of the El.

"And that's when the difference between the two brothers showed," my mother told me, way back. "Eddie went to get your father off the boat. He was crumpled, dirty, and sick after all that time at sea. But Eddie pounced! On what? Your dad's boots. They weren't polished, and were laced with binder twine."

"So Eddie was pissed?"

"Watch your language. Eddie was mixed up in something," said Mom. "I heard talk of guns. Your father told me a story about when he was a boy, going to the market with their father in the early morning. They came across Eddie doing lookout on the road. 'What's up?' your grandfather asked. 'Court martial,' Eddie said. 'They're in the field, decidin' whether they'll kill himself or not.' 'Have nothing to do with all this,' the father told the young boy."

She was convinced Eddie was still mixed up in something. Nobody could get that rich by legal means. Yet occasionally, when Dad was on a bender, he got so out of hand that Mom called Eddie, regretting it afterwards. Somehow Eddie knew how to whip Dad into line. And things would continue for another while. When it was over, Mom banged on about conversations she'd heard, money she'd seen handed over in cabs, and about a bar being the best place to launder money. "What do you know about laundering?" I often replied. "You got Jessica to do it for you!"

I regretted such remarks now, and wondered where she was.

In no time at all I reached Broadway, with its crowds and traffic and fruit displays. I liked it better here. This was home. Men on the sidewalk spoke Chinese and Slav and Arabic into cell phones. *Visit Queens and see the world.* Here was where the Nultys started out, in a small apartment over a busy junction. Young parents, two small children, plenty of stress, and plenty of fun. Dad drove a bus and binge-drank. One day he parked the bus full of passengers and went into The Beer Garten (there was no *garten*) and got drunk. There was hell at home and Eddie was sent for.

It was an icy winter's day when Eddie came up the steep narrow stairs wearing a black coat with some kind of fur collar, like a rich man in the movies. Mom wrung her hands. Dad was strangely obeisant as if to his own father, and it was all settled. The German wanted to sell up The Beer Garten. Eddie would buy and Dad would run it. He had to make it work and live on the proceeds. The word *autonomous* was bandied about.

From there on, Dad appeared to play the game, fitting in quite well with the bar routine and keeping our little family from the poor house. For years we lived over the bar. Later on, Eddie bought us the mansion and persuaded Dad to move. I never knew exactly how the accounts were handled, but Eddie engaged a hot-shit accountant from Manhattan and even a tax accountant in case Dad messed that up as well. For a long time Dad was strict as a sergeant major, rising before dawn, polishing his shoes himself, eating a raw egg before breakfast: all stuff Uncle Eddie favored or advised. Even then, I knew there was no way Eddie was shining his own shoes. But I said nothing, knowing The Importance of Shoe Shining in the Family. Back in Monaghan, nobody shined their shoes, if they had any. A school photo of Dad showed most of the kids had no shoes at all—only Dad in the front row had a good pair of black boots, black socks, short pants, and a black turtleneck. I reckoned he was taken out of school shortly after that to work in the fields, until Eddie sent him the ticket for Canada.

On certain sections of the streets there were signs of the usual fracas of the previous night: bottles and cans and over-turned garbage. In recent times, crowds of young local men gathered at night to drink and carouse, as if they belonged to a different species, married to the night. Sometimes they didn't even bother going to a bar. Sometimes bar owners use the tobacco ban to keep them out. Visitors slumming the bars at night made a helluva noise while they were there, then again as they revved up to leave. Residents complained about them as much as they did about the youngsters, who sold and smoked weed and giggled a lot, then kicked the garbage out of the cans and around the street. I had known most of them since they were kids—they were Sean's age. I wondered if Sean spent time with them, but didn't dare ask. So far they'd left me and the bar alone, and although there was increasing talk of hate crimes and savage attacks in the night, I couldn't see them being the perps. For the moment, anyone kicked down subway steps had been openly gay or Muslim—or even black—but I knew that could change.

"So you rich fucks get up for a little while every day?" My friend George was standing in the doorway of his restaurant.

"Gid adda here," I grinned.

"Whadaya like, I gad it," said George, waving me in.

"Check the shop and be right back."

I entered the dark interior of The Two Way Inn. It was quiet but for an Abba song coming at low volume from the juke-box: *I don't wanna talk . . . about things we been through . . .* The usual lineup of men drinking silently in the late morning never failed to remind me of a scene from an O'Neill play. There was no green, no shamrocks, no Irish beers, no black-and-white pictures of small villages, whiskey mirrors, leprechauns, shil-lelaghs, no objects made of bog turf, nothing Irish visible. The occasional token of a German past remained undisturbed, for here the Swamp Rat had no influence and didn't like the atmosphere. No fucking compliance here, feng shui or other-wise. For a long time a German firm continued to provide Ger-man songs for the old jukebox until we updated. One of these songs survived: "Oh Mein Papa," due to popular demand, had been remastered and now kept company with the Carpenters, Abba, Maureen McGovern, Roberta Flack, the O'Jays, John Denver, and—as they say—much, much more. The bar had remained untouched for so long that it was becoming popular with the yuppie crowd out from Manhattan. It was mentioned in one or two hip magazines in search of "awthennic" places to spend their money. The barmen were instructed to charge more in the evenings. I invested in chairs and tables for the sidewalk, and after being fined twice for putting them out, eventually paid for a licence. These days I pay smoking fines, although we try to stop 'em smoking till the cops have gone to bed. Because what interests the yuppies is the interior, and the music. If it's like a stage set for me, how much more must it be for them?

I waved through the open kitchen door to our Mexican factotum (Dad's title for him). He navigated between the kitchen here, the corridors of the apartments above, and the garden on 12th Street.

"*Buenos dias, Pepe*," I said. "*Que pasa?*"

"Land of the free and the brave," replied Pepe.

I nodded to the young man behind the bar, an ex-seminarian from the old country, solid as an Aran Island, robbing only exactly enough so as not to make it obvious and rock the boat for the other bartenders doing the same.

"Gimme a shot from the real bottle you keep under the bar," said one of the O'Neill characters. "The curate isn't cooperating."

I nodded again at the young man. "Go ahead," I said, "what they have there wouldn't fill a hole in their tooth."

The young man ran a round down the bar: He had instructions to give them every third drink free, but to go easy on the non-fiddled bottle.

"Come on, lads, put yer hearts into it." This was another of Dad's goads. "Ye'll never get cirrhosis the way ye're drinkin'."

The young man handed me the morning mail, which reminded me of the letter from Canada. I reached into a pocket, fished it out, and sat at a table. No one sat at a table except in the evenings.

The letter was typed. This didn't look good. It was from a lawyer. My eyes shot to the bottom paragraph: *It is with regret that we must inform you of the intention of Mr. Edward Nulty to dispose of his properties in Astoria.*

Alerted, no doubt, by press references to a property boom, I thought. More warehouse conversions and hoardings bearing the legend, *Jesus hates this building.*

Do not hesitate to contact us should you have any questions, the letter finished. It gave the coordinates of some fancy broker in Manhattan who would contact me instanter.

I hated the British tone of it all. I even hated their tight vowels up there. I wondered what had stung Eddie into action. I folded the letter and put it in my pocket. The O'Neill characters who had been studying me turned back to their drinks again.

I got up, nodded to the company, and made my way next door to George, who had lunch ready.

"You donna looka good."

"No."

"You dyin'?"

"No."

"Yo' family die?"

"No."

"So then!" George handed me a glass of his special heavy aperitif wine.

"*Ya mass,*" he said. I said nothing. "You looza all yor money?" George had been imitating his father's accent for so long and spending three months a year in Greece that it was second nature. He looked anxious. Money was serious.

"Maybe."

George was all attention. "Money is not love," he said slowly.

"I got neither."

"First, you eat."

It seemed to me there were more of the little white plates than usual. I told George my woes, as I often do. What had once been a place serving hero sandwiches had become a high-class restaurant. Through the kitchen door I could see two Indians hard at work. And I'm not talking about Native Americans. Behind a little desk sat George's brother Lazarus, once short-order cook and pea soup expert, and his sister Hermione. They were all getting on in years.

The phone in the kitchen rang. One of the Indians answered it. "007!" he said, and giggled. "Bond, James Bond!" He was laughing so hard the other Indian had to take the phone from him.

Above our heads hung photos of George's parents and grandparents on the whitewashed terrace of a modest house in Cyprus. The men were dressed as popes, the women in black. They'd heard that the house had long since made way for a pink Turkish villa. None of them had ever tried to go back, even when it became possible.

"Eat."

George forced food on me like I remembered my mother doing before she vanished. He raised his glass and said, "*Eleftheria i thanatos*."

I nodded, repeated the words, and drank deeply.

Freedom or death.

Me and George took a stroll in Astoria Park to walk off the wine. We stopped to lean on the rail and look at the garbage floating in the water below. I wanted to drop into the Noguchi Garden Museum. I loved the smooth control and order of the marble and granite pieces. It reassured me.

George refused. "The fuck? All that cold stone giva me the creeps."

"Some Greek you are," I said.

"*Malaka*. Irish fucks only let gays and lesbians into their parade this year, for the foist time! *St. Pat's for all*, my ass!"

"Greeks'd know all about gays."

"We're all getting old," said George.

We picked divine olives from tubs in about three emporia,

then stopped off at Noureddine's for mint tea before the evening crowd arrived to smoke hookahs loaded up with honey-dipped *sheesha*. I'd heard the Pole say Noureddine's place ran women behind closed steel shutters in the afternoon. I supposed it was possible. I supposed she'd know.

Noureddine was talking about an old lady who'd been robbed on her own stairs as she returned from the bank. The robbers were said to be local.

"You don't do that on your own turf," Noureddine said. He looked like he knew what he was talking about. Then he told us about a younger brother he was educating, who'd managed to get a job teaching Spanish in Texas.

"Sounds like sand to the Arabs to me," I said.

"We're from northern Morocco," he explained. "Spanish is like a mother tongue to us. We go where it pays."

We left Noureddine and headed off, George to Danny McGrory (my dad's name for Nana Mouskouri and now our code name for George's wife, also known as La Callas or La Diva) and me to the Swamp Rat, due back that evening.

"Bet you're sorry now you didn't finish your doctorate and get a chair of philosophy," George said. "Never get off your ass at all." His phony accent had disappeared. My problems were affecting him even more than me.

"Hit me now with the child in me arms," I replied.

"Till the white rose blooms again," he said as we parted.

Back on 12th Street, I surveyed the signs of Old Jessica's daily visit—more spray-on polish, more quick-fix polluting solutions. Jessica was a failed Irish immigrant ten years older than myself. She needed the money, I couldn't in all conscience fire her. The shine in the house was getting higher, but everything else was going downhill, except for the feng shui compliance.

Old Jessica appeared from the kitchen quarters. "You'd want to straighten up," she said. "Yer gettin' a dowager's hump."

"Don't shit a man who's already down," said Sean, skipping down the stairs and out the front door before either of us could react.

Jessica shook her head indulgently. "I'da made two pairs a pants outta his one," she said.

We mounted the stairs to Dad's room, where Naïma was bedding him down for the evening. Mitch Miller was playing.

"I'm goin' plantin' spuds tomorrow, will ye help me?" Jessica asked Dad.

"I will," he said.

"Have ye the tools?"

"I have." He counted on his fingers: "I have two spades, two graips, and a shovel."

"Right so," said Jessica. "Be ready at dawn."

I wasn't sure I liked this kind of fooling with a man's already fucked-up mind.

"Once a man, twice a boy," Jessica said as she went by me.

"I want to be taken to the Astoria Sanatorium," Dad said distinctly as soon as Jessica left.

Naïma smiled down at him. "They gave it a new name now. Mt. Sinai."

"You should never paint bricks," said Dad. "They do it all the time here." Then: "The sanatorium must've laid an egg." Then he spotted me. "Priest or minister? You're doing everything wrong today."

"What did I do now?"

"You sailed up the broad expanse of Killala Bay. Give me me box."

This was a tin box containing mementos that he pored over from time to time. He pulled a collection of objects out of it and spread them over the bed: a silver dollar wrapped in tissue paper, a Rockaway Playland token, postcards, beaded Indian leather (Native American). He indicated the display to me:

Eoin Roe O'Neill
Treads once more our land
The sword in his hand is of Spanish steel
But the hand is an Irish hand

"Wanna take a leak before I go?" Naïma asked.

"You only want to see my dick, that's what you're after."

I told her to go ahead and lifted Dad back into bed. He was light as a feather.

"Ain't you the big heavy lad," I said.

"What good is it to you when you're gone?"

We sat in silence. Then he said, without opening his eyes, "When did Da die?" I never heard Dad use that word before, and realized he thought he was talking to his brother Eddie.

"Long ago," I said.

"What'd ya kill her for?" he asked, opening his eyes, now noticing me. "I think I'll go to bed now," he said, then seemed to doze.

The Pole arrived, still threatening to quit. The weather had already turned heavy.

"A storm is brassing," she said. Sometimes I wasn't sure what language she was massacring.

Dad said, with his eyes closed, "You're a bitch and you never were anything else."

After that, the house settled for a while. I tend to sit in front of the TV when I want to think. People leave me alone. I haven't read a book in years, once my favorite occupation. My attention was drawn by an item on the World Cup about to be played out in Germany. Several players from the winning 1974 German team were paraded out, one a smart older business-exec version of his younger self with a name like Baking Powder, which is what me and George had dubbed him at the time. The other was a thicker-set man who left football in 1974 and opened a newspaper kiosk. *"I wasn't cut out for all that,"* the man explained.

Perhaps this was what Dad should have done, long ago: something simple, no overreaching. There were horses for courses and that was all. It would have meant no Irish education for me and my sister, but what did that change? And perhaps Mom would still be with us. I recalled vacations from university when Mom seemed to be having an early "change of life," as she called it to her friends (nurses with real problems and families to deal with). She talked of going into a convent, where she would have peace and quiet from them all. By then, Dad had settled down to controlled drinking, a cup with milk and whiskey under the bar at all times. As if trying to numb himself. At times I think she might be with some Little Sisters, atoning in peace and quiet, not far away. Unless she's dead. *Who was the woman Uncle Eddie killed?* Was this a reference to the Civil War, or something more recent?

At 9 p.m. the Swamp Rat was poured out of a cab, laughing. The Armenian gallery owner helped her out, laughing also, wearing a beige cashmere coat that was too warm for the weather. Then he took himself off in the cab.

I lit the lights and poured us a drink. The storm was beginning to crackle outside. A door opened upstairs, releasing a few bars of Al Martino, then closed again.

My wife's breath smelled of olives and feta and all kinds of Balkan fare, something she complained of in others in the past. She was excited, smoking. She'd clearly been fucking the Armenian satisfactorily all week. It was Setrak this, and Setrak that.

"The Matisses were breathtaking. I never realized they were so *big*." She pulled out a notebook with names written in Cyrillic in a baby hand, pronouncing them as if she spoke Russian fluently. They'd obviously discovered plenty of new, cheap talent to flog for their new gallery project.

I found myself getting angry, but this was nothing compared to what I felt when I discovered that the Armenian's parents had gone with them.

"He's a hotelier, he got a special deal, why not take advantage?"

I felt a pang for the demented man upstairs in the bed, and my lost mom. I was spoiling for a fight.

"It's a long way from coffin ships," I said.

"What does that mean?"

"That was your sales pitch when you met me, wasn't it?" She said nothing.

"Your stock-in-trade. Up from Florida with a Scots name, you quickly got the hang of things here and decided you were Irish. *Only the strong survive*, you used to say."

"So?" She was icily still.

There was silence. I wanted to bring something to a head. I got up to get another bottle from the fridge. I was still in the kitchen when the question jumped out like a genie from a lamp. "Am I getting a hump?"

"You always had one," I heard her laugh out from the next room. "I thought it was from all the reading and thinking you used to do. Big thinker."

I came back, the cold bottle in my hand.

"Didn't you know that?" she laughed again, throwing her head back.

I wanted to shove the laugh down her throat. Both of us had taken plenty of drink but I felt stone-cold sober as I swung the bottle. It caught her on the side of the head.

She slumped down on the sofa slowly and quietly.

In a panic, I felt her pulse, almost afraid to touch her skin. There was no sound from upstairs.

She was alive, breathing clearly, inclined to snore. Nat King Cole sang, *"I thought you loved me, you said you loved me . . ."* as I sucked air into my lungs and ran out of the house, forgetting to code in the alarm. It was raining to beat the band.

Old rancors and memories boiled up as I walked. Cars hissed by in the wet. My father's first car was an old Falcon, whereas even the shabbiest Two Way Inn customer could surprise by turning out in something decent like an ageing Cadillac for the odd expedition to Far Rockaway. My Dad loved those words, *Far Rockaway.* "Goddamnit!" The Falcon stalled at every red light, and before it did I went into an agony of apprehension feeling a giggle build up inside, knowing there was no way to stop it rumbling up and out to hurt Dad's feelings and make him swear even more, or even lash out and hit me. *Saving Face for Ireland.*

That was the "up-and-up" era. "We're on the up-and-up," Dad often said. That same year we went "home" to Ireland as a family, to thatched cottages and women in aprons and cardigans with anxious looks. I was put to sleep in a room full of bunk beds for students of Irish.

The males of the family laughed at jokes they didn't share and at Dad's hat. Nobody wore hats over there, at most they pushed a cap or beret around their heads when answering a question, as if it helped them think. I heard one of them say, "See any dollars fall outta the hat, boys?" We were overcharged everywhere we went. A vendor refused to tell Dad the price of an ice cream until he admitted we were "Yanks." Dad was oblivious, delighted with everything.

I could still feel this anger somewhere inside now, untreated. I walked and walked.

There'd been a trip to Nevada as well, to another relative. Mom and Dad took us to shows of people I couldn't stand, like Carol Channing and Buck Owens and Fats Domino. They watched these shows with the half-attention of people waiting for something more important to arrive, who expected better things of life and had the impression the real action was happening elsewhere. Me and Sis sniggered as Carol Channing threw imitation diamond rings into the audience, and Dad hissed, "Will you cut that out?"

A while later I found myself near the river, somewhere between the two big bridges. My clothes were sodden and the earth was muddy and smelled fresh. The world was washed down.

I heard my own voice quote A.E. Houseman aloud: "*Yonder lies the gate of hell.*"

"What's that, Daddyo?" a voice said, and I saw the outlines of eight young men in hoodies against the evening sky. "Didn't we see yo' down hea' the other day with yo' friend?"

I realized the urgency of the situation, slid and lurched onto the street, dropping my cell phone. I ran until I reached a late-opening grocery store but was stopped at the door.

"Sorry," the man said, "no can do."

"There's eight of them. I need to phone for help."

"If we let you in, they'll smash the place up." He shut the door.

They soon caught me again, forced me to the ground, then kicked me as I lay. They broke my eyeglasses and took my wallet. They'd already smashed my phone.

I heard a saxophone peal out clearly, cutting the air like a knife, before I eventually lost consciousness.

I woke up in Mt. Sinai with stitches on my face. "Those kids feel threatened," the nurse said. "They feel they're being forced out by neighborhood change. They're afraid of losing it to people from Manhattan, from anywhere."

"We're all going to lose it," I said to George when he arrived to take me home. I gave no info to the cop who came, refused to file a complaint.

At the house, all was quiet. The front door lay open as I'd left it.

George refused to come in because I'd told him I socked one to the Swamp Rat.

When I went in, she was nowhere to be seen, although I knew there'd be trouble tomorrow. I looked in on Dad. The Pole was dozing in an armchair in his room.

"Someone rattled your cage," he said, his eyes open. "I never saw a more miserable creature."

The Pole opened her eyes or woke, depending on what she'd been doing. "All quiet," she said too quickly, not mentioning my face. She stood up. "I'm going to get something to drink."

"See the ass on that one—it's far too big," Dad sighed.

I knocked lightly on my wife's bedroom door. We'd had separate rooms for years. There was no reply. I opened it as quietly as I could.

She lay on the white bed. The duvet (as she always liked to call it) had soaked up a lot of the blood, although I knew there was positively none when I'd left her downstairs. I approached, calling her name softly. She looked as youthful as the young Piaf I once loved.

This time there was no pulse.

I headed for the phone. As I shouted for an ambulance, I heard the Pole on the stairs and my father asking, "Am I dying?"

The police weren't as sympathetic as I might have expected. This was perhaps due to my face, which was beginning to bruise up nicely. My story was disjointed, with periods that I couldn't account for. They refused to let me call George, then changed their minds and called him themselves. He came, white-faced, but was of little help, as he hadn't entered the house with me. He was escorted out, promising me that he'd send someone straight away.

"Bail or bond?" he tried to crack wise as he left. It didn't work.

The Pole was bossy and informative, giving remarkably precise times and details of my comings and goings.

Naïma was hurried out of bed for questioning and arrived looking worried and hollow-eyed.

They even visited Dad's room, where Tony Bennett was warbling, "*If we never meet again . . .*"

"What are yis havin'?" Dad asked the cops. Then: "Have you a light on that bicycle?"

They went away and left him alone.

They took me with them.

Two days later I was home again. George went bail, with nothing proved or decided either way. The eight hoodies couldn't be found, obviously, although George and Noureddine were working on it. If those guys were from Astoria, they were dead meat. If they were from elsewhere, I was.

I was just thinking about lots of fresh coffee when I heard the door chimes and saw Jessica hobbling toward the door. I could see Pepe pretending to trim something with shears in the garden. Sean was slumped in a sofa, not sure whether he was more angry with me than he was sorry for himself. I spoke to him little. I didn't know how.

Jessica ushered four people into the hall, all looking like Jehovah's Witnesses on the way to a ball. They said they were real estate brokers, sent by Eddie to visit the house, swore blue that someone had given them an appointment.

It was certainly beginning to look like a plot. I felt more like Hamlet by the minute.

They checked out the house, came back to the hall again, and asked to see the cellar. I said there was no cellar. They informed me there was an extensive cellar. I changed my tune and asked Jessica to get the key. She shuffled off to the kitchen and returned after a while looking purple and perplexed. There was no sign of the key.

"Surely you have a second key," said one of the Jehovah's Witnesses.

I hate people who use the word *surely*.

"No surely about it," I answered. "The door is reinforced,

for the wine, and Dad lost the key before he lost his mind, or shortly after. There was one key left, in the kitchen, always in the same place. Nobody's been down there for a long time, the wine was my father's baby."

I didn't tell them about my own (poor) taste in wine, or the fact that Pepe thought the marquis on the bottles was my father.

George arrived just then, got the measure of the scene, and hooshed them out the door to their fancy car, saying, "It'll take a locksmith, it's reinforced. We'll call you already."

Jessica joined in then, and Sean. "This house is in mourning!" they shouted. "Get outta here!"

The suits were so astonished, they just left, saying they'd need an appointment to visit The Two Way Inn.

"Visit it," said George. "Anyone can. It's open from dawn to dusk." Then to me, he said, "What harm can it do? You're not married to 'em. Yet."

George spent the rest of the day calling the locksmith, calling Noureddine, keeping me on the wagon, and driving me to my bank, where a young man in a bad suit and eyeglasses told me the Swamp Rat had cleared out all of our accounts. I thought I caught a glimpse of the bank manager observing me through sanded glass somewhere, but George said I was paranoid. "Ye goin' perrenawd on me," was what he said.

The young man looked at me as if to say, *Ya ain't the first and ya won't be the last.*

"Curiouser and curiouser," said George, which wasn't how I'd describe it.

Back home Jessica fed us, then I tried to reach Eddie in Vancouver. It took me awhile to hunt up the number, and it cost me a great deal to dial it. Sean sat and watched. I'd never have managed it if George hadn't been there. Now I knew how my mother used to feel.

There was no reply. I didn't think it funny he wouldn't even have a servant, or an answering service.

We contacted several retirement homes for my dad. I thought there might be a problem with proof of income and all that, but George said it was best to have a place ready in case the worst happened.

"So what's the worst can happen?" I asked.

"You in the clink," said George. "The rest of the family can manage for themselves, your dad can't." Sean didn't look like he agreed much.

A locksmith friend of George's was due to turn up after work the following day and tackle the cellar door. I was all for cancelling him and forgetting about the Jehovah's Witnesses, but George thought we should go through the motions, at least till we contacted Eddie.

A lady came out from a home to check Dad out. I thought this untimely haste. She went up and explained to him exactly what she was doing there.

"No bother at all. Work away," he replied, as if he'd understood everything. Then he said, "What time is the tea? I'd eat a scabby child off the floor." He leaned over and put on Richard Harris singing "MacArthur Park."

The retirement home lady and George had gone when I went up to spend ten minutes with Naïma before she left.

"He's very restless," she said. "Something's upset him. He's been through his box three times already."

We agreed he might have understood about the retirement home.

As we settled him and fluffed his pillows, I noticed something odd on the white sheet, under his ass. It was a warm key.

"The ship's name was *Murphy* and the boat's goin' up a hill," he said, looking at me and giggling.

It turned out to be the key to the cellar, of course.

The Pole was in place and a thick fog had crept in from the river when George came by for a nightcap, later. I was sitting in my TV seat, as usual, watching nothing.

"Is The Two Way Inn running itself these days?" he asked.

"They'll rob no more and no less, they know the score."

I told him about the key. He was enthusiastic.

"Let's do it," he said, "before those assholes in the suits come back."

Armed with flashlights and warm pullovers, we headed down there. I thought we might bring up a few bottles of real wine as well.

The cellar had more rooms than the ground floor, since some of them had been made into smaller spaces for storage. I reckoned nothing down there but the wine would be usable after years in dust and damp. Even the central heating and air-conditioning had been installed in a building off to the side of the ground floor, so nothing varied the conditions down here. You could feel the fog oozing in from the street and garden. I noticed a half-dozen shed snakeskins.

George was going through the wine and I was giving a last check to each corner, when I almost stumbled on something soft that gave with my foot. It stank.

There were two bodies, one lying flung over the other. By their clothes, I could tell that the one underneath was a woman, the one on top a man. I gagged. George came running.

Before I even got a proper look at them, he waved me upstairs to call the cops.

I didn't think they'd believe me this time.

We all waited for them in Dad's room. I was still coughing stuff out of my throat.

"Throw it up," said Dad, "the chickens'll ate it."

"I quit," said the Pole.

"So do I," I replied.

I tried calling Eddie one more time. There was still no reply. I was beginning to think I knew where he was.

The cops took me with them again. It was more complicated, although they probably reckoned that even if I'd killed the Swamp Rat, it was still manslaughter and not first-degree murder. Much as I disliked her and wondered what she'd done with my money, I wished it was neither.

George and the Pole stood and watched me leave. They looked as if they were beginning to believe I'd done something bad. I felt I might be better behind bars for a while. I'd have time to think. It would force Sean to get serious, and reassure him that I was being punished for killing his mother, although I was still sure I hadn't.

I got back again some hours later. The house was crawling with forensics people, plugging the causal breach. I wondered if they'd sort this one out. Why was the cellar locked, and how come Dad had the key? What if Dad was the killer?

Soon they announced that the bodies had been down there for six months.

I did a quick calculation. "That's when Mom skipped out and Dad lost the plot."

"One of the bodies is your mother, Mr. Nulty, the other appears to be your Uncle Eddie, from Vancouver. Your mother was shot. We haven't found the weapon, but the bullet is an old-fashioned one."

"Sunuvabitch!" said George. "And the uncle?"

The cop ignored him and continued to address me. "Your uncle had his head smashed in by a blunt weapon."

There was a lot of legal stuff to handle after that. Eddie's estate was protected by some Canadian legal thing. It looked like no one would get at it for a while, least of all the inheritance-hunters who had set the ball rolling. It also looked as if his remaining brothers and sisters would inherit. The Irish legend of the Canadian uncle would become a reality. The real estate people were slapped down by my lawyer. House and bar were declared private for the receptions and funerals. (I did wonder if the Armenian would consider himself in or out, and then I wondered why he hadn't showed up lately.)

Sean began to throw his weight in and help with the arrangements.

Noureddine and George got a private investigator to come up with some loose threads: "An out-of-work Yugoslav brute called Niko is throwing money around. Turns out he got it from the Armenian. We're trying to find out why."

They got Niko up a dark alley one night. He admitted he'd found the door open and gone for it. He refused to admit anything else.

They called the cops, who found out the Armenian was in some kind of smuggling thing with Russia. The Swamp Rat was either in, or else she never knew about it. No one could figure out what had happened to the money. The Pole had disappeared and was suspected of working for the Armenian, among other things.

* * *

It didn't stop there. George and his pals found someone Niko'd boasted to about knifing my wife. It could never be proved that he'd done it for the Armenian, although the cops suspected this. They also suspected that Eddie had killed my mother, but couldn't prove that either. Nobody knew why, although she might have had something on him that she tried to use, or threatened to use. No gun was found. They reckoned my father had then killed Eddie, but couldn't prove that either. He might've hid the gun, but then why didn't he try to hide the bodies too?

"He lawst his mind, remember?" said George.

Naïma slept in the house until I found someone to replace the Pole. We got a clinic to take Dad for a week while the funerals were happening. The heat soared to over 100, and we mopped our brows and showered a lot and drank too much alcohol.

When all the bodies were buried—we did it the same day, same time, three hearses and three coffins had never been seen before except after an accident—Naïma and I went to see my father in the clinic.

"How are things at home?" he asked me. "How is everyone? How's She?"

I presumed he was talking about the Eternal Feminine, his mother, his wife, his daughter-in-law. Whatever.

"What kind of work are they doin' on the farm?" he asked.

"That's a great man for his age," said an Irish voice from the next bed. They keep 'em in twos so one keeps an eye on the other. Cuts down on staff.

I couldn't see its owner due to a screen, but recognized it as a Monaghan accent. I wondered if this was an accident, or if someone had actually tried to group them.

"Pray to Saint Theresa, she'll help you," the Monaghan voice said.

"She cured Patsy Gibney," said my father.

"It's 7 o'clock. Ye'd be doing the milkin' now," the voice continued.

"What?"

He repeated it four times before Dad got it.

"Indeed, an' I wouldn't," Dad replied. "I'm finished with all that now. I'm a suckler."

I tried to explain to Naïma my ideas about the agricultural metaphor outliving its context. She looked at me funny.

As we left, the two men thought they were preparing to dose an uncooperative beast from a bottle.

"Fuck him," muttered my dad. "Throw it all over him and let it soak in."

"We're off now, Dad," I said.

He eyed me for a moment, then he said: "The divine diarrhea of the dollar."

I recognized the words of Salvador Dali, and wondered again just how senile my father really was, and if it might strike me too.

But not yet, dear God, not yet. For the moment, me and Naïma were going to make a team. We'd get my dad home and whip Sean into some kind of shape. Rectitude was on the march again.

FIRST CALVARY

BY ROBERT KNIGHTLY

Blissville

The little girl is playing there by herself. She's off in a corner of the yard by the alleyway where the girls come out of the Good Shepherd School at 3 o'clock when the bell rings and walk through to the street. But it's already late, getting dark, time for all little kids to be home with their mothers. Nobody can see her there in the alley, he knows, because he's been watching her awhile from behind the iron picket fence. She doesn't see him, nobody sees him. For about the hundredth time, she takes her baby out of the carriage, fixes its clothes, talks to it, and puts it down again. He's on the move now, out from behind the fence, walking quick on stubby legs down the alley. She can't see him coming, she's got her head in the carriage again.

"Be good now, baby," he hears her say just as he reaches her and she straightens up and sees him. "Oh!" she says.

He pushes her hard and she flops down like a doll on her behind. He's down the alley, out the gate, onto Greenpoint Avenue almost before she starts bawlin'.

He crosses the avenue, pushing the carriage in front of him fast as he can along the high stone wall between himself and the dead people buried in First Calvary. He dares not look left for fear of the Stone Saints high up on their pedestals standing watch over the graves. Even though he knows they can't see him because their backs are turned to the street. He knows why this is so because his Nan has told him. Saints give fuck-all for the likes of the shanty Irish, Nan says. As he rolls across Bradley Avenue, he sneaks a look at the front door of the Cork Lounge, where Nan takes him and the dog on Saturday afternoons, after the stores for a growler of Shaeffer "to go."

The carriage is big as him but he can push it all right. He hurtles past the people sitting on the front stoops of the houses, there like always, the mothers hanging out the windows in their parlors, resting big folded arms on windowsills all up and down the block, watching. He knows this, so he keeps his head down behind the carriage, pushing it up the block fast as he can, up and on his toes, leaning into it like the football team he's seen practicing in the vacant lots off Review Avenue alongside the Newtown Creek.

Still, he feels the eyes on him, watching. He trips! Hits the pavement on hands and knees. The carriage rolls forward by itself, already two squares of sidewalk ahead, but he's up! *After it!* Tears stinging his eyes, he grabs the handlebars, just missing the cars parked at the curb. He rights his ship and sails on up the sidewalk. His hands are dirty, right knee scraped where his overalls ripped. They'll ask about that, he knows. He'll say: *I fell, it don't hurt.* At the corner, he wheels around onto Starr Avenue.

For the only time he can ever remember, there's nobody on his stoop. *Home free!* He backs up the stoop, dragging the carriage by its handlebars up the four stone steps and into the vestibule of his tenement, then down the long, carpeted hallway to the door to the basement stairway, and parks it there in the dark. No one can see him reach in and take the doll in its frilly dress into his arms.

"Be good now, baby," he cautions, then lays it back down

in the carriage, covering it, head and all, with the pink blanket so no one can see.

He climbs the four flights of stairs, holding tight to the wooden banister worn smooth by generations of hands, all the way to the top where he lives with Nan and Aunt May. Nan's his grandmother and Aunt May's mother and his father's mother. He knows this because they told him, and his home will always be with them as long as he's a good boy, and his mother drinks and his father's a whoremaster. He does not remember his mother because she dropped him off when he was eight months and didn't come back. Nan keeps house and Aunt May goes to work at the phone company. And Aunt May is the boss of all of them, Nan says when Aunt May can't hear her. There's an old dog named Dinah lives with them, it's Aunt May's dog, it won't let him walk it. He reaches up for the doorknob and goes inside.

"Young man!" Aunt May calls from the parlor. He goes in to her. She's in her housecoat, sitting in the arthritis chair by the window. Nan calls it that because Aunt May has that, and sits in it all the time. Nan's not there, she went to the store. He sees the open window and pillow on the sill, the sheer curtain wafting in and out on the summer breeze, before dropping his eyes to the little fox terrier sitting alongside the chair, studying him, alert as if also waiting for him to account.

"I found it," he says, staring at the dog who stares back, weighing his words with beady, angry eyes. Then, curling its upper lip to show fangs, growls from deep down in its little chest.

"Where did you *find* it?" Aunt May snaps.

"In the schoolyard."

"Liar!"

"She gave it to me."

Aunt May makes him push it all the way back. As he runs the gauntlet, he again keeps his head down, eyes to the pavement. The little girl is still there, bawlin', with her mother and a bunch of little girls. The other little girls are bawlin' too; he has no idea why. When the little girl sees him, she stops, runs to the carriage, snatches up her doll and hugs it. But when Aunt May holds him by the scruff of the neck in front of the little girl and tells her to give him a good slap right across his face, she starts bawlin' again. Staked out by bloodthirsty hostiles, his face burns under their piteous stares. In sight of the Stone Saints across the street giving him the ass, he prays with all his might that all the windows in all the houses on every block be nailed shut.

BOTTOM OF THE SIXTH

BY ALAN GORDON

Rego Park

Plaster dust fell lazily through the air. He watched it idly, betting on which finger it would land. His right hand was dominating his field of vision at the moment. His right hand, and the dust that drifted down from the crappy plasterboard someone had once used to patch up the ceiling, so old and crumbled that a loud noise could loosen it.

Like, say, a gunshot.

The dust fell on his ring and middle fingers, which twitched slightly when it hit them. That was a good thing, he decided. He moved the other three fingers, then rotated his hand on the floor where it rested. Even better. He was falling very much in love with the plaster dust, with his working fingers, with the hand and the wrist that turned it. He did a quick inventory of the rest of his body. Everything seemed accounted for, or at least attached. Something hurt around the right side of his rib cage.

Let's try breathing, he thought. Haven't done that for a while.

He sucked in air, and started to cough violently. The thing that hurt in his rib cage, which apparently had only been kidding before, began to throb badly. He used the right hand that he still liked so much to poke cautiously at the spot. It was tender and painful. But it wasn't bleeding. Protruding slightly from the inside of the vest was the mashed tip of a bullet.

Michaels pushed himself up from the floor, pointing his gun unsteadily in front of him.

"You okay?" asked Carter, who was getting to his feet.

"Basically, yeah," said Michaels. "Might have cracked a rib."

Carter looked at Michaels's vest, which had a neat entry hole on the front.

"Damn, those things actually work," he said. "Who knew?"

"Not that guy," said Michaels, pointing in front of him.

The man lying on the floor was groaning weakly, two bullet holes in his back and a pool of blood seeping out from under him.

"Shot his own man in the back," observed Carter. "Just because he got in the way. That's cold."

A pile of blue uniforms burst through the door, guns drawn.

"Oh good, now you're here," wheezed Michaels. "Tell me you got him."

"Got who?" asked one of the uniforms.

"Wasn't someone supposed to be covering the fire escape?"

"Yeah. Merck. He's still out there. He didn't see anything."

Michaels and Carter looked at each other.

"Two-bedroom apartment," said Michaels. "There's the door, which was us, and the fire escape, which is Merck. Where is the fucker?"

One of the uniforms called for EMS. The two detectives and the other three fanned out across the living room. Carter took a deep breath, then kicked open a bedroom door. He waited two beats. Nothing happened.

"Portillo, if you're in there, you know you ain't getting away," he called. "Make this easy. No one got hurt."

"Wait a second," protested Michaels.

"Shut up, I'm working," said Carter. He barged through the door, a uniform close behind.

"Clear!" they called a second later.

Carter came out and looked at the second bedroom.

"Portillo, I am not playing!" he shouted. "Don't get any stupider on me!"

There was no response. Carter sighed, then kicked the door in.

"Fuck me, it's empty," he said, peering inside. "Guy did a Houdini. Where'd he go?"

"Hey, detective," called a uniform from the first bedroom. "Take a look at this."

They all crowded in. There was a floorboard that wasn't quite flush with the rest. The uniform pulled, and a section of floor came up. The hole underneath was ringed by a dozen brick-sized packages wrapped in layers of plastic.

"Crawl space," said Carter, shining a flashlight into it. "Looks like it goes all the way to the elevator shaft. He's probably gotten to the basement by now."

"Not one of our finer days," said Michaels.

The EMS crew came in and went to work on the wounded man. Michaels took his first deep breath, regretting it immediately. He pried the bullet out of his vest and tossed it to one of the uniforms.

"Bag this," he ordered. "Bag the coke. Get Evidence Retrieval in here for prints. I'm gonna ride along with the Swiss guy."

"I thought he was Latino," said the uniform. "How do you figure he's Swiss?"

"'Cause of all the holes in him," said Michaels.

The ambulance screeched up the ramp to the emergency

room at Queens General, with Carter's Corvette pulling up right behind them, his bubble light flashing on top. Two RMPs brought up the rear.

"I want him guarded 24/7," said Carter to the uniforms. "Two men at all times, and heads up. If this guy wants to finish the job, he'll come in blasting."

They followed the gurney inside. There was a flurry of green scrubs and shouting, then the doors to the OR hissed shut, leaving the two detectives standing with a surgeon.

"How long for the operation?" asked Michaels.

"To take the bullets out, not long," said the surgeon. "But we got to get Neuro down to take a look at the spine. I don't think the guy walks again."

"He wasn't going anywhere, anyways," said Michaels. "We'd like him alive and talking."

"Don't worry, that's what we do," replied the surgeon. "Welcome to Gunshots 'R' Us."

He vanished through the doors. Carter tugged on Michaels's arm.

"What?"

"I figure that adrenaline rush you've been coasting on is about to run out," said Carter. "Let's get you looked at before you crash and get all whiny with it."

Cracked rib, said the ER nurse. Cracked rib, said the X-ray tech. By the time an actual doctor came by and peremptorily taped him up, the formal diagnosis was an afterthought. The doctor pulled out a prescription pad, then looked at him quizzically.

"How much do you want it to not hurt?" he asked.

"What's the tradeoff?" asked Michaels.

"You have any desire to be awake anytime in the near future?"

"Actually, I do," said Michaels. "But give me something for when I need to sleep without screaming."

The doctor scribbled something. "You're a lucky man today," he said as he handed it to him.

"I guess I am," said Michaels. "Not really feeling it yet."

He walked out of the ER. Carter was waiting for him.

"They told me you got a cracked rib," he said.

"So I heard," said Michaels. "How's our boy?"

"Still in surgery," said Carter. "And Birnbaum's here."

"He wants to debrief us?"

"That's one way of putting it."

Birnbaum's moods were measured on the Richter scale. From the looks of his complexion, which was veering into the deep-purple end of red, there was major activity happening along his faultline.

"Routine execution of a search warrant, that's what you said," he fumed. "That is what you said, isn't it?"

"Yes, captain," answered Carter.

"And now I got an escaped cop-shooter with no description," said Birnbaum. "Wonderful. Let's call the *Post* and share our little victory."

"I didn't really get shot," explained Michaels. "I got shot *at*. The bullet did not technically enter my body."

"And my foot will not technically connect with your ass," retorted Birnbaum.

"We did get twelve keys of coke off the street," pointed out Carter. "And one guy to charge them against."

"Oh, that was good work," said Birnbaum. "Did he put up a struggle as you put the cuffs on, or was he too busy bleeding on the floor? Get Portillo, and then I can start sticking medals on someone."

He stormed away.

"Ain't no winning with this one, is there?" said Carter.

The surgeon came out. "You need these for evidence or something?" he asked, holding out his hand. There were two bullets in it.

"Yeah, thanks," said Carter. "How's the patient?"

"He'll live, but he won't be out of a wheelchair until someone figures out how to reconnect spinal cords."

"That sucks," said Michaels. "How long until he wakes up?"

"Should be soon."

"Okay, doc, thanks," said Michaels. He turned to Carter. "So now that they've sewed him up, let's go see if he's willing to spill his guts."

"Not until I talk to him about his condition," said the surgeon. "He hears that from me, not from you."

"Look, doc, this is a serious case here," said Michaels. "We got a shooter on the run."

"My house, my rules," replied the surgeon. "I'll let you know when I'm through."

About fifteen minutes later, he came out and gave them a nod. They went inside. The man was stretched out on a bed, a number of different monitors beeping and blinking around him. He was staring up at the ceiling, but rolled his eyes toward the two detectives as they pulled up a couple of chairs to the bed. One of his hands was handcuffed to the siderail.

"How's it going, John?" asked Michaels.

"Who's John?" whispered the man.

"That's how they got you listed," said Michaels. "You're John Doe 375 until they find out your real name. Sorry about your situation. Guess your partner figured he didn't want you talking."

"I'm not talking," said the man.

"Look at that loyalty, will you?" beamed Michaels.

"Impressive," said Carter. "Gets shot in the back by his own boy, and still won't give him up."

"John—screw that, give me a name," said Michaels. "We'll have it by tonight with the fingerprints, so you might as well."

"Santos," said the man.

"Okay, Santos, nice to meet you. Here's the thing," said Michaels. "We took twelve keys out of the floor in the bedroom. That puts you deep into A-1 felony weight, which in real terms means a whole lotta years to life. Not only that, you get charged for what your buddy Portillo did when we came in the door."

"What do you mean?" wheezed Santos.

"I mean two counts of attempted murder in the— Hey, I guess it's first degree, isn't it?"

"He was shooting at police officers," said Carter. "Hit one. That makes it first degree in my book."

"So that makes it another whole lotta years to life consecutive to the first whole lotta years to life," continued Michaels.

"I didn't shoot anyone," protested Santos.

"Yeah, but it's this whole acting-in-concert thing," said Michaels. "Legal stuff, but I'm saying it means you go down for everything here."

"He's not my partner," said Santos.

"Then you shouldn't give a shit what happens to him," said Michaels.

"I wouldn't," added Carter.

"You see, here's what I'm saying, Santos," Michaels continued. "We can give up on him and let you take the weight, and that's a win for us. We go on to the next case, and you go upstate into maximum security . . ."

"That's on account of it being a violent felony," explained Carter.

"Where you will spend the rest of your life not being able to walk, piss, shit, or . . . which one am I missing?"

"Fuck," said Carter.

"Oh yeah, fuck," said Michaels. "On the plus side, when you get gang-banged, you won't feel a thing. You could get some reading done while it's going on."

"You are going to be one well-read man," said Carter.

"But, as you might have figured out by now . . ." started Michaels.

"Because you are an intelligent individual . . ." said Carter.

"There is a way of making this situation a whole lot easier."

"Portillo," said Santos.

"That's right."

"And you give me what? Witness Protection Program?"

"Not likely," said Michaels. "But we could just charge you with the drugs, and there's a lot of flexibility in the sentencing. Even probation comes into play if your info is good."

"I can get out?"

"We could drop it down a grade or three depending on the level of cooperation we get," explained Michaels. "This is Queens. We got a deal going with the Narcotics DA. Doesn't mean you can go back to selling, but yeah, you can get out."

Santos lay there, his eyes closed. "Am I ever gonna walk?"

"Not according to your doctor," said Michaels.

"Fuck Portillo," said Santos. "Fuck him up bad."

"We'll do our best," promised Michaels. "So what have you got?"

"His sister's kid," said Santos. "He's in Little League. He's a pitcher. Portillo was always bragging on how great his nephew is. He was talking about going to see him pitch on Saturday. There's a playoff game. He wouldn't miss it if every SWAT team in the world was after him."

"When? Where? What's the sister's name?"

"I don't know," said Santos.

"What's the nephew's name?" asked Carter.

"Portillo just called him Junior."

"And that's all you got? There are a thousand Little League fields in this city. How we gonna find the right one?"

Santos thought for a second. "Jews," he said.

"Excuse me?"

"He came back from this one game, I think it was last Tuesday night, and he was laughing about seeing all these Jews lining up for a bunch of school buses. He thought it was the funniest thing he ever seen."

"Jews in New York," muttered Michaels. "Well, that should narrow it down."

"You got him yet?" asked Birnbaum when they entered his office.

"We know where he's gonna be, sort of," said Michaels. He summed up their information.

"That's it?"

"Yeah, so far," said Michaels. "Doesn't really help. There are a lot of baseball fields and even more Jews to track down. Not sure how to narrow this one down in time."

"Maybe by asking the only Jew in the room, who has risen to his position of authority over you shmucks by means of superior intelligence," said Birnbaum.

"Enlighten us, captain," said Carter.

"When you or I say *Jew*, we're talking about a whole range of things," said Birnbaum. "But if a guy named Portillo is laughing about seeing Jews on a bus, he's means old-school Jews. I'm talking Hasids here."

"Those guys in the black coats and hats with the beards and the curly things on the sides," said Michaels.

"That sensitivity training really paid off for you," sighed Birnbaum. "Yes, those guys. Lubavitchers, Satmars, whichever sect, that's probably who he was talking about."

"So we're looking at Williamsburg or Crown Heights?" guessed Carter.

"Not necessarily," said Birnbaum. "They've branched out into a lot of neighborhoods. But if they're getting on school buses, it probably means either a synagogue or a seminary. Start calling precinct captains—those guys should be able to tell you if there are Hasid places near Little League fields."

"We're on it," said Michaels.

A few hours later, Carter hung up his phone and sighed. "Damn, when Cap's on, he's on. Got a likely from the 112."

"Forest Hills?" said Michaels.

"Forest Hills, Rego Park," answered Carter. "Proud home of the Forest Hills Youth Athletic Association, which is in Rego Park. They have their own fields on Fleet Street, and first round of playoffs is this Saturday."

"And?"

"Around the corner on Thornton, there's a Hasidic seminary. School buses line up to take the students back to wherever they live. The Captain at the 112 says they sometimes got complaints about the street getting blocked."

"Let's go take a look," said Michaels.

They drove to Fleet Street. There was a high mesh fence bordering the sidewalk, a concrete bunker of a clubhouse on the right. It was Friday, around noon, and the field was being mowed by a guy on a large riding mower. There was an old railroad bridge, overgrown with bushes and trees, and abandoned tracks ran along a path off the street, parallel to the left field line. Signs from local sponsors decorated the outfield fence.

"Looks doable," said Carter.

"Harder than it looks," countered Michaels. "There's another field there."

They strolled through the gate and up a hill. Sure enough, a second baseball diamond was set up above the first, and they could see two more past that one. A path stretched between Fields 3 and 4, running to residential neighborhoods in both directions.

"What's past that field?" asked Carter.

"Let's take a look."

There were woods, and a clearing. The tracks continued in that direction, heading toward a tunnel by the Long Island Rail Road tracks. A commuter train roared by as they watched.

"Someone's been having a party," observed Michaels, pointing to some empty beer bottles and crack vials scattered around a fallen tree.

"Our boy, or just the locals?" wondered Carter.

"Who knows? This could be a nightmare. We got three street entrances, the whole woodland frontier at the back, four fields going simultaneously for however many games, one very dangerous and armed cop-shooter, and civilians everywhere. Child civilians at that."

"Portillo spooks, there could be some bad headlines on Sunday," said Carter. "Shoot-out at a Little League game. Won't do anyone any good."

"We're gonna need a big team. Let's talk to the captain."

* * *

Saturday morning at 6:00 a.m., Michaels handed out satellite photos of the field that he had downloaded. "First games are at 8:30. Four fields going, and a new game every two hours until sunset. Every field will have two dozen kids, and three times as many family members watching. We're looking for a phenom, a Latino pitcher called Junior, and when we find him, we narrow down on that location and look for his uncle. We got twenty-five cops here. I want a car at the two side entrances at Thornton and Alderton, four guys up in the woods near the old railroad tunnel, two cars at the main entrance, and the rest of us wandering the location. If you see him, just phone it in. We'll grab him once he leaves. We don't want him to start anything when there's kids everywhere. Everyone got their cell phones charged up? We'll be keeping them on walkie-talkie mode."

"Won't that look kind of obvious?" asked a cop.

"Every parent on that field is gonna be giving play-by-play to Grandma," said Michaels. "We'll fit right in."

Sleepy six-year-olds wearing primary-colored jerseys and black pants over cups they wouldn't need for several years waddled up the hill to the T-ball field. Older children warmed up on the larger fields while their parents unfolded a wide variety of collapsible chairs. The caretaker trundled the chalk spreader from field to field, leaving foul lines in his wake. The tiny green snack shed's shutters opened, and the smell of coffee and hot dogs began to permeate the atmosphere. Michaels bought his first cup of coffee and promised to pace himself. There were going to be no bathroom breaks today.

International League. Pan-Continental League. Major League. Grandiose titles for small players, wearing their sponsors' names with pride. T-Bone Diner. Hancock Law. Fast Break—that was the best name for a team, Michaels thought. A basketball team, but still. He wandered around, listening in on coaches' instructions, looking for Junior.

"It's a beautiful day for a ballgame," came Carter's voice over his cell phone. "Let's play sixteen."

A burst of Spanish chatter caught his attention. A family had settled in to cheer their daughter on. A young woman, a young man, an older woman. The man had a beard. In the brief glimpse he'd had of Portillo, he hadn't seen a beard. He had a vague impression of height.

"Girls generally don't get named Junior, do they?" he asked into his cell phone.

"I'd say not," replied Carter. "Unless she's a real Griffey fan. But Santos did say *nephew*."

"Right," said Michaels. "I'm hanging by Field 3, Mom. I'll let you know when little Barney comes up to bat."

There were bleachers along the third base line, but he chose to stand by the fence near first. Families were still coming in as the pimply teenager who was umpiring the game yelled, "Play ball!"

Michaels glanced over the crowd, then watched as the pitcher plunked the first batter with his first throw. The crowd oohed in sympathy, then cheered as the batter swallowed hard to keep from crying and jogged down to first base.

"Settle down, Danny!" shouted a mom. The pitcher ignored her, and hit the next batter.

"One more and he's out," said a man sitting on a lawn chair by Michaels.

"That's the rule?" asked Michaels.

"Yeah, you can only hit two kids per inning. Safety thing."

"I guess you save it for the ones you really don't like," said Michaels.

"Yeah," said the man. "That's my boy in left. Which kid's yours?"

"Still on the bench," said Michaels. "They'll probably put him in halfway through."

"Well, they have to, don't they? . . . Hey, I know you."

"Yeah?" said Michaels.

"Yeah," said the man. "You're a cop, aren't you? So am I. Bill Stanley, 101st Precinct."

"Oh, yeah," said Michaels, shaking his hand. "Jim Michaels."

"Michaels, right. Didn't know you lived around here. And you got a kid my boy's age? Small world."

"Sure is," said Michaels.

"Yeah, I remember, you were working Narcotics," continued Stanley. "Still there?"

"Yup."

"Huh." Stanley's eyes narrowed. He stood by Michaels, keeping his eyes on the game. The batter popped up to third for the first out. "You don't have a kid, do you?" Stanley said softly. "Tell me you're not on the job right now."

"Sorry," said Michaels.

"Jesus, what's going down here?"

"Just looking for someone."

"There are children here," said Stanley. "What the hell are you thinking?"

"We're not going to take him down here."

"What if he freaks?" asked Stanley. "Did you consider that?"

"We did," said Michaels. "This is our only lead."

"Crap, crap, crap," muttered Stanley. "Is he at this game?"

"I don't know," admitted Michaels. "We were told he's got a nephew called Junior. Latino. A pitcher."

"Junior," said Stanley. "I don't know any Juniors in this game."

The next two batters struck out. Danny had settled down. The parents cheered, including Stanley. As the kids ran to the dugout, he motioned to his son, who quickly came to the fence.

"Billy, this is a friend of mine from the force. Jim Michaels."

"How ya doin', Billy?" said Michaels.

"Fine," said Billy.

"He was wondering about a pitcher named Junior," said Stanley. "Spanish kid. Know anyone like that?"

"Junior? He's in Majors," answered Billy. "This is Pan-Con."

"Which team?" asked Michaels.

"Yellowstone Tires. He's their best pitcher. I gotta go, Coach is yelling."

"Thanks, Billy," said Michaels.

The boy scooted away.

"Here," said Michaels, handing Stanley two bucks. "Buy him an extra ice cream on me."

"My son, the snitch. His mother will be so proud."

Michaels walked down to the league bulletin board and studied the schedules. Yellowstone Tires was playing at 10:30 on Field 1, the big one by the street. He pulled out his cell phone.

"Okay, Mom, I gotta see Junior play at 10:30," he said.

"You got him?" asked Carter.

"I don't know any other Juniors, Mom. Do you?"

"Haven't found any yet," said Carter. "Which field?"

"Yeah, Field 1, Mom, that's the nice one by the street."

"Well, I think we got to keep covering the others, just in case."

"You said it, Mom," said Michaels. "I'll call you when the game starts, give you a play-by-play. Put your feet up and go easy on the gin, okay?"

"If your mother is really like that, it goes a long way toward explaining you," said Carter.

Michaels bought a pretzel from the snack shack. The first base foul line for Field 1 paralleled the street, where a pair of ice cream trucks had parked and were doing brisk business. An apartment building loomed beyond the clubhouse. Michaels picked up his cell again.

"We should have someone covering the entrance of that building," he muttered. "Any Latino male coming out after the game ends should be tailed."

"You don't have enough people for everyone in Queens," said one of the backups. "And they all seem to be here."

Michaels sighed and hung up. A pair of three-year-olds ran screaming by him, their mothers following behind, chatting. No kid was being supervised, because every kid was safe. It was an oasis of security in the big bad city, and Michaels started hoping that he was wrong and Portillo was on his way back to wherever he was from.

The yellow jerseys of Yellowstone Tires began assembling by the field at 10:15, some tossing baseballs around, some cheering for their friends in the game winding down. There were several Latino kids on the team. A coach said something to one, and he nodded while a shorter, squatter kid dug a catcher's mitt and a baseball from the equipment bag. They went over to the side of the field and began throwing the ball back and forth. The Latino kid threw two easy pitches to the catcher. Then he brought his left knee up close to his chin and uncoiled. The ball hit the catcher's mitt dead center with a pop that echoed off the apartment building. Michaels pulled out his phone.

"I got Junior here," he said. "And he's got an arm, my friends."

"Right," said Carter. "Units 3, 4, and 5 to Field 1. The rest of you keep covering where you are, just in case we're wrong."

The early game ended, and the two teams lined up to slap palms in a display of ritualized sportsmanship. Yellowstone Tires and Wilco Hardware came onto the field to warm up. The parents of the Wilco kids gathered in the third base bleachers. Michaels grabbed a seat next to a woman who was surreptitiously reading a Harlequin romance.

"Which one is yours?" asked the woman.

"Oh, I got here too early," said Michaels. "Gonna see my nephew play, but my idiot brother got the time wrong. So I got a couple of hours to kill."

"That's my Tommy playing second," she offered.

"Good-looking kid," he said. "Looks like you."

"Are you one of those men who hits on divorced women at Little League games?" she asked hopefully.

"Nah, I only go for soccer moms. And they're out of season. Who's the kid pitching for Yellowstone? He's got some pop."

"That's Javier," she said. "His mom calls him Junior. He's excellent."

"Which one's his mom?"

"I thought you only went for soccer moms," she said, pouting slightly.

"Buddy of mine runs a travel team. He told me to scout for him while I was here. Javier might be a prospect."

"That's her in the yellow T-shirt," she said, pointing to the other bleachers.

He pulled out a pair of binoculars and scanned the Yellowstone supporters. A Latino woman was cheering loudly with some other moms. There were no Latino men.

The Wilco pitcher took the mound and threw his warm-ups. The catcher tossed the last one to second base, and then the game began. Yellowstone scratched out a run in the top of the first on three singles, the last by Javier, who was batting fifth. Then he took the mound for the bottom of the inning. He struck out the side on eleven pitches.

"This kid is good," said Michaels into his cell phone.

"You're telling me," said Carter. "Any luck on Portillo?"

"Haven't seen Uncle. I'll get back to you."

He stretched and stepped down from the bleachers. His colleagues were wandering around, pretending not to notice each other. He walked down to the street and bought an ice cream.

"Little League sure kills your diet," he said on his cell.

"It's our lack of will power," replied Carter. "I'm on my fifth hot dog, and I don't even like hot dogs. Any prospects?"

"Not yet."

Bottom of the second. Two more strikeouts for Javier, the batters flinching at each pitch. The last one swung late and hit a weak ground ball to the first baseman, earning a cheer from the Wilco parents.

Michaels sauntered over to the first base bleachers and took a seat in the top row, giving him a good view of both the game and Javier's mother. She kept up an animated stream of Spanish with a woman next to her, interspersed with cheers for her son and the other children. She did not look anywhere else.

The pitcher for Wilco, while not at Javier's level, was effective after the first inning, pitching in and out of jams without allowing another run. Javier struck out the side again in the fourth, and the crowd erupted in cheers.

"Do you realize that we're watching a perfect game?" marveled Michaels.

"Don't jinx it," warned Carter.

"Lucky bastards," said another detective. "The T-ball game is 18 to 4 in the second, and all the runs are unearned. I'm having flashbacks."

Word traveled, and kids and parents who were not committed to other games drifted down to watch Javier. Reluctantly, Michaels started scanning the crowd again, looking for possibilities. The ping of a bat distracted him, and he looked back at the game to see Yellowstone's center fielder racing toward the fence. At the last second, he stuck his glove out and the ball somehow landed in it.

Both sides and all the onlookers stood and applauded the effort, Javier as hard as anyone.

"Did you see that?" shouted Michaels into his cell phone.

"Unbelievable!" said Carter. "Game-saver right there."

Michaels stretched as the fifth inning played out. Javier was beginning to look fatigued. His pitches no longer popped, but his control was still with him. The Wilco batters were putting the ball in play instead of striking out, although the Yellowstone fielders were able to keep the perfect game going.

Only one inning left, thought Michaels. Then he saw a tall Latino male standing outside the right field fence next to a Hasid who had stopped to watch the game.

"Hey, Mom, I think Uncle Phil just got here," he said. "Down on the street side. I'm gonna go say hello."

"Got your back," said Carter.

He ambled over to the fence by where the Latino stood. Yellowstone did nothing in the top of the sixth. It was still 1-0, and Javier walked slowly to the mound, the crowd cheering him on.

"Good game," said Michaels. "That Javier is some pitcher."

The Latino man grunted.

"It would be a shame if something spoiled his big day," continued Michaels. "Like seeing his uncle get arrested in front of everyone."

"What the hell are you talking about?" asked the Latino man, turning to face him.

"Oh, sorry," said Michaels. "I wasn't talking to you."

"Then who you talking to?" demanded the man.

"Him," said Michaels, pointing to the Hasid. "And I suggest you give us a little space for a few minutes."

The Hasid glanced at him with a quizzical expression, sweat running through his beard. Then his eyebrows raised slightly.

"You were the one coming through the door," he said.

"That's me," said Michaels. "And I have friends all around you, so let's keep it quiet. There are kids here."

Portillo turned back toward the game, keeping his hands visible on the fence.

"Tell you what," he said softly. "Let's watch the last inning. Give me that, then I'll go quietly."

Birnbaum will ream me for this, thought Michaels.

"All right," he said. "Hell, I want to see if he pulls it off."

The first batter took a called strike. Then he glanced at the dad coaching third.

"Whadaya think, they put the bunt on?" said Michaels.

"Let him try," replied Portillo.

The bunt was on. The kid bravely squared around in the face of the onrushing pitch. It was a chest-high fastball, and it caught the top of the bat and went straight up. The batter, the catcher, and the umpire looked at it, then the catcher took a step forward and caught it.

One out.

"He read the play," said Michaels. "Smart."

The next kid gritted his teeth and took the count to three and two. Then he fouled off three pitches in a row.

"He's tired," said Portillo. "Come on, Junior, one good one here."

Javier brought his knee up high and whipped his arm around. The ball started chest high and broke down and to the left. The batter flailed. Strike three.

"I'm guessing he's an El Duque fan," said Michaels.

"Better believe it," said Portillo. "He was so happy when the Mets brought him back."

Wilco was down to their last licks. The batter, a muscular twelve-year-old, was the kid who had put the ball to deep center before. He swung confidently, then stepped up to the plate. He took Javier to a full count, then, like the previous batter, fouled several pitches off.

Portillo looked at Michaels and grinned through the fake beard.

"Gonna give him the hook again?" speculated Michaels.

"Just watch," said Portillo.

Javier reared back and threw it hard, right down the middle. The batter swung and connected, a line drive up the middle. Javier stuck his glove in front of his face in self-defense and managed to catch it.

Perfect.

Javier's team swarmed the mound and lifted him exultantly above them. His mother was screaming from the bleachers, and he pointed at her in triumph.

"Some game," said Michaels.

"Yeah," said Portillo, taking off the black hat and wiping his brow with his sleeve. "Okay, let's go."

They walked casually away from the field toward Thornton, the rest of the crew falling into place behind them. As they turned the corner, Michaels produced his handcuffs.

"Hands behind your back," he said.

Portillo complied, and Michaels cuffed him. The prisoner van pulled up. A uniform patted him down. "He's clean."

"Strip him when you get inside, just to be safe," said Michaels.

Portillo turned and looked at him as they put him inside. "Thanks," he said.

"You want me to tell them what happened?" asked Michaels.

"Nah," replied Portillo. "It's the best day of his life. Can't spoil those."

They closed the doors of the van and drove off. Carter stood by Michaels.

"How on earth did you know it was Portillo under that getup?" demanded Carter. "He looked kosher to me."

"See any Hasids up by the seminary?" asked Michaels.

"Well, no, as a matter of fact, I do not," replied Carter. "Why is that?"

"Because it's a seminary, not a synagogue. Seminary's where you learn, synagogue's where you pray. And it's Saturday morning. Hasids are in synagogues, not at ballgames."

"Damn. So what happened between you two?"

"We bonded," said Michaels. "Baseball does that . . . What do you say we get some lunch? I have this strange craving for bagels and lox."

THE FLOWER OF FLUSHING

BY VICTORIA ENG

Flushing

Let's get this party started!" Lily calls out to me from across the street. She's late, as usual. I've been waiting for her by the train station on the corner of Main and Roosevelt, breathing in the greasy aroma of hot dogs and frying noodles from various sidewalk carts. Sunlight washes over Main Street and its procession of festive store signs, all red and yellow with black Chinese lettering. As Lily approaches, the traffic lights change; cars brake at the crosswalk in succession, like they're bowing to her. She smiles brightly and bumps her hip against mine. I roll my eyes at her and don't bump back, but inside I'm relieved that she even showed up. Today is important: I'm determined to talk to my crush, Jimmy Lee, a junior at my school. I know he plays basketball at Bowne Park on the weekends, so I made Lily promise to come with me so that I could "run into him" there. We head down Main toward Sanford Avenue, weaving around weekend shoppers and double-parked trucks.

"Think he'll be there today?" I ask.

"Who? Yao Ming?" she says, her dimples showing.

"Stop calling him that." I poke her arm. "You know his name."

"Hey, look! There he is."

My breath catches in my chest. I look around without moving my head, hoping that he's too far away to have heard me talking about him. We're approaching the underpass of the Long Island Rail Road station and I expect to see him perusing magazines at the newsstand, or worse, walking right toward me. But Lily points to a store window with a life-sized poster of Yao Ming, the NBA player from China, and starts cracking up.

"Oh, reeeeally funny, Lil," I say with as much sarcasm as I can muster. I exhale through my mouth, the tension in my neck subsiding. "You almost made me puke, you know."

She's laughing so hard no sound is coming out of her mouth.

"Um, maybe you're the one who's gonna puke. You okay?"

She nods and gasps. I'm tempted to tickle her sides to make her throw up—she's always been sensitive like that—but I'm too anxious to get going.

Jimmy Lee looks nothing like the famous athlete, but he's 6'2"—way taller than most Asian guys—and he plays on the basketball team. That was enough for Lily to make fun of him. It made no difference to her that he's Korean.

"Really, quit calling him Yao Ming. Jimmy's not even Chinese."

"I know," she sighs. "Well, he's far from perfect. A *jock*. What's he going to do for you? Buy you pom-poms?" She catches her reflection in the window of a café and runs her fingers through her hair.

Lily Tong is the kind of girl who makes heads turn. She's only fifteen, one year older than me, but she looks at least twenty. She's curvy like the women in the music videos, and she wears her makeup and hair like she's one too. As usual, she's dressed in something slinky: an expensive, cut-up T-shirt that keeps falling off her shoulder, low-cut jeans that hug her curves, and black pumps. Dangling off her arm is a new purse, its print of interlocking letters broadcasting its expense. Along the street, old Chinese ladies carrying plastic bags full of groceries pause from scrutinizing vegetables to shake their heads at her disapprovingly. Men gawk at her from the open backdoors of restaurants; one worker almost falls from his perch on an overturned bucket into the pile of carrots he's peeling. As usual, Lily pretends not to notice, but she lifts her chin a little bit higher, and swings her hips a little bit wider.

I hold my head higher too, proud to be her best friend. At 5'5", I'm taller than Lily, but I look like a child next to her, in my maroon tank top and green Old Navy cargo pants. Even if I had the courage to wear the kinds of clothes as Lily, everything would just hang on me loosely. My hair falls straight down in stringy strands no matter what I do to it, so I never even bother curling it like Lily does. I'm glad that I chose to paint my toenails red instead of pink; at least my feet look grown-up.

As we turn onto Sanford, someone calls out Lily's name. We both turn around and see Peter Wong getting out of the passenger side of a gleaming black Cadillac Escalade.

He walks up to us casually and puts his arm around Lily's shoulders. The sun glints off the rock-star shades he's wearing. He's older, in his twenties or maybe even thirties; I don't know what he's doing talking to Lily, but I figure he must know her through her father, who owns one of the biggest dim sum houses in Flushing. As a big businessman, her father knows a lot of people.

"*Dai Guo!*" She smiles and kisses him on the cheek. She called him Big Brother, but the way he's looking at her is anything but brotherly. His hand lingers on her hair as he releases her shoulder. He barely looks at me when she introduces us.

I know he's headed to the park too; he and his friends are always there.

They continue walking together, Lily between us so I can't hear most of their conversation. He calls her *Xiao Mei*—Little Sister—and coos at her as if she's a baby. She's all giggly with him, which I think is gross. Still, I wonder what it would feel like if a guy like him paid so much attention to me, if I were that beautiful. He tells her about the kinds of things he can get for her from his "connections."

"I already have a Prada bag," I hear her pouting. "Can you get me a Louis Vuitton?" She pronounces it Loo-iss Voy-tahn.

As we near the entrance to the park, we can hear people on the basketball court, the slap of rubber on cement followed by occasional grunts and metallic dunks. The park, or Bowne Playground as it's officially called, is divided into sections separated by chain-link fences: The basketball court takes up the most space and is flanked by a kiddie playground and a treelined yard where old men pass their retirement days on its benches, reading Chinese newspapers or feeding pigeons. I scan through the trees for a glimpse of Jimmy, but I can't recognize his voice over the faraway laughter of children.

We reach the yard first and I see Peter's friends there—four guys and three girls. Most of them go to my school, seniors reputed to be gangsters. They have claimed the concrete chess tables set in the corner, but instead of chess pieces, there are mah-jongg tiles. Despite the heat of the day, the guys are in black and have spiky hair like Peter, and the girls wear their hair long and carefully frozen into voluminous curls. They're all smoking cigarettes; I wonder how smart that is, given all the hair spray in the air. Snippets of Cantonese, Mandarin, and Fujianese rise from their conversation.

I recognize one of the guys from my algebra class. He's a

few years older, but he's in my class because he doesn't speak much English. We've never talked to each other, so I just kind of nod at him. He gives me a strange look, as if he recognizes me but doesn't know why.

To my dismay, Lily follows Peter to the girls' table, where a new game of mah-jongg is about to commence. It's hard to look away from the mesmerizing whirl of pink and green, as pretty manicured hands shuffle and stack the jade tiles expertly.

"You play MJ?" Peter is actually addressing me as well as Lily.

"Uh, not really." I learned how to play from watching my mom and aunts, but I couldn't see myself doing it, here, with them. It strikes me as just so *Chinese*. I mean, sure, I'm Chinese, but not the same way they are, or even the same way Lily is. I was born and raised on Thirty-Ninth Avenue, but my neighbors were Dominican and Jewish, not just Chinese. My parents work in Manhattan's Chinatown and commute from Flushing on the dollar vans, my mom to a doctor's office and my dad to a TV repair shop. I grew up hearing almost as much Spanish as Chinese, whereas Lily's parents made sure that she stayed immersed in Chinese culture and cultivated friendships only with Chinese kids.

Lily nudges me and answers that of course we play. Peter motions for one of the girls at the table to make room for us as he goes to join the guys at the other table. One of the guys hands Peter something wrapped in a crumpled paper bag, from which he takes a swig. The girl, a senior I don't know, scoots right over and starts resetting the table, scowling at Lily. She's not the only one scowling, but Lily isn't fazed.

I look through the chain link to the other side of the park and finally spot Jimmy on the ball court. His brow is furrowed with intensity, his muscular arms outstretched as he motions for Eric Martinez, another junior, to pass him the ball. Eric responds, twisting away from his guard and whips the ball to Jimmy, who in one smooth motion catches it and shoots it into the basket for a three-pointer. Despite myself, I cheer along with the folks on the other side of the fence, which gets me strange looks from my seatmates, Lily included.

I lock eyes with Lily and talk to her under my breath.

"Are you coming with me or not?" I tilt my head ever so slightly toward the court.

"No! I'm staying here." She presses her lips into a fine line and whispers, "You should stay too. Forget about Jimmy. *This* is cool." She accepts a Newport cigarette from a spiky-haired senior whose name I still don't know.

"Fine. I'm going to go watch the game." I get up, nod at the table, and walk away. There's a large enough crowd over there that I feel comfortable heading over by myself. I take a seat at the edge of the bleachers. By now I'm so irritated with Lily that I don't even have time to get nervous when Jimmy plops down next to me. He has a towel wrapped around his neck and his cheeks are flushed.

"Hey! What are you doing here?" He is speaking to me. He knows who I am.

"Oh, you know, just visiting a friend." I look down and tuck my hair behind my ear. If I were Lily I would look up at him through my eyelashes and flirt. But I'm not, so I focus on how red my toenails are.

"You mean those gangsters over there are your friends?" He jerks his head in their direction. A few of the guys are talking with some Latino kids from the neighborhood. They all stand stiffly in a semicircle, menacing expressions on their faces. Peter seems to be negotiating with their leader, a dark, stocky guy with a shaved head and an oversized basketball jersey. They all relax when Peter and the guy shake hands, which they do in a hip-hop sequence: fists up, they grasp each other's hands as if they're going to arm wrestle, yank themselves toward each other, and bump chests. As their palms separate I catch a glint of light off little plastic bags.

"Those guys? Nah. I'm here with my friend Lily." Who is over there with those gangsters, I'm thinking. Lily is studying her tiles, but even across the park I can tell she's watching me from the corners of her eyes. "I didn't know you were going to be playing here. You're really good."

"Um, thanks . . ." He's pulling the ends of the towel, rubbing it back and forth over his neck. "I uh . . . I'm glad you're here."

Before we can say anything else, he's called back into the game. The sun feels good on my face.

And now, a couple of hours later, the sun is starting to set. The basketball game is winding down, without him for the last hour—Jimmy ended up leaving the game to come back to me on the bleachers, and we just talked about everything. He told me he thinks I'm the most mature sophomore he's ever met. I played it cool and did not tell him how I've been practically stalking him.

Eric yells to him that it's time to go, and as he turns to leave he bends and quickly kisses me on the lips.

"See ya at school!" He grins at me, then heads toward Union Street. I am too stunned to reply, so I just smile weakly at him.

But as the two of them walk off with some of the other ball players, one of the spiky-haired guys struts up to him and bumps him with his shoulder, hard enough not to be an accident. It's my algebra classmate. Eric looks at him as if to say, *What the fuck?* but once he realizes who it was that bumped him, he just mumbles, "Excuse me."

"Why you bump into me, man?" Algebra says. His voice is louder and shriller than I've ever heard it, but then again, he hardly ever speaks in class.

"I'm sorry. It won't happen again." Jimmy has his hands up the way basketball players do when they're trying not to foul out. Behind him, Eric Martinez and the other guys who were on the court stiffen. Smiles disappear as fists tighten. Jimmy backs away, holding his arms out from his sides to keep them at bay. His friends back off too. They're not stupid.

"What's your problem? Get the fuck out of my face!" Algebra is clearly drunk and enjoying the moment of power, but he doesn't push it any further. He holds up his hand, thumb and forefinger out, and pretends to shoot Jimmy in the head.

Back at the chess tables, Peter and his friends are chuckling amongst themselves. The mah-jongg tiles have been packed up and the table is littered with several more of those paper bags.

An unfamiliar emotion washes over me as I watch Jimmy leave with his friends, who are no longer laughing and joking. My eyes burn with tears and the words come to mind: *fear, shame, anger.* There was just no reason for that, I'm thinking to myself. And *this* is what Lily thinks is so cool? I look over at her, now leaning languidly against Peter's arm. Her fingertips are at her lips and I can tell that she's as shocked as I am, but she's trying to hide it, to look grown-up and still perfect.

"Let's go, Lil." I don't even want to make eye contact with anyone else. She nods and reaches for her bag, but as she slides away from Peter, he grabs her arm and pulls her toward him in a gesture that's meant to look gentle but isn't.

"Don't leave me, Little Sister. It's early. We're going to a party. I want to show you off." He looks me up and down. Without his sunglasses his eyes look dead serious and kind of scary. "*You* can go home."

"No, Tina's my best friend. I can't go without her." Lily shakes her hair as if to clear her head of cobwebs. "Where are we going?"

"There's a party at Kuo's place, the Tulip. It'll be fun. We'll make a karaoke video." His voice is too sweet when he speaks to her.

A lump forms in my throat. Even I've heard of that nightclub, the Yellow Tulip. It's always in the news; it's been raided several times for prostitution and there's a shooting there every other weekend. Of course, I can't say any of this. These are probably the people who do the shooting.

"Isn't that a bar?" I ask innocently. "Lily and I can't go. We're not twenty-one."

This makes everyone laugh. Except for Lily, who is staring at me as if I should spontaneously combust.

"*What?* They know how old you are," I whisper to her.

"No they don't," she hisses. She pulls me aside as darkness descends on the playground. Most of the group staggers out of the park, but Peter lights up a cigarette. His cell phone blares an electronic waltz and he answers it, leaning against the gate. The streetlights cast a shadow of the chain-link fence, crosshatching Lily's face.

I whisper to her: "Lil. You can't be serious. Isn't he like thirty? He knows your dad, so he's got to know you're only fifteen. He's not someone you should be messing with."

"Look. If you want to go out with a nobody, that's your problem. I think you can do better. But don't you ruin this for me. I really like him."

"You mean, you like 'Big Brother's' connections." I point at her expensive purse. "By the way, it's pronounced Loo-ey Vee-tawn." Her face twists, and she looks like she's going to cry. I've pressed her button. Her dad didn't always own his restaurant; he started out in the business as a dishwasher. "I'm really sorry. It's just—"

"It's just that you're jealous," she states flatly. "They chased your little boyfriend away and now you don't want me to have any fun. Well, I'm sorry if they want me at the party and not you. Maybe we're just too different. Maybe you're not my best friend after all. Maybe you're nothing." She steels herself for a fight. The defiant set of her chin makes me think of her mahjongg partners.

It's the liquor talking, I tell myself. I imagine what would happen if she were to go with them to the Tulip. Peter Wong and the drunk, sexy, teenaged daughter of his business associate. Algebra shooting invisible bullets with his thumb and forefinger. I imagine her beautiful hair splayed out across a dirty, beer-soaked stage.

With a grace worthy of a professional athlete, I reach under her arms and tickle her. At first she looks at me as if I've gone crazy, but as she begins to giggle she realizes what I'm doing, and her laughter turns intense, and then furious. She tries to fend me off but she's too drunk and I'm too quick, having trained myself since childhood to know her weak spot. Laughing and sputtering uncontrollably, she can't even turn away from Peter when a stream of vomit erupts from her mouth and all over his Bruno Magli shoes. The look on Peter's face as he studies his sopping shoes, before he turns and walks away, says it all.

The party is over.

CRAZY JILL SAVES THE SLINKY

BY STEPHEN SOLOMITA

College Point

When the over-muscled hulk in the studded leather jeans smacks the fat guy in the polka dot sundress, the eight patrol officers gathered around the small TV in the muster room cheer loudly. The body builder is a prostitute, the fat guy a prominent New York politician. The video is evidence discovered in the apartment of an extortionist.

Groans and cat calls greet the white guy's flabby thighs and flaccid penis when the hulk tears off his dress. When the fat guy turns to reveal a cotton-white ass the size of a watermelon, the boys nearly fall off their chairs.

I'm the only woman in the room, Officer Jill Kelly, and I feel sorry for the fat slob in the dress. I wonder what it's like to be a City Councilman, a Catholic, a husband, a father, a transvestite in a hotel room with a leather boy. The truth is that I can smell his desperation. The truth is that some cop's gonna leak the tape and the fat guy's life is gonna drop out from under him like a body through the trap door of a gallows.

"Jill? The captain wants to see you."

"Thanks, Crowley. I need to get away from this."

Bushy enough to conceal small game, Sergeant Crowley's eyebrows rise to form lush semicircles as he jerks his chin at the TV. "I woulda predicted this was right up your alley."

* * *

Captain McMullen's office is another world altogether, a quiet, clean world-unto-itself. Instead of peeling green paint, the captain's walls are lined with expensive paneling. Instead of scuffed linoleum, his floor is covered by a Berber carpet flecked with beige and gold. His walnut desk is big enough to land helicopter gunships.

I close the door behind me, shut out the squeals of the fat politician, the mindless comments of my peers. Captain McMullen is nowhere to be found, but the man seated behind his desk is very familiar.

"Whadaya say, Uncle Mike?"

Deputy Chief Michael Xavier Kelly offers a thin smile. He has a very narrow face with a prominent jaw that dominates veal-thin lips, a button of a nose, and blue glittery eyes that rarely blink. Uncle Mike is Deputy Chief of Detectives and heads the Commissioner's Special Investigations Unit, an attack-dog bureau far more terrifying to ranking officers than Internal Affairs.

"Jill Kelly," Uncle Mike squawks, "in the flesh." Thirty-one years ago, as a rookie on foot patrol, Uncle Mike took a bullet that passed from left to right through his neck. Now he can't raise his voice above a hoarse whisper. "Take a seat, Jill. Please."

I do as I'm told. "So, how's Aunt Rose? And Sean?"

"Fine, fine." Uncle Mike walks his fingers across the desk and over a bulging file. "I hear the boys have taken to calling you Crazy Jill."

"I consider it a compliment."

My admission evokes a raspy laugh, immediately followed by the most somber expression in his repertoire. "I came here for a reason," he announces. "Tell me, do you believe in redemption?"

Ah, right to the point. I was a naughty girl, a girl in need of punishment, but now I can make it up. Just do Uncle Mike this unnamed little favor—which will not turn out to be little—and retrieve my working life. Uncle Mike will pluck me out of the 75th Precinct in the asshole of Brooklyn. He'll restore me to the Fugitive Apprehension Squad and the SWAT team. I only have to do this one little favor.

It was last August and blazing hot. I was in an uninsulated attic, looking out through a window at the house across the way. The man in the house, George Musgrove, had butchered his ex-wife, then taken his three children hostage, naturally threatening to kill them as well. At the time, I was part of a SWAT team assigned to eastern Queens, a sniper, and my orders were to acquire a target a.s.a.p., then notify the boss. The first part wasn't a problem. When I came into the attic, George was standing in a bedroom window, completely exposed. He wanted out by then, but didn't have the balls to kill himself. That's what I figured, anyway. Just another suicide-by-cop.

I had my partner call down to the CO and explain that I was thirty yards away with a clear target, and that I couldn't miss. But Captain Ed McMullan—known to his troops as Egg McMuffin—turned me down flat. The hostage negotiator, he told my partner, was confident. Musgrove would be talked out eventually. There would be no further loss of life.

All through this back-and-forth, Musgrove stayed right there, right in front of the window with a cordless phone pressed to his ear. And I started thinking, Yeah, most likely he'll give it up without hurting the kids. Maybe even nine out of ten times he'll surrender. But when you consider what happens if he ends up in the wrong ten percent, a hundred percent is a lot better than ninety. I was in a position to guarantee those kids would survive and I exercised my options.

If Uncle Mike hadn't intervened, I would have been charged with disobeying a direct order, and might have faced criminal charges. But that was Uncle Mike's way. Clan Kelly first became prominent in the NYPD a hundred years ago, when Teddy Roosevelt was Acting Commissioner. Clan Kelly is still prominent today. This was especially relevant to Uncle Mike, who fully expected to become the next Chief of Detectives. Obviously, the Kelly name could not be besmirched. We were a self-policing family and a Kelly could be punished only by another Kelly. Thus, at Uncle Mike's behest, my gold shield was taken away and I was exiled to the Seven-Five, there to languish until he needed a favor.

As for me, I want back on the SWAT team and the Fugitive Apprehension Squad. I want both of those things and I want them bad enough to play along.

"Anything I can do for you, I'm ready," I finally say. "You know that."

"It's about your cousin, Joanna."

"The Slinky?"

"Pardon?"

"That's what I call her, Uncle Mike. The Slinky."

He bursts out laughing. "Yes, I can understand why you'd say that."

Joanna Kelly embodies the concept of slender. Her fingernails are slender, her elbows, her teeth. On those rare occasions when I'm with her, I feel like the Incredible Hulk.

"It wouldn't be so bad, Uncle Mike, if she didn't wear those dresses."

He nods agreement, his narrow smile widening slightly to indicate genuine amusement. "Ah, the dresses."

Joanna likes plunging, short-skirted designer frocks. When she attends family gatherings, male attention drifts her way like dust to a vacuum cleaner.

"So what about Joanna?"

"Paulie assaulted her last night."

"I thought Paulie was in prison?"

"He was paroled a week ago."

"So pick him up and violate him. What's the big deal?"

Paulie Malone is Joanna's ex-husband. He's an all-around knucklehead and he pretty much beat Joanna from the earliest days of their marriage until she finally called down the wrath of Uncle Mike and the rest of the Kelly clan. Then, within hours, Paulie was off the street, his bail denied, his lawyer made to understand that no plea bargain would be forthcoming. A short trial was followed by a conviction and a three-year sentence, the max for second-degree assault.

"I could have him picked up eventually," Uncle Mike concedes, "but I'll tell ya, Jill, if he hasn't gotten the message by now, he'll never get it. He's incorrigible."

"So what exactly do you want from me?" The words have an air of defiance, but my tone is resigned. Do it, or else: That's how I understand the offer.

"Your cousin needs protection."

"Only if you let Paulie stay on the street."

"Okay, I won't argue. Joanna needs protection until Paulie is taken into custody."

"You're telling me Paulie's not to be found?"

"He never reported to his halfway house or his parole officer. His whereabouts, as we in the policing business like to say, are unknown."

I look out the window at a nondescript street in a nondescript neighborhood. The stores on the other side of Pitkin

Avenue survive from month to month. A barber who makes book, a candy store that hawks cigarettes smuggled in from Virginia, a cop bar named Melvin's Hideaway.

"Jill?"

"I'm still listening, Uncle Mike."

"Then I'm still insisting. Joanna needs twenty-four-hour protection."

"And you want me to do the protecting."

"I think Joanna would be more comfortable with a woman, and you're the only woman I trust to do the job."

The rumor in the Kelly family is that Uncle Mike continued to offer Joanna his support long after Paulie went to prison, that Joanna found a suitable way to express her gratitude. I'd never cared enough to check it out, but now it begins to make sense. Under no circumstances would Uncle Mike allow his main squeeze to be locked in, 24/7, with a male cop.

"Am I gonna do this in uniform?"

"Sad to say, the job doesn't provide bodyguard protection to battered women." He shakes his head. "I've arranged for you to take your vacation. Later, I'll make it up to you."

I've got a big mouth and I say the first thing to enter my mind. "Ya know, I really wanna tell you to go fuck yourself."

Uncle Mike leans forward, his blue eyes twinkling, "Well, darlin'," he croaks, "don't waste your breath. If I could, I'd already have done so." He gets up, comes around the desk, and offers me his hand. "Let's take a walk, Jill. I feel the need of some fresh air."

He's right about the fresh air. Spring has penetrated the steel-and-concrete heart of the city. Tight buds crown every twig, and weeds push up through cracks in the sidewalk. For a few minutes, I keep pace with Uncle Mike, who walks with his hands behind his back as if pondering some weighty matter. Then, mostly because I'm getting bored, I decide to give him a break.

"You want me to kill him, Uncle Mike? That what you want?"

"That's harsh, Jill."

"If you were gonna bust him, send him back to the joint, you could just make Joanna disappear until Paulie surfaces."

He bares his teeth and grips my shoulder, stopping me in my tracks. "The Kellys don't run," he announces. "Never."

The effort to raise his voice makes him sound like a spooked chicken, but the point is clear enough. Paulie Malone has defied the Kelly family for the second time and he's not gonna get another warning. The other part, about taking him into custody, was pure bullshit.

"That makes Joanna the bait." When he doesn't respond, I add, "And me the executioner."

"Well, it won't be the first time, will it?" That said, Uncle Mike shifts gears. "Sooner or later, Paulie's going to kill her. We both know that, Jill. You may not like Joanna, but you can't deny that she has a right to her life." He takes a deliberate step, then another. "The sad truth is that I wouldn't trust anyone else in the family to handle this."

I ignore the flattery. "What if he shows up without a weapon, Uncle Mike? You want me to shoot him down, maybe go to prison for the next fifteen years?"

"Last thing on my mind." He reaches into his pocket, comes out with a battered .38, holds it up for my inspection. The grip, hammer, and trigger guard are wrapped with cloth tape. "I'll be able to control the post-shooting investigation. You just make sure this is laying on the ground next to Paulie and that you call me first." Suddenly, he takes my hand and grips it hard. His fingers are bony and cold. "Do this for the Kellys, Jill. Do it for us."

Repulsed, I pull my hand away. "So where's Joanna living these days?"

"She has a little house in College Point."

Again, it makes sense. I got to know the small neighborhood of College Point well in the two years I worked at the 109th Precinct in Queens, my first assignment out of the Academy. The Point's white working-class population is protected on one side by the East River, on the others by a solid wall of industry. The Asian explosion in Flushing, only a few miles away, has barely made a dent in the community's ethnic makeup. To Joanna, who was raised in Howard Beach, the mix of Irish, Germans, Italians, and Jews must seem like home.

But I know that Joanna's comfort is a secondary concern to Uncle Mike. Far more important is getting to and from her bed without being spotted by anybody who knows them.

Uncle Mike fancies himself the Kelly patriarch, and his authority goes unchallenged for the most part. Even as a Deputy Chief, he still has the ability to grant favors and deliver punishments. So the clan doesn't object to his relationship with Joanna, as long as he doesn't throw it in his wife's face.

"Yes or no," Uncle Mike finally declares. "I need an answer."

I take the .38 and shove it into my pocket. Though I haven't decided what, if anything, I plan to do, I don't have the *cojones* to refuse outright. I don't have the balls to seal my fate.

"Yes," I tell him.

Joanna has a right to her life, small and miserable though it may be. It's the only part of Uncle Mike's argument that holds up. It doesn't matter that a minute after I walk through the door, Joanna tells me I should let my hair grow out and change the color. Or that she wears a slinky jogging suit that cups her breasts and butt as though paying homage. Or that her arms and legs are firm without being muscular and she's so perfectly made up, the black-purple bruises on her face look as if they're part of the overall design. Joanna has a right to her life.

After a perfunctory air-kiss, Joanna leads me into the kitchen, where she evaluates my potential as if I was a coat on a rack. "So, you seein' anybody?" she finally asks. When I don't respond, she says, "I could fix you up, but you scare the kind of guys I know."

"Actually, I've got a boyfriend, Joanna. Joey Kruger. He's hung like a horse and he can hump all night. What more could I possibly ask from life?"

As usual, my words, no matter how crude, have no appreciable effect on Joanna. Instead, she opens a cabinet next to the refrigerator, withdraws a can of Colombian coffee (the one with the likeness of the grateful peasant), and fits it into an electric can opener. I note that her arms appear boneless, then turn away.

"I'm gonna go outside, take a look around."

Ten minutes later, I'm back in the kitchen, hoisting a cup of coffee. "When did the fence go up?" I ask Joanna.

"Three months ago."

"What about the outdoor lights? When were they installed?"

"The same time."

"And the window bars on the first floor?"

Joanna glances into my eyes, the gesture sly, then looks down at her coffee. "Me living here by myself, Uncle Mike thought it would be a good idea. For my security." She rubs the back of her hand across her brow, as if to erase the lie.

"It's getting warm in here. Do you think I should turn on the air-conditioning?"

Instead of answering, I lower the metal blinds, then set tables and lamps in front of as many windows as possible. When I finish, I'm nearly certain that Paulie won't be able to see into any room. Then I go back through the entire house, including the basement, checking every lock on every window and door. As I work, I become more and more pissed off by the obvious fact that Uncle Mike set this up months ago, that he knew Paulie was coming out, that he made his preparations well in advance.

When I reenter the kitchen, I find Joanna touching up her nail polish. I lay Uncle Mike's taped .38 on the table, say, "If Paulie gets past me, you're gonna have to use this."

Without looking up, Joanna asks, "How's he gonna get past you, Jill? I mean . . ."

What she means is that I'm a trained sniper, that there's not a cop in the city who can shoot with me. What she means is that the way Uncle Mike arranged things, Paulie's gonna have to come through the front door and he's gonna make a lot of noise in the process. What she means is that if I do my job, if I decide, mercilessly and without warning, to execute Paulie Malone, she won't need the .38.

Joanna inspects the nails on her right hand, then blows softly across the drying polish. Her fingers are as supple as her arms and shoulders. If she has knuckles, I can't see them.

"From here on out," I tell her, "I want you to stay upstairs as much as possible."

"Fine by me. I was gonna go up and change for dinner anyway."

"Joanna, it's 3 o'clock in the afternoon." I glance at the stove. "And you haven't started cooking yet."

The corners of her mouth pull down and she rolls her eyes. "I'm gonna take a bath," she announces. "I need to calm my nerves."

I wait until Joanna's in the tub, then toss her room. Beneath a pair of lime-green panties in her second lingerie drawer, next to a .32 caliber automatic and a box of ammo, I find a small bundle of letters written on prison stationery.

It only takes me a few minutes to read through them. Like every wife beater, Paulie is both contrite and optimistic. He knows he's done the wrong thing, but now he's straightening himself out. He's in therapy. He goes to Mass every Sunday. His shrink loves him. Father O'Neill loves him. Even the warden loves him.

None of this interests me very much because I saw a lot of domestic violence when I worked patrol. Once you put them in cuffs, wife beaters are always remorseful. But what does capture my attention is Paulie's reference to a note sent by Joanna: *Your letter gave me hope for the first time. I know I don't deserve another chance, but when you wrote that you never stopped loving me . . .*

I slip the .32 and the ammo into the pocket of my blazer, scatter the letters on Joanna's bed where she's sure to notice them, and finally go downstairs to open the blinds on a window in the living room. From a chair set back in the shadows, I can see most of the front yard. I note that there are no trees and no tall shrubs between the house and the seven-foot fence. The newly mown lawn is a killing zone.

By the time Paulie Malone opens the gate, steps inside, closes it behind him, I'm sure of only one thing: I'm not gonna whack him before I give him a chance to mend his ways.

I understand the implications. This means that I have to

speak to Paulie close up. It means a dedicated knucklehead with two years in prison behind him might decide that I'm the enemy and beat me to a pulp. But as I rise from the chair and head for the front door, I know I'm just gonna have to take the chance. My one consolation is that if Paulie gets past me, he'll probably murder Joanna, who's still in the bathtub.

I meet Paulie just as he reaches the top step of the little porch. He jerks himself to a halt, but neither of us is willing to be the first to speak. I drop my gaze to the middle of his chest and wait. Two seconds, then three, then four, then ten, until there's nothing left to us but violence. I watch his torso rotate slightly, then I grab his balls, drop to one knee, and yank down as hard as I can. When his body naturally follows his jewels, I snap my head up and catch him flush on the mouth.

He goes over backwards, slams his head into the porch railing, and drops, facedown, on the floorboards. I pull my Colt and jerk the slide back to draw his attention to the bottom line, his miserable life. He pulls himself to a sitting position, then leans against the railing and brings his hand up to his bloody mouth. Finally, he raises his eyes to look at me.

I have to blink twice before I can meet his gaze. Paulie Malone has the saddest eyes I've ever seen, a fact that a moment before completely escaped me. Now I remember him when times were better, at Christmas and Thanksgiving. Even in the best of moods, even laughing, the pain never left his eyes.

"You comin' back here, Paulie? Huh?" I center the Colt on his forehead. "Because if you do, I'm gonna personally serve you with the only order of protection that really matters."

But my words don't penetrate the wall of his obsession, and Paulie responds by listing his grievances. Although he once made forty bucks an hour working the high steel at construction sites, Joanna spent every penny and more. She openly flirted with men, even with family members, even in his presence. She not only refused to cook, clean, or do laundry, she wouldn't lift a finger to augment the work of a weekly housekeeper. Worst of all, though she'd known how much he wanted children, she'd had an abortion without his permission or knowledge.

Nice, right? But not relevant. I lower the Colt and shake my head. "Shut up for a minute, Paulie." When he quiets down, I continue: "Look, I don't like Joanna either. But I handle it by avoiding her as much as possible. Whereas you, Paulie, you keep comin' back. What's the point? You can't win."

I squat down about six feet away and lean against the front door. While it's nearly 6 o'clock and the sun has dropped behind the house, the air is still warm enough to caress my neck and face. From down the block, I hear children arguing, the echoing clang of a basketball against a hoop. "What's the point?" I repeat.

Paulie strips off his T-shirt, wads it up, and presses it to his mouth. "I can't let her go."

"Why not, Paulie? It's not like she's the only game in town."

"I know she loves me, Jill. The letters she wrote . . . She always said she loved me."

"The letters were a setup. You understand that? Joanna doesn't love you because she doesn't love anybody except herself." When he doesn't respond, I push his buttons again. "Joanna was your punching bag for eight years. You can't get her back. You'll never get her back. I'll kill you first."

After a moment, Paulie opens up. "I don't understand it," he admits. "When I was with my counselor or with Father O'Neill, it always seemed easy. Turn my back, start over, there's a new life right around the corner. But at night, after the final count, Joanna would march into my brain like a storm trooper. It was an invasion, Jill. I'd try to throw her out, think about something else, but she stuck to me like a leech. You ever get so mad you felt as if you were gonna fly apart?"

"Recently, Paulie. In fact, just this afternoon, when I saw what you did to Joanna's face."

He pulls the T-shirt away from his mouth and stares down at his own blood. "Something's wrong with me," he says, "and I can't fix it. When I think about losing Joanna, I feel like my heart's gonna fall out." He probes his ribs, as if checking for leaks. "I came here yesterday sure that Joanna really wanted me back. I thought she was gonna give me another chance. When she wouldn't let me in the house, I was just blown out of the water. I asked her about the letters, what she'd written, and she told me she wrote them because she was bored. She said, 'I shouldn't have done it. Like I'm sorry, all right?' Jill, I went nuts. I couldn't help it."

Any sympathy I might have felt dropped away with the last bit: *I couldn't help it.* That's what all the wife beaters say. *I couldn't help it. She made me do it. It's not my fault.*

"There's still a way out, Paulie. Go to your parole officer, tell him what you just told me, get yourself violated. That way you'll have some time to think it over." I'm wasting my breath. I can see it in his eyes, see the pain marching back through a hundred lifetimes.

After a struggle, Paulie manages to stand upright. He limps across the yard, through the gate, and out into the street. When he releases the gate, it snaps back into place so hard the fence quivers on either side. "I came," he calls back over his shoulder, "to tell Joanna how sorry I am. I came to make it up to her."

* * *

Joanna comes down at 6 o'clock to throw a pair of frozen dinners into the oven. She's wearing navy slacks over a pale blue top, an outfit that not only complements her jewelry and her eyes, but the sheen in her inky-black hair. She keeps her back to me as she unwraps the dinners and sets the timer on the stove. "You want a drink?" she asks.

"I want," I tell her, "to get so drunk I aspirate my own vomit."

"Does that mean yes?"

"It means no."

She fixes herself a stiff one, three fingers of Wild Turkey and a splash of ginger ale. "Are you gonna tell Uncle Mike about the letters?"

"He doesn't know?" It's the first time Joanna has ever surprised me. Before this moment, I'd always assumed that her brain and body were equally free of angles.

"Uh-uh."

"Tell me why you wrote him, Joanna, if Uncle Mike didn't ask you to. Make me understand."

"I don't know. Paulie sent me a couple of letters and, like, I was bored."

"Then why'd Uncle Mike secure the house? If he didn't know about the letters?"

"Uncle Mike knows about some of Paulie's letters because I showed them to him."

"But not all of them?"

"Not the ones that said about me writing back."

"And if he finds out, he'll make you wish you were still living with Paulie. That about right?"

Joanna's crimson lips fold into a childish pout. The effect is nearly pornographic. "I'm not like you, Jill. You can't expect other women to be like you."

"Yeah? Well, answer me this, Joanna. How come Uncle Mike didn't arrange for your protection before Paulie knocked on the door yesterday? How come he waited until after you took a beating? You think maybe he used you to set Paulie up? Or do you think he forgot to check his calendar?"

That night, long after Joanna has gone to bed, I'm lying awake on the living room couch. I'm not worried about Paulie getting past me. By the time he breaks through the door, I'll be ready. No, it's Joanna who keeps me awake, Joanna and Michael Xavier Kelly.

I slip into a T-shirt and jeans, then walk out onto the porch. The quiet eases over me, comfortable as an old sweater, the one you only wear in the house. A few fireflies, the first of the year, dance above the lawn, and I can smell, very faintly, the lilacs blooming in a neighbor's yard. There are no nightclubs in College Point, no theaters, no after-hours bars. The locals are committed to work and church, to the small, neat yards that surround their small, carefully maintained homes. There's not a lit window anywhere.

A few blocks away, MacNeil Park leans out into the East River. I ate more than a few meals in the park when I was stationed at the 109. I liked the sullen odor of the sea on summer nights and the slap of the waves against the bulkhead. The view, on the other hand, is less than spectacular. No glittering skyline. No ladder of bridges. Across the river, the South Bronx is a jumble of low-rise warehouses and isolated tenements. To the left, the many jails of Rikers Island rise into the night. They do glitter, those jails, because the lights are on 24/7. But they somehow lack the panache of Manhattan.

Suddenly I find myself wondering what, if anything, Joanna feels when she undresses for Uncle Mike. Does she pretend she's somewhere else? With someone else? Uncle Mike is past sixty and Joanna's still four years short of thirty.

Maybe, I think, I've got it all wrong. Maybe she basks in his approval. Maybe she can see it all in his eyes: admiration, gratitude, even worship. Maybe she likes what she sees.

But what I can't imagine is Joanna being aroused in any way, and I know that sex is a chore that brings out the actress in her. I know that she squeals in the right places, urges him on, groans with delight, screams when he comes. And then she defends herself by saying, *I can't be like you, Jill.*

So what am I gonna do? I'm as bad as Paulie now. I can't get Joanna Kelly out of my mind.

I fall asleep somewhere in the early morning hours and wake up at 8 o'clock when Joanna comes down. She's wearing a gray terry cloth robe and plaid, down-at-the-heels slippers. No makeup, no jewelry. Maybe this means she's in a sober mood. For her sake, I hope so.

Without a word, I rise, head upstairs to the bathroom. When I come back down, Joanna's sitting with her elbows on the table and her chin cupped in her palms. Her eyes flick toward me, then back to the tabletop. "What a mess," she announces.

The coffeemaker emits a final burst of steam, then goes quiet. I fumble through the cabinets until I find cups and saucers, spoons, and sugar, then set the table. Joanna leans back in the chair and crosses her legs.

"You think about what I told you last night?" I ask as I fill the cups. "That Uncle Mike's risking your life? Because one of these times, Paulie's gonna come to kill you. It's just pure luck that it didn't happen the last time."

"Well, that's what I mean," Joanna explains, "it's gotta stop."

"Maybe it's gotta stop," I say, letting the words drop like wet sponges into a dirty sink, "but I'm not gonna be the one to stop it."

Joanna nods, as if at something she figured out a long time ago. "Tell me what to do."

I reach down into my pocket for Uncle Mike's throwaway and Joanna's .32. I put the throwaway on the table, then eject the .32's magazine and the round in the chamber. Finally, I hold up the .32.

"Did Uncle Mike give you this weapon?"

"Yeah, for protection."

"He show you how to use it?"

She takes the .32 from my hand, grasping the butt with two fingers like the weapon is a shit-filled diaper she wants to be rid of in a hurry. "First, you push this thingy here . . ."

Suddenly, I'm tempted to reach across the table, grab a handful of Joanna's hair, slam my fist into her mouth. Suddenly, I'm Paulie Malone.

"Jill?" Joanna's lower jaw is hanging open. "It scares me when your face gets like that."

"Yeah." I force my shoulders down, take a deep breath. "I was just trying to demonstrate what happens when you get emotional." I press the automatic's grip into her palm, force her to grab the handle, flip the safety, curl her index finger through the trigger guard. "I scared you, right?"

"Yeah," she admits.

"Good. Now point the gun at the center of my chest."

"What?"

"Do it, Joanna. Point the gun at the center of my chest and pull the trigger."

She wouldn't be Joanna if her hand didn't tremble, if she didn't say in her precious little-girl voice, "Jill, I can't."

"You better. Because if you don't, I'm gonna kick your Slinky ass from one end of the house to the other."

Joanna's pupils go flat, as if they've suddenly decided to absorb instead of reflect light. Her mouth tightens into a sneer and she yanks on the trigger.

Clack.

The principle established, I take the .32 back and hold it up for her inspection. "Now, this gun, it's really small, Joanna. That's good because it won't jump out of your hand when you pull the trigger." My goal is to keep it simple, and I wait until she nods her head. "But it's bad, too, because one shot won't necessarily stop a grown man. So what you have to do is center the gun on Paulie's chest and keep pulling the trigger until it's empty."

"How will I know that? I mean, when it's empty?"

I consider this for a moment, then say, "Put the gun in your mouth and give it one last pull. If you're still alive, it's empty."

"Very funny." Joanna glances down at her hands. Her mouth works for a moment, before she speaks. "You really think I can do this, Jill?"

"Tell you the truth, Joanna, I don't see as you have a lot of choice. But you might wanna think about this: If Joanna Kelly shoots Paulie Malone, Uncle Mike's never gonna be sure that at some point Joanna Kelly won't shoot Uncle Mike. It's an edge you can use to your advantage."

Joanna thinks it over, then says, "Now I know why they call you Crazy Jill."

I ignore the comment. "Two things to remember. First, this gun with the tape on it? Put it somewhere close to Paulie's hand. Second, call Uncle Mike. *Not 911.* Uncle Mike."

She looks at me for a second, then mutters, "Uh-huh."

"Now, I'm going outside to sit in the sun before it gets too hot. If Paulie shows up, I'm not gonna stop him. I'm not even gonna slow him down."

Joanna's tongue slides over her lips. She raises her hand and flicks her fingers in a little wave. As I open the door, she finds her voice. "Jill," she says, breaking into a heartfelt smile, "I just want you to know. If I ever decided to go to bed with a woman, I'd pick you."

I expect Paulie to charge up the walk, but when he comes through the gate he's limping noticeably and his swollen mouth is the color and texture of chocolate cookie dough. Still, his features are twisted with rage and the sledgehammer he grips with his right hand makes his intentions abundantly clear.

By the time he sees me, Paulie's halfway to the door. He stops abruptly and throws out his chest as though offering a larger target. But when I circle him, heading for the gate, he becomes confused. He glances toward the front door.

"Whadaya doin'?"

"I'm going home, Paulie." I want to add something about him maybe doing the same thing, but I find that at the moment I don't care what happens to him. Or to Joanna. I step through the gate, turn right, and start walking. Maybe, I think, I can get away before it happens, though I'm still short of the neighbor's yard when Paulie crashes the sledgehammer into the front door. A moment later, I hear him shout, his tone still defiant, "What are you gonna do, Joanna? What are you gonna do with that gun? You gonna kill me?"

I count the gunshots, one through nine. They come faster toward the end. Paulie cries out once, early on, a short choking moan that ends almost before it begins. Then silence and, very faintly, the acrid stink of cordite through the open door.

Bye-bye, Paulie.

I drive to a gas station on College Point Boulevard, pull up at a pay phone at the back. There's somebody using it, but I don't mind. I nod to the jerk on the phone when he flashes an apologetic smile. I even thank him when he finally hangs up.

I take my time getting out of the car, searching my pockets for a quarter. I feel there's no hurry, that Joanna will shut her mouth until Uncle Mike arrives, that Uncle Mike has no choice except to keep me out of it. I punch Joey Kruger's number into the keypad, wait as it rings three, four, five times. I know Joey's been working the late tour for the last week and he's most likely still asleep. I realize, too, that I have no idea what I want Joey to say when he eventually answers. I have no idea until he finally says it.

"Baby," he whispers, his voice dulled by sleep, "when are you coming over? I've been dreaming about your ass all night."

LAST STOP, DITMARS

BY TORI CARRINGTON

Ditmars

R
ule #37 in the P.I. handbook: Never eat where blood's been spilled.

"I want you to find my husband's killer."

I knew what words the woman would say even before she said them. I knew the instant she spotted me, said goodbye to the man she was talking to at the counter of the Acropolis Diner, and headed straight for my table. She was dressed all in black, her mascara smeared because she'd been crying. I figured that since she was only two days into her new role as widow, she was entitled.

I sat back in the booth, considering her where she had taken the seat across from me. I'd also known what she was going to say because I knew her. And had known her husband. Mihalis Abramopoulos had owned and operated the Acropolis Diner on Ditmars Boulevard in Astoria, Queens, for the past thirty years. Ever since he'd come over from Greece in the early '70s. Not unlike many of Astoria's Greek population that had been trying to escape military coups and martial law and were looking for a safe environment in which to raise their kids. Hey, my parents had done it in the '60s, before the colonels had staged a military junta in Greece and taken over control of a country that was still trying to get its shit together after the civil war. I'd been seventeen at the time, but I'm told I still speak like I'd just arrived on the last plane over the Atlantic. Usually after

I've had one too many glasses of Johnnie Walker Black and was trying to figure out the mystery of my life rather than one of the many cases on my desk back at the agency.

But I'm getting ahead of myself here. My name's Spyros Metropolis and along with my silent partner, Lenny Nash, I run Spyros Metropolis Private Detective Agency, which is located on Steinway Street halfway between Broadway and Ditmars. While most of my family gravitated toward the Broadway end of Astoria, I preferred Ditmars. Mostly because my family gravitated toward Broadway. I didn't live in the rooms above the agency, partly because they'd need extensive restoration to make them livable. Mostly because I preferred to keep my business life separate from my personal life.

I eyed the widow across from me. So much for that philosophy.

Then again, being a twice-divorced P.I. with alimony and child support payments, where else was I to take my meals if not a diner?

"My condolences, *Kiria* Abramopoulos."

Hermioni blanched, possibly tired of like sentiments even though her husband wouldn't be lowered into the ground until the day after next, when the M.E. officially released the body. "Can you do it? Find my husband's killer? I'll pay your going rate."

Probably she didn't know what my going rate was. Probably she would change her mind if I told her. "*Kiria* Abramopoulos, I'm sure the police will find your husband's killer."

And I had every confidence that they would. Not because I was a big fan of the NYPD, but because I used to count myself as one of them.

"The police have their hands full with the blackout. Mikey's death is a low priority."

The blackout. Over 100,000 Queens residents had gone without power for almost two weeks, predominantly in the Astoria area. LaGuardia Airport had been closed down, parts of the subway, and even Rikers Island's jails had to rely on backup power for the duration. Many businesses were forced to close their doors. But the diner had remained open, Mike relying on propane burners and a grill set up out back to offer a short menu of items, and a generator to operate a couple of fans and a cooler.

The blackout had coincided with a heatwave that left residents scrambling to find someplace with air-conditioning or sweating it out. And all my good shirts bore sweat stains to prove it.

Then the night before last, the lights came back on. Revealing Mike Abramopoulos lying on his diner floor in a pool of his own blood. The floor I was looking at filled now with white orthopedic shoes as Petra, the young Albanian waitress I'd come to know since she hired on eight months ago, approached to top off my coffee cup. I noticed her smooth alabaster arms as she poured, as well as her other fine parts; she was a very attractive kid. She asked if Hermioni wanted coffee. The widow waved the girl away.

There had been a rash of restaurant robberies in the Astoria area of late, perhaps blackout-driven, perhaps not. Chances are, Mike was a random victim. Greeks worked hard for their money and were loathe to give it up. Especially to a masked man who would make in two minutes what it had taken the Greek all day to earn. It was the principle of the thing.

It was also what tended to get Greek business owners into heaps of trouble.

Hermioni covered my hand with hers where mine held

my coffee cup, a damp Kleenex between her skin and mine. I grimaced and pulled my arm back and pretended to fix the right cuff of my white long-sleeved shirt that I had rolled up to my elbows. My wardrobe was limited to white shirts, plain ties, and dark slacks in the summer, and varied little in the winter except for the addition of a black trenchcoat and hat. My appearance had never been a priority for me beyond staying neat. I'd been cursed with a Greek nose that my brother said you could see turning a corner at least half a minute before I did. And the march of time on my hairline couldn't be stopped with a lifetime supply of minoxidil.

"Please, Spyros. I . . . need to know who killed my husband. I need justice."

Dishes and silverware clanked where Stamatis, the busboy, cleared the table behind Hermioni. The widow slanted him a glance that told him he could have picked a better time. I agreed. Stamatis ignored us both.

I drew my attention back to Hermioni. "Did Mike have any enemies?"

"No, no." She smiled feebly. "Aside from me, of course." An attempt at humor. "But you know I could never do that to him."

Did I? Over the course of my career, I'd seen a lot of things I'd originally thought were impossible. Learning that Hermioni did away with Mike so she could take over the diner and move in with an Ethiopian half her age would rate somewhere on the less-shocking end.

"So you'll take the case then?"

I told her my going rate.

I had to give the old gal credit. She didn't even blink.

"I'll bring the retainer by the agency this afternoon," she told me.

My intention had been to scare her away. Instead, I'd just let her in the front door.

Murder cases didn't make up a large percentage of my case-load. Mostly because they were best left to the boys in blue and it wasn't a good idea to get in their way when you were a P.I. But those I had worked had taken a great deal of detective work that rarely included any fancy crime lab results. Fact was, a lot of evidence was contaminated and untraceable. And the results on most of the potential evidence they collected was slow in coming. New York's forensics labs were so backed up that a suspect on a case stamped low priority could have skipped to a foreign country and started a new family by the time the authorities caught up with him.

As far as I was concerned, solving any case almost always came down to pounding the sweltering NYC pavement and examining a few rocks to see which way the moss grew, in order to find the answers.

Later that afternoon, I stopped on the corner opposite the diner and lit a cigarette. Whereas before I might have taken a seat in the restaurant opposite to watch the joint, now New York City law had chased me outside. Oh, a lot of places had smoking areas. Usually outdoors in the back surrounded by neighboring buildings and glass. But I didn't particularly like the feeling of being walled in, put on display like a smoking turtle in a terrarium for the other diners to stare at as they ate. Which was probably a good thing, because I didn't smoke half as much as I used to. But I wasn't going to admit this to anyone that mattered.

I drew deeply on my cancer stick and slowly released the smoke, watching as Petra updated the chalkboard propped outside announcing the dinner specials. I had half hoped that Hermioni Abramopoulos wouldn't come by the agency. But she had, putting down the retainer I'd asked for. Which meant I was pretty much in this till the end.

Inside the diner I could make out at least seven regulars. Whereas before I might have viewed them simply as fellow diners, now each and every one of them was a suspect.

Could a customer have been upset at his burned steak—earlier thrown out of the house by his wife, fired from his job—taking his rage out on an unsuspecting Mike? Or, in the case of the young couple holding hands in the first booth and sharing *moussaka*, could an argument have grown loud, causing Mike to intervene and become victim rather than mediator?

At any rate, I didn't have many resources to dedicate to this case. Sure, Hermioni was paying me. But I was in the middle of a sticky job that commanded most of my attention.

Since Mike had been a friend of sorts, however, and a fellow Greek, I figured I could give him at least a fraction of the time I'd spent eating at his establishment.

I looked up and down the street. To my left, Ditmars Boulevard would take me toward the East River and Astoria Park, the Hellgate Bridge looming as a reminder of history in a city full of history. To my right, the street would take me to LaGuardia Airport.

But it wasn't the river or the airport I was interested in now. I turned and walked east, crossing 31st Street, the squealing brakes of the N train announcing its arrival at Ditmars station, the last stop on the elevated line, a regular sound that blended with the din of cars and airplanes sweeping down from the northwest. I stopped and bought a fresh peach from the Top Tomato on 35th, then walked further up still, to the only spot I'd been able to find in this parking-challenged area. I climbed into my old Pontiac and pointed the car in the direction of the 114th Precinct on Astoria Boulevard at 34th Street.

A little while later, I sat opposite Detective Sergeant Tom McCurdy, who I'd learned was the guy in charge of the case after a quick call to my NYPD mate, Officer Pino Karras. If the files littering Tom's desk were any indication, Hermioni was right: It might be some time before anyone got around to finding out who had killed her husband.

Of course, I hadn't ruled Hermioni out as a suspect yet. Call me jaded, but there was something about the human condition that allowed some folks to believe that if they hired a private dick, it deflected suspicion away from them, no matter how damning the evidence. One of my former clients had learned the hard way that guys like me weren't wired to look the other way. While I wasn't a cop anymore, the basic principles that had led me in that direction were still very much intact.

Besides, I knew enough about life to know that you took order where you could find it.

Tom McCurdy finished a phone call, sighed, and then nearly dumped the contents of his coffee cup over the files covering his desk as he reached for a pen.

"Looks like you've got your hands full," I remarked.

"That ain't the half of it. That goddamn blackout has us backlogged two weeks. We're investigating every death until we can rule out those that were heat-related." He fingered through one pile, then began on another, pulling out the file on Abramopoulos. "I thought you might be by for this. Ugly case, this one. Steak knife to the neck. Real mess."

I'd known Mike had been stabbed. Only I hadn't known

where or with what. "You wouldn't happen to have handy the list of the vouchered evidence and crime scene photos, would you?"

"Probably. But you know I can't let you see them."

I crossed my arms over my brown tie and grinned. "I don't think I have to remind you that you owe me."

Tom frowned, plainly remembering the hit on a prominent Greek politician I'd helped him thwart a year ago. "I think you just did." He squinted at me. "The widow hire you?"

I indicated she had.

He swiveled in his chair and pulled out another file. The evidence itself had been collected by the Crime Scene Unit and was probably at the NYPD lab waiting to be tested. After that, it would be sent to the prosecutor's office, once a suspect was named. I looked over the list Tom handed me and the photos. One shot was of a steak knife, the blade coated with blood. Another showed a short-sleeved blue shirt stained with blood in a pattern I guessed was consistent with a neck wound. I squinted at the third shot.

"The knife was still in the side of his neck." Tom tapped a spot near his left carotid artery.

"Any idea if the attacker approached from the front or the back?"

"Nah. Still waiting on the M.E. for that. But this guy was a fighter. Scooted at least ten feet toward the telephone on the wall before he blacked out. Hit the left carotid head on. There ain't no bigger bleeder in the body."

I nodded, my gaze catching on a small, blood-caked item featured in the third shot. A dime had been placed next to it to indicate scale.

"Don't know what in the hell that is yet," Tom said. "Maybe after the guys scrape the blood off we'll get a better clue."

I already had a good idea what it was.

"What's your take on who did it?" I asked.

"Cash register emptied, hour late. Robbery gone bad, is my best guess."

"That's what I figured you'd say."

I again looked through the photos that had been printed out on regular paper. Not very good detail. But with digital cameras and computers nowadays, there was very little need for hard photos, unless you wanted to make a point with a jury. Needed to know something? You used a computer to zoom in on it.

While originally I had been reluctant to add the new technology to my inventory, in the past few years I'd become quite proficient, updating my software every year and a half or so to make sure I had the latest.

I held up a photo. "Prints on the knife?"

"Only those of the victim. Probably he tried to take it out. Made a real mess of things. Which is why he bled out."

"How about footprints in the blood?"

"Only those of the victim."

"Was the knife clean or dirty?"

Tom grimaced. "Do you mean, did someone use it to cut a steak or something before burying it in Abramopoulos's neck?" He shrugged. "I don't know."

I eyed a shot of the entire diner and then handed him back the photos. "Thanks."

"That's it?"

"I'll be in touch," I said over my shoulder, heading for the door.

I sat back in my office chair, staring at the notes I'd made. Was Tom right? The killing the product of a robbery gone bad? Mike *was* the kind to resist.

Hermioni had provided me with a list of the staff—names and Social Security numbers; I'd checked them out. Nothing but minor traffic violations. Hermioni had also told me about a customer Mike had argued with the morning before he was killed, but she didn't have a name, so I'd have to ask around if I was to pursue that lead.

I personally knew of other strange regulars who kept to themselves. But to spotlight them was like shining an unflattering light on myself.

Was Mike the victim of some psycho agitated by soaring temperatures and the blackout? No, I didn't think so. The problem with that as the scenario was that while Astoria—the entire city of New York, for that matter—hadn't always been safe, now it was a nice place to raise a family, the Manhattan skyline near enough to appreciate across the East River, but far enough away to escape the problems of too many people crammed into small spaces.

Yet the real reason I rejected all the theories was because I was pretty sure I knew what had gone down that night in the Acropolis Diner.

I grabbed my notepad, purposely leaving my pen behind, and decided it was time for dinner.

Mayor Bloomberg and I didn't agree on much, but our take on Greek diners was in sync. He'd said in a recent interview in the *Times* that if he had to eat at only one New York restaurant for the rest of his life, it would be a Greek diner, because the variety of food was impressive and the ingredients fresh.

I concurred. And it wasn't just because I was Greek. Having been single for the better part of my life, I'd come to appreciate the range my compatriots offered up. While tonight I'd ordered only *yemista*—rice-stuffed tomatoes—that could rival my own mother's, since I ate at diners every day I often mixed it up with meatloaf and fried chicken. While none of the meals would win any awards, they were pretty close to what Mom would make, if, indeed, Mom made these dishes.

My mother had been living with my younger brother Pericles and his wife Thalia ever since the old man had cashed in his lottery ticket for a big exclusive condo in the sky. She still cooked, but rare were the times when I got to enjoy it. Call me a coward, but I didn't like the way she looked at me across the table even as she told me about some distant cousin or other from the Old Country who she could fix me up with.

Of course, my life probably would have been a whole hell of a lot simpler had I just taken her advice from the beginning. Instead, I'd married two American women who had thought me exciting and exotic in the beginning, plodding and boring at the end.

The topic of marriage brought my brother Pericles's oldest daughter, Sofie, to mind. She'd just announced her engagement to a good Greek boy, much to the family's delight. She'd done some odd jobs for me on and off over the years whenever she got fed up with working in my brother's restaurant or her maternal grandfather's café, both on Broadway. I remember thinking she would make a good P.I. That is, if wedding cakes, color swatches, booking good bouzouki bands, and trying to be a good Greek girl weren't what currently populated her list of priorities.

Personally, I thought she could do better.

I finished my food and pushed my plate away, craving a post-meal cigarette. But I just sat back and waited for the waitress to take my plate and offer me coffee.

When she popped up like clockwork, I motioned toward

the empty seat across from me. "Sit with me a minute, please, Petra."

Her movements slowed and her expression was pinched. She glanced around as if seeking an excuse to refuse my request. But I'd purposely come into the diner just before closing, so there were no other customers to be waited on, aside from an old man at the far end of the counter who was reading a newspaper and nursing the same cup of coffee he had been for the past hour.

Petra reluctantly sat down.

"You know that Mrs. Abramopoulos hired me, don't you?"

She looked down at where she had her hands tightly clasped on the table in front of her, then nodded.

I took out my wirebound pad and pretended to consult notes that didn't exist even as I looked in my pockets for a pen that wasn't there.

Petra removed a pen from her apron pocket and held it out to me with her right hand. Her wrist was not only minus the Greek evil-eye charm that had been covered with blood in the crime scene photo, but the bracelet that had held it too.

"Did you lose your bracelet?" I asked, taking the pen.

Her face burned bright red. She nodded again.

I took a sip of black coffee. "There were times when you and Mike didn't get a long all that well, weren't there?"

Big green eyes looked up into mine.

"Yeah, I saw it. The old man making passes. The swats on the ass." I shrugged. "Kind of hard to miss."

"Mr. Abramopoulos was a nice man," she said quickly.

Of course she would say that. Since I hadn't been able to dig up much on her, I'd guess that Petra Ahmeti was illegal. Chased from a struggling homeland like the Greeks had been a generation earlier. Mike had paid her in cash, and since she was good worker, she took home good tips. Better than the other two waitresses who would just as soon dump your plate into your lap as serve you.

Maybe the night Mike was killed he had pushed things beyond an ass-swat with pretty Petra. And paid for it in spades.

A price exacted *not* by Petra, I was sure.

"When did you lose your bracelet, Petra?"

She began rubbing one of her thumbs hard against the other. "I didn't. Lose it, I mean. I . . ." She appeared to be searching for the right words, as any non–native speaker might. But I guessed her hesitation grew more out of her not wanting to tell me what she had to say than her limited English.

I heard the sound of a tub of dishes being put down heavily on the table behind me.

"She gave it to me," the busboy said. "So just leave her alone."

Bingo.

You see, Petra had never been on my radar as a suspect. She was just too gentle. Someone had killed on her behalf. And it was a sure bet that the guy was Greek. Because while it wouldn't be unusual for an Albanian girl to be wearing a Greek evil-eye charm on her bracelet, I'd gotten the impression from the way I'd seen her play with it that it had been a gift. From a Greek guy. And since Mike hadn't been the gift-giving kind, that left one other Greek guy in the diner.

Stamatis came to stand next to my booth, his hands fisted at his sides. "What do you want with Petra? Why are you asking her these questions?"

I kept my gaze on Petra's pretty face. "Sweetheart, why don't you go in the back and see if you can scare up a piece of fresh *baklava* for me. Not the pieces that have been in the display all day."

She briefly met my gaze and then scooted from the booth, disappearing into the back of the diner.

"How long you been working here, Stamatis?" I asked the kid as I peeled off a twenty from my clip.

The question was rhetorical. I already knew how long he'd been working there. Exactly eight months. Hired on the day after Petra, after the previous busboy had met with a hooded mugger in a dark alley.

Now, you might say that was just a coincidence. Then I would have to remind you of Rule #2 in the P.I. handbook: *There are no coincidences.* My inquiries had revealed that Petra worked at another restaurant in Jackson Heights prior to coming to the Acropolis. And so had Stamatis. And through NYCIS, that the young man also had two priors, violence-related. A name-check by my buddy McCurdy had produced that tidbit. Of course, being illegal, Stamatis had no Social Security number.

Enter Mike Abramopoulos, restaurant owner, husband, father of three, and pretty much harmless, if a bit lecherous. Being of the male persuasion myself, I knew that many of us appreciated the value of a pretty girl. I'm not saying it's right. I'm just saying that a man's primal desire to spread his seed is, well, it is what it is.

As for the steak knife, it was an even bet that the forensics lab might discover that it had been used for its normal intended purpose—even though the photos of the entire diner post-murder had shown the tables and counter cleared of all plates, glasses, and utensils. Stamatis may have cleared the tables for some reason after using the steak knife to stab Abramopoulos.

A crime of passion, and a mundane weapon ready to hand.

Then he may have emptied the cash register to make it look like a robbery gone bad.

I noticed that Stamatis hadn't answered my question, and his fists were still clamped tight at his sides.

I pushed from the seat, tucking a copy of the *Queens Tribune* under my left arm. Stamatis had to either back off or make good on his unspoken threat. I wasn't sure how he'd play it. But he blinked.

I eyed the kid. A shame, really. He was all of nineteen and had his whole life ahead of him.

A life that would now include a sojourn at Rikers before a long stretch upstate.

"Tell Petra I changed my mind about the *baklava*," I said, putting the twenty on the table and heading for the door.

A little while later, I watched from the opposite corner as Sergeant Tom McCurdy and his partner pulled up in front of the diner and went in to arrest Stamatis. While no confessions had yet been extracted, nor solid evidence produced, I'd suggested to Tom on the phone that a little pressure applied *just so* would get him both.

The homicide detectives led the kid out in handcuffs and nodded in my direction. I nodded back and then took a long pull off the cigarette I'd just lit. I coughed, stared at the burning end, let it fall from my fingers to the pavement, and ground it out under the heel of my shoe. As I turned to head to my car, the N train squealed to a halt on the elevated tracks a half a block up on 31st. I didn't have to hear to know that inside the train the announcement was: *Last Stop, Ditmars.*

And for Mihalis Abramopoulos, Ditmars had been his last stop.

I looked at the sea of people coming down the platform stairs on their way home, and others out on the warm night with families and friends, gathering in cafés and restaurants and Astoria Park. For other immigrants and locals alike, Ditmars represented a beginning . . .

PART III

FOREIGN SHORES

AVOID AGONY

BY SHAILLY AGNIHOTRI

Jackson Heights

AVOID AGONY: *Let me investigate the morals of your child's intended before the sacred blessings of Marriage are arranged in America. Make sure your future son- and daughter-in-law are of pure values. Based in New York. $US 200 per report.*

T he week after he placed the advertisement in the *India Today* matrimonial pages, he received fifty-six requests. Not all, of course, had paid the $200 he charged through PayPal. But twenty-one had. He did a criminal background check of the ten men and eleven women. He ran their credit histories and sent the reports:

Dear Sir:

It gives me great pleasure to report that the match for your daughter/son should proceed as planned. My investigation has revealed no character flaws in the intended.

If you need further assistance, please advise. I should note that I also offer astrology guidance in selecting the date/ place for marriages, children, and the like.

Jai Hind,

Raj Kumar

With the astrology business and now the Matrimony Investigating Agency up and running, things were looking good.
Raj treated himself to a *masala dosa* at India Grill. "Add more
mirshe," he always reminded them, or else the *dosa* lacked the
requisite zing. He relished the spiced potatoes and the sweet
masala tea. All around, families, business people, and ladies
sat and gossiped, some in English, some in Punjabi, and some
in Gujarati. Almost everyone was Indian. *Why,* he sometimes
thought, *Queens is more Indian than India.* He took out some
quarters, left two as a tip, and went to the register to pay.

It was a Saturday; he would sit and wait for any walk-in
business. He headed into the Sari Palace, past the mannequins
in *langas* and *saris,* nodded his greeting to the ladies setting up
the register, and up the stairs to his office. It was best not to
speak to them, he had realized, or else they'd draw him into
their gossip. Then he'd have to listen to the not-so-subtle sug-
gestions about some cousin or niece who was ready to marry,
who cooked so well and sang beautifully. *Would you like to see
her photo?* Best to avoid the tedious talk.

The walls of his second-floor office were bare but for
three posters of the most beautiful woman who had ever
lived, the 1950s Indian film star, Meena Kumari. When he
procured the lease to the office, he had allowed himself the
extravagance of taking some publicity photos he'd had since
his teens to the copy center and enlarging them. Her gaze
never escaped his.

He flicked on the neon *Open* sign in his window, under a
hand-lettered one that read, *Vedic Astrology,* and checked his
e-mail.

He scanned the few requests for matrimonial character
checks. One e-mail caught his eye:

Dear Sir,
I am in urgent need of your investigative skills. Tell me, are
you based in New York? I need a full report on a person
living there who has entangled my son. I must get a full
dossier on the woman in question to save my son from this
match. Please advise as to your services and fees.
M.S.

Raj read the e-mail over several times and mulled the "full
dossier" request. What should be the quote for such a report?
$400? This one doesn't want a report that reassures him that
his child will be fine coming to America and marrying his intended. He wants dirt. The salacious detail of depravity. That
she drinks, smokes, and dances.

He responded:

Dear Sir,
Thank you kindly for your request. The services you re-
quire can be had for a fee of $340. Please supply details,
names, date of birth, and the like for the girl in question.
Please use PayPal to arrange these transactions.

Within ten minutes, he received confirmation of a payment and a name: Ritu Rani. *Ritu Rani?* He smiled and dug
through the stack of *Little India* magazines on his desk, finding
the one from four months ago. There she was on the cover:
Miss Little India, Queens 2006—Ritu Rani. He remembered every curve of her delicate body. She was back in his life again.

He waited two days before responding:

Dear Sir,
I am saddened to inform you that Ritu Rani is of question-

able moral character. She has been known to smoke, and further, participate in beauty contests. She was awarded the title of Miss Little India after performing a dance on the stage. Her sign is one of a woman with much ambition and greed. I would advise avoiding further alliance between your son and her.

Within minutes of sending his report, he received a most pleasant offer.

I am disappointed to hear of the adventures of the lady in question. However, these facts of smoking, beauty pageants, and dancing in public will not dissuade my son, as he has come under her spell. Please consider an extensive investigation with more meaty facts. MONEY IS NO OBJECT.

This time it was signed with the full name: *Manny Sharma.*

"Lakshmi, praise be to you," Raj said out loud. Manny Sharma. *The* Manny Sharma needs his services. How fortunate is his cusp. He must do his horoscope to see what other good karma is coming his way. Manny Sharma needs him. A wayward only-son entangled with a woman. Well, one man's bad luck is another's good fortune.

Dear Mr. Sharma,
Thank you very much for your kind e-mail regarding the plight of your son. Of course, as a man who values the auspiciousness of marriage, I can understand your deep concern. This is an unfortunate set of circumstances. God willing, I will be of assistance to you. Kindly send me your son's vitals, date of birth, time of birth, and of course his

current address. I will never let him suspect that I am in any way involved with his affairs. I will simply ascertain, based upon my understanding of human nature, what set of facts will dissuade him from pursuing this unholy alliance.

My hourly rate for this in-depth work will be $95 US. Please advise how much time you wish for me to devote to this investigation.

Raj read his work over with care and wondered whether the $95 was high enough to show his worthiness but not too high to make him seem greedy. He changed it to $85 before sending the e-mail.

Raj was so pleased with himself that he left right away for some *paan*. It was important to sweeten one's mouth at good news so that it would linger longer. He walked to the corner of 74th Street and Roosevelt Avenue. Vinod had set up a *paan* stand inside the sweet store. Raj came here a few times a week, as nothing was as satisfying as the taste of a freshly made *paan*. As Vinod wrapped the betel leaf and added areca nut and mineral lime, then sprinkled some spices, sweet mixture, and whatnot, they chatted. But Vinod was always looking for some free advice. *What's an auspicious date for buying stock? Good dates for traveling?* Today Vinod wanted to know about his sister's marriage. *What good dates are coming?* Nothing annoyed Raj more. Astrology was an ancient and sacred art. It required precise calculations. It was not gossip material. But he loved *paan*, and Vinod was the only game in town, so he held his tongue and gave general information. "Well, till the eclipse on the thirteenth, not good to set the date." He finally got the *paan*, plopped it in his mouth, and chewed.

As he walked back to his office, he stopped at the DVD

store at the corner of 37th Road to see what latest Hindi movies they had. All the usual trash. He rented two and headed to
his office, feeling satisfied that now his moment had come and
Manny Sharma himself would be the vessel.

Manny was around fifty, ten years older than Raj. Manny
had made a fortune in the Indian steel business. When Raj
had taken his correspondence course in astrology a few years
before, Manny's horoscope had been his final project. Raj remembered that even with all of Manny's money, the chart
showed difficulty in the fifth house—some fracture with a
child. And since Manny had but one son . . . Well, well, well,
Manny and Raj's fortunes intertwined.

Now Raj did a more extensive moon chart of Manny,
which showed him to be a ruthless man who destroyed his
competition and cared little for others. So it is only fair, Raj
reasoned, that though he have a fortune (he was, after all,
born in the Shukra ascension), his lack of humility must bring
him pain in some other area of his life. And nothing would
concern the great Manny Sharma more than the thought of
his prince marrying a loose woman.

Neal Sharma was an MBA student at the Stern School
at NYU. Raj had no trouble locating him the next day. Raj
presented himself in the lounge of the Stern building and
waited. Soon classes were over and he spotted Manny's son
with a group of other young men. Neal was handsome, slim,
and decidedly casual for being the son of one of the wealthiest families in India. Raj watched and studied him. Was he
a good kid? He seemed to be enjoying the company of his
friends. No pretentiousness. Not the strongest personality
in the group. Not the most handsome. But a good enough
fellow.

Raj continued his investigation by doing Neal's chart. His

instincts were correct: Neal was a boy of unquestionably good moral character. Would have a happy family life. Three children. And, of course, lots of wealth. How to play this out? Raj wondered. He felt he was still missing something and so he'd sleep on it. He dreamed all night of Miss Little India, Queens.

Raj woke up with a plan that made him feel young. He knew where his destiny lay. He did not doubt the stars. He went to the electronics store and haggled a digital camera. He knew where Ritu lived and went to her apartment building five blocks away. Soon enough, he saw her. She wore a skirt that covered her knees and a simple pink top. No makeup. Flat sandals. Just the sight of her made his heart beat faster. He moved to the other side of the street.

And took her picture.

Dear Mr. Sharma,
I have started the surveillance you requested. The girl in question is difficult to track and will require many days of observation. I attach a photo of her I took just this morning.
RK

For the first time in years, he was hungry for something. His brain—which, as a young man, had been routinely praised for its discipline and quickness—was perhaps going to be used again. Maybe it had just been resting till now. Wearing a hat and dark glasses to obscure his appearance, he went in search of the couple. It wasn't hard. He waited outside her building, and soon he saw Neal buzzed in. They came out together not ten minutes later, and he took photos of them walking. They went to lunch at Chat Hut. He slid into the table behind her, and she never noticed him. How could she, when all she did was look at Neal and smile? They were chatting about this and that, in the meandering way young couples do when smitten. He had a paper due, she had a job interview; he wanted to go to a movie that night, she said earlier was better. Neal was eating *channa* with *puri* and she had a *dahl chat* plate. She fed him a spoon full of her *chat*.

"Ritu, I can't wait to take you to the *chat* place in Delhi, baby, you will love it," Neal said as they got up to leave.

Raj waited a few days and sent the photos to Manny. With an email:

> *Dear Sir,*
> *I am distressed to inform you that your son is in fact seriously entangled with the girl in question. Their contacts are substantial and plans of going to India together were discussed. If you advise, I will speak to this girl, who is known to be greedy, to see what I can work out—for the sake of your son and your family honor.*
> *RK*

Manny replied instantly:

> *Understood. Range of $25,000-$50,000 approved. Send details for money transfer.*

Raj e-mailed again two days later—at night so it would be received early in the morning in Delhi:

> *Dear Sir,*
> *I met with the girl and had to go the maximum range of the*

offer as she was determined to get more after marriage or possible divorce. So you see how she thinks. If approved, she wants funds quickly and will move away from this city.

RK

Almost immediately, Raj received a response:

My son's happiness is my duty to ensure. Thus, $50,000 is my obligation to pay. Send details and wire transfer will take place. Thank you for your diligent service.

The money was in Raj's account within twenty-four hours.

He put on his best suit with the red tie and first went to the Lakshmi Temple when he knew there'd be no long, drawn-out prayer ceremonies under way. He wrote a check for $201 and left it in the donation box. Bowed to Lakshmi, took a bit of *parshad* to sweeten his mouth, and left. He knew the right thing to do. And God blessing him for doing the right thing would bring good karma.

Time to visit Miss Ritu. He had with him her astrology chart. Ritu lived in a small studio apartment. It was simple and tastefully decorated. She had taken his call and his request for a visit in a relaxed way. "So nice to hear from you again," she'd said. She's all class, he thought.

"Mr. Raj, would you like some tea?" she asked when he arrived. He accepted her gracious offer. When they were seated at the dining table, he opened up the astrology chart.

"Dear Ritu, I have some news I must share with you," he said. "With the moon on the eclipse and the house of Rahu on the cusp, I urge you to marry quickly. If you need help finding a suitable mate, I will help. You should be with a doctor or businessman . . ."

She was listening intently. "No, no, I appreciate your offer of help—but I'm—"

"Oh, so you are involved?"

"Yes," she whispered.

"Good news. Good. Then arrange hastily, if you must. Arrange quickly to marry. It is so written and must be done before the full moon or you risk . . . Let's not discuss that. Marry immediately, you must." He noticed how her delicate fingers twirled the silky strands of her hair as he spoke. He departed then, leaving the chart behind.

Four months before, he had been the judge for Miss Little India, Queens. He had been one of the sponsors of the contest—having given $550 to place his name prominently in the advertisement for the event. For his money he had expected flirting from the contestants, hints of romance, some ego stroking—and these of course had come—but nothing prepared him for the pressures of the final round. It ended up that for the last stretch of the two-day contest, he was the sole judge. So he decided that the five girls in the finals would each dance to a song from the Hindi classic film, *Pakeezah*. It was enchanting, haunting music that Meena Kumari, the loveliest actress to ever grace the big screen, danced along to with stunning grace. Raj had picked his favorite movie and favorite actress as the challenge. There could be no greater challenge, as the audience, too, knew every gesture and movement that Meena Kumari danced in the film. It was the highlight of Indian cinema—the beauty of the camera movement, the music, the story, Meena Kumari.

During the day of the event he was visited by two contestants, and the fathers of two others. He drew a bit more than just attention from one of the two girls. Her breasts were round and firm and he enjoyed lingering there for a moment. The other, a young woman named Geeta, had kissed him and he'd put his hand on her thin waist when she leaned into him. The fathers left envelopes with cash. One $350, and one $500. Only the fifth contestant failed to visit him or send her father.

And, of course, she won.

It wasn't just that Ritu didn't visit: It was the dance. Ritu seemed to possess the characteristics of the Ideal Indian Woman. Her curves were generous, her movements minimal. She didn't strive too hard, instead the music just swayed her. She smiled at him from the stage, which had excited him even more than the touching or the money. It was the warm smile of innocence untouched by the crass world. He avoided her after that, lest she disappoint him. Or perhaps he would disappoint her. But he thought of her often, alone in his bed.

She deserved abundance—and to be married to the rich only-son of one of India's wealthiest families. That bastard Manny couldn't appreciate a classy girl like Ritu. He represented all that was wrong with these situations: the brutish man keeping his son from happiness.

Of course, Raj knew that he, like all the other players, had a predestined role. He was to teach Manny Sharma some humility—and if that humility came with humiliation, so be it. He was to help Ritu in her life. First the contest, then the husband. And he was being rewarded for his good deeds. But it wasn't just the money; it was knowing that he, not Manny, was in charge of the way this would end. When he was in charge, the good won out. Don't rest on your laurels, he reminded himself. Destiny was calling.

He turned on his computer and started by changing his

e-mail and PayPal accounts. Then he opened a file entitled *Wealthiest Indian Bachelors* and considered Davinder Shah, son of the pig-headed Minister of Defense, Terjinder Shah. Years of graft had left the family very well off. Davinder, the eldest son, was also enrolled in the Stern School at NYU. Raj had noted his presence among the young men hanging out with Neal Sharma. Raj plugged Davinder's vital dates into his computer program and printed out his astrology chart. While anyone could run numbers to get a chart, an analysis of the planet positions, the lunar asterism, the ascendants—understanding their relationships with one another was a gift that few possessed. And clearly, Raj knew, he was one of the blessed.

His chart showed Davinder as a weak man, tending to be swayed easily. No great intellect. A bit lazy. Not a great person, petty really. Of course, Raj would find his match. There is, after all, a match for every person. Raj consulted his folder marked *Eligible Indian Girls*, studying the photo of Geeta. He studied her curves and her look, which was a tad cheap—though he had no regrets about enjoying her wet kiss. He had only chosen her as a runner-up, but he would make it up to her now.

He e-mailed her immediately.

My Dear Geeta,
Good news is coming your way. I have a perfect match
for you. Please do visit my office tomorrow at noon. I will
discuss specifics and plans with you then.
RK

Then he e-mailed another:

Your Excellency, Minister Shah,
I write to offer my humble services to you. I believe your

son may be in some entanglement that does not suit the son of the honorable Minister of Defense. Please advise if you seek my assistance to avoid the agony of such an embarrassment.

RK

Later, as he watched India-Vision in his office, Raj was interrupted by a knock on his door.

Ritu and Neal walked in, arm in arm.

"How do you do, young man?"

"So nice to see you again, Mr. Raj," Neal said.

"Yes, yes, we did meet at the Miss Little India pageant, right?"

"Yes. And thanks to you, I met Ritu that night."

"Oh no, these are all events that fate has ordained," Raj demurred.

"Mr. Kumar," Ritu said, "Neal and I were married this morning at City Hall."

"Congratulations, congratulations."

"We need your advice. You see, Ritu and I, well, we . . ." Neal began.

"We got married . . ." Ritu added.

"Blessings, blessings."

". . . without my father," Neal continued. "Well, he doesn't know yet and I want to seek your advice to smooth things over."

"Oh, I see. But your wife is a blessing to your family."

"Yes sir. But my father—"

"I will tell you, young man, that only a few get to be married to a girl as lovely, honest, and wise as your bride. Treasure her. Once you have children, I guarantee you all will be well."

"Children?"

"Yes. I know Ritu's chart. And all happiness unencumbered by obstructions will be yours in this union. Wait till you have good news of a grandchild and then go to India. All will be well."

"I shouldn't tell my father then?"

"No. Wait a few months. Then you will have two good things to tell him."

Ritu looked at Neal and gave him that sweet smile that Raj knew so well.

"Go and enjoy each other," Raj counseled. "Give it time. All will be well. All will be well."

Neal reached for his wallet, "Can I give you something?"

"Oh, please. Please . . . it's my pleasure."

Neal shook Raj's hand, and the happy newlyweds left his office.

Raj watched the couple from his second-floor window. As they walked away, arm in arm once again, Ritu turned to look up at his window. She met his gaze for a moment and held it. She nodded slightly and then turned her attention once more to her husband.

He was now alone in his office above 74th Street, with all the hustle and flow of life below. With his posters of Meena Kumari. With his foldout chairs. With his TV and DVD player on a stand. He flicked off the *Open* sign outside his window.

From his desk drawer he took out the DVD. He needed some pleasure too—life could not only be work. He dimmed the lights and sat on the floor cushion, as he always did to watch. Nothing could interrupt him for three hours. He put on the movie *Pakeezah*. The music stirred and then there she was. Looking for her love. Full of grace. Dancing her pain away. Her soul unappreciated by the wealthy patrons. She is a courtesan who doesn't get to be with her love, the prince. The callous king forbids it. She has no one to help her. And Raj weeps for her once again as he hears his beloved sing:

> I, silently, o sir, will open the gate.
> Darling, slowly shall I open the gate.
> Stay awhile, o handsome friend.
> O save me from agony . . .

VIERNES LOCO

BY K.J.A. WISHNIA

Corona

It's never good when you open your front door and the first thing you see is uniforms. Only this time, they were military dress green, not 110th Precinct blue, and lucky for us they wanted the house next door. Bad luck for the Mantilla family, whose oldest boy, Freddie, joined up seeking the fast track to citizenship. And now he's going to get it—posthumously.

The following Thursday I'm standing with the family as the flag-draped coffin is about to be lowered into a hole overshadowed by the Long Island Expressway and a recycling plant. The last notes of "Taps" float by on the wind, mingling with the Doppler-shifting *wee-oo-wee-oo* of a passing police siren. Someone's not at peace with the Lord out there.

A white-gloved finger presses the play button on a boom box, and the crash of angry Spanish ghetto rap rips the stillness to shreds. Freddie chose this music as his final shout-out to the world, and, if I know Freddie, as a final screw-you to all the white boys in his unit who would have gone with "Amazing Grace." The honor guard salutes stiffly as cars roar by on the overpass.

I go up to the cops who brought Freddie's uncle here, and ask them to take the guy's handcuffs off for five minutes so he can hug his family. It takes a moment, but they do it for me.

"You on a case?" says Officer Sirota.

"Friend of the family."

"Uh," he grunts. "Say, you know what that's about?"

There's a group of mourners dancing around a grave across the street in Mount Zion Cemetery. I tell him it's a splinter sect of Orthodox Jews who believe that their former leader, Rabbi Aaron Teitelboym, is the Messiah, so every year they gather at his grave on the anniversary of his death to celebrate his imminent resurrection.

"That so?" says Sirota. "How long's he been dead?"

"Nine years."

"*Nine* years? Man, it only took Jesus three days. So I guess that's one up for our side."

The lieutenant presents Freddie's mom, Irene, with the purple heart and bronze star, and salutes her. She presses the medals to her chest, and hugs a color photo of her smiling boy, the sharp-eyed soldier who waved his comrades away from the roadside bomb that shattered his skull and left a smoking crater of that handsome young face. It was a closed casket service.

Too soon, they snap the cuffs back on Uncle Reynaldo and escort him to the squad car. I wait my turn as close relatives go up and hug my neighbor. She's clutching Freddie's brother Felipe, who's already sprouting a teen mustache and getting pretty big for a twelve-year-old.

Felipe wrenches his arm away from her and seeks out the masculine ritual of swapping greetings with his cousin Ray Ray, who I once helped dodge a graffiti rap that could have gotten nasty if the cops had felt like pressing it. Just being caught with "graffiti instruments" is a Class B misdemeanor, and it doesn't help that in order to get proper respect as a graffiti writer in the *barrio*, the supplies have to be stolen. Reparations were costly, but worth it, since that dark-skinned Dominican kid is now working on a twenty-one-game hitting streak carried over from his previous season at Newtown High School, and the rumor is that he's being scouted by the Mets.

That night we climb up onto the roof so Felipe can look at the glittering crown of Shea Stadium on the horizon.

"Yo, Filomena," he says. "I hear *los Mets* are gonna put their game on real thick this year."

"They definitely have a shot at it."

"Remember the subway series when that *cabrón de Yanqui* Clemens threw the broken bat at Piazza?"

"Sure."

"Freddie got some tickets for me and Ray Ray. We was in the upper deck, the three of us doing mad daps all around." He points at the bright lights as if the exact spot is marked for all time, which I suppose it is, in a way. I know what he's thinking, but he says it anyway. "Some day Ray Ray gonna be playing center field out there."

The next morning, I'm training my new part-time office assistant, a tanned and freckle-faced sophomore at Queens College named Cristina González. They're putting her through the wringer at that school, making her take two semesters of Composition, which is encouraging since half the college kids I see lie to me on their resumés and think they can get away with writing crapola like, *My mother's a strong women and roll model for all American's*, which doesn't look too good in a report.

The last applicant didn't mention his credit card scam and drug convictions when I asked him if there was anything unusual in his past that I should know about. When I caught it on a routine background check, he said, "Hey, in my neighborhood, that's nothing unusual."

"You mean, I beat out a convicted felon for this job?" says Cristina. "Gee, thanks."

It's hard to find good help for $6.50 an hour, which is all I can afford to pay. But striking out on your own is risky at my age, and I wouldn't even be able to pay that much if my former bosses at Davis & Brown Investigations didn't toss a few heavy bones my way, continuing a long-standing American business practice of subcontracting out to cheap immigrant labor like me.

So I'm sitting in my eight-by-fourteen storefront office, directly beneath the flight path of every other jet approaching LaGuardia Airport, trying to debug the Hebrew font we installed for a case involving an Orthodox congregation in Kew Gardens Hills. The font's right-to-left coding has defeated the security protocols and migrated to some of the neighboring programs, causing system commands to come up randomly *in Hebrew.*

Oy vey, couldn't it have at least been Yiddish?

I look up as a man in a light gray business suit who I've been expecting knocks on the glass. I buzz the door open for the junior executive, who looks like he's worried about contracting malaria through the soles of his wingtips from walking on these cracked sidewalks.

"Miss Buscarella?" he says.

"Close enough. It's Buscar*sela.*"

He doesn't seem to be listening as he sits in a chair that was once bright orange and hands me his card, which says his name is F. Scott Anderson, and his title is Assistant Director of Product Security for the Syndose Corporation.

"What can I do for you on this fine spring day, Mr. Anderson?"

He snaps open his briefcase and pulls out a plastic bottle of dandruff shampoo with a blue-green label you can find in any drugstore in the northeast.

"What's wrong with this?" he says, holding up the bottle.

I check the label and tell him, "That used to be an eight-ounce size, and now you're selling six and a half ounces for the same price."

He doesn't bite. He just places the plastic bottle on my desk and pulls a seemingly identical one out of his briefcase. "How about this one?"

I study it for a moment, and it's obvious that the blue-green color isn't as saturated as it should be, and the white lettering isn't perfectly aligned with the other colors on the label.

"It's counterfeit," I announce.

Cristina butts in. "What kind of dumbass would counter-feit shampoo? Ain't no money in that."

I'm about to tell her to keep out of this, but Mr. Anderson beats me to it. He says, "Counterfeiting and product diversion cost my company several million dollars a year. The police just raided a store in Jackson Heights and seized 24,000 bottles of counterfeit shampoo. In *one* store. That's a tremendous eco-nomic loss."

"To say nothing of the babies who get sick from diluted baby formula," I say.

He smiles. "Mr. Davis told me that if anyone could find an illicit manufacturing operation in Corona, you could."

"I'll take that as a compliment. What makes you think Corona's the place to start?"

"Because the store owner in Jackson Heights gave the po-lice an important clue. He said one of the suspects had dark hair, a gang tattoo, and listened to Spanish music."

I wait for more. Nothing doing.

"That's your clue?" I say, because I practically fit that de-scription myself.

"Well, no. Not just Spanish music, some special kind. It's in the report. It also said something about the tattoo indicating that he's Ecuadorian. Anyway, they figure he's a member of a street gang like the Latin Kings or MS-13."

Wow, that's some terrific random profiling there, Mr. Anderson. But the rent's due, so I try to keep a placid surface. And tell him, "The Latin Kings are Puerto Rican, the *Maras* are Salvadoran, and they rarely let anybody else in. I don't know of any Ecuadorians who've jumped in with them, but you never know what could happen as the new generation gets Americanized. I'll check it out for you."

He gives me the cocksure grin of a man who just bought exactly what he wanted, as always. But after we sign and file away our copies of the contracts, this glorified errand boy looks like he can't wait to bug out of the jungle before the headhunters get wind of his scent.

I usually meet the reps from the big clients at the cushy offices of Davis & Brown in downtown Jamaica, but I was getting a weird vibe from this bunch so I just said screw it, I'll take their money, but I want this guy to come to me and have to drag his skinny white ass to the *barrio*. Let him feel what it's like to be a stranger, on alien turf. And I must say, I'm awful glad I did that.

I start with the police reports of the big shampoo bust and other recent crimes relating to counterfeiting, product diversion, and the rest of the gray-goods racket covering the area between Elmhurst and Corona south of Roosevelt Avenue, and Jackson Heights and East Elmhurst north of Roosevelt. That's right, East Elmhurst is due *north* of Elmhurst. What do you expect from a borough where you have to know a different language on every block, where pigeons ride the A train to Rockaway Beach to scavenge from the garbage, where you know that Spider-Man lives at 20 Ingram Street in Forest Hills? No, really. He does.

Most of the cases deal with pirating—unauthorized duplication of CDs, DVDs, and computer software—which are of no interest to my client. The counterfeiting is mostly luxury items like watches, perfume, and designer handbags peddled by West African immigrants on fold-up tables, and the occasional case of Mouton-Cadet with labels made on a laser printer that fool the eye but not the fingers (they lack the raised embossments). But five-and-dime products like shampoo and antibacterial soap? Not much. Time to check out the shelves at the local *farmacias*.

Latinos take their music seriously, especially on Roosevelt Avenue east of 102nd Street. There's a music store on every other block, and the cars—from tricked-out pimpmobiles to body-rot jobs with plastic wrap covering the gaping holes where the passenger windows should be—have top-of-the-line subwoofers pumping out *bachata* and *merengue* loud enough to compete with the 7 train roaring by overhead. And not one noise complaint is ever called in to the boys at the One-Ten. Though I do think that a spoiler on a battered Toyota Corolla is kind of pointless.

The store owner in the police report described the suspect's nationality based on his choice of music and a tattoo of the Ecuadorian flag on his left bicep. But the only music style around here that is exclusively Ecuadorian is *pasillo*, which is too old-fashioned and sentimental for any self-respecting gangbanger to listen to. He probably meant *reggaetón*, the Spanish version of gangsta rap, which crosses ethnic borders in all directions, to the dismay of proud parents everywhere.

And the flag is not a "gang" tattoo. Most people don't know the basic difference between the Colombian and Ecuadorian flags, which boldly fly yellow, blue, and red from second-floor windows and storefronts. (And to anyone who complains about Latinos in the U.S. flying the flags of their homelands, I dare you to go down Fifth Avenue on St. Pat's Day, or to Little Italy during the Feast of San Gennaro, and try to take down the flags. See what happens.)

I stop by a few *farmacias* and *botánicas* and find a number of Syndose knock-offs, including a tube of minty toothpaste with the brand name Goldbloom misspelled *Goldvloom*, a mistake that only a Latino would make.

The *panadería* and *ferretería*—that is, the bakery and hardware store—are displaying handmade posters of Ray Ray in his Newtown High uniform, with his full name, Raymundo Reyes, keeping track of his hitting streak, which after yesterday's ninth-inning blooper now stands at twenty-two games. Go, Ray Ray.

We take our sports seriously too, although soccer's the favorite among Ecuadorians. It didn't get much press up here, but a coach back home was shot when he didn't select the ex-president's son for the Under-20 World Cup in Argentina. Yeah, in case I haven't mentioned it, Ecuador's major exports are bananas, cocoa, shrimp, and unstable politicians, which is why so many of us come here hoping to catch a piece of the American dream. And sports offers a way out for many, even if it remains a distant dream most of the time. Either way, the bright lights of Shea Stadium cast a long shadow over the neighborhood.

Interviewing the store managers yields a range of responses. One *Salvadoreño* says the cops told him not to discuss the case without the state attorney general's consent, but he won't give me a name or a badge number, or sign a statement to that effect, even though I tell him it's a bunch of *tonterías*. You know, B.S., but even the legal immigrants don't want to tangle with the authorities when their citizenship applications are pending.

Another place is staffed by sullen teenagers making minimum wage who don't seem to know anything but one-syllable words, and the next place has employed some fresh-off-the-boats who are still having trouble telling the difference between five- and ten-dollar bills. Then I hit a place on 104th Street where the manager talks a Caribbean mile-a-minute about *beisbol* and the pride of Corona, but he clams up when I ask about the antibiotics in the faded yellow boxes.

"How'd they get so faded? You leave them lying out in the sun?"

Dead air.

I make a show of flipping through my notes, writing a few things down *very slowly*.

"They've just been on the shelf a long time," he says.

"Then it's probably time to replace them," I say, picking up one of the boxes. The expiration date is two years down the road. I mention this. "They can't have been here that long."

More silence.

I like the silence. It tells me a lot. "I'll be back," I say.

Next up is a drugstore run by a *Colombiano* whose attitude is: It's the same stuff for half the price, so his customers buy it. What's the big deal?

The next guy's a *compatriota*, a *paisano*, an *Ecuatoriano* like me, who turns into a walking attitude problem when he accuses me of helping the big *gringo* corporations protect their money instead of going after the *real* criminals, like the *hijos de puta* who charged a couple of hundred would-be immigrants $5,000 each for a boat ride to Florida, then left them floundering in rough seas about 200 miles from the coast of Mexico; or the *sinvergüenzas* who hire day laborers and abandon them without pay in the middle of Nassau County because they can't go and complain to the Board of Labor; or the *perros* at the Hartley Hotel in midtown Manhattan who laid off one-third of their employees after 9/11 and told the rest of them to work double shifts if they wanted to keep their jobs, because business was bad. So they were just using 9/11 as an excuse to run the old speed-up.

A ring on my cell phone interrupts this tirade. It's Felipe, and he must be in big trouble if he's calling me instead of his *mami*.

His school is only a few blocks away, so I can fit it in. I head over on foot, crossing under the El tracks as the train rattles by, thinking about the changing seasons, time passing, and my own parental obligations. Yeah, my generation was supposed to be different. I never thought that my daughter would be growing up in an era when rock stars are dying of old age, or that I would come to know the joys of having a teenage daughter who goes from manic to suicidal on an hourly basis. It all started a few years ago when she was in eighth grade. We had ten minutes to get to some school function, and Antonia was in the bathroom putting on makeup. I asked her, "Do you want to take anything to eat? Some fruit? A sandwich?"

"No."

"No?"

"I don't have *time*," she replied, in that universally adolescent don't-you-know-*anything* whine that drives parents up the wall. And I knew right then that my daughter had reached the age where makeup is more important than food. God help me. And after all these years, I can *still* recite *Green Eggs and Ham* word-for-freaking-word.

* * *

Every school cafeteria in the country smells the same, a uniquely American blend of rotten apples and plastic, evaporating floor cleaner, ripening half-pint cartons of milk, and other food garbage. No wonder the kids all live on chips and soda.

The halls are filled with thirteen-year-olds plugged into the current fashion of low-slung jeans and hip-hugging thongs. I never thought I'd use this expression, but *in my day*, it took some work to see a girl's panties. Now it's pretty much on display, and all I can say is that, fortunately, pimples and braces are God's way of saying you're not ready for sex.

And you know you're in a public institution when you pass a classroom with a sign taped to the blackboard saying, *Do Not Tape Anything to This Blackboard*, which is clearly a test of the logical skills needed to survive in the absurd bureaucracies of the information age.

Felipe is sitting by himself in a tiny interrogation room in the assistant principal's office.

"Are you his guardian?" asks the secretary, whose plastic ID plate says her name is Evelyn Cabezas.

"I'm the person he called."

"Do you know why he's here?"

"No, but I'd like to hear it from him first."

She makes me sit across from Felipe like a court-appointed lawyer with a three-time loser, then she leans on the doorframe with her arms crossed.

"*Dime lo que pasó*," I say.

Ms. Cabezas interrupts. "I'm sorry, but we're not allowed to speak Spanish to the kids inside the building."

"Why not?"

"The principal sent out a memo saying that the underachieving students bring our test scores down and we'll lose funding. So, no Spanish. English only."

"What about the parents who don't know enough English?"

"Hey, I just do what they tell me, like when they had us opening the mail with rubber gloves during that whole anthrax scare."

I don't push it. I just ask what happened.

"I didn't have my homework," he says.

"You didn't call me in here for that."

"Yeah, well, it's the third time this week."

"And now you're in trouble. Tell me why."

"I got mugged."

"Mugged? A couple of hard cases said, 'Forget the cash, we want the English homework'? Try again."

Same sentence, he just changes a crucial verb: "Okay. I didn't *do* my homework."

"Why the hell not?"

He gets all tight-lipped, like he's taken a vow of silence, but I'm not the one looking at serious detention time, so I just sit there letting the emptiness fill the silence until he says, "Ray Ray and his crew was hanging with his *primo* who works at the gas station, gearing up for some mad *viernes loco* action."

He means those crazy Fridays near the end of the school year when kids push their parents' tolerance to the limit.

"You know Ray Ray, he got that pretty-boy face, always looking all ghetto fabulous. He'd go up to Deirdre, the boss, and just put his game on her fat, ugly self. Yo, we be doin' some crazy stuff."

"Keep talking."

"Man, we be a-capellin' and buggin' out. He had us laughing up a lung, smoking the *sheba* with his *primo*."

"You were smoking in a gas station, *pendejo*? Let me get this straight. You went out and partied with your friends the night of your brother's funeral?"

"Well, Ray Ray had a game that day. And we always party after a game."

"So it's sort of like a tradition."

"Don't tell my mom, okay?"

"Don't put me in that position."

"I mean, this is like confession, right?"

"Go on."

"Ain't that what Jesus said?"

"I'm thinking Jesus would be kicking your ass right about now."

"It don't say that in the Bible."

"Sure it does. Check out chapter forty-one, verse three: *And thou shalt kick the asses of all those that offend thee.* So what did you do next?"

He tells me they went on a shoplifting spree and got away with a few bags of chocolate chip cookies, a six-pack of Bud Light, and a couple of sixteen-ounce bottles of Coke, which proves what a bunch of idiots they are. I mean, if you're going to boost the merchandise, at least grab something worth stealing.

So he didn't do his homework because he was busy emulating Ray Ray, and he doesn't want to roll over on his cousin and—at this point—his primary male role model. What am I supposed to say? Some platitudinous crap he won't listen to? Still, it falls to me to be *el malo de la película* and teach him a life lesson. So I tell him, "Listen *chico*, you better not do anything that freaking stupid ever again. And if you're going to hang out with older kids, you better make damn sure you do your homework first, you hear me? . . . I asked if you heard me."

"Yes."

"Yes what?"

"Yes, I heard you."

"Good, because you've still got a lot to learn, *hijito*, and dropping out of high school is a joke in a world that has no sense of humor, unless you've got some rich celebrities in the family I don't know about. You think the cops are going to give you some special treatment when you screw up? Let you off with a warning?"

"Hey, you got Ray Ray off."

"Is that a reason to start a Juvenile Offender record? 'Cause maybe the judge won't be so kind-hearted next time. And I'm going to give your *mami* the same message. After that, it's up to her. I've got my own kid to raise."

I've also got to have a little chat with the pride of Corona.

But all that has to wait. Something was clearly hinky about the pharmacy with the faded-yellow antibiotics. It takes a couple hours of expensive online searching, billable to my deep-pocketed clients, but I find it. Late last year, a sixteen-year-old boy died of septicemia—a galloping blood infection that rode right over the diluted antibiotics the *curandera* bought for him. At first, the cops thought it was a drug overdose, but the autopsy didn't turn up any known street drugs in his system. By all accounts, he was a good kid who studied hard, kept his grades up, and made the varsity wrestling team. He lived about three blocks from the pharmacy. There's no visible connection, but a dead teenager gives me all the motivation I need to stop playing nice and kick it up a notch or two. This goes way beyond watered-down baby formula.

The victim's name was Edison Narvaez, which sure sounds

Ecuadorian. His parents found him in his bedroom. He had already turned blue. I can't imagine anything worse than that. My heart goes out to them for having to come face-to-face with every parent's worst nightmare. It's a professional hazard, I guess. I feel the urge to pull the plug on all the technology, stop traffic, and run home to hug my daughter for the rest of the afternoon.

But I have to swallow my maternal instincts and check the police report first.

It's impossible to find out what the victim's parents actually said, because the detectives didn't know any Spanish, and the report isn't even signed. I could talk to the Narvaez family myself, though I wouldn't want to put them through that unless it's absolutely necessary.

But I do know someone else I can lean on.

"Where'd you get this?" I say, holding the yellow box under the pharmacist's nose.

"I don't know."

"You don't *know*?"

"I mean, a guy who worked here during the holiday season handled it, but he was gone by the end of December."

"He only worked here for one month?"

"Yeah."

"And you let him handle bulk orders of prescription medicine?" I'm not letting him get an inch of breathing room.

"He said he had a source, and the price was right."

"What was his name?"

"José."

"I'm running out of patience here."

"We all called him José."

I turn on my patented X-ray eyes and burn a hole clean

through the back of his head into the wall behind him. "Do you have a pay stub?" I suggest.

"We paid him in cash."

"Of course you did. Did he fill out a job application? A health care plan? Anything with a name and address?"

A customer comes in and starts browsing around the lip glosses, which breaks my hold on him for a moment. So I use the opportunity to dig out the camera and snap a bunch of time-stamped photos of the counterfeit merchandise in close-up, medium, and a really nice wide-angle shot with him in the background. Then I take out a couple of quart-sized Ziplocs, double-bag a handful of the fake medicine as evidence, and stuff it in my bag.

The customer makes a choice, pays for it, gets her receipt and change, and heads out the door. The pharmacist's hands are trembling slightly as he opens a drawer and pulls out a file folder full of invoices and crumpled sheets of pink and yellow paper. He goes through them one by one, wetting his fingers for each sheet, trying to get a grip or else maybe buy the time to come up with a plausible story. Another customer comes in, but I don't take my eyes off the pharmacist for an instant. Finally, he produces a coffee-stained job application form.

I grab it and smooth it out on the counter. *Antonio José de Sucre*. Someone's got a sense of humor, because that name belongs to the heroic general on Ecuador's five-*sucre* note. Other warning signs that a legitimate employer should have spotted include out-of-state references with no phone numbers and a list of previous jobs with companies that went out of business years ago. But the price was right, I guess.

There's an address that's got to be a fake, and I wouldn't put too much faith in the phone number either. "This number any good?"

He's having trouble concentrating.

I repeat, "Did you ever call him at this number?"

"I guess I might have. I don't remember."

"Don't you remember anything? Because you're not getting rid of me until you give me something. You know that, don't you?"

The woman gets in line behind me with a bag of cotton balls and a bottle of baby shampoo. I think the shampoo is one of the fakes. He says, "Let me take care of this customer first." Buying more time, the bastard. When the woman's gone, he says, "I just remembered—some of the cartons the medicine came in might still be in the storage room."

Sounds almost too good to be true. I'll follow this guy, but I'm not going to turn my back on him. I open my jacket so I can get to my .38 revolver quickly as we go down the back stairs to the storage room. Then we toss the place until we find a couple of boxes with the Syndose logo on them. The shipping labels have been torn in half. Another red flag. Who gets a delivery and tears the shipping label in half? Not the whole thing, just the return address.

"Tell me something. Did this guy have a tattoo of the Ecuadorian or Colombian flag on his left bicep?"

"I don't know."

"How could you not know?"

"It was Christmas and we couldn't afford to keep the heat up high, so we were all wearing long-sleeved shirts and sweaters."

"It seems like you can remember things if you try."

"What are you going to do?"

"I'm going to send this guy to a place where he can't choose his neighbors."

"I mean about me."

"That depends. Maybe we can swing a deal if you cooperate."

"I'm cooperating."

"Yeah? Well, I know another word for it."

The phone number's no longer in service, but a quick search turns up the previous owner's name, Julio Cesar Gallegos, which just might lead somewhere. A lot of career criminals in my culture favor such grandiose names, as if they stand to inherit the power of the name by sympathetic magic. The biggest one, of course, being *Jesús*. I mean, there are a lot of Muslims named Mohammed, but nobody names their kid *Allah*.

The name, it turns out, doesn't connect to an address in any of the usual places—motor vehicle and property records, bankruptcy court, government benefits—and I'm starting to get a feeling about this guy. Seems like he only used the name once to get the phone. Nobody makes themselves that invisible unless they're working hard at it, and the kind of swagger he showed on the job doesn't sound like a timid illegal trying to stay off the radar. I don't give the street gang theory much credence. The *pandillas* are into curbside extortion, jacking cars, and drug dealing. They might have a piece of the street action on this, but staking out a one-month undercover in a local pharmacy seems a little beyond their scope. No disrespect.

But I figure if he is my guy, he's *got* to have had a brush with the law at some point, even if it's just a speeding ticket. I do a county-by-county search of the tri-state area and come up with nothing. I finally catch a break and match his name with an accident report that gives a recent address on Queens Boulevard, a wide thoroughfare that more than seventy people have died trying to cross in the last ten years, giving it the catchy nickname of the Boulevard of Death.

I call with a pretext about an insurance payment from the accident, and a woman named Gloria confirms Gallegos's existence by telling me that he's not in right now. But people will tell you anything if they think it'll lead to money, and she practically offers to FedEx me a sample of his DNA. She says he's watching the game in a bar a couple of blocks from the stadium. She doesn't know the exact address, but it's under the elevated tracks, which means from what she's told me that it's on Roosevelt Avenue east of 108th Street. I know the place.

The setting sun paints the store windows with an orange glow that transforms them into heavenly palaces for about a minute and a half. Dueling sound systems thump out *bachatas* from storefronts and apartment windows, while men in sweat-stained T-shirts hang out on the steps, laughing and enjoying the end of another work day with bottles of *cerveza Pilsener*, a taste of the old country. The hardware store owner is changing the numbers beneath Ray Ray's dark Dominican features to include the results of today's game, showing that he's just extended his hitting streak to twenty-three games, while the 7 train shakes the sidewalks as it thunders on toward Flushing.

The big blue-and-orange Mets banner tells me I'm in the right place, and only one of the guys hunched over the bar matches the description I extracted from the fast-talking pharmacist. There's a spot next to him, opposite the big color TV. I slide onto the empty stool as the Mets take on their archrivals, the Atlanta Braves. Glavine's on the mound, facing his old teammates. Top of the third, one out, no one on. Both teams scoreless.

The bartender comes over and asks me what I'll have.

"I'm fine, thanks."

"You gotta have something if you're gonna sit here."

"Oh, I've got to pay rent, huh? Okay, I'll have a seltzer with a twist."

He doesn't try to hide his annoyance with me for ordering something so girly-girly and cheap, and unlikely to result in a big tip. I keep a close watch to make sure that's all he's giving me, and leave a few extra bills on the bar.

The batter pops up to center field, and Beltran gets under it with plenty of time.

"*Así se hace!*" says my neighbor.

"*Vamos Carlosito!*" I chime in.

He looks at me. I toast him with my seltzer. He returns the salute with his beer.

"Do I know you?" he asks.

"You've probably seen me around. I think I've seen you around too. How's it going?"

"Me? Just trying to get through the day."

"It's good to set realistic goals."

Díaz comes up for Atlanta. He takes a few practice swings, then gets into his stance. Glavine throws low and inside. Ball one.

"So, *a qué te dedicas?*"

He says, "Oh, this and that. *Y tú?*"

"I've got my own business."

"Uh-huh. Doing what?"

"I'm a private contractor."

Glavine shakes his head. Lo Duca spreads three fingers and taps them against his right thigh, pinky extended. Glavine takes his time, then fans the guy with a devastating curveball.

"Yeah!" My guy pumps his fist in the air, and his T-shirt sleeve slides halfway down his bicep. I gently slide it the rest of the way. No tattoo.

He looks at me. "You like that?" He can't resist making a muscle for me. "Want to see more?"

"That depends. Is your name really Julio César Gallegos?"

His face darkens. "Hey, what is this?"

"Well, it started out as a counterfeiting case, but I think it's turning into a homicide investigation, although a good lawyer would probably get the charges reduced to second-degree manslaughter."

He goes hard on me and swallows the stale beer at the bottom of his glass, then says, "I have no idea what you're talking about."

"And I always know I'm getting close when the guys I'm interviewing start thinking about what they're going to say in court. *Uh, your honor, my client's remark, 'I'll blow his fucking head off,' was taken out of context,*" I say, mimicking a typical mob lawyer, then wave it all away like bad smell. "Give me a break."

"You got nothing on me."

"I also know I'm getting close when they start talking in clichés."

"This is entrapment."

"I'm not the law, dude. I told you, I'm a private contractor."

I give him a brief rundown of my activities for the past few hours, solidly connecting him to a shipment of counterfeit medicine at the pharmacy on 104th Street and implying an equally strong connection to the death of Edison Narvaez, with suspicion of possible intent, unless he comes clean with me.

"Now, what do you know about the stuff that killed that boy?"

"It's always the one you least suspect, right?" he says, trying to make it into a joke.

"That would mean Brigitte Bardot did it. She's pretty low on my list of suspects. No, I'm looking for a guy with a tattoo of the Ecuadorian or Colombian flag on his left arm." I let him catch a glimpse of the .38 under my jacket. Díaz connects and sends the ball sailing over Delgado's glove, but Chavez gets to it quickly and holds Díaz at first. While the place erupts with cheers, Gallegos looks at his shoes and says the words very quietly, "It's the Ecuadorian flag."

I nod. "Why are you telling me this?"

"Because I knew one of these days someone like you would be walking through that door." He looks around. "No cops, all right?"

"Aw, shucks. And I just called them."

"What the *fuck* did you do that for?"

"Yo, buddy. Your language," says the guy two stools over.

"Yeah, it's English. What the fuck's your problem?"

"Settle down, guys," says the bartender.

I tell Gallegos, "You've got about three minutes, unless you give me some sugar, *comprendes?*" I'm making that up, but screw it—it's working. The next batter hits a hard one up the middle and Reyes stops it cold to end the inning. That's José Reyes, hometown: Villa González in the D.R.

Gallegos says, "We could have worked something out."

"Before all this, maybe. Not with the Narvaez kid dying from tainted meds, or whatever the hell you guys sold him. Tell me where to find him."

"I can't do that."

"Do you hear sirens?" That's kind of a trick question, because you *always* hear sirens in this part of Queens. "Look, if you point me to someone else further up the ladder, I'll leave you out of it."

"I've been wanting to get out of the life," he says. "'Cause me and Gloria are gonna get married, and we're planning to have babies."

"You can *plan* to have babies? That's news to me."

"I want immunity."

"Then tell me something that'll take the focus off you, *hermano*."

"For real?"

"For real."

The lights are on at Shea as twilight turns to darkness, and we can hear the fans cheering in the distance as a ring of cops closes in on a clandestine warehouse near the boat basin off Willets Point Boulevard. The police find what they're after: a conveyor belt, pill counters, stacks of empty bottles and jars, state-of-the-art printing equipment, boxes of fake labels, crates of ready-made knock-offs from Pakistan, Vietnam, Malaysia— talk about the effects of globalization—drums of raw chemicals from Colombia and China for mixing up everything from cough medicine to horse steroids, as well as invoices, account books, and a list of contact names, including delivery boys.

Ray Ray's name is right in the middle of the list.

They're willing to let me talk to him first, but Ray Ray's out celebrating his twenty-three-game hitting streak, and by the time he comes home from his *viernes loco* a couple hours later, the cops have gotten a warrant, stormed right past me, torn up his room, and are tramping down his front steps with their arms full of cases of counterfeit steroids. And I have a sick feeling that the lab is going to find significant traces of the active ingredient in Edison Narvaez's blood samples.

"What the—" he starts to say, but he knows what's going on.

I tell him, "I was on my way over to talk to you, but I guess it's too late for that now."

They read him his rights under the harsh lights of Shea while the fans cheer somebody's throw-beating play. The cheers that he'll never hear. And I can just imagine Felipe when he finds out tomorrow. When they all find out: "*Dime que no es cierto, Fil.*"

Which translates roughly as, "Say it ain't so."

OUT OF BODY

BY GLENVILLE LOVELL

South Jamaica

Phisto remembered it like it was yesterday. The first time he saw a dead body. It was in the embalming room of his father's funeral home. He was almost twelve years old, already bored with school and given to playing hooky, cruising around in stolen cars with his new friends from a Bloods gang that controlled the Baisley Projects.

That day the police had stopped them in a stolen green Caddy on Archer Avenue and had taken the older boys off to jail. He later found out the only reason he'd escaped a trip to the lockup was because one officer had known his old man. Turned out the tough-love cop wasn't doing him any favor by not taking him to jail.

The cop drove him home and he almost bluffed his way out of trouble. But the guy refused to release him without first speaking to his parents. The house was empty that afternoon. His mother had died earlier in the year, and soon afterward, his eighteen-year-old sister ran off with the pastor who conducted his mother's funeral.

The cop took him down to his father's funeral parlor over there on Guy Brewer Boulevard about a mile away from where they lived on 178th Place, a quiet leafy neighborhood of one- and two-family homes dense with Caribbean immigrants like his father who'd settled there in 1960.

Phisto had never visited the funeral home until that day.

He knew what his father did for a living. He knew that his father buried people. And made a pretty good living from it, evidenced by the latest appliances and new furniture they had in their one-family brick house, but it was never talked about in his company.

While the officer explained to his father why Phisto had arrived there in the back of a patrol car, his father showed no emotion, merely nodding and shaking his head. Moments after the blue-and-white drove off, his father exploded, displaying a temper that Phisto had heard his mother talk about but had never seen before.

His father took him down into the basement and ordered him to strip. Defiant, Phisto grabbed his crotch, aping the bad-boy posturing he'd picked up on the street. With this bluff, he tried to walk away. His father grabbed him in a choke-hold and slammed him to the ground. Phisto was surprised by his father's strength. The slightly built man from the island of St. Kitts, though no more than a few inches taller than his son, was well-muscled with surprising power in his upper body from cutting sugar cane and working construction in his youth. With a piece of electrical cord, he tied his scrawny son to a chair next to the dead body he was preparing for burial and proceeded to rip Phisto's clothes from his body until he was naked in the cold room.

Then the mortician went back to his work. The smell of embalming fluid soon filled Phisto's lungs. The prickly odor knifed through his toughness and singed his palate until he puked all over himself. His father paid no attention to him at all. Singing cheerfully and going about his business, stepping over Phisto sitting there in his own vomit, admiring how craftily he'd restored the young woman's face, mutilated by a jealous boyfriend after he'd killed her.

With nothing left in his stomach, Phisto leaned against the table leg. He was weak and bleeding where the wire chafed his wrist. Slime dripped from the corners of his mouth. From where he sat he could see the blood and fluid draining from the woman's body, flowing down into the waste receptacle.

He glanced at the corpse's face and felt a strange relief, a sort of bonding with something outside of himself. Quietly, as if he'd somehow acquired the facility to remove his spirit from his body, he stared at the pathetic little boy with spittle drooling from his mouth, trembling at his father's feet. He saw himself, the pathetic little boy, rise up and walk over to his father and put his arm around the man's shoulder and whisper, *Thank you.*

Then he headed out of the room, pausing at the door for one final glance at the sniffling kid sitting in vomit.

Phisto stored that dead woman's face in his mind, embracing that stillness characterized by death as a part of himself. By the time his father released him two hours later, the smell of vomit and the sickly odor of embalming fluid had disappeared from his senses. He wasn't even aware of the cold anymore. He could've sat there for another two hours as comfortably as if he were lounging poolside at the Four Seasons in Miami.

Years later, he came to realize that in those two hours he sat in that frigid room while his father worked on that body, he'd formulated the virtue that would rule his life: Feel no pain or remorse.

In 1984, he quit school at sixteen and started selling weed. In three months he had moved onto powder, making as much as $8,000 off an ounce. He struck a deal with some Colombians and by the end of the year was flipping $100,000 a week with rock houses in South Jamaica. In two years, he controlled the large housing projects which dominated the two sections of the southside. But he knew that this game wasn't going to last, so he started taking business classes in sales and real estate. By the time the crack craze was over, he'd amassed a fortune and an army, and while maintaining his stranglehold on the drug trade, exporting to as far away as Texas, he had diversified his holdings into real estate in Atlanta, Miami, and the Caribbean.

People saw him as a drug lord. A gang leader. A killer. A psychopath. He laughed whenever he read those kinds of descriptions in the news. America worshipped psychopaths and other miscreants in the name of business. Just pick up *Business Week* or the *Wall Street Journal* or any major business magazine and you found profiles of men who ran businesses, who on the surface appeared to be legal, but with a little digging were discovered to be looting the companies, stealing employee pensions, and knowingly selling products that killed people. The newspapers and magazines lauded those muthafuckers as visionaries, but condemned people of a similar personality profile like himself, who did business on the margins of society. *Ain't that some shit.*

Was he any different from the CEOs of big corporations in this country? He was just as charismatic, as visionary, as tough as a Steve Jobs. In fact, you could say he was tougher. He had never operated any business at a loss. If his businesses were listed on the stock market, the share values would rise every year. His underlings worshipped him just as shareholders worshipped the Bernie Ebberses or Jack Welches of the world. He did whatever he had to do to get the job done. Just as they did. And just as they were celebrated and applauded by their peers and profit-worshippers for their willingness to take chances, to be aggressive and visionary, so was he by the many people who depended on him for their survival.

There were two codes he lived by. They were ruthless, but effective. His first motto: *Snitches must die*. The silencing of witnesses was the rule he lived by and everyone in his orbit, including all the Baisley Projects, paid heed. Neither the NYPD nor the Feds had ever built a case against him.

The second motto: *Accept no disrespect*.

Which was why he had no choice but to put down Fred Lawrence in view of everyone in the playground in Baisley Pond Park. It was as necessary as any CEO firing a junior executive who disrespected him in public. As much as he liked the youngster, if he let the upstart get away with this, the mystique of being Phisto Shepherd would be destroyed. Forever. The youngster had stepped to him in a way that no one in their right mind should be tempted to do. And bragging on top of it. You disrespect Phisto and walk around bragging? That's asking to be cut down. There's no surer way to commit suicide than to disrespect Phisto Shepherd and brag on it.

When Phisto claimed a woman, she was his for life. Only when he said the relationship was done could the woman walk away. And until such time, all other suitors were expected to wither way, to drop into the gutter like rats running from the exterminator. This young pup, Fred Lawrence, had laid some pipe on one of his women and then told the world that the girl had begged to be his bitch. Said she would give up Phisto and all his money for another night with him.

Phisto had reached a point in his life where he seldom handled disputes personally. There were any number of young guns in his organization he could call on to quash a beef. Of any sort. If the resolution needed to be quick and permanent, he had enough specialists for every day of the week. If gentle nudging or mediation was required in a sensitive matter, there were people who could be trusted to be discreet.

But he had to show the world that he was still Phisto Shepherd. That the Phisto who survived his father's beat-down, who remade himself into a fire-breathing dragon to create the baddest outfit in Queens, wasn't finished, as many were beginning to whisper on the street after word got around that Fred the baller had fucked Phisto's woman. He'd taken on the dreaded Jamaican Shower Posse for turf and sent them scampering back to Miami. He'd ordered the hit on a corrupt cop who tried to shake him down, and he'd gotten away with it. Why hadn't this youngster heeded his warning? When the message was conveyed to the kid, he'd signed his own death warrant with a laugh.

Once in a while, even with the large army at his disposal, Caesar still had to go out and slay somebody to remind his soldiers why and how he became Emperor. This one wasn't a head-cracker. The youngster had to be bodied, and he would do it himself.

Fred Lawrence was a talented young baller who'd just finished his senior year at LSU. Some pundits thought he was sure to be drafted by the NBA. Maybe not a first-rounder, but definitely a second or third. He was that good. Phisto had seen him play and didn't like the kid's game as much as others did. Not enough range on his jumper, but the quick first step and the physical nature of his game reminded Phisto of Stephon Marbury. Fred could have gotten his shot.

That is, had he not come back from Louisiana thinking he could spit in King Kong's eye. Thinking he could steal Fay Wray and not suffer the consequences. Thinking his dribbling skills would get him a buy after dissing Phisto.

Like everyone else who tried to fuck with Phisto's program without considering the consequences, the young man had to pay. The beating and humiliation Phisto took from his father that day in the mortuary taught him never to bluff. Once you bluff you have to back down. And when you back down you lose respect.

His core crew had advised him to let the matter drop. Why knuckle up with this young stud? But he knew they were begging for the youngster's life simply because they were in love with his game. Phisto knew they converged on the park on Saturdays and Sundays, just like everybody else, to watch the muscular youngster play. Everyone on the southside loved this young man, wanted to see one of their own make it in the NBA. Putting the grip on him wouldn't go down well with the residents.

Nevertheless, Phisto's code was his code. The situation reminded him of when his father was shot to death on 121st Avenue during a robbery in 1995. By that time his father had disowned him and he and the old man hadn't spoken in more than ten years. But everyone in the neighborhood knew this was Phisto's father, and accorded him due respect. Phisto found the young killer, and in sight of other customers spaded him as he sat in the barber's chair. Phisto was arrested the next day. But the case never made it to trial. The man who had identified him to the police was Bobby Tanner, a retired postal worker. Tanner got a bullet in the back of the head for his trouble. Word soon got around that Bobby Tanner got tagged for snitching. The next Sunday, Phisto visited the church where another of the witnesses worshipped. The bloated man saw Phisto's six-foot, 275-pound frame blocking the sidewalk and, fortunately for him, fell down in the street from sheer fright. No one ever appeared in the grand jury to finger Phisto.

Contrary to what his advisors believed, Phisto didn't actually want to put the youngster under at first. He would've let the matter go had the young stud not been stupid enough to woof that he had more dog in him that Phisto. After that, his hands were tied.

That summer evening, the sun had left a band of endless purple across the sky. An unusually high wind curled the young tree limbs and stirred leaves and dust in the park. It blew hard and heavy against the houses on Sutphin Boulevard, rattling the sign on the Crowne Plaza Hotel on Baisley Boulevard.

A storm was coming. Colored balloons, left over from an abandoned family picnic, hung from tree limbs. Yet the approaching inclement weather wasn't enough to delay the fitness fanatics doing laps around the track, or to arrest the pick-up game on one of the three courts behind the racquetball wall.

The few daring souls on the sidelines that evening who'd scoffed at the looming bad weather witnessed a near flawless performance from Fred Lawrence on the court. The perfection of his long lean body, snaking through small spaces, piercing the tough wind and a tougher defense, twirling and swerving around defenders with precision, left most people shaking their heads in disbelief.

Fred scored on a driving, twisting lay-up off the glass, using a classic crossover move that left his defender flat on his back. The small crowd screamed. Fred ran back down the court pumping his fist in the air, yelling, "You forgot your jock, bitch!"

The next time down the court, Fred took a pass on the wing and without breaking stride elevated past a closing defender for a rim-rattling dunk.

People were whooping and hopping up and down and spinning around in circles of disbelief.

"Did you see that?"

"No he didn't!"

"Replay! Replay!"

"Jordanesqe."

"*Better* than Jordan."

Phisto's black BMW pulled up on 155th Street behind a white Explorer. The doors of the truck were open and Jay-Z's latest joint was blasting full force. Phisto wanted to tell the idiot to turn his music down, but decided to ignore the disturbance and walked the short distance across the grass to the courts.

There was a hush as Fred got the ball back on a steal. He veered left and was met by an agile defender. He slipped the ball between his legs and dribbled backward, looking for another opening. Shifting the ball from side to side, through his legs, and then a glance to his left as if searching for someone in the crowd. Everyone knew what was coming. Fred jabbed to the right and the defender bit on the fake. The elusive youngster changed direction and in a split second flew by his defender for another dunk.

Oh, the ecstasy of the crowd. Fred soaked up their response for a full second, posing under the rim.

And then, *praack! praack!*

Heads jerked around. Too loud for a firecracker. Too close to be the backfire of a car. People scattered when they saw Fred stumble and fall to the ground. Even his friends on the court ran and left him.

Seconds later, only five people were left. Phisto handed the .45 to someone in his three-man posse to dispose of it. He walked over to the only person who hadn't run away.

"Do I know you?" Phisto said.

"I don't know."

Phisto took hold of the man's face, digging his fingers through his scraggly beard into his jaws. "Do you know me?"

"Yeah, I know you."

Phisto laughed. "Why didn't you run away like the rest?"

The man hesitated. "Why?"

Phisto's eyes screwed up and he lifted the man's dark glasses from his face. "What'd you say, muthafucker?"

"Why? I didn't think the game was over."

Phisto laughed. "You think you're funny."

"I mean, he was so amazing, the way he defied gravity. I thought he was Superman. I thought he would get up and fly above that rim again."

"He *was* amazing, wasn't he?" Phisto said.

"Yeah. Amazing."

Phisto said, "Did you see anything else here?"

The guy took his sunglasses from Phisto's hand and put them back over his eyes. "What do you mean?"

"Exactly. That's what I mean," Phisto replied, turning away. "You better bounce. Cops gonna show any minute."

"I *am* a cop," the man said.

Phisto turned slowly, his face scarred with a dark smile. "For real?"

The man adjusted his dark glasses and smiled. "Just fucking with you."

Phisto relaxed. "I should kill you for fucking with me."

"Actually, I wasn't. I'm really a cop."

The man opened his jacket. An NYPD detective badge hung from a chain around his neck. Phisto also noticed the 9mm stuck loosely in his waistband.

Phisto gauged the distance between him and the man. "You gonna arrest me?"

"No."

"If you ain't gonna arrest me, what you gonna do?"

"Shoot you between the eyes."

Phisto laughed.

The man wriggled his fingers. "What's so funny?"

"You're gonna shoot me between the eyes?"

"Yeah."

Pointing at the dead baller, Phisto said, "For him?"

"No."

"Is this personal?"

"Remember the cop you ambushed in that crack house?"

"I don't know what you're talking about."

"He had a son. That son became a cop."

"And that son . . ."

"Would be me."

Phisto turned to the member of his crew holding the .45. "Shoot this muthafucker."

Nobody moved.

Phisto made a quick grab at the .45. His hand closed on the grip and that's when he felt a jolt to his chest as if he'd been kicked by a mule. He bounced against the white wall of one of the racquetball courts and slid to the ground on his back.

Phisto had often thought of what this moment would be like for a person. The moment that separated life from death. Was there some brilliant light to illuminate your path into the next world, as some people claimed who'd had so-called near-death experiences? Was there such a thing as coming close to death? He knew what death looked like. His father had made sure of that.

He looked up and saw streams and streams of white clouds. And then he felt a strange relief swell in his chest, a sort of bonding with an energy entering him. A sadness overcame him and he wanted to cry. He saw the faces of his crew and knew that he'd been betrayed. By one or all of them. He also knew it didn't matter anymore. The light was approaching fast.

LIGHTS OUT FOR FRANKIE

BY LIZ MARTÍNEZ

Woodside

Frankie tapped his foot and wished the clerk would hurry up. How long could it take to scan a couple of items and punch the keys on the cash register? He lifted his baseball cap and wiped the sweat off his forehead, then slipped it back on, pulling the bill lower. The heatwave was taking its toll on everyone. The air-conditioning inside the store helped a little, but the customers still looked like they were wilting.

Finally, the cashier got her act together. She handed him the transaction slip and her pen. He scribbled *Gerry Adams* in the signature space. In the past, Frankie had passed himself off as Billy Clinton, Charles Prince, and Johnny Depp. The cashier counted out crisp currency and gave it to him along with a command to have a nice day. Her name tag read *Rochelle*.

"Thanks, Rochelle," he said, and asked her for the receipt. She stared vacantly at the piece of paper. "Oh. Sure," she said, then handed it to him and wandered off.

Frankie glanced around the customer service desk. What a misnomer. The three clerks behind the counter were doing anything but servicing customers. One was chatting on her cell phone with her back to the store. Another was deep in thought, staring intently into the middle distance. The third mindlessly folded and refolded the same article of clothing. He spied a roll of thermal cash register tape sitting out on the counter. Somebody had probably started changing the tape and then forgot about it midstream. Nobody was paying any attention to him, so he swiped the tape and tucked it into the white plastic bag. He was sure he could find some use for it.

He hopped into his black SUV and merged into traffic on Northern Boulevard. He headed toward his next stop near the Queens Center Mall. Most of his NYPD colleagues worked extra jobs on their RDOS. Having regular days off gave them an opportunity to land good gigs like guarding one of the Commerce Bank branches. Stand there for eight hours in uniform, flirting with the tellers. *Nice.*

Frankie sighed and looked at the list his wife had made for him. This was how he spent his RDOS—running from store to store. He thought about his wife and their two kids and sighed again. For the millionth time, he questioned the way his life was unfolding. Shouldn't he try to land a private-pay job with a bank for his days off? Or maybe with a store? He grimaced. It was only July, but the kids would need new school supplies soon, and then Christmas . . . Always something.

He pulled into the left lane on Queens Boulevard and waited for the light to change. One of the guys in the livery cab that sailed through the light on his right looked familiar, but he couldn't be sure. He tried to think who it might be. The memory came to him just as he pulled into the Marshall's parking lot.

On his first day in the Police Academy, Frankie had buddied up with three other recruits: Thompson, Edwards, and . . . the third guy's name escaped him. The group had coffee before classes, studied together, and ate lunch in a diner two blocks from the Academy. The man in the black car reminded Frankie of the last member of the Fearsome Foursome. (How young they'd been! That name had sounded so cool at the time.) He was a lanky, raw-boned shit-kicker from the hills of West Virginia. The guy had heard an ad for the NYPD on his short-wave radio and had spent a day driving northeast to take the test. Everybody thought he was stupid because of his hillbilly accent, but Frankie copied his homework every chance he got.

Williams—that was his name. Frankie must have been the first Mexican-American Williams had ever seen. Right off the bat, the guy made a remark about Frankie's nose. Frankie, who thought his nose was regal, like the profile on the statue of an Aztec warrior, was slightly insulted. "What do *you* know?" he'd asked Williams. "Your last girlfriend was probably a sheep."

The other guys chuckled, but Williams took it seriously. "We never had no sheep in our family," he said. "I had an uncle once, kept goats. He was pretty tight with one of them—called her Priscilla." He looked puzzled when the other three recruits doubled over with laughter. He must have figured he'd made a slight miscalculation because he tried to backtrack. "I don't think he was improper with Priscilla or nothin'," he protested. "They was just real good companions."

Frankie could hardly catch his breath, he couldn't stop laughing. "They never got married, huh, Williams? Your uncle and his goat?"

"That's disgusting," Williams said. He refused to speak to the other three for the rest of the day.

One of the guys found out later that Williams had a degree from some Bible college, but it was too late. He'd earned himself the nickname Officer Goatfucker. Nobody called him that anymore. He was a captain now, working out of the 115th Precinct. Now they called him *Captain* Goatfucker. Behind his back, of course.

Frankie smiled, thinking about the old days. Fifteen years had slipped by. He sometimes regretted that he didn't have more to show for the time besides a few gray hairs and occasional heartburn. He'd been so naïve when he first came on the job. Thought everything was the way they showed it on TV. Boy, did he know better now.

Frankie pushed open the heavy entrance door to the store and made a beeline for the customer service desk. "I'd like to return this merchandise," he told the clerk, and handed her a receipt. This one's name tag said *Shaquanna*.

She gazed blankly at the clothing he pulled out of his shopping bag and lifted her electronic scanner. She passed it over the tags and pressed a key on her register. "A hundred and eighty-six dollars. Would you like a store credit?"

"Cash, please," he said.

She ripped both layers of register tape off and held them together with her thumb and forefinger. Her nails were painted tomato-red and had rhinestones embedded in the polish. "Fill out your name and address and sign on the line here." He scrawled on the paper and handed it back. The clerk pressed a button on the register with her long, fake fingernail. There was a noise like a lawnmower starting, then everything went dark.

Silence enveloped the store for a long moment, then shouts erupted. Frankie's first thought was another terrorist attack. He'd spent 9/11 pulling people out of the World Trade Center. A part of him had been on edge ever since, always halfway expecting a repeat performance. His heart raced into fourth gear. He whipped out his phone, praying that the cell towers were still relaying calls.

"Seven-three Precinct," a voice snarled. Frankie never thought he'd be so glad to hear PAA Malloy's nasal twang.

"Hernandez here. What's going on?"

"I'm busy. Whadaya mean, what's going on? With what?"

Lovable old Malloy, the best police administrative aide in the department. Frankie gritted his teeth. "With the lights. The lights are out. Is it citywide? What's happening?"

"I don't know nothin' about no lights out. We got plentya light here. Whyn't ya come in and use the lights here? Maybe you could see to make out the reports right once in a while. Say, is that it? I gotta get back. *Somebody* has to do some work around here."

"Yeah," Frankie said, "that's it." He pressed the *End Call* button.

His heart downshifted to third gear. The chaos that had threatened to erupt calmed to a dull murmur. Late afternoon light streamed in through the front windows, diluted by the grime. Drawn like moths to a flame, shoppers swarmed in the sunlight, their intended purchases clutched uncertainly to their chests. Store security was already in action. Uniformed guards gathered with the store managers near the exits to make sure no one took advantage of the power outage to sneak merchandise past the electronic monitoring pedestals.

Electric signs on businesses across Queens Boulevard were illuminated, so maybe it was just the store's system that had given up the ghost. That's why the PAA at Frankie's Brooklyn precinct didn't know anything about it. He smiled grimly, gently chiding himself for jumping the gun and heading right to thoughts of disaster. He turned back to the cashier. "Uh, what about my refund?"

She looked at the cash register without focusing. "It won't open without electricity," she said.

"I understand that," he said slowly, patiently. "How can I get my money?"

"We'll mail it to you, I guess." She consulted the tape

where he'd identified himself as Colonel Parker, with an address at 12 Finger Lickin Lane in Fried Chicken, Kentucky.
"You're from Kentucky?" She squinted uncertainly. "They got
mail there, I guess. We'll send it to you."

A knot formed in Frankie's stomach. "I need it now," he
said.

She shrugged. "I can't give it to you. Hey, I got kids. I
better pick them up from day care." She shuffled off, leaving
Frankie standing at the customer service counter by himself
in the dark.

Fuck! Who would have thought giving a wrong name and
address would come back to bite him in the ass? No cop in his
right mind handed over that information to strangers. Now he
was out the money and the merchandise. He glanced behind
the counter, but efficient old Shaquanna had hustled his returns to the back, so he couldn't even take them with him.

The crowd thinned rapidly as people poured outside. Maybe
he could find the manager. And then what? The guy would
grab the money out of petty cash and hand it over to Colonel
Parker? Shit. Frankie cursed himself silently. He'd just fucked
himself out of almost two hundred dollars.

He got back into his family-sized gas-guzzler and took off
to finish the rest of the errands on his wife's list. Her family came from the Mexican state of Puebla. Frankie's family,
which hailed from the West Coast state of Jalísco, secretly
looked down their regal noses on Puebla, which they considered to be the asshole of Mexico. (When you looked at Puebla
on the map, it really did look like the end of the long intestine,
which made Oaxaca and Chiapas and a few other states the
shit end of the country, as far as Frankie's parents were concerned.) Frankie himself didn't really have an opinion, having
never spent more than a few school vacations in any part of

Mexico. All he knew about the people from Puebla was that the food they cooked in the local Woodside restaurants wasn't as good as his mother's.

He had to admit that his wife came from a long line of savvy politicians. In Mexico, that meant that they stole with both hands and lied out of both sides of their mouths. Some of the family had emigrated to the States, where they continued the family tradition by becoming involved in New Jersey politics.

María was a perfect blend of North and South. She ran their little tribe with an iron fist, the way the matriarchs in her lineage always had. And she was clever, much like the rest of her family members. She had a number of friends, but the relationships were always transactional, rather than emotional. María had no interest in socializing with anyone who didn't trade in the currency of favors. If she couldn't get something on somebody, she wasn't interested in pursuing the friendship.

Of course, she had plenty to hold over Frankie's head. She was also bewitching. She would dazzle you with her smile and enchant you with her personality. Once in a while, Frankie caught glimpses beneath María's charming veneer to a heart of stone. Other times, he thought he must be imagining things and that she was the best thing to ever happen to him. Occasionally, he thought that if it weren't for María, he could have had a much different—probably better—kind of life.

He followed the directions on his list, the chores taking him out to Nassau County, on Long Island but close to the Queens border. He listened intently to the radio, changing stations to catch any news about the power situation. The oppressive heatwave that was plaguing the New York Metropolitan Area was taking its toll. A blackout was focused mostly in western Queens, caused by excessive demands on the power grid. Too many people in illegal apartments running extra air conditioners. Astoria, Woodside, and Sunnyside bore the brunt. But, the announcer said, residents in that area shouldn't feel too badly—people in other areas of the city were also suffering.

Frankie felt much better hearing that. Wow, other people were suffering too. Yippee.

His wife called his cell to report that their lights were still on, but their neighbors' houses had lost power. "Thanks for the update," he said. "Does that mean you're gonna cook dinner?" She hung up on him.

On his return trip to Queens, he was going against rush-hour traffic, but the cars still crawled. He decided to stop on the other side of Woodside before heading home. He owed Tía Alba a visit. He lived only a five-minute drive away, but didn't see her as much as she wanted. He parked outside Seán Óg's, the Irish pub on Woodside Avenue. It was 8:30 and the darkness was settling in slowly. He loved the way the day took its time ending during the height of summer. The extended daylight brought back memories of riding his bike at dusk and playing ball with the other children. Remote, simpler times, when the most important decisions he made revolved around which kids to torment for the day.

Most of the businesses on Woodside Avenue were dark, but a few had lights. Weird how the power grid worked, skipping over certain places but hitting the ones next door. He briefly wondered whether someone got paid off to keep the lights on in certain places. Nah. That was too paranoid, even for him.

The big wooden sign on the side of Seán Óg's read *Drinking Consultant*. He wondered about that every time he saw it. He could picture the scene inside: A guy walks up to the bar, says, "I want to consult you about drinking." The bartender says, "Yes, sir, what would you like to drink?" Frankie wondered if the consultation cost fifty bucks an hour, like a shrink. Probably, he thought, if you downed the booze fast enough. Then again, you'd probably wind up lying down in Seán Óg's, just like at a shrink's, you drank enough. He remembered when the place was some other Irish joint where you could bet on soccer games and horse races. Of course, the son of a bitch running the place taped the soccer games and got suckers to bet on the losing team when he rebroadcast them, but it only took a couple of losses for people to wise up. The guy went out of business years ago, go figure.

Frankie's family had been among the first wave of Latinos to settle in Woodside. He'd gotten his ass kicked a few times before the other kids in the Irish working-class neighborhood accepted him. It helped that his family was Catholic. Also that his old man brought them here when Frankie was young enough that he didn't grow up speaking with an accent. His pop, on the other hand, had the whole Señor Wences thing going.

Now, of course, it didn't matter. Aside from a few old, entrenched Irish families, the neighborhood was predominantly Latino. Not too many Mexicans, but a few here and there. Mostly Dominicans, Salvadorans, Guatemalans, some Puerto Ricans. Plus your Indians, Pakistanis, and Koreans, of course. Most of those were in neighboring Jackson Heights, but a lot of them had slipped over into Woodside. And now the Russians were discovering the neighborhood. Not to mention the blacks who were swarming into the projects the next block over from Frankie's house.

He glanced up Woodside Avenue and suddenly felt old. He could remember when almost every business had been something else. Except the Astoria Federal Bank. They'd been annoying people in the same spot for years. A fee for this, a fee for that; *I'm sorry, sir, we've misplaced your records* . . . He couldn't think of a place that gave him more heartburn than that bank. Well, maybe the DMV, but it was close.

Get a grip, Frankie told himself. He knew his thoughts were careening crazily because he had to go see his aunt. She wasn't his real aunt, of course; that was just what everybody called her. At the corner of Woodside Avenue and 62nd Street, he glanced at the building on his right. The lights dotted the windows of The Jefferson. It figured Tía Alba's building would still have electricity. She would keep the power on through sheer force of will. He stepped into the vestibule and took a deep breath. He pressed the buzzer for her apartment. After a pause for whoever was manning the door to look at him through the camera, he got an answering ring. He dragged himself up the three flights, prolonging the inevitable.

Tía Alba threw open the door. "*Ay, Paquito!*" she squealed. "*Ven acá!*" She held her arms open. Paquito was Spanish for "Frankie." He hated to be called Paquito. His aunt smelled of lavender water. He was mildly allergic to the scent and felt his nose tickle uncomfortably. He hated lavender water. He embraced her quickly and stepped back.

"Come in, come in," she said. "Sit down. I have some *empanadas* heating up." She bustled toward the kitchen.

"*No, gracias, tía,*" he said. "I'm not hungry, really." He patted his stomach to indicate how full he was. He hated her *empanadas.*

"Okay, some coffee then, *sí?* You'll have some *café conmigo?*"

Sure, he would have coffee with her. Her coffee was tolerable. Besides, it would take her a few more minutes to pour.

But no, she was back instantly with two steaming cups. "Just perked," she said. She still used a stovetop percolator, rather than a coffee machine, although God knew she could have had a new one every week. She claimed the machines didn't brew the coffee properly. "I knew you were coming."

This prescience was less a function of her mind-reading abilities and more the result of the phone call he'd made to her in the morning before leaving the house, telling her he planned to stop by later.

And now it was later, and he owed her money, and he didn't know how to tell her he didn't have it.

She got right to the point. "What did you bring me?" She beamed at him.

"Well, listen, *tía*, it's like this . . ." he started.

Her face darkened like a storm cloud. "Don't tell me any stories, Paquito. I'm not in the mood for stories. Just give me what you owe me."

Don Pedro stuck his head out of the back bedroom. "Trouble?" he asked. He and Tía Alba had been together for longer than Frankie could remember. Hardly anyone saw him unless something bad was about to happen. Don Pedro had an uncanny sense of when things were going to shit.

"No, no trouble," Frankie croaked.

"Depends on what you mean by trouble," Tía Alba said. "I think Paquito is a little short today."

Don Pedro hauled his bulk into the living room. "Short? How can that be?" He looked genuinely puzzled.

"Well, listen," Frankie said, looking up at the big man. Don Pedro towered over everybody, especially when he was standing and they were sitting. "I ran into a little trouble today. Because of the blackout." He shrugged, letting them know that he could hardly be held responsible for the vagaries of Con Edison.

"No excuses, Paquito," Don Pedro said. "We don't tolerate excuses here. You know that." He sounded almost regretful.

"I have almost all of it. Here," he said, and pulled out his wallet. "I owe you another two hundred. Less, even." He handed over a fat wad of bills.

Tía Alba counted them quickly. She shook her head. "Two hundred dollars. That's not acceptable." She brightened, as though struck with an idea. "Why don't you go down to the bank and get the rest?" She turned to Don Pedro. "Walk him down to the ATM. You could stand to get a little air. You've been inside all day."

"That's a fine idea. Come, *m'ijo*." He beckoned toward the front door.

"I . . . I can't," Frankie said. He swallowed hard. "I don't have that much in my account."

Don Pedro loomed over him. "Listen, *cabrón*, you better figure out a way to get the two hundred. Or we'll have to figure it out for you, *comprende?*"

"I don't have it," Frankie repeated. A voice in the back of his head told him he was being ridiculous. He had an NYPD shield in his pocket and a gun in a holster. He had nothing to fear from this lug. The voice of reason cut in and told the other voice to shut the fuck up. He cleared his throat, started to explain.

Don Pedro got red in the face, but Tía Alba spoke calmly. "It's all right, Paquito. These things happen. Don't worry, Pedro, we'll work it out. Paco's a good boy. We can make some arrangement."

Don Pedro looked like he wanted to arrange Frankie's face in a new configuration, but then he nodded. "As always, you are right, Alba. I will leave it to you to work something out with the boy." He wandered back into the bedroom.

"Now," she said, "what can we work out?" She closed her eyes for a moment. "I know! We are in need of a guard. You will be the guard."

"A guard? You already have a security system here."

"No, no. More of a . . . bodyguard. Yes, a bodyguard." She nodded. "It's settled. You will go down to the second floor and make sure that everything is all right with our guests. Then we will be even."

"Oh, no, *tía*. Not that. I can't . . ."

She clapped her hands. "You can, and you will." She checked her watch. "Starting now. And you will come here every night this week. Then I will see you next week, as usual," she said, beaming again. "Now, come. I will bring you downstairs."

Frankie trailed her down the flight of steps, feebly protesting the whole way, although he knew it was useless. If only he had been able to get that refund, he wouldn't be into Tía Alba for the two hundred. He'd started out working in this enterprise at his wife's insistence. At first, it had been a way to earn easy money, just a simple method of stretching their budget a little further. Somehow, he'd wound up behind the eight ball, into Alba for more money each week. It reminded him of that Tennessee Ernie Ford song "Sixteen Tons": *Another day older and deeper in debt . . .* And now he did indeed owe his soul to the company store.

That store, in this case, was Tía Alba and her merry band of fences, who specialized in moving hot—or at the very least, lukewarm—goods. He had a sneaking suspicion that the profits somehow got sent back to the land of the camel jockeys and the home of the ragheads, but his ass was so deep in the alligator pool that he was in no position to do anything about it, even if he knew for sure, which he didn't. He made damn sure he didn't. Which was another reason he didn't want to go downstairs.

He stopped his thoughts as Alba led him into her other apartment on the second floor. The place was jammed, mostly with women, but quite a few men swarmed around as well. It had the feel and sound of a casbah or bazaar. Merchandise was selected, haggling ensued, and deals were finalized. A Middle Eastern–looking man in Western dress approached Alba. She made the introductions quickly, calling the man Mohammed. She turned Frankie over to him, saying, "Mohammed will show you what to do. Now you visit me again tomorrow night before you come down here." She squeezed his cheek before she left. Hard.

Frankie rubbed his face. Mohammed's hands snaked over Frankie's torso and legs expertly. Before Frankie could smack the guy, Mohammed said, "Ah, you are armed. It is good to be prepared. Come, I will show you what to do."

Frankie glared at him, but what choice did he have? He followed Mohammed to a stool next to the front door. Frankie was to sit there and guard the place for the next four hours.

I can't stand this, he thought. *What am I doing here?* His life started flashing in front of his eyes. Was he dying? Or just wishing he were dead? He knew that was a sin, but at this point, what was one more? He pictured María at home, working comfortably at the laptop, using the scanner like a pro, churning stuff out of the color printer like a one-woman Kinko's.

He sighed and tried to pretend he was on a shit-fixer—a post in the bowels of some shithole in Brooklyn where you got sent if you fucked up. Well, that was apt. He'd ridden out a couple of assignments to shit-fixers in his time, and he supposed he could do it again. Of course he could. He pulled himself up taller. Just another . . . he glanced at his watch . . . three hours and thirty-eight minutes to go. He opened the door to let a stout Dominican woman with three gold teeth leave. She waddled out with a bundle of clothing wrapped in string. Frankie spotted the store tags still hanging from the items.

As soon as he closed the door, the buzzer rang. Mohammed appeared and inspected the visitor through the closed-circuit TV system. He nodded to Frankie. "It's okay, my friend. You can let her in. She is good customer." He disappeared into the throng, calling out, "Ladies, ladies! No fighting. We have plenty for everyone."

There was a smart rap at the door. Frankie peered through the peep and saw the same woman who had just been spotted on the CCTV. She was a petite Latina wearing jeans and a red T-shirt with a denim vest that had embroidered flowers on it. The hairs on the back of his neck stood up. He didn't know why, but his cop intuition kicked in and told him something was wrong.

She tapped on the door again. Mohammed appeared, glaring at Frankie. "Let her in, my friend. That is what you are here for." Before Frankie could protest, Mohammed opened the door and ushered the woman in. "Hello, my friend," he said to her, taking her hand between both of his. "We have fine selection today. Check it out."

The woman smiled at him. Frankie noticed she had good white teeth. No gold. The alarm bells clanged in the back of his skull. He looked for Mohammed and spotted him bent over a clothing rack in the back, making a deal with a heavy-set lady in a purple pantsuit.

Frankie tucked his hand in the crook of Mohammed's elbow and pulled the man upright. "I am making deal," Mohammed spit at him. "You go back to door."

Frankie pulled the man roughly out of the crowd. "I need to talk to you," he hissed. "There's something about that woman that's not right." He indicated the newest arrival by lifting his chin in her direction.

Mohammed glanced her way. "She is good customer. She has shopped here many times before. You go back to door." He shook Frankie off and lost himself among the shoppers.

Frankie stood there for a moment, unused to people ignoring him. He headed back to the door, thinking to let Tía Alba know what was going on. She was a businesswoman, yes, but she was also smart. She obviously ran the show, and she would be able to straighten out Ali Baba.

He whipped out his cell phone, ready to ring her upstairs. Before he could press the button, however, the door flew open. "Police! Put your hands up!" A sea of blue uniforms fanned out, screaming the order a second time in Spanish. "*Policía! Manos arriba!*"

As one, the female shoppers let out a high-pitched wail. No doubt they were all illegals worried about being sent back to their countries on a bus. Frankie could have told them not to worry about it. They'd be out of Central Booking and on their way back to their Queens apartments before the cops finished the paperwork for the bust. The women were crying and screaming. All except one. The petite brunette in the flowered vest had whipped out her gun and was herding the others back against the wall.

He knew it! No one in her right mind would be wearing an extra layer in this heat—unless she needed the vest to conceal her shoulder holster. The vest, plus the fact that she had good teeth, were the clues he'd picked up on subconsciously. He'd known she didn't fit in with the rest of the women. Fat lot of good it had done him.

He felt a gun pressing in the small of his back. A man yelled, "Hands up!" into his ear.

"I'm a cop!" he shot back, and reached for his shield.

"I know who you are," the voice said. Hands reached for his gun and slid it out of his holster. He felt the sweat slide down his sides. Now he was naked.

"I'm a cop!" he said again. The same hands spun him around.

"I know who you are," the man repeated.

Frankie's eyes flew open. "Captain Goatfucker!" He winced at his own stupidity. "Er—ah—I mean, Captain Williams. How the hell are you?"

"Better than you, Frankie, m'boy," the captain said as he snapped the cuffs around Frankie's wrists. "Better than you."

"Hey, Williams, whadaya doing here? It's me, Frankie. From the Fearsome Foursome, remember? I'm on your side. One of the good guys." He tried a weak grin.

"Oh no, Frankie. You done crossed over to the other side a long time ago." Williams shook his head. "My Organized Retail Crime Task Force has been watchin' you, m'boy. We got videotapes, still photos, receipts with your fingerprints on 'em—you name it, we got it. Your ass is fried." He made a kissing noise. "You can kiss that pension goodbye."

Frankie felt dizzy. "But—but my kids. My wife . . ."

"Tsk, tsk. You should have thought about your family while you were committing fraud."

Frankie wanted to throw up. The cops were hustling the wailing women out the door. He was gratified to see Mohammed trussed up like a chicken in ankle cuffs and handcuffs—the guy should have known better than to fight a cop, Frankie thought. Meanwhile, he was standing there with his hands behind his back like some two-bit perp. "Come on, Williams. We can work this out. You're a cop, I'm a cop . . ."

"Oh no, that's where you're wrong, Frankie. You're no cop. Not no more. Least, not when we get through with you. I'd say you were the next candidate for protective custody." He squinted at Frankie. "'Less you wanna go straight into population and spend your days playin' Drop the Soap with the Bloods and Crips." He grinned sorrowfully.

Frankie scrambled frantically for the magic words that would get him out of this mess. "No, hey, look, you came in here to make a bust, I'm a cop, I'm helping you out . . ." he tried.

Williams shook his head. His voice became businesslike. "No good. You're caught, Hernandez. Game over."

"Williams, please. For old times' sake?" Frankie was disgusted with himself for pleading, but he was out of options.

Williams gave Frankie a pitiful glance. "I'll tell you what I can do. For old times' sake." Frankie looked at him eagerly. "I'll let you ride in the back of the RMP instead of the van with the rest of the perps."

Williams handed Frankie over to the small female officer with the vest. "Guzman, bring this one in. Let 'im ride in the back of your car."

Officer Guzman wrinkled her nose as though smelling something rotting. But all she said was, "Yes, sir."

As she shoved him out the door, Frankie turned back and yelled, "Fuck you, Goatfucker! *Chinga tu madre!*"

Guzman clucked her tongue at him. "That's no way to talk. Captain Williams would never do that to his mother. He's a very religious man, you know."

"I want my delegate!" Frankie snarled. "Call the PBA and tell them to get my delegate down here pronto."

"Don't worry," Guzman said. "We'll make the call once we get to the precinct." She lowered her voice confidentially. "Although the way I hear it, the delegate's not gonna be able to do much for you. Your wife's already down there, singing like a canary." She glanced sideways at him. "Course, if you wanna tell me about it, I can maybe work out a little something for you."

Frankie wanted to cry and scream and throw up, all at the same time. How could she think he'd fall for that trick? He'd used it often enough himself—get a perp to talk by pretending his confederate was giving him up. But what if it was true? What if María was selling him down the river even while he was being hustled into the backseat of the RMP? He wouldn't put it past her. The blood of generations of corrupt Mexican politicians ran through her veins. She had probably learned how to sell out her partner while other kids were playing hopscotch.

Within ten minutes, Frankie was being hustled toward an interrogation room in the 115th Precinct. Jackson Heights was just a stone's throw from Woodside, so it didn't take long. As he passed one of the other interrogation rooms, he glanced inside and saw his wife sitting at a table, chatting with a bunch of detectives. Her jacket was draped over her shoulders in defense against the air-conditioning, and she warmed her hands around a steaming paper cup of coffee.

"María, you bitch!" he screamed as he passed the window.

Guzman shoved him into the next room and plunked him into a hard chair. "You wanna tell me about it?" she asked, pulling out a notebook.

"You bet," Frankie said. "It was all her idea."

Guzman held up her hand. "You sure you don't want to wait for your delegate before you talk to me? You don't want me to Mirandize you?"

"Hell no!" Frankie replied. He missed the small smile that curled up at the corner of Guzman's mouth for a fleeting moment.

"Okay, then," she said. "Go ahead. I'm listening."

Officer Guzman opened the door to the neighboring interrogation room. "Thanks for coming down and waiting, María," she said. "I'm sorry. It doesn't look too good for Frankie. He's confessed to a lot of crimes, and he didn't wait for his delegate before he talked."

María shook her head. "My father told me not to marry him, but I thought I knew better. What am I going to tell the kids?"

Guzman patted her hand. "I know it looks tough now, but you'll make it through. Can you take your children to your parents' house tonight? It's only a matter of time before the press comes knocking on your door."

"That's a good idea, thanks. Does Frankie want to see me now?"

"I don't think that would be for the best. You can see him once he's booked."

María stood up. "Well. Thanks for everything."

"You're welcome. And it will all work out. You'll see."

You bet it will, María thought.

As she slid behind the wheel of her car, she mentally ran through the contents of her home office. She had packed up the laptop, scanner, and printer and stashed them in the trunk of her car as soon as Roberta Guzman called. She'd had a mental escape plan in place since the day she and Frankie had gotten involved in what she thought of as "refunding for profit."

Her family and Roberta's had been close for at least two

generations, but the two women hadn't seen each other very often since Roberta went on the job. She had let María know that she would have to take a step back because she was going to play it straight. (Roberta's family had treated her like the proverbial black sheep—*What's wrong with the girl that she isn't open to taking bribes? How could we have gone so wrong?*)

María only pretended to understand her friend's choices. She heard about Roberta's successes in the department through her parents and aunts and uncles, but like her relatives, she always puzzled over why her longtime friend would work harder than she had to.

Well, no matter. She'd held Roberta's marker from when they were teenagers. María held the key to a moment of youthful indiscretion on Roberta's part, and Roberta owed her for keeping her mouth shut. She knew she'd collect on it someday, but she'd always hoped it would be for something bigger than this harmless little scam.

She fingered the tickets in her handbag. Tomorrow morning at 6 a.m., she and the kids were taking off for a long-overdue vacation to visit relatives in Mexico. Depending on what happened with Frankie, she might just stay there.

NEW YORK DAILY NEWS
August 30, 2006

Jackson Heights, N.Y.—Roberta Guzman, an NYPD spokeswoman, revealed today that Francisco Hernandez, the police officer who was arrested last month on multiple counts of fraud and was to be prosecuted under the Federal RICO (Racketeer Influenced Corrupt Organizations) statute for conspiring with al-Qaeda terrorists to resell stolen merchandise as part of a fundraising scheme, has committed suicide while in protective custody at the federal Metropolitan Correctional Center. "Mr. Hernandez appears to have wound a bedsheet around the top bunk in his cell and used it to strangle himself," Guzman reported at a press conference late yesterday afternoon.

Other members of the alleged fraud ring include Alba Terremoto, Pedro Volcan, and Mohammed al-Yakub, who is also suspected of having links to al-Qaeda and is charged with funneling profits from illegally sold merchandise into terrorist activities.

JIHAD SUCKS; OR, THE CONVERSION OF THE JEWS

BY JILLIAN ABBOTT

Richmond Hill

Ramzi Saleh wondered how this nation had become the most powerful in the world. The despicable little urchins who turned up to harass him at Richmond Hill High, where he taught math to ninth graders, were indifferent to his lessons. They cheated him of his time on earth.

It was with no little pleasure that he contemplated being an instrument of their demise, those cocksure boys and strutting girls. Now that winter had set in and the sidewalks were treacherous with ice, he was spared the exposed flesh that assaulted him every warm day. What sort of parents let their daughters out wearing less than what would pass for acceptable underwear at home? And the boys were little better. He found their lack of modesty and wayward attitudes blasphemous.

Ramzi pulled the collar of his overcoat tight against a biting wind. Above him, the 7 train rattled by, its brakes screeching as it pulled into the Roosevelt Avenue station. Beneath his feet the sidewalk trembled. Two levels underground, a subway train, maybe the E he'd just gotten off, was pulling up or leaving.

He knew no one here, at least not in person. He kept walking, and soon caught a whiff of fennel as he approached his destination: the *paan* seller on 74th Street. It seemed that

Satan himself had a hand in his being here. How else could he explain the impulse that had propelled him to the E train? He told himself that he was going to pray, but when he got to Sutphin Boulevard, instead of leaving the station and making his way along Jamaica Avenue toward Azis's mosque tucked away on 146th Street, he'd raced onto the E, which brought him straight here to Roosevelt Avenue, Jackson Heights.

This neighborhood meant peril. At how many points along the way could he have abandoned his quest and gone to Azis's, or even home to Liberty Avenue? But now his destination was Little India. He stopped outside the *paan* shop. Why not? He'd resisted for as long as he could, but the first time he'd slid the *paan* inside his cheek to an explosion of flavor, he'd known he was lost.

He was supposed to avoid his countrymen and spend his time among the *gora*. Not that Richmond Hill was Infidel Central. But many of the Asians there were West Indians who had lived in the Caribbean for generations before coming to America. The neighborhood was mixed, not exclusive, and while the *roti* shops had few rivals, the *paan* could not compete. He should take it home. He should eat it unobserved in his recliner, but he couldn't.

At times it seemed to Ramzi that America offered nothing but temptation. Could a man be wise, let alone moral, living among such sirens? Was his sophisticated Jackson Heights palate evidence that the Great Satan had corrupted him? Perhaps he should buy two *paan*? One for now, and one he could put in the fridge for after dinner.

As he pressed toward the *paan* seller, his worst fear was realized: He recognized a man ahead of him in the line. They had been at camp together in Afghanistan. The fellow licked his lips and inched closer to the booth as if mesmerized by the vendor's red-gummed grin and nimble fingers as he smeared red *kathha* and *chuna* on a fresh betel leaf. The veins in Ramzi's neck throbbed. Even if the fellow recognized him, they would not acknowledge each other.

His breath quickened. Their time at camp was long ago, and he wondered if this man was part of the same mission? He knew little about his task other than that he was to assimilate and wait. On that glorious day of victory, when, with the rest of the world, he'd watched the Twin Towers fall, he'd hoped his time among the infidels would end. But it was not to be.

The man from camp took his *paan*, looked around with the sly delight of a thief, and, using his thumb, thrust it inside his cheek and disappeared into the throng.

The *paan* seller remembered Ramzi. "*Meetha paan*, no coconut," he said, his eyes bright with the pride of a man who knows his customers.

Despite his inward panic at being known, Ramzi smiled and nodded. "How do you do it?" he asked. "Every time, your *paan* is delicious."

"It is all in the balance of *chuna* and *kathha*," the *paan* seller said, rolling his head from side to side as he smeared a leaf with his special *masala*.

The proportion of betel nut to lime paste was crucial to a good *paan*, but Ramzi came to this fellow for his perfect *masala*—no one around mixed the spices and chutneys quite like he did. Now he behaved as if Ramzi was one of his regulars. Was that good or bad? To leave one or two footprints might be for the best. Ramzi imagined the *Queens Chronicle* story following his mission . . . They'd quote this man. *A paan seller on 74th Street described Ramzi Saleh as a polite man, quiet and predictable. "He loved my meetha paan, but it was always, 'Hold the coconut.'"* Ramzi smiled to himself. Not a bad epitaph.

He stuffed the folded packet inside his cheek and turned toward the street to watch the bustle of rush-hour traffic nudge by. The heady smells of curry leaves, cardamom, and incense wafted from the many restaurants and swirled around him. In his time at Richmond Hill High, he had not met one child—well, there was one—who was grateful for the education his cover required him to provide. His teaching was scrupulously average, he knew. His biggest challenge: to remain invisible.

He had a talent for teaching. He had been plucked from the rubble of an earthquake, all his parents' properties ruined, and had been educated by the charity of the Great Satan itself. But it had promised and not delivered. Before the earthquake his family had been among the wealthiest in the village; afterwards they had nothing. When the American aid workers left, he was no longer hungry and ignorant, he was hungry and educated.

When the *mujahideen* entered his village in western Pakistan as they fled the Russians, he had seen fear in the village elders' eyes. He had vowed to teach all who wished to learn, so that no Pakistani would ever again know ignorance and hunger, but he was still hungry himself, as were all his pupils. He craved to be the cause of that fear he saw in his elders—he saw the respect it inspired. From the day he joined the jihad, he lost the knowledge of hunger. That was nearly twenty years ago.

Saliva stimulated by the *paan* built in his mouth and he spat a stream of red liquid onto the sidewalk. Behind him a door opened and Hindi music spilled out to compete with the sounds of traffic. Ramzi's nose twitched at the blasphemy. Bloody Hindus with their Devil's music, idolatry, and fuzzy logic. *There is no God but Allah. Praise be to Allah.* And yet lounging in the street, chewing *paan*, and feeling contemptu-ously superior to Hindus brought a deep comfort and satisfac-tion to Ramzi. Oddly, it was like going home—his real home, not the squat little one-bedroom, eat-in-kitchen apartment on 115th Street off Liberty Avenue. There were Hindus in Richmond Hill, but not nearly so many. He lingered to drink in the sights of brazen, sari-clad Hindu whores, their faces fully exposed to him, and to the world.

Allah is merciful. He led Ramzi to Azis. Azis had helped him find the righteous path. At the training camp he had learned the art of destruction. The American education taught him that he would always be less than they were. When the time came he would play his part.

The earthquake had taken everything from his parents and denied him his future as a landowner. But this loss left him free for jihad. In due course, the Americans would lose their livelihoods. Husbands would lose wives, though Ramzi wondered if that would cause them pain. He doubted it. In this godforsaken nation, whores were elevated and virtuous women despised. A young girl in *salwar-kameez* skipped by clutching her mother's hand. Something about her brought back the image of his laughing sister the day before the kitchen collapsed on her, and a sharp pain stabbed at his chest as if someone had slammed a knife into his heart. Soon *their* sisters would be taken away: a mass of bloody, twisted bodies and tangled limbs all that remained.

The Great Satan was so naïve—had helped him to immi-grate when he had shown them his certificate from the Peace Corps. And now, between his salary as a teacher and his pay-ments from al-Qaeda, he would be able to take another wife, maybe two—virtuous Muslim women to keep his current wife, Fatima, company and produce more *mujahideen* for the cause.

A group of women wearing saris and *salwar-kameez* glided by. How much more beautiful and elegant than the jeans and T-shirts of Richmond Hill. He should not have come to this neighborhood. The sight of these glorious hussies stirred long-dormant yearnings in Ramzi and he silently cursed himself for giving into temptation. Tears welled in his eyes, but he steeled himself. He missed his wife and children, and understood he might not live to see them again, let alone take another wife. He had pledged his life to this holy war and would do whatever was asked.

He turned back toward the subway and headed for Azis, exchanging the noise and crush of the street for the noise and crush of Mexicans, blacks, and West Indians packed like sardines into the E. Perhaps there would be word. Perhaps today his long wait would end.

He remembered the anticipation he felt when he first arrived in Queens. Back then, he thought his mission was imminent, and he would take the stairs down from the J train two at a time in his rush to get to the mosque. Always his heart pounded in his chest as he waited for Azis. Was today the day? He would catch Azis's eye, his own face hot with anticipation, but Azis would shake his head discreetly and lower his eyes. Ramzi waited. He undertook reconnaissance as instructed. He reported to Azis. Time passed. In his daily life he was indistinguishable from every other Pakistani immigrant. Familiar, reliable, recognizable, known by no one.

He knew that he should stop by the mosque on the way home. There was no excuse. He'd be right there at Sutphin Boulevard and Jamaica Avenue. But he felt no enthusiasm, no anticipation. Jihad had become rather like his day job. He went through the motions.

By the time he got to Liberty Avenue it was dark, and

the roadway was treacherous to cross. In the shade of the elevated A line, the ice never melted, and if he slipped and fell in his haste to be out of the cold, it wouldn't be the first time. He turned onto 115th Street and climbed the steps to his front door. In his mailbox he found the usual array of bills and magazines. He clicked his tongue. What a country this was, so many magazines, so much information. The day an issue of the *Herald* arrived in his isolated village, the men would gather at the tea house and Ramzi would read it out loud. It was never less than six months out of date, but they were hungry for its wealth of knowledge.

The *Smithsonian* had arrived. He went inside and dropped into his recliner. Such luxury, if only Fatima could see his leather chair. He flipped through the magazine to examine the pictures. Then he read the headlines and breakout paragraphs. He always did this to decide the order in which he'd read the articles. Then he'd put on a pot of coffee, slide back into his recliner, and read every word. Today he broke his routine. Five pages in he found a piece on the science of biological weaponry. The infidel never tired of telling him all he needed to know. He would not rise again until he'd read it at least twice.

Ramzi Saleh basked in the fortune of having the staff room at Richmond Hill High all to himself. This was a first. The place was always overcrowded and stuffy. Heat blasted from the radiator, and the musty odor of too many bodies lingered. Ramzi headed for the coffee machine, found a clean cup—*Praise be to Allah, this is a great day*—poured his coffee, heaped in four spoons of sugar and extra cream, and made his way toward his cramped cubbyhole at the back of the room. He raised his mug in thanks for the twenty-five-percent absentee rate due to Monday flu and dropped into his chair. Just as he finished arranging his desk exactly the way he liked it—coffee on the left, pens on the right—he heard the door fly open. Too good to last. The sound of women's voices reached him over the thump and hiss of the radiator. He identified them instantly. Beryl Johnson was a science teacher; Lucy Gruber a fellow math teacher.

They kept chatting. Perhaps they couldn't see him back here.

"You're too ordinary?" Lucy said. "*Hello.* He's an assistant manager at Home Depot."

"Manager. They promoted him just before he left."

Ah, thought Ramzi, they were talking about Beryl's husband. What a scoundrel. He'd run out on her two years ago for a girl just six years older than their daughter. Why would he do such a thing? Beryl was a nice enough woman, nothing special, but for an infidel whore she had a good heart. It never ceased to surprise Ramzi the way even the most humble citizens here tried to live like movie stars—to their ruin.

He should speak up, let his presence be known, but the godless fornicators fascinated him, so he continued to eavesdrop. As they loitered by the coffee machine, Ramzi could see their bobbing shadows on the linoleum.

"It makes me sick to admit I went to an online dating site, but what could I do? I was so lonely," Beryl said, her voice choked with emotion. "I wanted someone to hold me, to be tender."

"I know," Lucy replied.

Ramzi detected a catty undertone. Beryl should hold her tongue—this Lucy was no friend, and besides, why would anyone publicize their shame in this way? Living among the godless affected him, moderating his true beliefs. He knew Beryl was contemptible, but he pitied her anyway. He had known her from his first day at this school. He had been bewildered, not knowing where to go and what to do, and Beryl had found him wandering in the corridor.

She took him to his classroom and introduced him to his students. She had a way about her that put Ramzi at ease. He felt he could talk to her about almost anything. An involuntary shudder moved through him as he thought back to that day. He had told her more about himself than he ever meant to. After that, she had adopted him, helping him become part of the school community, helping him to follow his prime directive: *Blend in, attract no notice.*

"This isn't the place. We can't talk here, someone might overhear," Beryl said.

Ramzi scrunched himself up as small as he could, even gritting his teeth and grimacing like a kid trying to make himself invisible. He didn't dare look in their direction.

"Look. It's empty—not a soul here. Come on, you're going to crack up if you don't tell someone."

"I'm so ashamed," Beryl said between sobs. "When I started it wasn't so bad. I mean, I thought it was terrible, those boring dates with fat guys. But this one, Mike, he didn't just rape me, he beat the hell out of me, and then robbed me."

"You should have said something. When was this?"

Ramzi craned his neck in their direction to hear better.

"The beginning of summer. The marks faded just in time for the start of school in September." Beryl's sobs drowned out the wheezing radiator.

Lucy responded with those little clucking noises women make when they comfort each other. The thought of someone raping Beryl brought heat to Ramzi's cheeks. Who would do such a thing? Beryl's rape caused him a dilemma. Yes, he knew the infidel whore deserved what she got—she was divorced, a matter of shame for any decent Muslim woman.

She had brought shame to her whole family, in fact. Yet Beryl was kind, and raised her children with no help from their father. Though jihad had separated him from his Fatima, she was provided for and had staff to help run the household. If he died in jihad, she would be taken care of, and if, Allah forbid, he fell out with Azis, he had paid a great uncle in Karachi enough to ensure she would disappear and be safe. But no one was there for Beryl. Ramzi struggled for control of his mind. He must banish thoughts of Beryl's goodness. Her loneliness presented him with an opportunity. Her fate was in Allah's hands.

"But what was the alternative? I was lonely. Do you know how many single women there are out there? I didn't stand a chance. Who'd look at me?" Beryl said, a bitter edge to her voice.

Ramzi had looked closely at Beryl when they first met, and he liked what he saw. Though a bit older than he, she was still a handsome woman. Rich, black hair (although he knew it was probably dyed, as all of the women in this country colored their hair), complemented by deep blue eyes. A soft face, lines around the eyes and mouth. To him the lines indicated character.

Beryl had a lush figure, and this was so much more appealing than the skinny, barren women so highly prized here. American women were either stick-thin or waddling giants. The women of Islam were robust and fertile.

Beryl blew her nose loudly, bringing Ramzi back to the present. He struggled to keep his breath even, to remain undetected. Before either spoke again, the school bell went off. The room would be crowded within minutes.

"Come on," Lucy said. "Let's get out of here."

He heard the door flung open. Teachers flooded into the

room, talking, laughing, heading for their desks. Ramzi, with two free periods back-to-back, waited until the room filled up to slip out.

Ramzi kneeled on the carpet in the corner of the large prayer room at the mosque. Azis, his imam, kneeled next to him, smiled indulgently, and took Ramzi's hand in his. The warmth and strength of Azis's touch comforted Ramzi.

Ramzi guessed the imam was in his mid-forties, the wiry black beard showing streaks of gray. Azis's leathery skin fit tight over his facial bones, a result of early deprivation, a testament to years of living in the harsh light of Pakistan's mountains. He had a cruel mouth and Ramzi was pleased he could not see Azis's eyes. The times when he had, he'd been unnerved by the black void that stared back at him. *Warm hands, cold heart.*

"I'm confused," Ramzi said, searching the room with his eyes. It was empty but for the rich, blood-red carpet and three low squat desks along the opposite wall. The faint odor of working men emanated from the worn rug.

Azis stroked the back of Ramzi's hand with his index finger. Ramzi watched this, and for the first time in his life he felt uncomfortable with the physicality of it. Among the people of the Great Satan, when one man touched another it led to the abomination of homosexuality. But in Pakistan, men never hesitated to express their affection and concern for one another in this way. Watching Azis's hand, Ramzi wondered if this was how Adam felt once he had eaten from the forbidden tree. The Great Satan corrupted all that was good, even to the point of undermining the purity of his contact with Azis.

"If your feelings for this woman are strong, you should take her," Azis counseled, "but remember that Americans pride themselves on turning their wives and daughters into whores, and that any goodness you see in her is an illusion. This woman, the Jew, Beryl, is a whore."

Ramzi glanced then at Azis. Being an imam had freed Azis from the need to assimilate. The infidel seemed to expect him to retain his ethnicity, and he hadn't disappointed. His perfectly white turban was arranged so skillfully it appeared to be an extension of his brow. Azis wore a long beard which extended to his ears. He shaved it almost to the edge of his jaw line, leaving his face exposed and causing the beard to jut out at an angle from his chin that gave Ramzi the impression that Azis's face grew out of his facial hair instead of the other way around. Azis shifted slightly and the glare left the bifocals he habitually wore. Ramzi saw that Azis was contemplating him fondly.

Ramzi turned his hand over, allowing him to wrap his fingers around Azis's. Why had he doubted? He let his breath out and with it went his anxiety about Beryl. *Allah is all-knowing.* Azis was wise indeed. Richmond Hill High bragged at its role in producing fallen women. Mae West and Cyndi Lauper were two of its proudest alumni. He need not fear becoming too involved with the hussy, Beryl.

He smiled at Azis, who smiled back.

"You came to me with the idea to take this Jew woman. It is a good idea. It will deepen your cover, and I see in your eyes you know it is right. Now that you are sure, there are things I must tell you, things you need to know about these fornicating She-Devils . . ."

A week later, Ramzi waited by the staff room door. "Heading out?" he asked, trying to sound casual when he saw Beryl. He fell in with her as she left for the day. When he pushed the door open for her, his jaw was tight and his stomach fluttered. It was ridiculous; he was forty years old, after all. Beryl wore a tight skirt and a low-cut blouse, and as she sauntered along beside him her coat flared open revealing cleavage. Ramzi looked away discreetly. "How's it going?" he asked.

"Not bad. How are you doing with 9B? Have they settled down?"

"Yes, thanks to you. You told me to get on top of Kasan and you were right. Once he was under control the others fell in line."

Beryl grinned. "He's a tough customer that one. Way too big and strong for his years. His father is in the Russian mafia."

Ramzi raised his eyebrows and shook his head as if he were shocked, although he knew all about Kasan's connections.

Beryl's heels clicked pleasantly to the end of the hallway and then stopped as she paused inside the door to do up her coat. Their eyes met and Ramzi smiled at her. He felt a pang of guilt. But why? Beryl was an infidel hussy, and he had Azis's dispensation. Ramzi opened the outside door and held it for her. As Beryl passed him, he caught a whiff of perfume. It brought to mind lilacs and spring.

The air was frigid, turning their breath into clouds of vapor. Azis's warning haunted him. He caught himself staring at Beryl. He blushed and forced himself to focus on the ground as they walked in silence to her car. The moody sky threatened snow, and it would be dark by 4:30 p.m. Beryl drew her scarf tight around her neck. Her cheeks, ears, and the tip of her nose had turned red; her beauty made him ache. If her husband were a real man, if he'd stuck by his wife, then Ramzi could never have contemplated using her in this way. The thought that it was Jeff's fault, not his, comforted him.

Taking a woman would help deepen his cover. Handled

correctly, it would make him even more invisible. Beside an American woman, his surveillance wouldn't draw suspicion. And there were other benefits. He could go to the beach and to the Museum of Natural History and all the other places in New York he wanted to see, but felt too conspicuous to go alone.

Beryl pushed the key into her car door. It was now or never. He cleared his throat.

"Beryl, would you do me the honor of accompanying me to dinner and a movie this Saturday night?"

She looked confused, then slightly amused—he had been too formal, he knew. He had met Fatima on their wedding day; today was the first time in his life he had asked a woman out. He was more nervous than he expected to be and cursed himself for this.

She smiled. "Dinner and a movie. Why not?"

It was all Ramzi could do not to high-five her.

Ramzi swept inside the mosque amid a flurry of coats and scarves and wet umbrellas. Azis stood against the wall surrounded by his followers. Ramzi tried to control his expression. He wanted to appear his usual calm self but his emotions were in turmoil. He raised his eyebrows in inquiry when he caught the imam's eye. Azis shook his head and lowered his gaze.

Back on the street, Ramzi realized Beryl's acceptance had left him cranky. A woman her age shouldn't be dating at all. Azis had not only approved his plan to take a woman, he had encouraged it. But now Ramzi no longer wanted to go through with it.

The wind picked up, and icy needles attacked his exposed cheeks. He moved quickly and almost went flying when his foot hit ice and shot out in front of him. By the time he got to his apartment, he was moving at a steady trot. He paused on his stoop, ripped open his mailbox, and flipped through the contents. He sweated and his legs twitched from the run. What must it feel like? His breathing didn't slow even though he'd been still for several minutes. To his eternal shame, there was movement in his trousers. He must complete his mission and leave this country. But first, dinner and a movie with Beryl.

Ramzi squeezed Beryl's hand. To think he'd once dreaded dating her. She had become as familiar to him as his leather recliner. Today she wore her cobalt-blue jacket open, revealing a long-sleeved T-shirt that looked perfect with her jeans and sneakers.

He parked on Utopia Parkway near the off-ramp of the Cross Island Parkway. Behind them was an entrance to Little Bay Park that followed the water's edge to Fort Totten and then on to the Bayside Marina. On his first visit he had discovered that if you keep walking south, the path leads beneath the Long Island Rail Road and up onto Northern Boulevard.

He got out of the car, opened the trunk, and grabbed a picnic basket and blanket. Beryl scanned for the entrance. Along the road, just inside the park, was a dark wooded area where the spring grass was unkempt, and several ragged trees made it seem unwelcoming.

"Follow me," Ramzi said. He headed back up toward the off-ramp and waited for her by two rectangular brick piles that marked the entry to the park. "This is the back way, but you get a nice view of the bridge and water."

"How do you know so many beautiful places? I've lived in Queens all my life and I never knew this was here," Beryl said.

As they entered the park, Ramzi touched his finger to

his lip to silence her. A crumbling concrete trail began at the entrance, but petered out within fifty yards of the gate, leaving them to walk through grass. Ramzi breathed in the scent. Fresh cut grass, blossoms, and manure, it all added up to spring. It was barely April, but the forecast said seventy, and already it was warm and sunny. The sky was the richest blue, and the water, though grayish-green, was mirror-still, reflecting the bridge.

"I came from the mountains in what is almost desert, not this lush green and expanse of water," he said by way of explanation.

Had he made a mistake? Yes, it was a good idea to use this woman for cover, but he should have chosen a more brazen, less likeable one. It was a constant struggle to keep her at a distance. It troubled him. He had to remind himself this was a She-Devil, however kind, and that he was performing his duty to Allah by deceiving her. But he couldn't banish the thought that she was a good woman trapped in an evil culture. He felt her round hip rub against his, and despite himself he was aroused. The first time they'd slept together he'd been terrified. He had listened to Azis's warning, and read *New York* magazine every week. The sexual habits of New Yorkers repelled, yet fascinated him.

He had been content with his wife. In truth, sex wasn't something he'd given much thought to before coming to live in Queens. Americans seemed obsessed with it, as if it were the most important thing in the world. It was true that he enjoyed sex. When he and Fatima did it, he felt close and safe. No one in Pakistan ever talked about love. That was something for the blasphemers of Bollywood to churn out in their endless stream of movies. Seeing Fatima was often accompanied by a feeling of warmth and longing, and if he'd ever given it any thought, he'd have been happy to call that love.

Beryl turned to him and smiled. He knew she looked forward to these outings. She'd lost fifteen pounds from the exercise and claimed to be fitter than she'd been in years. Even in winter, Ramzi had led her along the water's edge, although one day in early March he'd had to abandon his plans because the path was slick with ice. Instead, he'd taken her on a luxury water cruise. He felt a twinge of guilt when he remembered Beryl that night—giggling like a schoolgirl, posing for his pictures. She couldn't have guessed that the true subject of those photos were the bridges and buildings and port facilities in the background. He'd taken enough photos to fill a 256MB memory card. Their expeditions became more frequent as the weather warmed up. They'd explored the whole length of the Long Island waterfront from the Brooklyn Bridge to today's outing at the Throgs Neck Bridge.

"What's that?" Ramzi asked, pointing to a chicken-wire enclosure about the size of a residential building block.

The park was crowded with people, some lone walkers, some in groups, and some on bicycles. The slope down to the water was dotted with sunbathers who had dragged fold-up chairs to the park and sprawled in their swimsuits. Two women in leotards power-walked, while another couple glided by on rollerblades. Inside the enclosure he'd pointed at, the grass had been worn to dirt. It was mobbed with people and dogs, and the stench of animal excrement, fur, dog breath, and urine wafted from it.

"It's a dog run."

"A what?"

"A dog run. In New York City you have to keep your dog leashed most of the time. Inside *that*, you can let it run free."

"Really?" Ramzi was appalled: In his country, dogs were

rabid curs. Here they were more pampered than children.

They made their way down the gentle, sloping lawn toward the path, and met up with it under the bridge's pylons. The tide was low and the air had a decidedly fishy tinge to it.

"Look at this bridge," he said. "What a magnificent achievement. Look at the pylons, they're solid. And the cables could hold it up on their own."

"I suppose I should be grateful we're not discussing piston engines," Beryl said.

Ramzi turned his attention from the bridge to his companion. He glared at her. "You know how much I admire these bridges, not just the engineering either, they are magnificent." He slid his arm around her. They passed under the bridge and beside some soccer fields where elementary and middle school children battled it out. The shouts from the parents fought with the noise of the traffic on the bridge overhead.

Ramzi's mission loomed before him, and the thought of it filled him with dread. The longer he stayed here, the harder it was to maintain his rage. Jihad had saved him from shiftlessness and had given him direction. Of course, he despised Beryl, but until he started to date her he hadn't realized how much he missed a woman's touch. Then, despite himself, Beryl had begun to mean something to him. In time, he began to know the infidel, and had developed a liking for many of them.

Beryl's hand crept around his waist and she kissed his cheek as they strolled along. At the same time, he was fully cognizant that a war was being fought and he had chosen a side. Beryl was a weapon the Great Satan had abandoned in the field. He had merely picked it up where it lay and was putting it to good use.

They rounded a bend. "Let's look for a place to eat," Beryl said. There was a hilly section where man-made mounds of earth had long since become part of the landscape; grass and trees grew on them.

"Let's eat up there on the plateau," he suggested. "That way you can watch the view and I can watch the soccer." Ramzi laid out the blanket and Beryl spread the food on it. She'd made sandwiches, brought sodas, and packed grapes into Ziploc bags. She'd gotten used to Ramzi not drinking alcohol, and had given it up herself. For dessert, she'd bought a pie at The Stork in College Point.

After they ate, Ramzi lay his head on her lap and stared at the sky. Several trees were just coming into blossom and filled the air with a heady but pleasant scent. Immediately, an image of Beryl on her knees before him, her mouth clamped firmly around his penis, came to mind. He remembered the fear he felt when she did it the first time. Ramzi had never hit a woman, but looking down on Beryl's soft, shiny hair, her head bobbing at his crotch, he wanted to knock her across the room and scream, *Have you no pride, woman? No fear of God?*

Azis had given Ramzi absolution when he first warned him this would happen. They had prayed together. In the end, Ramzi grew too ashamed to face Azis. Perhaps God would forgive him. After all, he had submitted to serve Allah. But Beryl would go to Hell.

He feared telling Azis the worst. This abomination had given him the most intense pleasure of his life, while the shame crushed him. How could he ever speak with a decent Muslim woman again? Azis's dispensation meant nothing. He was tainted, dirty, and the shame of it would never leave him.

"It's so beautiful, isn't it?" Beryl said.

He turned his face toward hers and hoped his anguish didn't show. "Not compared to you."

"Flatterer."

"Truthteller."

"You *are* free next Sunday, right? There's no reason to miss my mother's party. You'll enjoy it, it's a fundraiser for the Jewish orphans of Kazakhstan. That's your part of the world."

Ramzi didn't bother to hide his annoyance. "Oh yes, Pakistani Muslims and Kazakh Jews, we are almost brothers. And clearly we all look the same to the Jews of Scarsdale, New York." He had bolted upright, his muscles tense and his neck throbbing.

"Oh Ramzi, this is America, that sort of thing doesn't matter. Besides, the only religion I've seen you practice is the same one I do—lapsed. Lapsed Jew, lapsed Muslim, what's the difference?"

Ramzi had no retort. In truth, he could not be bothered to find one.

"She wants to raise money to bring the orphans here for six months to get the medical help they need and to learn English, math, and Hebrew so they might get a better start in Israel. My mother's getting on. She thought maybe you could teach them. We both could. Maybe we could move in with her and look after her and teach the Kazakh children. You speak Aramaic."

"How do you know I speak Aramaic?"

"You told me, remember? The first day at school when you were lost and I told you some of our students were from central Asia."

He'd forgotten. What other lapses was he guilty of? It was all too much for him. Great *levivot* and *off tapuzim* to die for was one thing, but no amount of knish was sufficient to entice him to embrace the Jews, except for Beryl, of course. Then Ramzi had the merest glimmer of a thought.

"All right already," he said, taking pride in his mastery of

New York speak, "I'll come to the party. But only if you let me take your picture."

Beryl laughed good-naturedly.

"Stand here," he said, positioning her so that his shots would take in the undercarriage of the bridge.

While she fussed and clucked over her hair, he took a dozen photos, from all angles. Beryl wasn't in half of them.

As Ramzi walked home on Liberty Avenue that same evening, he spied standing in a doorway the same man he'd recognized so many weeks ago at the *paan* sellers. As their eyes met, the man left the cover of the storefront and slowly approached, his right hand inside his overcoat even though it was much too warm to be dressed that way.

The man was called Mohammed, Ramzi recalled in a flash. He had been foolish and naïve to think he could avoid Azis. He would not get away that easily. The best he could hope for was that Mohammed had come to question his absence from the mosque. Mohammed's expression gave Ramzi little reason to hope for the best. If he made a run for it now, he would die. He would never see Beryl again. Then he admitted the truth to himself: He had abandoned jihad. He was a changed man, an infidel, a fornicator. He wanted to live.

"There is no God but Allah. Praise be to Allah," Ramzi said in greeting.

"The true believers are those only who believe in Allah and His messenger and afterward doubt not, but strive with their wealth and their lives for the cause of Allah. Such are the sincere," Mohammed said, closing the distance between them.

Ramzi knew the quote from the Qur'an, and the guilt it produced in him squeezed his chest like a vice. At first he thought to reply: *Allah, most gracious, most merciful,* but that implied a certain culpability, and so instead he said, "Allah is all-knowing, all-aware."

He approached Mohammed, careful to keep his movements steady and nonthreatening.

Mohammed's face flashed uncertainty, and taking advantage of this brief moment, Ramzi added, "I have taken a woman." His tone meant to convey that this explained everything.

"A Jew," Mohammed said, his mouth pulled tight with contempt.

"A whore," Ramzi agreed, although it pained him to speak the words. "A controlling She-Devil to whom I must account for my every movement. And yet, Azis knows the value of the hussy and encouraged me to take her."

"No man cowers before a woman. What have you become?" Mohammed's small eyes narrowed to slits and his glare felt like a laser beam slicing into Ramzi. He moved toward Ramzi.

"I serve Allah through jihad. That is who I am," Ramzi said, standing very still. He hung his head as if the shame of his dalliance with Beryl was tangible weight.

"You are a favorite with Azis. I have seen him have a man killed for less than what you have done. I would be happy to oblige my imam should he change his mind. You are expected at the mosque tomorrow at 4:00 p.m. Fail to come and I will be given my chance." He took two more steps toward Ramzi, meeting him head on, then sidestepped and walked past.

When Ramzi was sure Mohammed had gone, he headed up the stairs to his apartment. As he put keys to the lock, he caught the end of a message being recorded on his answering machine. *"I know you're probably tired but I've got to run a bunch of chairs and plates and flatware over to my mother's. You wouldn't help, would you? I could really use you."*

Ramzi dashed into the apartment and grabbed the phone. Life was mysterious, and he, merely a fallen leaf tossed and blown on the wind. "Beryl, my love, of course I will. And why don't we visit awhile?"

Had it really been six months since his meeting with Mohammed? The first class of Kazakh orphans were about to graduate. As they fed the pet rabbits and turtles kept at the school behind the Chabad, he realized he'd grown quite fond of them, and was sad to think they'd soon be leaving for Israel. What a pleasure to teach children so hungry to learn.

He glanced up as Beryl entered the classroom. She leaned against the blackboard beside him and smiled at the children. He wanted to slide his arm around her but knew he couldn't do that in front of the orphans. He stroked his beard. He'd been surprised by how quickly it had grown in. He'd dyed all of his hair silver, making him look at least fifteen years older than he was. This may be America, but he still equated age with wisdom, and was happy to think of himself as growing wise.

"Almost done?" Beryl asked.

He nodded.

"Good. Mom's cooking up a storm. She loves you . . . almost as much as I do."

Ramzi's world had shrunk in the relocation. He felt safe here, and he kept to the neighborhood. He walked each day from Beryl's mother's house, which was now his home, to the Chabad and back, occasionally stopping at the local deli to pick something up for the evening meal. Except perhaps for the *paan*, he didn't miss his old life at all. Beryl was due to move in with him when school ended in June, and he looked forward to that.

It was Hanukkah and the menorah would be lit tonight. As with many converts, the rituals of Judaism seemed to have more meaning for him than for those who'd practiced from birth. Most of all, he was looking forward to Gloria's (he had begun calling Beryl's mom by her first name) famous *levivot* and applesauce.

The last few orphans left the room and he took Beryl's hand as they strolled home to Gloria's, the chill air turning Beryl's nose bright red.

THE INVESTIGATION

BY BELINDA FARLEY

Jamaica

So Edwin Stuckey had *not* believed in miracles. Couldn't
have. By the third hour of services at the Crusading
Home of Deliverance in southeastern Queens—when
the bellow of the preacher rang out like a toll that beckoned
to repent and reform, and the congregation of twenty-eight
had sprung to their feet in a fervor—I, who had so often
scoffed at organized religion, was on my feet as well. All
about me, the jiggle-jangle of tambourines being slapped on
open palms reverberated. Shouted *hallelujahs* stung my ear-
drums. Tears were shed; wails directed heavenward. Was I
praying?

I should've been taking notes.

Instead, I now found myself exercising total recall on the
F train. It had been a week since the call had come in on the
police scanner: a "1010" announcing a possible death at Guy R.
Brewer Boulevard and 108th Avenue. I was a reporter, a novice in the newsroom of a weekly in Richmond Hill, where the
Maple Grove Cemetery kept us a safe distance from Jamaica, the
neighborhood of this particular call. Jamaica, Queens intimi-
dated the other staff reporters—all four of whom were white—
for no other reason than its inhabitants were largely black, and
so we tended not to report there. The paper was a rag anyway,
housed in bright yellow corner boxes and valued mainly for its
classifieds. I worked there to prove to my folks that the money

they'd shelled out for my J-school tuition hadn't been a complete waste.

I still lived with my parents, and a great aunt, in a Brooklyn brownstone that had been in my family for three generations. I'd been happy there. We were privileged upper-middle class, or, rather, my parents were, being members of fraternal organizations, committees, and social clubs with established roots in the African-American community of Bedford-Stuyvesant. Despite my precarious employment, I was still considered a catch within my circle; I'd escorted no less than three females to their debutante balls. I supposed that sooner or later I'd have had enough of my journalism career and would join an uncle on Wall Street.

The call came in while I was alone in the office. Later—when things had run their course—I thought of a photograph that I had tacked to the wall in my college dorm.

The picture showed a house on a hill in Hollywood, California, circa 1962. It was taken by Diane Arbus, so, of course, it looked like no other house on a hill in Hollywood, or anywhere else. The hill was all tangled vine and bare tree limb, and the house was appropriately dark and stoic, and made of cardboard. It was a prop. But the sky above it was lovely. Who, what, when, where, why, and how: No photo—or story, for that matter—ever told the *whole* truth. The most important lesson I learned in J-school.

There was no ambulance nor squad car at the scene when I arrived. I didn't feel too confident as I rapped on the door of the modest wood-frame house. You could feel on the street that the neighborhood was tight: Loungers on their front porches eyed my unfamiliar self with suspicion. But I needed to get a byline under my belt.

"Yes?" The door swung open immediately and a man who

appeared to be in his late fifties eyed me over his glasses.

"Evening, uh, morning, sir," I stammered, to no acknowledgment. I hoped I wasn't too late. "I'm a reporter for the—"

"Who is it, Gershorn?" A thick, squat woman with a hairdo that looked as if it had been roller-set for two days appeared at the man's side. With her elaborate coif, and skin the color of a gingersnap, she could've been an aged starlet. In reality, she was a housewife, as evidenced by the formality of an apron tied over her blue housecoat.

The man bristled. "We were expecting someone, but not you," he said. "What is your business here, young man?"

Where the skin of the woman remained taut and unlined and shone with the assistance of petroleum jelly, every second thought and hardship that had ever befallen the man was noted in some wrinkle or frown line that caused his face to sag like a deflated mahogany balloon. His gray hair was coiled in tight, generous ringlets on his scalp. He was tall, standing nearly two heads above her.

"I'm Doug, Douglass Nichols, and I'm a reporter for the *Weekly Item*." I extended my hand. "I'm responding to a call that came over our police scanner regarding a possible death . . . ?"

The man stared at me blankly. He did not shake my hand. I glanced at my notepad to confirm the address.

"Sir, was there an incident here tonight? The police came?"

The man contemplated my question before opening the door to me. "A crime, young man, not an incident. Come in."

I stepped inside. He closed the door behind me and clasped his hands behind his back.

"Claudette," he called to the woman. "Tea. Tea for our guest."

In no time at all the woman reappeared with a lone cup on a saucer, which she extended to me. I balanced it on my notepad. The man motioned for me to take a seat.

On either side of the doorway stood a pair of ivory ceramic Rottweilers like sentinels. Potted plants generously dotted the living space, barely allowing me room to sit down upon a brocaded sofa sheathed in plastic. It was positioned between two end tables that supported lamps bearing shades of heavily braided fringe that must have smoldered every time the light was switched on.

The walls were teal; the lamps were gold. I committed the room to memory, to be described later in my story.

"Do you take sugar?" the woman asked haltingly.

I shook my head.

The man sat down beside me, and the woman took a seat across the room at a dining room set of heroic proportion. It spoke of some other time—a time in which there were castles and feudal systems—with elaborate inlaid carvings, mounted on claw feet. An unframed oil painting of a Caribbean landscape hung above it.

"The Bel-Air Mountains, yes," the man nodded approvingly as I studied the painting. "That was once the view from my own window. See there?" He rose to his feet and approached the image, pointing. "Those mules, those pigs foraging in the garbage pits? Those palms, those coconuts? Is all Haiti. Is my home."

He turned to face me, scrutinizing me.

"I am Mr. Stuckey," he said finally. "And this is Mrs. Stuckey."

I nodded and waited for him to continue. He did not.

"You say your son was murdered," I ventured.

Mr. Stuckey nodded, satisfied with my inquiry. "In that

room, there." He pointed down a darkened hallway.

Now it was my turn to give him the eye. *What's going on here?*

Noting my skepticism, the man rose to his feet. "Follow me."

Midway down the hall, he paused and flicked on a light switch. A door stood open adjacent to it, though the other doors on either side of the room were closed. Warily, I peered into what appeared to be a child's bedroom or, rather, the room of an adolescent boy. It was painted a dense, cornflower blue, and decorated with outdated pop culture posters. A large, weathered Table of Periodic Elements hung on one wall, attached with brittle and yellowed tape.

"That once was mine," Mr. Stuckey noted proudly, indicating the poster. "When I was a boy, it hung in the classroom of my secondary school, the Petion National Lycée." His back stiffened with pride at the mention of the name. "It was given to me by the headmaster, a gift. I was to be a great scientist, then." He paused. "As was Edwin too."

The room was small. Shoved under a window that opened onto brick was an unmade twin bed, and not two steps from it stood a modest desk, bowed by a stack of books whose titles were turned away from me. A boom box also sat perched atop the desk, and there—*How had I not seen that!*—rested an overturned chair and a noose hanging limply from a light fixture above it.

"*Jesus!*" I stepped backward and clutched the doorframe in reflex.

"Yes," Mr. Stuckey nodded solemnly. "My son was murdered right here. He was twenty-two years old."

"Same age as me," I whispered.

Mr. Stuckey turned off the light and we returned to the

front of the house in silence. I took my seat back on the couch. My tea had grown cold.

"You will help us?" Mrs. Stuckey piped up.

"What time did the police arrive tonight?" I asked, pen poised to record the details in my notepad.

"The police," she clucked dismissively with a wave of her hand.

"The police do not come here anymore," Mr. Stuckey added.

Anymore? "Were you home then, when the intruder broke in?"

"The intruder was already here," Mr. Stuckey corrected.

"So there *are* suspects?"

"Oh," he nodded enthusiastically, "there are suspects."

"Nice," I added, in spite of myself. "If you could give me a list of the names you gave to the police . . ."

"The last time the police were here, they took no names. No. Nothing from us," Mrs. Stuckey fumed.

The last time? "The last time this evening, the last time . . . ?"

"The last time one month ago," Mr. Stuckey said stoically.

"A month ago?" I closed my notepad. "Sir, listen. I'm not sure what exactly is going on here, or what it is you want me to—" I fell silent as I shifted my position on the sofa, making sure that I had all of my belongings. The Stuckeys looked at me helplessly, and I was beginning to feel spooked.

At that, a girl stepped into the room from the hallway.

"I'll talk to him, Papa," she said. "I'll tell him what he needs to know." The girl was brazen. She stood with her hand on one hip, and she blinked her eyelashes once she was done taking me in. She wore denim cutoffs and a T-shirt that was knotted tightly in the center of her back. Her speech was not the patois of her West Indian parents, who only nodded as she signaled me with a beckoning finger to the door.

Once we stepped off the porch, she immediately lit a cigarette. "I heard everything," she said, exhaling.

"I'm a reporter for the—"

"I said *everything*." She rolled her eyes. "Walk with me."

The girl pirouetted gracefully as a ballerina and took off down the block. She was short, like her mother, barely over five feet, and though I was nearly six feet, I had to jog to keep up with her.

"So, you from around here?" I asked, falling back on my usual opening line. *Dumb! Some reporter I was, but I didn't know where to begin with this girl.* I was ecstatic just to be walking with her. In an instant, my street cred had risen to the umpteenth degree, and the few brothers hanging out seemed to be getting a kick out of watching a dude like me, in my skippies and Polo, pursuing a sister like her, whose mane of naturally red ringlets blew behind her like a superhero's cape.

She didn't respond to my lame attempts at flirting, and we walked along Jamaica Avenue in silence, passing the gated entrances of fast-food restaurants, 99-cent stores, and discount clothing outlets with names like Foxy Lady and Tic Tock. The sky above us had a chunky, textured look about it; mounds of cloud clung stubbornly to the midnight blue, as often happened after a storm. It had been an uncharacteristically stormy summer. A crushed can of Colt 45, however, still balanced precariously on the fence post of King's Manor.

"I don't know why people drink that swill!" I knocked the can over in an attempt at irreverence, accidentally splashing my sneakers with stale beer. *Shit.*

The girl led me a little further to a Salvadoran café with Christmas bulbs and plastic flowers in its window.

"I'm Janette," she said, as we slid into an upholstered booth.

"Dougie," I grinned.

"Dougie, huh? That's cute." She drummed her fingernails on the table between us. "I hate that you can't smoke anywhere anymore."

"Been smoking long?"

"Since I was thirteen."

"Nasty habit."

She raised an eyebrow and pursed her lips. I ordered beer for both of us. Music and words incomprehensible to me floated from a juke box somewhere in the place.

"My brother committed suicide," Janette said suddenly. My beer caught in my throat and a bit of it dribbled down my chin. "You're conducting an investigation here, right?"

"Yeah, but—"

"So, here." Janette reached into her back pocket and shot a scrap of paper across the table at me. "That's the name of the detective."

"Detective?"

She shook her head at me in disbelief. "What the fuck? Are you a reporter or what?" She rolled her eyes. "The detective working my brother's case, you moron."

"Right, right." I took a pull on the neck of my beer, trying to recover. "Here's the thing," I said, leaning toward her across the table. "Your pops said this happened a month ago."

"A little less than a month ago. We're just really stressed about how long all this is taking, you know?"

"Right, but a month ago?" I sit up straight. "A month ago is not a story today. After a month, there's no story. I'm sorry."

"But my brother is dead." Janette's aggressive demeanor crumbled.

"You're talking suicide here." I shook my head sympa-thetically. "That's tragic, but I can tell you straight up: If your brother chose to kill himself, we ain't gonna run it in the paper now, know what I mean?"

"My brother did not choose to kill himself." Janette's eyes flashed angrily.

"What are you saying?"

"I'm saying, call the detective."

"Wait." I wave the waiter over for another round. "If you already have a detective working the case, why the call on the scanner?"

Janette ignored my question and turned to the waiter. "I'll have a Jack and ginger."

"And," I continued, "if you already know he took his own life, why not just grieve and clean out that bedroom and move on?"

She remained silent.

"I'm sorry. I didn't mean to offend you."

"I'm not offended," she shrugged. "Your questions are valid."

"Any answers?"

"If I had answers, would I be sitting here talking to you?" She smiled slyly. "I think not."

I never cared for police precincts. Not that I'd had much ex-perience with them.

Occasionally, I was sent to the local station house to clarify a fuzzy docket that'd come over the teletype, but the officers always seemed less than welcoming. I usually got out of there as soon as I could, which was what I intended the afternoon following my interview with Janette. In a moment of hopeful lust, I'd promised I would speak to this Detective Spurlock, and she, in turn, promised she'd speak to me again. So here I was in the 103rd Precinct at the detective squad.

"Come on back." Detective Spurlock motioned toward one cluttered desk among many. With a swish of a burly arm, he cleared a chair of paperwork for me to sit. "You got good timing, kid. Caught me right before sign-out. Minute later, I'd a been gone for the night . . . Coffee?"

I glanced over his shoulder at a stained-glass pot that contained what looked to be black sludge. "No thanks."

"Smart," he shrugged, sipping boldly from a chipped mug. "What can I do for you?"

"I'm here about the Stuckey case."

"The Stuckeys." Spurlock ran a pink hand through a thick head of white hair. "Listen, I don't know what your connection to this family is, but—"

"I'm a reporter for the *Weekly Item*," I interrupted.

"That so?" He nodded. "Well, good luck. Once they've got your number, you're getting no peace from then on. My advice: Steer clear. There's no story there."

"That's what I'm thinking too, but if there was," I lean in, "what would it be?"

Spurlock furrowed his brow. "Meaning?"

"The parents seem to think their son was murdered."

"Okay, kid, I'll indulge you, I've got nothing but time, right?" He shuffled through a stack of bulging file folders before selecting the thinnest one. "Here we go." He took a swig from his mug and whipped on his reading glasses. *"Edwin Stuckey, age twenty-two, found hanged in his own bedroom, March 2."* He paused at the date, gave me the once-over, continued reading from his notes. *"Apparent suicide, no suspicious circumstances,* blah, blah, case closed."

Spurlock sat back in his chair and folded his arms across his chest.

"Wait a minute." I flipped through my own notebook. "If you began your investigation on March 2, why did the call come over my scanner just two days ago?"

"Ahh," the detective laughed. "They won't stop, these people. I closed this case one week after it happened, and they've been phoning 911 ever since." He shook his head. "Hell, I'd arrest the two of them for Aggravated Harassment if it weren't so damn sad."

"So there's nothing? Nothing to suggest the murder that the family thinks occurred?"

"Nope." Spurlock reopened the folder and flipped through the paperwork. "The sister gave me a couple a names of some friends of his, who turned out not to be friends at all. The boy didn't have any friends." He handed me the list. "Church members. A bit too pious for my tastes, but hey, to each his own." He closed the folder and switched off his desk lamp. "Like I said: case closed."

Of course, there was no story. But I went ahead and crafted a lead and pitched it to my editor.

> *Jamaica, Queens—A twenty-two-year-old man was found hanged in his bedroom under mysterious circumstances. Family members suspect foul play.*

He glanced at it before tossing it aside. "We don't do suicides."

Still, I wanted to see Janette again. I steeled myself for the journey. It took me nearly two hours: the F train, then the Q76 bus to the end of the line. The bus wove its way down residential streets before groaning to a halt at the concrete 165th Street terminal in Jamaica, Queens.

It was bedlam. Greyhound on crack. People mobbed each designated bus slot, frantically directing the drivers into their respective spaces. An open, buzzing vegetable market operated behind the commuters, and as the day was a hot one, clouds of flies swarmed crates of long onions and collard greens. An old woman wearing a hairnet sat on a folding chair selling spices and exotic remedies sealed in plastic baggies. There was too much going on here; I was used to separation: a bus terminal being a bus terminal, a vegetable market being a vegetable market. Here, in Janette's neighborhood, everything was everything all at once.

I cut behind the terminal through the Colosseum Mall and down tight aisles displaying brightly colored skirts and cell phone accessories. Out on the other side stood the First Presbyterian Church of Jamaica; Edwin's funeral had been held there.

"Yo, man, you good?" A guy about my age peered at me from beneath an open car hood.

"What? Oh, yeah man, yeah." I kept moving.

Jamaica Avenue, almost there. On the "Ave," all the girls resembled Janette, with their manicured hands, toes, and eyebrows. Women sashayed bare-legged, wearing tight clothes; streaked, braided hairdos; metallic purses; chatting casually on headsets while munching on meat kebobs and cubes of sugared coconut.

I was tripping.

"Help? A little help?" A thin, thin, thin woman with a red cap pulled so low that she had to raise her chin to look at me blocked my path. "Ice-e?" She extended a cart toward me with a brutal shove. A regulation grocery cart, sealed in duct tape, enclosed with a plastic lid, a cardboard cut-out of brightly colored ice creams taped to its sides.

"Whoa," I muttered, gripping the cart to keep from being run down. A plastic wheel jumped the rim of my sneaker, leaving a marked trail.

"Ice-e?" the woman repeated sternly.

I hadn't noticed the man next to her. The old cat was just squatting there on the balls of his feet, arms extended at awkward angles from where they rested on each knee. In front of him stood a stack of newspapers and, atop the stack, a neat pile of quarters. I recognized the paper, a freebie like mine, but here on the street it cost a quarter.

I slapped some coins in his palm and snatched up a copy. The lead caught my eye:

Jamaica, Queens—A young man recently found hanging in his bedroom has been identified as Edwin Stuckey, age twenty-two. Family members say the list of suspects is numerous and have sealed off the scene of the crime—the home—until further notice. The police have no comment.

The Crusading Home of Deliverance was located in a sprawling Victorian residence. It wouldn't have been recognizable as a church were it not for the small cardboard sign and handmade cross posted in a none-too-clean bay window. I checked Detective Spurlock's directions several times before rapping on the front door.

I'd tried to contact Janette after seeing the brief article about her brother in the competition, but she wasn't taking my calls. So what was I doing? Seems I needed to know what happened to Edwin Stuckey after all.

"Are you here for evening service?" A smiling elderly

woman dressed in white opened the door. I could see behind her into a drab parlor containing metal folding chairs, a podium, and what looked like a small organ.

"No, ma'am," I said. "I'm here to see Reverend Pine."

Did I have an appointment? she inquired, continuing to smile.

I admitted I didn't but assured her it was important, that I was here about Edwin Stuckey.

"Edwin. Yes." She bowed her head. "We are still mourning his loss, but happy for his deliverance."

"Yes, well . . . Reverend Pine?"

I followed the woman into the room and took a seat in the back row. The room was large and half-filled, all its occupants black, conversing in hushed voices.

"Son?" A slim, natty man dressed in a three-piece suit charged toward me with his hand extended. "I'm the Reverend Pine, and I welcome you to our sanctuary." He shook my hand with an intense vigor before adjusting his chunky glasses and straightening his tie. "We can speak briefly in my office. I've got service in an hour and I must prepare." He cleared his throat. "You understand."

I studied the hallway he led me down. On either side of the wall were photographs of the reverend with parishioners and community dignitaries. His office, lined with two bookcases of theological texts, contained more of the same.

Reverend Pine took a seat behind his desk. "You're here for Edwin?"

"Yes, sir." I shifted in my seat. "I'm a reporter for the—"

"*Weekly Item*. I know." He smiled wryly.

I peered up at him sharply.

"I keep myself informed, son." He laughed and adjusted himself in his seat. "See, my congregation is this here community, and we are all interested in Edwin's well-being. We even trust that *you* are interested in his well-being."

I was suddenly growing wary of this man and his glib talk of dead Edwin's well-being.

"Look, I don't know what kind of shop you're running here—"

"There's no need to be disrespectful." Reverend Pine pinned me with his gaze. "What do you want to know? Edwin Stuckey saw a flyer for our church revival last summer, showed up at our doors, and we welcomed him."

"So why does his family think he was murdered? Why did his sister give the names of members of your congregation to the police?"

Pine shrugged nonchalantly. "Why? You best ask Edwin's sister, Janette, yourself. Before he came to us, Edwin had no friends. He had no interests. He had no hope. He was very depressed. We tried to comfort him."

"He killed himself."

"No, he didn't." Pine took off his glasses and rubbed his temples. "There's a problem in our society, son, that I'm sure you're familiar with. Loss of hope."

I stared at the man, attentive despite myself.

"Let me be clear here." He held up his hands in a defensive gesture. "I do not advocate suicide. I did not encourage Edwin Stuckey to kill himself. I pray for his soul every day. But Edwin and his family are the reason I do what I do: People *do* lose hope and not all of them regain it. And not all of them can accept when hopelessness claims one of their own."

"Look, Reverend Pine, that's a nice sermon and all, but I'm just here for the facts," I said.

He opened his arms. "Sadly, those are they."

* * *

To my everlasting surprise, I sat through all three hours of Reverend Pine's service. It was motivating, it was uplifting, it was hopeful. The tears, the tambourines, the shouting. Most importantly, though, it did not compel me to commit suicide. It made me want to get on with my life.

When the door of Deliverance closed behind me and I stepped onto the cracked sidewalk beyond its front stairway, I decided to phone Janette one final time. I watched a group of middle school girls skip double-dutch further down the street. The clothesline they were using for a jump rope slapped the pavement fiercely and their chants rippled down the block: *"All, all, all in together, any kind of weather . . ."*

The father answered, said Janette was out. "Mr. Stuckey, this is Douglass, the reporter," I began.

"Yes?" His voice rose to an expectant pitch. "Any progress?"

"See the teacher looking out the window. Dong, dong, the fire-bell . . ." The girls picked up their volume, feet racing the rope.

On the line I let out a sigh, and I heard Mr. Stuckey deflating in the silence. "Unfortunately, sir, I am no longer able to pursue this story." Across the street, a dude carrying a basketball under one arm shouted after a car rolling past on a wave of bass line.

"That boy who did that to himself was not my son, he was someone else. Somebody did something, or said something that—" Stuckey cleared his throat. "Someone should be held responsible."

I hesitated, then snapped my phone shut.

"How many ringers can you take? One, two, three, four . . ." The girls ticked off their chant behind me.

ABOUT THE CONTRIBUTORS

Eileen Kelly

JILLIAN ABBOTT'S short stories have won awards in the United States and Australia. She is a reporter at the *Queens Chronicle* and her writing has appeared in the *Washington Post*, the *New York Daily News*, the *Writer Magazine*, and many other publications. She's currently at work on a new mystery series as well as her second Morgan Blake thriller. She lives in Queens.

Joshua A. Gaylord

MEGAN ABBOTT is the Edgar Award–nominated author of *Queenpin, The Song Is You,* and *Die a Little,* as well as the nonfiction study, *The Street Was Mine: White Masculinity in Hardboiled Fiction and Film Noir.* She lives in Forest Hills, Queens.

Miraya

SHAILLY AGNIHOTRI was born in India, grew up in Baton Rouge, and now lives in New York City. She is a filmmaker and recently completed a documentary entitled *Three Soldiers.* Her other projects include a feature film, *Sangrita* (in pre-production), and a novel, *East River.* She likes to consult Vedic astrologers, buy silver jewelry, and eat spicy *chat* in Jackson Heights.

Tony O'Shea

MARY BYRNE was born in Ireland and now divides her time between teaching, translating, and writing. She collaborated with Lawrence Durrell on his final book of essays, and her short fiction has been published in Ireland, England, France, Canada, and the United States. Byrne won the 1986 Hennessy Literary Award and currently lives in France.

TORI CARRINGTON (a.k.a., Lori and Tony Karayianni) has published nearly forty titles, including those in the Sofie Metropolis, P.I. series, which are set in Astoria, Queens.

JILL EISENSTADT is the author of two novels set in Queens, *From Rockaway* and *Kiss Out*. She is an occasional contributor to the *New York Times*, among other publications, and is a part-time writing professor at The New School's Eugene Lang College. Her *Queens Noir* story, "The Golden Venture," is based on a real event in the borough's history.

Roberto A. Herrera

VICTORIA ENG was born and raised in Chinatown and Queens. She is a graduate of Hunter College and holds an MFA in Writing from Columbia University. Her work has been published in *The NuyorAsian Anthology: Asian American Writings about New York City*. She lived in New Mexico and Costa Rica for seven years, and is currently back in New York working on a historical novel set in Chinatown.

Mickey Estep

MAGGIE ESTEP has published six books and is working on her seventh, *Alice Fantastic*, which came to be when Robert Knightly asked her to write something for *Queens Noir*. Her favorite parts of Queens are the Kissena Velodrome, Aqueduct Racetrack, and Fort Tilden in Rockaway.

Pavla Serifoglu

BELINDA FARLEY resides in Harlem, not Queens, and is currently at work on a novel.

Bruce Infantino

ALAN GORDON is the author of the Fools' Guild Mysteries, including the forthcoming novel *The Moneylender of Toulouse* and, most recently, *The Lark's Lament*. He has been a resident of Queens' second oldest co-op since 1987, and is a defender of the borough's alleged miscreants as a lawyer with the Legal Aid Society. Gordon is the father of one genuine Queensian, and has been a Little League coach for six years, which has taught him all he needs to know about hard-boiled types.

JOSEPH GUGLIELMELLI grew up in Jackson Heights, Queens. He cultivated his love of mysteries by reading golden age classics found while browsing in tiny bookstores in the shadow of the elevated tracks of the 7 train. For the past thirteen years, Joe has been coowner of The Black Orchid Bookshop, which was the 2006 recipient of the Raven Award given by Mystery Writers of America.

DENIS HAMILL writes a column about Queens for the *New York Daily News* and has written ten novels, including, *Fork in the Road,* recently purchased by Alexander Payne's company for a feature film from Fox Searchlight. He lives in Queens.

PATRICIA KING is the author of four books on business subjects, including *Never Work for a Jerk.* Her forthcoming book—*The Monster in the Corner Office*—will be published in 2008.

ROBERT KNIGHTLY moved to Jackson Heights in 1995 and works as a Legal Aid criminal defense lawyer in the Queens courts. As a teenager, he dug graves one summer in First Calvary Cemetery in Blissville, where he set his story for this volume. His short story "Take the Man's Pay," from Akashic's *Manhattan Noir,* was selected for inclusion in *The Best American Mystery Stories 2007.* As an NYPD officer and sergeant he patrolled Brooklyn and Manhattan for twenty years.

GLENVILLE LOVELL has published four novels: *Fire in the Canes, Song of Night, Too Beautiful to Die,* and *Love and Death in Brooklyn.* His stories haved appeared in *Conjunctions, Shades of Black, Wanderlust: Erotic Travel Tales,* and *Hardboiled Brooklyn.* For more information, visit www.glenvillelovell.com

Jeff Robles

LIZ MARTÍNEZ has lived in Woodside, Queens, for the past fifteen years. She is currently collaborating on a mystery anthology with fellow award-winning Mexican-American writer Sarah Cortez. "Lights Out for Frankie" was inspired by an organized retail crime case solved by legendary police detectives Eric Hernando and Sergeant Louie Torres of the Holmdel, New Jersey police department.

Jim Sitvers

STEPHEN SOLOMITA is the author of sixteen novels. He was born and raised in Bayside, Queens, not far from College Point, the setting for "Crazy Jill Saves the Slinky."

Ron Rinaldi

KIM SYKES is an actress and writer who lives in New York City. She frequently works at Silvercup Studios.

Bob Hall

K.J.A. WISHNIA'S first novel featuring Ecuadorian-American P.I. Filomena Buscarsela, *23 Shades of Black*, was a finalist for both Edgar and Anthony Awards, and was followed by four other novels, including *Soft Money* and *Red House*. He lived in Ecuador for several years, and taught English at Queens College, CUNY. Wishnia gives special thanks to his students at Suffolk Community College, especially Victor Nieves, for providing him with the authentic ghetto phraseology.

Also available from the Akashic Books Noir Series

BROOKLYN NOIR
edited by Tim McLoughlin
350 pages, trade paperback original, $15.95
*WINNER OF SHAMUS AWARD, ANTHONY AWARD, ROBERT L. FISH
MEMORIAL AWARD; FINALIST FOR EDGAR AWARD, PUSHCART PRIZE

Brand new stories by: Pete Hamill, Robert Knightly, Arthur Nersesian, Maggie Estep, Nelson George, Sidney Offit, Ken Bruen, and others.

"*Brooklyn Noir* is such a stunningly perfect combination that you can't believe you haven't read an anthology like this before. But trust me—you haven't. Story after story is a revelation, filled with the requisite sense of place, but also the perfect twists that crime stories demand. The writing is flat-out superb, filled with lines that will sing in your head for a long time to come."
—Laura Lippman, winner of the Edgar, Agatha, and Shamus awards

MANHATTAN NOIR
edited by Lawrence Block
260 pages, trade paperback original, $14.95

Brand new stories by: Jeffery Deaver, Robert Knightly, Lawrence Block, Liz Martínez, Thomas H. Cook, S.J. Rozan, Justin Scott, and others.

"A pleasing variety of Manhattan neighborhoods come to life in Block's solid anthology . . . the writing is of a high order and a nice mix of styles."
—*Publishers Weekly*

BRONX NOIR
edited by S.J. Rozan
368 pages, trade paperback original, $15.95

Brand new stories by: Jerome Charyn, Lawrence Block, Suzanne Chazin, Terrence Cheng, Kevin Baker, Abraham Rodriguez, Jr., and others.

"Akashic's latest city-themed crime anthology successfully captures the immense diversity of the Bronx, from the mean streets of the South Bronx to affluent Riverdale . . . Rozan, herself a contributor, has put together one of the series' better entries."
—*Publishers Weekly*

LOS ANGELES NOIR
edited by Denise Hamilton
360 pages, trade paperback original, $15.95
*A *Los Angeles Times* Best-seller

Brand new stories by: Michael Connelly, Janet Fitch, Susan Straight, Héctor Tobar, Patt Morrison, Robert Ferrigno, Neal Pollack, Gary Phillips, Christopher Rice, Naomi Hirahara, Jim Pascoe, and others.

"Akashic is making an argument about the universality of noir; it's sort of flattering, really, and *Los Angeles Noir*, arriving at last, is a kaleidoscopic collection filled with the ethos of noir pioneers Raymond Chandler and James M. Cain."
—*Los Angeles Times Book Review*

NEW ORLEANS NOIR
edited by Julie Smith
298 pages, trade paperback original, $14.95

Brand new stories by: Ace Atkins, Laura Lippman, Patty Friedmann, Barbara Hambly, Tim McLoughlin, Olympia Vernon, Kalamu ya Salaam, Thomas Adcock, Christine Wiltz, Greg Herren, and others.

"The excellent twelfth entry in Akashic's noir series illustrates the diversity of the chosen locale with eighteen previously unpublished short stories from authors both well known and emerging."
—*Publishers Weekly*

BALTIMORE NOIR
edited by Laura Lippman
294 pages, trade paperback original, $14.95

Brand new stories by: David Simon, Laura Lippman, Tim Cockey, Rob Hiaasen, Robert Ward, Sujata Massey, Jack Bludis, Dan Fesperman, Marcia Talley, Ben Neihart, Jim Fusilli, Rafael Alvarez, and others.

"Baltimore is a diverse city, and the stories reflect everything from its old row houses and suburban mansions to its beloved Orioles and harbor areas . . . Mystery fans should relish this taste of Baltimore's seamier side." —*Publishers Weekly*